"SO YOU RIDE LIKE A LANCER AND NO DOUBT SMOKE LIKE A BLACKGUARD AND HANDLE A PISTOL LIKE A DRAGOON!"

His blood raced hot in his veins, not from the hard ride, but from anger at being made a fool of. "Do you also sport bloomers beneath your riding habit?"

She pursed her lips. "What I wear beneath my habit is none of your affair," she replied.

Jon's eyes moved over hair that gleamed with twists of russet gold in the shafts of sunlight sifting through the evergreens. Tracing her lips with the pad of his finger he said in a quiet voice, "And now I intend to collect on your promise."

"What promise?" she asked, her heart pounding.

"This." His mouth covered hers.

She splayed her fingers to shove him away, but instead found herself gliding her palms over his shoulders and curving her hands around his neck. It was as if a world of sensation were awakening inside her . . .

Other **AVON ROMANCES**

COME BE MY LOVE

PATRICIA WATTERS

To Jane —
    I hope you enjoy
my book — it should
add a little spice to
your life —
    Best
        Pat Watters

AVON BOOKS ◆ NEW YORK

7-27-93

COME BE MY LOVE is an original publication of Avon Books. This work has never before appeared in book form. This work is a novel. Any similarity to actual persons or events is purely coincidental.

AVON BOOKS
A division of
The Hearst Corporation
1350 Avenue of the Americas
New York, New York 10019

Copyright © 1993 by Patricia Lynn Watters
Published by arrangement with the author
Library of Congress Catalog Card Number: 92-93921
ISBN: 0-380-76909-3

First Avon Books Printing: April 1993

AVON TRADEMARK REG. U.S. PAT. OFF. AND IN OTHER COUNTRIES, MARCA REGISTRADA, HECHO EN U.S.A.

Printed in the U.S.A.

RA   10   9   8   7   6   5   4   3   2   1

For you Mom—

It's hard to imagine that this story takes place the year Grandaddy was born, and four years before Mère was born. I want to dedicate this book to the Victorians in my life: Grandaddy Watters, who gave me a glimpse into the life of a horse-and-buggy doctor; and Mère, who with humor and diligence tried to make a southern lady of me.

But most of all to you and Daddy—Daddy for leading me to believe I could be anything I wanted to be; and you for your love, support, and incredibly positive outlook on life.

And a special thanks to my own hero, Ed, who polished the prose, refined the grammar, and weeded out the anachronisms; to my agent, Elizabeth Cavanaugh, whose enthusiasm and efficiency got the manuscript into the right hands; and to my editor, Ellen Edwards, whose editing expertise made all the difference.

Come live with me, and be my love;
And we will all the pleasures prove
That valleys, groves, hills, and fields,
Woods or steepy mountain yields.

And I will make thee beds of roses
And a thousand fragrant posies,
A cap of flowers, and a kirtle
Embroidered all with leaves of myrtle;

A belt of straw and ivy buds,
With coral clasps and amber studs;
And if these pleasures may thee move
Come live with me, and be my love.

—CHRISTOPHER MARLOWE

Prologue

Aboard the Mariah
September 1863

Harriet Galbraith braced a hand on the door frame and peered down the passageway, her pale blue eyes searching the shadows. She waited, listening for sounds of footsteps, but heard only the rhythmic creaking of the ship as it rolled with the relentless ocean swells.

Her thin lips curved in anticipation as she slipped into the stateroom. Scanning the quarters, she searched for the journal in which she'd seen Sarah Ashley write several entries. Unable to locate it, she moved to the trunk and raised the arched lid. Inside lay silk stockings richly embroidered with satin threads; muslin drawers, camisoles, and petticoats trimmed with dainty tucks and delicate lace; and preformed corsets with satin ties, one of black silk with red stitching. They were garments of the sort she had expected to find in the trunk of an unchaste woman like Sarah Ashley.

Hastily sorting through the undergarments, Harriet, to her delight, found the leather-bound book. A flush of excitement rose in her cheeks. Lowering her angular frame to the berth, she fanned the pages, selecting at random an entry dated August 4, 1863.

1

The authorities have closed the doors to the business, Dear Diary, and because I cannot show my face in polite society, and I no longer have a future in San Francisco, I have decided to set up my own business in Victoria. With the prospectors bringing in so much gold there, I know I shall soon be wealthy ...

Harriet arched a brow. So the rumors were true. Of course, she'd known it all along. She'd watched the woman bedevil the captain, caught the seductive innuendos, seen the sin and wickedness in her enormous green eyes with their sweeping lashes. A hideous creature who colored her lips with rouge and her eyelids with bister; and after painting her face like Jezebel, she dressed her hair ... hair that was far too shiny, unquestionably dyed. No hair was the color of a polished copper pot.

And her scandalous gowns would lure the most righteous of men into sin. Such garish colors! No respectable woman would combine poppy-red and purple, or emerald-green and peacock-blue. Nor would she dare wear trousers, or go without crinolines. Shocking! Very shocking indeed!

And the governor's daughter ... latching on to the woman. It was no wonder the girl was as wild as a March hare. And one could say the same for her father. He was not much better than the savages. It was shameful. That's what it was ... him being the governor and all. Poor Dorothy. Imagine a woman of her standing in the community having to put up with the likes of that son. And now, when she learned about this ...

Thinking she'd heard someone coming, Harriet snapped the journal shut, slipped it into the trunk, and lowered the lid. Her mouth tipped upward with righteousness, and she skulked quickly out of the stateroom and up the darkened passageway.

Chapter 1

Victoria, Vancouver Island
September 1863

The rusty cries of gulls announced the arrival of the clipper ship *Mariah*. As the tall vessel glided into Victoria harbor, main and topsails furled, royals and skysails set and pennant flying, the raucous birds swooped down and dipped into the murky water, snatching debris that rolled in the wake.

Bracing her feet against the rocking deck, her coppery hair streaming in the breeze, Sarah Ashley inhaled the sea air and felt the sting of the wind on her cheeks. All day, a thick mist had enveloped the ship, then shortly before it had sailed into the harbor, the mist had lifted, like a curtain opening to a bright new world . . . and a fresh new life.

Sarah had no idea what her stepbrothers would do when they learned she'd liquidated her savings and fled from San Francisco, but she prayed they would not come looking for her, at least not in Victoria. Tyler she didn't fear, but Hollis was not one to issue idle threats—he'd already proved that. If he did find her, his revenge would be shrewd, inventive, and unmerciful.

She trusted the servants to keep their word and

3

lead Hollis to believe she'd gone to New York in search of her mother's family. Which, for her, was not an option. Ever since her eastern relatives had learned of her ignoble birth, they'd refused to have anything to do with her.

Gazing at the scene before her, she was almost too excited to breathe. Everywhere, she saw signs of growth. In the distance, tall stands of cedar and fir made a jagged profile against a gray-blue sky. And vast areas, recently cleared for pasture and crops, bordered patchwork fields of homesteads. Closer in, stores, hotels, saloons, and other buildings lined an orderly network of streets, the entire landscape appearing planned, organized. A city on the threshold of prosperity.

But in the foreground, the scene changed dramatically. On the quayside between the aging palisade of Fort Victoria and the warehouses at the water's edge, ragtag tents and makeshift hovels housed prospectors waiting for passage to the Cariboo goldfields. Shabby-looking men carrying knapsacks laden with picks, shovels, and iron buckets crowded the wharf. And hacks, carts, and peddlers' wagons; jobbers, brokers, and fishmongers—all come to profit from the gold seekers—jammed the thoroughfares.

Anxiously fingering the smooth handles of her reticule, Sarah scanned the passengers on deck, looking for her maid. She saw the young colored woman sashaying past a handsome seaman with skin as black as pitch, his dazzling white grin coaxing a demure smile from her in return. It wasn't the first time a man had rested appreciative eyes on Mandi. With mirthful black eyes fringed with long curling lashes, beautifully sculpted lips the color of rich burgundy, and a smooth unblemished complexion the shade of dark walnut, Mandi possessed uncommon beauty.

Even so, she'd turned down several good offers of

marriage because she carried in her heart false hopes of one day finding her ideal man. An improbable fancy, Sarah thought. The man of Mandi's dreams did not exist except in her mind. Quixotic, sentimental, daydreaming little fool.

As Mandi approached, Sarah gave her a sharp look. "Where have you been? It's almost time to disembark."

"Ah heard Miz Galbraith sayin' to a couple of the ladies aboard some things about you and the captain," she tattled, her voice excited, "so Ah just had to keep on listenin'."

"Oh, for heaven's sake. Captain Sweeney's old enough to be my grandfather. You must have heard wrong."

"No, Ah didn't," Mandi insisted. "Miz Galbraith was sayin' that you really is one of them loose women from San Francisco. Ah hopes she don't do like Mister Hollis and Mister Tyler did in San Francisco . . . spread ugly things 'bout you like that. She seems a right spiteful women for a preacher's wife."

"She may be a preacher's wife," said Sarah, "but she's also a harridan, a snoop, and a busybody. I'm sure the people in Victoria will disavow anything she might say."

"Not accordin' to Ida—that's Miz Cromwell's maid. Ida says that the ladies of Victoria have nothin' else to do but sit around and gossip 'bout one thing or another . . . that word spreads so fast, one lady can start a rumor one afternoon, and by the next, it's bein' talked about in every parlor in Victoria."

Sarah chuckled. "Then let's look on the bright side. Think of how quickly the word of our business venture will spread. Besides, if the women have nothing better to do than gossip, they should be eager for new ideas on ways to occupy their time, which is exactly what I've been counting on."

"But that's not all. Ah heard Miz Galbraith say, loud enough so's other folks on the boat could hear, that the guv'nor's sister ought not be in your company, her traveling with the guv'nor's daughters and all. And that's apt to get back to the guv'nor's mother, since Ida said she and Miz Galbraith are special good friends."

Sarah felt a sudden twinge of uncertainty. If Lady Cromwell—the Dowager Viscountess of Haverhill, the woman at the pinnacle of Victoria's polite society—believed such aspersions as Harriet Galbraith might spread, Sarah might once again face the very situation she'd left in San Francisco.

Mandi looked beyond Sarah. "Well, we'd best not be discussin' it now. Here come Miz Cromwell."

Sarah glanced back and saw Esther Cromwell walking toward them, the skirt of her plain brown traveling dress swishing back and forth with each quick step. Esther and her nieces, Louella and Josephine—teenage daughters of Governor Cromwell—were returning to Victoria after a holiday in San Francisco. During the voyage, Esther and Sarah had become friends. A spinster in her early forties, Esther wore her mouse-brown hair parted in the middle and dragged back into an unadorned chignon at her nape; her light brown eyes were without bister, her pale cheeks and lips devoid of rouge.

On first seeing Esther, Sarah had felt sorry for the woman, being so plain, and she'd suspected that her personality was as lackluster as her appearance. Instead, Sarah had found a warm, humorous lady hidden beneath the colorless exterior.

As Esther approached, her face held a look of grave concern. "I insist you come to our home and stay with us," she said to Sarah. "Look at them all."

She motioned toward the multitude of bearded, hard-looking men milling about on the wharf, most of them visibly armed with revolvers and bowie knives. "These men are a very rough lot—the absolute dregs of society—and it's simply not safe at the hotel for an unmarried woman."

Sarah perused the men. She, too, had misgivings about staying at the hotel. But she expected to be so busy setting up her business, she didn't anticipate spending much time there. "I'm sure we'll be fine," she said, hoping she sounded more confident than she felt.

"You don't understand," said Esther. "Several women have disappeared . . . single women snatched right off the street. And no one knows what's happened to them—there's not a trace. Jon suspects they've been carried off to the goldfields and sold to the prospectors up there."

Sarah stared at Esther, incredulous. "Sold? Like . . . white slaves?"

"Precisely. It's a horrible thing. Now the women here are afraid to go out in groups of less than three, and of course everyone guards their daughters constantly. So far, all of the women who have disappeared have been prostitutes, but one never knows when a decent woman might be abducted."

Sarah eyed the disreputable-looking throng. Until now, she had not realized how untamed the city was. The thought of staying alone in a hotel crowded with these men was becoming increasingly unappealing. She looked askance at Esther. "Well, if it's really no imposition."

"I assure you, it's not," said Esther. "So it's settled. Now I must find Louella and Josephine . . ."

As Esther walked off, Sarah nearly recanted, raising her hand with hesitation, but she said nothing. Esther had mentioned earlier that her brother, the governor of Vancouver Island, was opposed to the influx of Americans coming to Victoria to make their fortunes. And there was no question, Sarah was another American doing just that.

Thirty minutes later, as Sarah stood on the wharf with Esther, Mandi, Ida, and the two girls, a great commotion arose among the crowd in the street above. Shouts erupted and a horse reared, breaking its ties. The horse bolted forward, toppled a wagon, and rushed headlong toward a small child. Suddenly, a horseman on a blood bay bounded over the toppled wagon, overtaking the riderless horse, and in one fluid motion leaned low astride the horse and scooped up the child. Reining to an abrupt halt, the horseman comforted the crying child for a few moments, then lowered him into the arms of his distressed mother.

Esther slapped both hands to her face. "Good God! It's Jon!"

Sarah stared at the man, too stunned to speak.

Tall and powerfully built, with a crop of unruly black hair, broad massive shoulders, and muscular thighs evident beneath his tight breeches, the man did not look like a governor—at least not in the sense Sarah would have expected. But then, Jonathan Cromwell governed a wild, untamed frontier, a land that seemed as raw and rugged as the man himself.

For an instant, he looked directly at her, and Sarah found herself staring into a pair of intense, dark eyes. Her cheeks grew warm, then her entire body seemed to respond. The sight of him awakened something inside her, stirring and warming her—and scaring her, too. Danger lurked in those dark eyes, not the kind of danger she'd felt when she'd gazed at the men on the wharf, but another kind of danger, one capable of

piercing her heart and finding its way into her very
soul.

Never in her life had she seen a man who exuded
so much strength—a bold strength that was evident
in the firm angle of his jaw and the almost brutal line
of his mouth. Then his mouth softened and his eyes
brightened, and she knew at once he'd spotted his
daughters running toward him. Swinging his leg
over the horse, he sprang to the ground, ran down to
the wharf with his horse loping behind him, and
gathered Josephine and Louella in a fierce embrace.

Esther took her arm. "Come on," she said. "I'll introduce you to Jon."

Only then did Sarah realize she'd been holding her
breath. Feeling a vague uncertainty, she walked over
to meet the man.

"Jon," said Esther, pulling Sarah toward him, "may
I introduce Miss Sarah Ashley. I've taken the liberty
of inviting her to be a guest in our home for a few
days, and she has agreed."

Captivated by those same dark eyes, now luminous, that seemed to be assessing her, Sarah extended her hand and rested it against the governor's
broad palm. "I'm very pleased to meet you."

His large fingers closed around her hand. "This is
indeed a pleasure," he said, his eyes reflecting the
lazy grin on his tanned face as he held her hand a
shade longer than propriety allowed. "Am I to assume you have no friends or relatives here?"

"Well . . . yes," replied Sarah, a hint of strain creeping into her voice. "That is . . . no, I have no relatives
here in Victoria. Most of my family lives in the East,
except for my two . . . that is . . ." She paused. After
what Hollis and Tyler had done, it seemed inconceivable that she could consider them family. Trying to
dismiss the anger and bitterness, she said, "Two stepbrothers live in San Francisco."

The long pause that followed led Sarah to surmise that Governor Cromwell was trying to adjust to the idea of his sister having invited an American to stay in their home. "Then you're here on holiday?"

Sarah hesitated. "Well, no ... not exactly. That is, I'm moving to Victoria. I've heard that the town offers many opportunities."

His expression hardened. "Yes, I suppose it does. Many Americans feel that way," he said, his voice now cool, impassive. "I understand that many of them are deserting families, jobs, and country in favor of gold."

Sarah couldn't dispute that. She'd heard talk of merchants and farmers quitting work, lumber mills shutting down, sailors jumping ship, Union and Confederate soldiers fleeing from battle—all swarming to outfitting stores and steamship ticket offices, then funneling up the Fraser River to the goldfields. When she'd left San Francisco, the city had been a madhouse: men standing in long lines to board vessels, merchants of outfitting houses selling goods at inflated prices ...

Fourteen-year-old Louella, a pretty child with a sharp, pointed face and a pouting mouth, raised her flaxen head and looked up, fixing anxious blue eyes on her father. Tugging on his arm, she said in an impatient voice, "Please, Papa, may we go home now? It's been dreadfully long since I've seen Taffy and her kittens."

Jon gave his younger daughter a warm smile. "Yes, poppet." He curved his arm about Louella's shoulders, took his horse by the bridle, and motioned for everyone to follow. Sarah gathered her skirt and petticoats. Lifting them clear of the dirt on the wharf, she and Mandi traipsed behind the governor and his entourage as they marched up the plank roadway ascending the quay.

On the street, two carriages waited—a dark green depot wagon drawn by a pair of dappled grays and an elegant midnight-blue town coach bearing a crest on the door. A team of four whites with patent leather collars and silver rosettes on their face pieces pranced nervously in place before the town coach.

Sarah smiled inwardly. A coach-and-four, and a footman and coachman smartly dressed in fine livery: silk top hats perched on their heads, dark blue greatcoats with rows of shiny brass buttons, and matching trousers tucked into high black boots—a mark of distinction and prosperity. Only a colony with wealth could afford to provide its governor with such refinement. At least, she assumed the colony had provided it. Governor Cromwell didn't seem a man who would waste money on anything as frivolous as a luxury coach.

She'd made the right choice in coming here, she was certain. Victoria would indeed bring her wealth and the security she needed.

Mandi, Ida, and the girls climbed into the depot wagon. Then, to Sarah's surprise, the governor turned his horse over to one of the footmen and said, "Tie him behind, Hayworth. I'll be joining Miss Cromwell and Miss Ashley for the ride home. But first, I have to talk to Mayor Harris. I'll be back in a few minutes." With little more than a nod to the women, he left.

Esther climbed into the coach, but Sarah remained outside where she could peruse her new surroundings. She scanned the buildings lining the waterfront. A small brick building—the kind she envisioned as housing her clothing business—caught her eye. It appeared unoccupied. Curious, she wandered over to where a tall, rather nicely dressed man stood just outside the front door. She smiled politely. "Is this building by any chance for let?"

The man's gaze meandered down the full length of her and wandered back up. "For you, little lady, it could be arranged."

Sarah wasn't certain how to take the man's comment. "Then it is available?"

The man stepped closer. "Yes. Come inside and we'll talk about it."

"Inside?"

The man gave her a furtive smile. "I never discuss business on the street. If you're interested in leasing this building, you'll have to step inside." He reached out and took her arm.

At first she started into the building with him, then she became frightened. "No . . . not now. I have to go." She tugged on her arm, and to her relief, the man released her. As she walked away from him, he called after her, "Then I look forward to seeing you . . . soon."

She didn't respond, but when she looked up, she found Governor Cromwell's eyes fixed intently on her. The dark look they held, and the hard line of his mouth closed around his cigarette, left no question as to how he had interpreted what he'd just seen. His eyes still on her, he pinched the cigarette butt from his lips and flipped it into the street. She gave him an uncertain smile, scurried past him, and climbed into the coach, sitting beside Esther.

Once settled against the tufted-velvet upholstery, Sarah inspected the interior of the coach, the ornate silver card cases, the velvet drapes, the door pulls covered with morocco. Yes, she'd definitely made the right choice.

The coach dipped as Governor Cromwell swung inside and sat opposite the women, his broad-shouldered frame and long muscular legs seeming to fill every available space in the coach. The odor of smoke and horse and oiled leather filled Sarah's nostrils, the earthy presence of the man seeming to infuse her body. Unsettled by his nearness, she crossed her ankles, but when her foot rubbed against his calf, she quickly withdrew her foot and clamped her knees snugly together.

He looked steadily at her, his slow, sensual smile leaving no question in Sarah's mind that he had been aware of the casual contact. "You said Victoria offered many opportunities, Miss Ashley? Does that mean San Francisco does not?"

"Well, yes, I suppose it does mean that ... for some people," she said, unsettled by his close perusal.

"You being one of those people?" He rapped on the window behind him, and the coachman cracked his whip, giving the command. The four whites strained at their bits and moved forward, the high wheels of the coach clattering and rumbling over coarse cobblestones. His gaze fixed on Sarah, Jon folded his arms across his broad chest. "It surprises me that you expect to find something here in Victoria that a thriving city like San Francisco lacks. What, may I ask, would that be?"

"It's not that I expect to find anything ... exactly."

"Then, if you don't expect to find anything here, I assume you meant to leave something behind."

Sarah looked at him with a start, and he returned her wide-eyed stare with a knowing smile. She had no idea where this conversation was leading, but she most definitely did not want to reveal the reason for her hasty departure. "What exactly are you implying, Governor?"

His smile widened. "I'm only curious why a beautiful woman would leave her home and family and travel alone to a town that is barely more than an outpost. Unless, perhaps, she was ... running from something."

"For heaven's sake, Jon!" Esther snapped. "Why are you interrogating Miss Ashley as if she left San Francisco under shady circumstances."

For a long moment, he looked at Sarah, then he slowly arched one dark brow. "I apologize, Miss Ashley. I certainly didn't mean to imply that."

But Sarah knew from the perceptive look in his eyes and the rueful curve to his lips that that was precisely what he'd meant. It was also the bitter, unspoken truth. She *had* left San Francisco under a cloud.

Was she so easy to read? Or was Governor Jonathan Cromwell unusually adept at proceeding directly to the core of things?

Ignoring his last comment, she turned away from his assessing gaze and the unsettling effect his presence seemed to have on her. Staring out the window, she studied the row of false-front brick and wooden buildings lining walks of fresh-cut cedar planks. Everywhere, stores displayed American names: San Francisco Baths, American Bakery, California Saloon. The colony seemed far more American than British.

Her heart beat a staccato rhythm as she looked out at the bustling town. It resembled San Francisco in the days of the gold rush. And she, too, would build a successful business, just as her father had.

No, not father . . . stepfather. Stepfather!

It was so easy to forget, to slip back to a time before her mother had died when she hadn't known the truth, but had struggled to comprehend the enigma of her father: trying to grasp a resentment that seemed to have no basis, reaching for a love that was never returned, attempting to understand a soul she could never touch.

Her throat tightened and the deep, dull pain that seemed to have no source rose in her breast, the restless, desolate emptiness, the unnamed longing that made her feel disarmed and vulnerable. Why couldn't her mother have spared her the truth? Spared her the deathbed confession? Sarah could almost see her mother's pallid face, eyes ghostlike in their sunken sockets. There had been no quavering in her mother's voice, no trace of emotion, only the harsh reality of cold facts as she'd said, "Your father is not your real father."

Sarah had sat in stunned silence.

"Your real father was a captain in the British navy—a man with fiery red hair and restless green eyes. When he sailed away, I fancied myself in love. By the time your stepfather came along, I realized my captain wasn't coming back, so I accepted your stepfather's proposal. But shortly before the wedding, your father sailed into port again. It was a brief, impetuous affair—I had to know how I truly felt—and your stepfather found out. He took me back because he needed a mother for Hollis and Tyler. Shortly after we were married, I realized I was pregnant, but I didn't know which man was your father.

"When you were born . . . your green eyes and copper hair . . . well, there was no question. I'm telling you because you need to know why your stepfather has always resented you. You're a constant reminder of the man I betrayed him with. That's why no matter what you do, you'll never gain his acceptance, or his love. It's not your fault, it's mine. When I next saw your father, I told him about you, but he denied it . . . called me a whore and said you could be any man's . . . Well, that's not important. He denied it and left. I never saw him again."

Sarah had looked at her mother's gaunt face and thought: *Why did you wait so long to tell me? Why are you leaving me now with this terrible burden?*

Then a morbid elation began to grow. At last she

understood her stepfather's rejection. Over the years, she'd tried desperately to gain his love, but nothing seemed to please him. She'd worked long hours in his clothing manufactory, but the harder she tried, the more he resented her presence.

"You are not in your stepfather's will," her mother added. "But I've been saving money. Use it to build your own business, and to be independent like I've tried to teach you to be. And *never* let your stepfather or brothers know about it. They'd take it from you."

How well she knew!

Now Sarah must make a success of her business. And she had faith that the Cariboo gold rush would be her means to that end. Glancing at Esther, she commented, "I don't believe I've seen a women's apparel store here."

Esther shrugged. "Most of the women here fashion their own garments or buy ready-made wear from the Hudson's Bay Company store."

Sarah smiled, pleased. It was as she had anticipated. Women would be flocking to her store for shirtwaisters and bloomer costumes, glad to shed their corsets and petticoats.

Esther looked across at her brother. "Have any more women been abducted since we left?"

"Yes, two ... both prostitutes," he replied. "It's assumed they left of their own accord for the goldfields."

"Assumed?" Sarah glared at the governor, annoyed with his callous attitude. The women were, after all, human beings, many of whom had no doubt been cast into their demeaning profession by ruthless men. "Does that mean the authorities are not searching for them?"

He looked visibly annoyed, as if she were accusing *him* of something. "It hardly warrants a search," he said. "The women will practice their trade whether here or in the goldfields. We're more concerned with stopping the smuggling of contraband rum and whiskey to the goldfields and arresting Americans trying to avoid the purchase of mining licenses." He turned to look out the window, seeming to dismiss the discussion.

Sarah eyed his firm profile and the unruly black curls on his neck that had escaped the barber's shears . . . if in fact he ever went to a barber. It looked more as if he'd been to a horse clipper. "I wasn't aware that the provincial government levied a discriminatory tax on Americans," she said.

"I assure you, Miss Ashley, the license is required of all who seek gold. Americans who tread on British soil are no exception, although they frequently forget that."

Sarah absorbed that rebuttal. Miffed, she replied, "Perhaps you should consider what the American prospectors did for California. Because of them, land values escalated, thousands of new buildings were built, and the railroads went in. The British could certainly do worse."

The line of his mouth hardened almost imperceptibly. "Perhaps," he replied. "But right now our concern is with the recapture of revenues lost through smuggling and the avoidance of the mining tax."

Regarding him with vexation, a hint of irony creeping into her voice, Sarah said, "Yes, I suppose you would find that more important than the welfare of a few women of questionable character." Although initially she'd found the man disarmingly attractive, his petty attitude reminded her how deceiving looks could be. Clamping her mouth shut, she intended to say nothing more for now. After all, she was to be a guest in the man's home.

As the coach turned off the main street, the grating racket of wheels on cobblestones ceased, and they followed a hard-packed dirt road skirting the bay. Several minutes later, the carriage swerved around a gravel drive and pulled to a halt in front of the governor's home—an impressive two-story white house shaded by several grand old oaks and surrounded by a modest stretch of park and lawn.

When they entered the house, Sarah noted the elegant interior and lovely carved furnishings. Jon excused himself, and Esther gave Ida instructions as to where Sarah should stay. Gathering her skirt, Sarah followed Ida up a wide stairway, down a long hall, and into a room with a window facing the bay.

After Ida left, Sarah raised the window, and a gentle sea breeze billowed the lacy white curtains. It was obviously a woman's room: a striped floral bedcover of soft pinks and dusty blues; a dressing table with an ornate silver brush, comb, and hand mirror; a turned-wood bed with a grouping of decorative needlework pillows. She lifted a scrap-work screen from the desk and examined the forget-me-nots and other miniature pressed flowers, the cutouts of rosy-faced cherubs, and the snippets of delicate lace with satin ribbon. A meticulous person had planned it, and a steady hand had tediously pieced it together.

Her eyes were drawn to a large oil painting above the fireplace. In the scene, a woman of exceptional beauty, with skin as pale as a lily, sat on a sofa, her golden hair caught in a coronet of braids and flowers about her head, her icy blue eyes staring out at the world. In her hands, she held a piece of embroidery, and beside her, two young girls looked on. The younger of the girls—a child with wide blue eyes and flaxen hair—bore an incredible likeness to Louella; the older, a comely young girl with large dark eyes and dark brown hair, resembled Josephine.

Peering into the eyes of Jonathan Cromwell's deceased wife, Sarah had an almost overwhelming urge

COME BE MY LOVE

to withdraw from this room. Those eyes were so like her stepfather's: so distant, so austere. With no trace of warmth or affection.

With no trace of love.

During the year after her mother's death, Sarah had kept trying to touch her stepfather's heart ... kept waiting, and hoping, until she realized he looked at her as if she didn't exist.

Even when his health began to fail, he didn't look to her to run his business. Instead, he turned it over to Hollis and Tyler. By the time he died, Hollis and Tyler had depleted the capital, running up large debts from gaming. When the banker—one of Hollis's gambling cohorts—tipped Hollis off about the existence of Sarah's savings, Hollis immediately started proceedings to obtain the money. So she liquidated the account and fled. By now, they'd know, and she prayed they wouldn't come looking for her and press the lawsuit.

She needed the money to start her business so she would never be dependent on a man again. Only then could she put aside the uncertainties and the unwilling tug of jaded emotions that always seemed to drag her down: the hopeless inability to come to terms with the fact that her entire life had been a lie.

She was a love child, conceived in lust.

The only truth she knew was that her real father had not wanted her, the man she believed was her father had not wanted her, and her stepbrothers despised her.

Men were an abject, contemptible lot, she decided.

Within the hour, Sarah's trunks arrived. While she was unpacking, a light rapping on the open door of the room startled her. Turning, she saw sixteen-year-old Josephine standing in the doorway.

Josephine's dark eyes gleamed with anticipation. "Miss Ashley, may I see them?"

Sarah smiled. "You certainly may." Josephine had come to examine a pair of bloomers. On the ship, Sarah had described her shirtwaisters and bloomer costumes to Esther and the girls, and Josephine had shown particular interest.

Josephine sallied into the room and at once noticed Sarah's hoopskirts collapsed on the bed. She fingered one of the wide steel hoops. "Louella wants one of these," she said, "but I think hoopskirts are the absolute height of absurdity; props for yards of unnecessary material; sweeps for gathering dirt and dragging it into the house."

Curious, Sarah looked at Josephine. Her statement, which sounded vaguely familiar, seemed far too opinionated for such a young woman. "Louella can have that one if she wants it," she said. "I had intended to leave it behind, but it found its way among my things when my maid packed."

Josephine shook her head. "Papa wouldn't allow it. He says when they swing back and forth they show the limbs, and that's not good. And of course Grandmother agrees—insists Louella and I wear layers and layers of petticoats instead. But Aunt Esther's not as strict as Papa and Grandmother," she added. "She would have bought Louella a hoopskirt when we were in San Francisco, but she won't go against Papa or Grandmother's wishes."

Sarah shook out a gown of emerald-green duchesse and hung it on a hook on the door of the armoire, next to a gown of plum and fuchsia foulard. She ran her hand over the skirt of her green gown to smooth away the wrinkles, then looked askance at Josephine. "Does your grandmother always agree with your father?" she asked, curious about the older woman, wondering if she could find an advocate there.

"No, not always," replied Josephine. "At least not

in our schooling. Grandmother thinks we should go to St. Ann's Academy, where we would have the benefit of a virtuous upbringing. But Papa insists we go to Madame Pettibeau's Seminary for Young Ladies, so we can learn to be poised and proper . . . like Mama was."

Seeing the melancholy expression on Josephine's face, Sarah promptly distracted her by whisking out a pair of black bloomers. "Well, here they are." She offered the bloomers to Josephine. "This pair should fit you, and you may have them if you'd like. You wear them over your pantalettes and under a short skirt or tunic."

Josephine giggled, draping the bloomers from her waist. "I wonder what Papa would say if I wore them," she mused, "since we're to be in all respects ladylike?" Peering into the mirror, she curved her lips in a devious smile. "But if he didn't see me . . ." A mischievous twinkle crept into her eyes. "Can I really have these?"

"Yes," said Sarah. "But you mustn't wear them unless your father approves."

Josephine gave a vague nod of agreement. Walking over to the armoire, she touched the sleeve of Sarah's plum and fuchsia gown, then trailed her hand lightly down the skirt of the green duchesse. "These are surely pretty," she said. "I've never seen such bright colors."

Sarah smiled at the look of wonder in Josephine's dark eyes. "They are some of the new dyes—vivid colors are the rage in Paris."

Josephine traced her finger along the neckline of the green gown. "The front is surely low."

"It's the latest fashion," said Sarah. "In the boxes at the San Francisco opera, the woman whose dress is not décolleté is presumably a maid or a theater attendant."

"It sure is pretty. But Papa would never let us wear anything with the front so low. He'd say we were trying to tempt the devil, yielding to base sin. Papa's a God-fearing man."

"Then you'd best listen to your papa," said Sarah, finding Josephine's comment somewhat incongruous with what she'd seen of the man thus far. Jonathan Cromwell seemed anything *but* a God-fearing man.

After Josephine left, Sarah reached for her diary and made an entry dated September 3, 1863:

Dear Diary,

Victoria is everything I dreamed it would be. Every woman we passed on the ride through town wore yards of skirt, and I am here to change that. In fact, I have just decided that to-night will be my overture. I shall wear a brightly-colored décolleté gown to dinner— without the usual layers of petticoats. No doubt Governor Cromwell will regard it as indecent, when, in fact, it is really quite in vogue. But I shall not let the man dictate my fashion. In fact, I rather look forward to seeing his reaction.

Chapter 2

J on poured a brandy and walked over to the parlor
window. Slowly swirling the spirits in the snifter,
he watched the sun creep lower on the horizon, the
crimson-gold sky reminding him of the rich hue of
Sarah Ashley's hair. He couldn't deny it. The American woman with her emerald eyes, high cheekbones,
and firm but delicate chin possessed uncommon
beauty.

He tossed back the brandy and swallowed with a
gulp.

Uncommon beauty, hell! With hair that flamed like
the fires of Hades and eyes that could bewitch the
devil himself, she could lead a man straight to the
gates of hell. He knew her kind. Only too well.
Snatch a man's heart, suck out his lifeblood, and toss
him away.

He also suspected she'd left San Francisco under a
cloud of notoriety—no doubt a sexual scandal of
some sort. Her startled look when he'd implied as
much all but told him so. And he had good reason to
imply. Five minutes off the ship and she'd cornered a
merchant and arranged a tête-à-tête . . .

Certain other facts also supported his conjecture.

She, a single woman, had arrived in a town where
she admittedly knew no one and had no relatives.

Yet she apparently arrived without a letter of introduction. She obviously had money, because her clothes were of good quality and she had a personal maid. And although she observed proper etiquette, she was not a product of an old, aristocratic family, but rather someone who had recently acquired wealth. Her protocol was not spontaneous, she seemed more a comrade to her maid than a mistress, and she'd been in awe of the coach.

Definitely questionable circumstances.

Admittedly, he was a cynic now. But he hadn't always been. Before, he'd simply been a guileless fool replete with utopian notions. All his youth, it seemed, he'd been waiting for something, something elusive and intangible and of extreme importance, yet he hadn't known what it was.

And then he saw Caroline at the cotillion.

Dressed in a gossamer gown, she was an exquisite fairy creature with eyes of crystal blue that sparkled with gaiety, and hair of spun gold that glittered with diamonds. And as he stared, absorbing her dazzling beauty, he fell in love. Passionately. Desperately. Irrevocably.

The blood-heat of possession began to pump in his veins until he burned with the desire to make love to her, to possess her body and soul. Then came the realization that the elusive, intangible something he'd been waiting for was love—abiding, eternal love. And she, and only she, was the woman who could give him this love and make his life whole.

So theirs had been a fairy-tale wedding . . .

What a blind fool he'd been, so susceptible to her whims that her every request became his promise, her every notion his impetus to action. He'd been ambitious because he'd wanted to be everything *she* wanted him to be, something of each of the suitors he'd bested. He'd have the esprit de corps of one, the grit of another, the enterprise of yet another, until he wasn't certain who he really was.

And then came the fire ... and the truth ...

And he awoke to the realization that the elusive, intangible thing he'd waited for during his romantic youth did not exist. Love happened in fairy tales, not in life, and he accepted that.

Now he didn't hate women because of Caroline, nor did he avoid them. He romanced them, dallied with them, used their soft, willing bodies for his pleasure. But he'd never again indulge in impossible dreams or search for the myopic love of his youth, never again give his heart and sell his soul, or find himself caught up in the futile emotional labyrinth in which he'd been trapped with Caroline. He would not be that fool again ...

Short, quick footsteps brought his head around.

Too stunned to speak, he stared as Sarah Ashley approached wearing a satin gown of the most brilliant shade of green he'd ever seen. Richly embroidered in purple and blue, her dress disregarded all convention of color and style. And the neckline plunged low, generously exposing high, round breasts. She wore her hair parted in the middle and pulled back over her ears, and a coppery bun decorated with silk pansies rested near the curve of her neck—an exquisite neck that beckoned a man's lips.

She could indeed lead a man to the fiery gates of hell. And she knew it. She walked toward him with all the stealth and wile of a sleek, lissome feline: furtive eyes assessing her prey, claws retracted but poised for attack.

Alluring. Mesmerizing. Lethal.

He rather looked forward to dallying with this enticing little hellcat. "Good evening, Miss Ashley."

She smiled. "Good evening, Governor." The glow from the fixture above emphasized the high set of her cheekbones and sparkled in her magnificent eyes, wide-set eyes with an upward slant that made them seem almost feline, drawing his gaze into their golden-green depths.

Although her initial demeanor had been one of reserved modesty, she presented quite a different picture now. One that unquestionably caught his attention—an alluring, seductive *fille de joie* who undoubtedly knew her way around the bedroom, and who had the experience to thoroughly satisfy a man's needs. And do it with savoir faire.

A titillating thought: that luscious body, soft and warm against him; the act performed, of course, without the distraction of sentiment to muddle his perception. With nightbirds like Miss Sarah Ashley, it was just a game, a sensual, hedonistic game. As he fantasized on that intriguing thought, a lazy smile tugged at the corners of his mouth. "Please sit down," he said. "My mother and sister will be joining us presently. Can I offer you a glass of sherry, or perhaps Madeira?"

"Yes, thank you," she replied. "Madeira would be lovely." Lowering herself to the sofa, she glanced around. "Louella and Josephine? Won't they be joining us?"

Jon moved to a silver tray with a cut-crystal decanter. "I'm afraid not. They'll be taking supper in their rooms and retiring early."

"Oh. I rather looked forward to seeing them tonight."

Pouring a glass of wine, Jon offered it to her, his eyes resting where her gown dipped dangerously low on her bosom. "Yes, I did too, but my sister allowed them far too many liberties while they were on holiday," he said, taking in the sight of creamy white breasts pushing upward from her low bodice. The scent of blossoms wafted to him, sending a sultry heat rushing through his veins. Had she placed a cloth with essence between the lovely mounds?

He filled his lungs with the sweet woman-scent of her.

"Governor, is there something wrong?"

Raising his gaze, Jon peered into dangerous sea-green eyes fringed with dark, coppery lashes. He stood straight, realizing he'd lost himself for a moment. The fact was, Sarah Ashley, with her provocative smile and enticing curves, primed his body for action; lustful, passionate action. "No," he said. "There's nothing wrong," *that a lively romp in the hay wouldn't cure.*

A glaringly idiotic idea, he decided. She was, after all, Esther's guest, not a common tart. A tart perhaps, but not a common one. Best to divert his thoughts to safer ground. He focused on the confrontation he'd had with Josephine before dinner, an argument concerning the purchase of a gown that dipped low in front. He knew now where the idea for the gown had originated. "My daughters seem very impressed with you," he said.

"Well, I'm impressed with them, too," she replied. "They are both truly lovely. Josephine is so . . . spirited. An absolute delight."

Jon took a swig of brandy and rolled it around in his mouth. "She's also very impressionable . . . easily distracted from what's expected of her, and determined to have her way. And I am equally determined to instill in her"—his gaze dropped to Sarah's bosom—"high morals."

Sarah opened her fan and fluttered it at her throat, masking the décolleté neckline. So Governor Cromwell thought her immoral. Well, he was obviously unaware of the latest fashion, living as he did surrounded by trappers, prospectors, and Indians. "Both girls seem especially anxious to please you," she said. "That should make you very proud." She saw his mouth lift slightly with the barest hint of a smile.

The smile vanished. "Proud, but concerned," he replied. "Josephine sometimes finds it difficult to accept her position in life."

"Her position?"

"As a woman. She's overly headstrong and independent."

Sarah gave him a cool, crisp smile. "And you think she should be less assertive? Better yet, a servile creature without an opinion of her own?" she said, her voice calm in spite of her agitation.

His mouth curved in a cynical, one-sided smile. "Josephine is entitled to her opinions," he said. "It's her manner of expressing them that concerns me. She's far too forthright and outspoken."

Sarah pursed her lips, annoyed with his condescending attitude. "Forgive me, Governor," she said, "but I fear I, too, have been outspoken. After all, Josephine is your daughter, and you have a perfect right to be an autocratic, overbearing father if you so choose."

He cocked a dark brow. "When I deliver my daughters to the altar, I assure you they will be"—his gaze dipped to Sarah's bosom again and rested there momentarily—"untouched. And if it takes an autocratic, overbearing father to accomplish that goal, that's exactly what I'll be."

Sarah's lips tightened angrily. So he based his wrong assessment of her character on the fact that she wore a stylish gown.

Or . . . had the dreadful scandal followed her here?

The disturbing thought settled over her like an ominous shadow. Please, dear God, no. She couldn't bear the shame and humiliation again . . . endure the disgrace . . . feel herself stripped of all pride and dignity . . .

To her surprise and alarm, Jonathan Cromwell brushed a finger along her jaw, smiled a broad, devastating smile, and said in a low, suggestive voice, "Innocence, however, is only for my daughters. I prefer a more experienced woman."

Shocked by his implication, Sarah struggled to think of a proper retort, one that would exonerate her virtue while putting the man in his place. But before she could respond, Esther appeared, accompanied by a small, white-haired woman who stepped with a lively gait. "I would like to present our mother, Lady Cromwell," Esther said, directing the dowager viscountess to where Sarah slowly stood to receive the older woman.

Lady Cromwell stared first at Sarah's gown. Then she raised the gold-rimmed spectacles that were attached to a gold chain pinned to her bosom and propped them on her nose. Her white brows arched, and her thin lips gathered with distaste as she scrutinized Sarah's dress more thoroughly. A glint of fire came into her eyes. "My daughter informs me that you are removing to Victoria, Miss Ashley." Her cool tone seemed unusually husky for such a frail-looking woman. "Why, may I ask, have you chosen our city?"

Sarah caught the jaded overtones and noted the glint of challenge in the woman's eyes, and wondered again if the scandal had made its way here. Or if, perhaps, Harriet Galbraith had already stopped by. Trying to dismiss that uncomfortable thought, she said, "With the goldfields up north drawing so many people to the area, I feel that in Victoria there are many opportunities for success."

Lady Cromwell's eyes narrowed, and she gave her a brittle smile. "Unfortunately, the best claims in the Cariboo have been taken. And when those play out, there will be another exodus from the city. As in '59, stores will close, merchants will leave, and Victoria will slip into an economic depression. But even if that does not happen, certainly your American cities, with their wealth of modern comforts, offer more than our meager colonial outpost."

Sarah looked into a pair of cool, unfaltering eyes and pressed her lips into a polite smile. "I'm afraid our modern cities also attract problems," she said. "Swindlers, rowdies, and overcrowded streets."

"But we have all of that right here in Victoria with the prospectors," parried Lady Cromwell.

"Yes, I see you do," Sarah admitted, trying to hold her voice steady, feeling a growing unrest in the face of the woman's blatant hostility. As gracious as Esther had been on the ship, Sarah had not expected anything less from her mother. Struggling to hold her voice calm, she said, "But when the goldfields play out and the prospectors move on, they should leave behind a prosperous city."

Lady Cromwell pinned her with an icy glare. "They will leave behind a city populated by greed-driven Americans."

Esther took her mother's elbow. "Come, Mother. Dinner is ready." She looked over her shoulder at Sarah, giving her a contrite smile. Lady Cromwell looked over her shoulder at Jon and scowled, obviously miffed that he was not the one to escort her into the dining room as protocol demanded.

Jon ignored her. Gathering Sarah's hand, he tucked it into the crook of his elbow. Covering it with his palm, he looked down at her with hooded eyes. When he spoke, she could feel the heat of his breath on her temple. It smelled of smoke and brandy. "You'll have to excuse our mother," he said. "She was unprepared for visitors." He ushered her toward the dining room.

Sarah's palm, trapped beneath his large hand, rested against a rock-hard forearm. "Yes, I can see that everyone was," she said, finding her attention divided between the gist of their conversation and the feel of his unusually muscular arm. As he swept her across the floor, she was vividly aware of his powerful masculine presence, and it was with some effort that she forced herself to focus on his comment. Looking up at him, she said, "My maid and I will see to finding other quarters at once."

Something wickedly dangerous flickered in the dark depths of his eyes. "That would be a bloody shame," he said, "and would hamper things greatly. If you spirit yourself away, how are we going to conduct a proper dalliance?" His gaze dipped lingeringly to her mouth, which he observed with candid interest.

She gave him a faint, insolent smile. "We aren't."

He leaned toward her. "Now there's a grim thought, which I'll simply dismiss."

She looked at him sharply, and he gazed steadily back at her, giving no indication that her sharp look had affected him in the least. Rather, he seemed to derive amusement from it. Ignoring him, she focused on a table graced with exquisite porcelain dinnerware, fine crystal goblets, and a pair of elegant silver candelabra.

Adjacent to the table, a richly carved sideboard displayed an ornate silver tureen filled to the brim with steaming green pea soup; a silver tray with a poached salmon fancifully decorated with black olives, small onions, and egg slices; a white and gold porcelain platter holding a honey-baked ham garnished with whole cloves and pineapple slices; several elegant silver serving bowls and trays containing glazed carrots, steamed chard, muffins, banana fritters, rhubarb tarts, cheeses, and an assortment of small cakes.

After the soup was served, Lady Cromwell, who sat opposite Jon at the end of the long table, took a dainty sip, swallowed, then looked down the table at her son. "Jonathan, there is need for more illumination in the streets. There was another incident in town. Young John Work stumbled on the planks on Government Street and fell into the ditch."

Snickering, Esther took a banana fritter from the platter offered by Ida. "Young John Work was no doubt dizzy as a goose and had probably stumbled out of the Brown Jug shortly before he fell into the ditch."

Lady Cromwell shot a stony glance at her daughter, which sobered Esther immediately. "Be that as it may," the older woman said, "the problem still persists."

Sarah, certain she'd noticed lamps lining the main thoroughfare as they'd driven from the docks through the streets of Victoria, looked at Jon and asked, "Does the city not have gas lighting?"

"Yes," he replied, "but the lights are not in use, as we have been plagued with air leaking into the mains. But the problem will soon be remedied and the streets should again be well-lighted, at least in the mercantile district."

"I'm relieved to hear that," said Sarah, reflecting on the tall storefront she'd fancied as one day being hers—a building with two brass lanterns adorning its fine brick facade. "It's most important that the mercantile district be well-lighted."

"Is there a particular reason for your concern about our mercantile district?"

"Yes," she replied. "I plan to establish my own business."

Amused, he arched a brow. "A business that requires lighting at night?"

Deciding she'd put up with his offensive insinuations long enough, she gave him a tepid smile. "Perhaps, at times. I plan to establish a clothier's, which will be supervised and operated by women, for the manufacture and sale of women's garments. It will frequently require my being in the building at night."

He steepled his fingers, studied her for a moment, and said contemplatively, "Why, I ask myself, would a woman who is obviously capable of finding a husband burden herself with such a task? It seems senseless, if not downright absurd."

Sarah looked steadily at him. "I am doing it because I want to do it," she said simply.

He broke off a piece of muffin and chewed it thoughtfully. "Have you operated such a business before?"

She raised her chin. "My father was a very successful clothier."

"I'm not asking about your father—the manufacture of clothing is a man's trade. I'm asking about you."

She held his gaze. "I spent countless hours working with my father in his business and helping with his books. I even drove the delivery wagon on many occasions."

He eyed her with wry amusement. "Many women in Victoria also help their fathers and husbands," he pointed out. "However, none burden themselves with the sole management of such a business."

Sarah bristled. Obviously, the man believed that women should stay at home busying themselves with all manner of tedious handiwork, as his wife had no doubt done. Well, that might be fine for some, but for her it was not enough. "A woman is more than a mere butterfly content to lead an aimless, frivolous life," she said. "That we are incapable of handling a man's business is a most absurd bit of twaddle. We are responsible, intelligent beings, Governor, so why should we not be allowed to make our own way in this world?"

Jon stared steadily back at her. "Because women, as the gentler sex, are not conditioned to the harshness and brutality of the business world."

Sarah's mouth twitched with suppressed anger. "I beg to differ with you, but through the ages, women have borne greater harshness and brutality from drunken and abusive husbands. Men lead women to believe that as the gentler sex they are incapable of honorable independence. But, in truth, men fear that if women were given equal education and allowed to work in men's professions, they might excel and, in fact, be capable of performing all the duties in the positions men now hold exclusively, including those in government."

Jon eyed her with mounting interest. There was more to this particular nightbird than he'd initially found. She was articulate and astute and obviously intelligent. And she most definitely had an independent streak. But she was also illogical, impractical, and unrealistic. He leveled his gaze at her. "Surely, Miss Ashley, you don't truly believe a woman can hold public office?"

"I most certainly do. I assure you, we have the ingenuity, creativity, and skills for achievements higher than cooking, darning, and washing!"

Jon pondered her brash statement, but soon became distracted. The glow from four tall candles accented the fine planes of her delicate face and sparkled like amber jewels in her stunning green eyes. And golden highlights glistened off her rich coppery curls, dusting them in gilt, the overall effect

reminding him how exceptionally beautiful she was
. . . and how much he'd like to bed her.

Focusing again on her statement, he said, "American women, it seems, are restless. Wisely, the women
of Victoria choose to rely on their men rather than
face untold obstacles and dangers while learning
how difficult, if not impossible, it is to stand alone."

"That may well be," she replied, "but nevertheless,
I intend to try."

Esther looked at Jon. "Perhaps you should heed
what Sarah says and not underestimate today's more
independent woman. I suspect you have at least one
daughter who shares her views."

Jon gave a faint, ironic smile. "Josephine is naive
and impressionable, as are all young women her age.
She may believe she shares Miss Ashley's views—
though she hasn't been brought up with such unconventional notions—but I trust it will pass eventually,
and she'll come to her senses."

Lady Cromwell looked on with a disapproving air.
Her voice had the sharp snap of a whip. "That is precisely why the girls should attend St. Ann's Academy, where they would receive moral guidance, or
the next thing we shall see is Josephine flaunting herself in trousers like a man."

Esther gave Sarah a bland smile, then promptly
changed the subject. "Sarah has brought with her
two Singer sewing machines, and she has offered to
teach the girls and me how to operate them."

Lady Cromwell peered over the gold rims of her
spectacles. "There is no need," she said. "Both of the
girls have a deft hand with the needle."

"But with the sewing machine," said Esther, "a
seam can be stitched in a fraction of the time."

"Which will undoubtedly create a crude, uneven
seam," countered Lady Cromwell.

"On the contrary," Esther parried, "the seams are

quite straight. Sarah showed us a sample. You will be greatly amazed when you see for yourself. I'm anxious to give it a try." She turned to Sarah. "When do you expect to have the machines operating?"

Sarah dabbed her mouth. "Very soon, I hope." Turning to Jon, she said, "Perhaps you'd be so kind as to tell me where I might go to apply for a business license. I'd like to get started at once."

Jon hadn't expected her to pursue her venture so soon. "Applications for licenses are at the legislature building." He steepled his fingers and regarded her speculatively. "I'm curious about one thing," he said. "What makes you think you can compete with the Hudson's Bay store? It stocks a complete line of women's apparel."

Sarah gave him a confident smile. "Oh, I won't be competing with the company store," she assured him. "I'll be selling apparel that women cannot buy there or in any other store in Victoria . . . items such as bloomer costumes and shirtwaister dresses. I've brought a wide selection of sizes. The women won't be difficult to convince, once they see the practicality of my products."

Jon's mouth spread in a wide grin. "Bloomer costumes?" Her announcement brought him to the brink of outright laughter, and he struggled to keep from giving way to it. "I doubt you'll find a woman in Victoria who'd be inclined to wear something as ridiculous as bloomers."

A faint flush rose in her cheeks. She pinned him with eyes darkened by renewed anger, eyes that took on vast ranges of greens and azures. "You, being a man, might see it that way, which is to be expected," she said. "And, of course, I have taken that into account."

"My being a man has nothing to do with the facts," said Jon. "The ladies here are traditional, conservative women who adhere to popular sentiment. I assure you, they won't be inclined to condone anything as unconventional as bloomer costumes."

"Perhaps at first," Sarah admitted. "But I intend to change that way of thinking. Women need freedom of limb and motion if they aspire to higher levels of employment, to move out of sewing circles and into the professions that men now hold. Dress reform is one of the most important aspects of our emancipation. So in addition to selling my costumes, I shall strive to enlighten women as to what is considered healthful attire. Of course, I plan to discuss with them other aspects of liberation as well."

Jon noted the spark of determination in her eyes and the firm set to her mouth. It appeared she was on a crusade of sorts, though he questioned if she had the stuff to survive as a female merchant in a male profession in a town populated mostly by men. Perhaps he'd throw a few minor roadblocks in her path, just to see how gutsy the lady really was. Then later, of course, he'd come to her aid and allow her to repay him in the best way she knew how.

Ah, yes . . . the best way . . .

"To obtain your license," he said, "you'll first have to offer your business plan to the city council, members of which are openly opposed to women in business. I'm afraid you won't find them very supportive."

Beneath his burning gaze, Sarah's cheeks warmed, and she hoped he had not caught the telltale sign. But from his roguish grin, she realized he had. Dismissing the unwanted effect he seemed to enjoy having on her, she said, "Is there an ordinance prohibiting a single woman from setting up and operating her own business venture?"

"No," he said, "but you won't be setting up anything without a license, which must be approved by the city council and signed by me. I'd hate to find you locked away with scurrilous men, but, as yet, we have no facility for women in our jail, and we do· strictly enforce the law regarding business licenses."

That wasn't truly the case, he knew. In fact, they were actually quite lenient in that regard. And the legislature and the city council were currently at odds about the city's power to levy such fees. But he intended to thwart her efforts, at least until he learned more about her and her objective.

Sarah sensed a battle brewing, one she had no intention of losing. She looked at Jon, aware that her eyes were locked with his, but she refused to break the contact and give him even that small edge over her. "Then, if I end up in jail, you shall have that on your conscience," she said. "Make no mistake, Governor. I *will* sell my garments to the women of Victoria. And if you think you can stop me just because I am a woman, you'll soon find yourself with a fight on your hands."

Jon's mouth still held that faintly amused smile Sarah was coming to know. Curving his large fingers around his goblet, he raised it in a silent toast. "Then, shall I assume it will begin tomorrow at the legislature building?"

The way he looked at her—the aggressive boldness in his gaze—made Sarah's breath catch and tiny hairs bristle on the back of her neck. Attempting to mask any hint of emotion in her voice, she replied, "Yes, Governor, you may assume that, unequivocally."

Chapter 3

Sarah dragged her largest trunk to the middle of the room. "Get out my lilac bloomer costume with the braided trim, Mandi." Although initially she'd planned to wear conventional dress to the legislature building, Jon's high-handed attitude the previous evening still rankled her. Now she was determined to introduce her bloomer costume to the women of Victoria as soon as possible.

Mandi giggled as she opened the trunk. "Ah was wonderin' when you was goin' to start in showin' off your things."

Sarah sat at the dressing table and started brushing her hair. A smile played about her lips. She could just imagine what Jon would think of her unconventional attire. Even though the bloomer costume she planned to wear was really quite lovely, he would, of course, disapprove—the man was far too insular for her to expect otherwise. But if she intended to promote her garments, she must get on with the business of introducing them.

After Mandi finished arranging Sarah's hair, Sarah stepped into the pale lilac bloomers, which gathered about the ankles of her high-topped, white kid boots. Over the Turkish-style trousers she wore a tunic of matching foulard, the silk fabric richly embroidered

39

with shades of purple and lavender and amethyst. A band of purple braid trimmed the loose garment at the wrists of the bishop sleeves and along a full hem that reached just below her knees.

Standing in front of the mirror, she positioned on her head a small aubergine straw bonnet trimmed with lilac chiffon, leaf-green ribbon, ostrich plumes, and deep purple roses. "What do you think?" she asked Mandi when she stepped back to view herself.

Mandi held up an overjacket of matching lilac foulard. "Ah think you look real nice," she replied. "And Ah 'spect you'll cause quite a stir."

Sarah slipped her arm into one flared sleeve. "Yes, I imagine I will." She hoped she wouldn't cause too much of a stir. But once the ladies of Victoria saw how lovely and practical a bloomer costume could be, she felt certain they'd be anxious to own one. She opened her parasol and twirled it against her shoulder. "Well, wish me luck."

Mandi eyed her with mild concern. "Ah 'spect you'll need it ... this bein' your first time goin' to town dressed in your costume and all. Ah'll sho' be anxious to know what happens."

Sarah arched a dubious brow. "So will I." Closing her parasol, she grabbed her gloves and reticule, and left.

Esther met her in the entryway. "I've ordered the coach to be brought around for you," she said, gazing with interest at the bloomer costume. She stepped back to observe it more thoroughly. "Your costume is really lovely ... and so sensible."

"Thank you." Catching the gleam of envy in Esther's eyes, Sarah said, "I'd like very much to give you a pair of bloomers, if you'd accept them."

"Oh ... thank you, but I don't think so. Mother would positively have a fit of the vapors." Esther's forehead puckered with a contemplative frown. "But

... perhaps if I were to wear them only in the privacy of my bedroom. Yes, that's exactly what I'll do!"

So ... Jon's sister had a streak of rebelliousness in her, too. Sarah entertained the idea of Esther crawling out of her drab cocoon and doing something quite shocking, like applying a bit of rouge to her lips and cheeks while parading about in bloomers. Yes, her mother would indeed have a fit of the vapors.

Esther eyed Sarah with mild concern. "I had no idea you planned to wear your costume today."

Sarah pulled on a white kid glove. "Well, actually, neither did I. But then, I decided it's as good a time as any to introduce it." She only hoped the women of Victoria would be as receptive to the attire as Esther and Josephine had been.

Esther placed her hand on Sarah's arm and squeezed. "I do wish you well," she said. "But it won't be easy."

"I know that," replied Sarah. "But I'm not one to shy away from obstacles."

"It's a good thing," said Esther, "because I fear there will be many for you. Right now, Jon and his cabinet are having some rather monumental problems with political and governmental issues, mainly the threat of unification with British Columbia."

"Well, I hardly see how my selling bloomer costumes and shirtwaister dresses could possibly have any bearing on unification with British Columbia or any other governmental issues," said Sarah, pulling on the other glove.

Esther gave an empathetic sigh. "It does seem a bit peculiar," she admitted. "But, you see, Jon is strongly opposed to unification—he's determined that Vancouver Island remain independent from the mainland—and he feels that only by maintaining a stable economy can he prevent unification. To do that, he must have the support of his cabinet, the city council, the House of Assembly, and the merchants—most of whom are Hudson's Bay men—and they don't want a woman merchant among them. And Jon's efforts are further aggravated by caustic editorial attacks in our newspaper, the *Colonist*. The editor is Jon's political enemy, and he can be quite brutal at times."

"Well, I'm sorry about that," said Sarah, "but I have no desire to become a teacher or a seamstress, and since today's woman has few other options, I have little choice. So in spite of the men of this town, I intend to pursue my business and see it become a success."

"I rather share in your sentiments," said Esther. "So I hope, for your sake, you do succeed. However, Jon feels otherwise. He believes that a single woman in business would be a threat to the merchants' integrity . . . that she would create contention and unrest in the community."

"He told you that?"

"Well, not in so many words. But from last night's conversation, you must know what his views are on where a woman's place is supposed to be—at home. I suspect he may be your biggest obstacle."

"I simply cannot believe I could possibly be a threat to anyone," said Sarah, "so I will proceed with my plans, and Jon, and his cabinet, and the merchants of this community will have to deal with that as best they can."

Esther stepped onto the porch. "I suspect they've already initiated something," she said. "Jon left unusually early . . . said he was meeting with his cabinet and the mayor. He's up to something. I just know it."

"Well, at least he's true to his word," Sarah mused

on a note of disgust. "The fight is most definitely on."

Esther gave the coachman instructions, then again wished Sarah well. As Sarah rode, she felt a growing sense of resentment. She refused to believe that she had managed to liquidate her savings, flee from Hollis and Tyler, and make her way to Victoria, only to be defeated by a haughty governor and his flock of bootlicking bureaucrats before she had barely begun. She had no idea what to expect—her options ranged from being issued a business license, then later facing whatever obstacles Jon and his council would concoct, or not being issued a license at all. But since Jon admitted there was no ordinance prohibiting a woman from running a business, how could the council refuse?

It was some moments before Sarah, her brows gathered in concentration, realized the coach had pulled to a halt. The footman helped her out, and when she looked up and saw the legislature building, she simply stood and stared. The architecture— part wood, part brick—combined a confused agglomeration of styles fancifully painted in various shades of red. The footman, following the direction of her gaze, smiled in amusement. "It's a bit of a controversy around here," he said. "It's been described as a Dutch toy, a Swiss cottage, a Chinese pagoda, and a Chinese wash house. But most folks around here call it the Birdcages."

Sarah arched a brow. "That seems appropriate."

She marched up the wide stairs to the main entrance. Once inside, she located the room dubbed House of Assembly and stepped up to a desk displaying a sign carved with the name Joseph Porter, Esq., Clerk of the House. Leveling her gaze on the man behind the desk, she said, "I'm here to obtain a business license."

The man inspected her costume critically. Reaching into a long drawer, he retrieved a bundle of papers and offered them to her. "Supply the information required," he said in a cool, dry tone, "secure the necessary signatures, and bring everything back here for the legislative council to review."

Sarah stared in bewilderment at the bundle of papers. "You apparently misunderstood. I'm only trying to get a business license."

"If you wish to be issued a business license," the man said, his voice growing impatient, "then you must complete the papers I have given you."

Expelling a weary sigh, Sarah sat on a long wooden bench. Paging through the documents, she noted that they had been hastily drawn.

She scanned the information requested—copious details about the location of the building and the nature of the business; an agreement to abide by oppressive restrictions and specifications for privies, including exact hours when offal matter would be moved; a schedule for beating or shaking rugs, cleaning and maintaining the board walkway in front of the building, and disposing of ammoniacal liquor, soap lees, and other offensive matter; character references and signatures from six local merchants; the backing of two local banks; signatures of the mayor and each member of the city council; and, finally, the signature of Governor Jonathan Cromwell.

She stepped over to the man behind the desk. "There's no way a person could possibly follow all of these rules. I cannot imagine that every merchant in Victoria has been subjected to *this*"—she waved the papers in front of him—"in order to obtain a business license."

The man blinked dispassionately. "If you wish to discuss it with a member of the legislative council, I'll schedule an appointment for you. The council is occupied with governmental matters at this time, but they might see you in, say, three weeks."

Glancing around, Sarah noticed that several men had gathered to gawk at her in amusement. Obviously, they had been a party to this little scheme. Her mouth compressed in a harsh line, she drew in an extended breath through flared nostrils and said, "I do believe I understand." Gathering her reticule and parasol, she left the room, the voluminous document clutched in her hand, a scowl on her face.

Marching down the hallway, ignoring the snickers and curious glances following her as she went, she located Jon's office and swept into the room. She was at once aware of the rugged, virile man sitting behind the desk. With his crop of unruly black hair, his unshaved chin with the shadow of a day-old beard, and his broad, square hands covered in short, dark hair, he looked more like a frontiersman than a governor. She was also aware of the penetrating dark eyes appraising her. But she refused to let that distract her.

She stood before him, her eyes stinging with suppressed tears of rage. "You and your prestigious legislative council must take me for a complete noddy!"

Jon leaned back in his chair, a smile creeping across his face. Sarah's overtunic and the baggy trousers draped beneath it were comical, almost clownish. The entire costume gave her a diamond-shaped outline—her bonnet with its tall plume forming the apex. On another woman the ridiculous costume might look sexless and frumpy. But on Sarah, it looked provocative. The soft silk draped between and around her lovely round breasts, which were rising and falling with her vexation, and followed the gentle taper of her hips, making him vividly aware of the enticingly sensuous woman beneath . . .

"Are you quite through ogling?" she snapped, her foot tapping a staccato beat.

Jon raised his heated gaze to meet a pair of militant emerald eyes. "I was just admiring your . . . unconventional attire."

Her soft lips tightened angrily and she waved the bundle of papers before him. "I refuse to let a group of underhanded pettifoggers prevent me from achieving my goal."

"Underhanded pettifoggers?" He smiled. Too true. The lot of them were exactly that. And he was enjoying it immensely. "Am I to assume you were not granted your request?" he asked with mock innocence.

She slapped the bundle in front of him, sending papers scattering about. "You already know that!"

He stood and walked around his desk, then circled her slowly, eyeing her closely. Everything about her glowed, her flushed red cheeks; her moist, angry lips; her shimmering silk costume. His nostrils filled with the sweet woman-scent of her—the fragrance of rosewater, the aroma of talcum powder, a vague touch of something spicy he couldn't identify. He folded his arms, resisting the urge to drag her against him. He would in time, but not yet. It was too soon. "I told you last night that the city council was opposed to women in business . . . that you wouldn't find them very supportive."

"But you didn't tell me they would stoop so low as to undermine my efforts."

"Undermine?" A one-sided smile curved the corner of his mouth. "Isn't that a bit strong?"

Sarah caught the devil-look in his dark eyes and found the effect disturbing, unsettling. Toying with the handles of her reticule, she said, "What exactly do *you* call it? I'm obviously being singled out as a scapegoat."

He moved toward her, his white smile accented against his sun-bronzed skin. "A scapegoat is one who bears the blame for others," he said in a low, husky voice. "Is that what you feel you're doing? Bearing the blame ... being a martyr for all the women who have suffered throughout the ages for their misfortune of ... being a woman? What a pity. I find it most fortunate that you *are* a woman."

Sarah had to swallow before words could come. The man was trying to distract her, drag her attention away from the fact that he and his men had fabricated the papers in an effort to stop her. "A scapegoat is also one who is the victim of unreasonable hostility."

He laughed lightly. "Believe me, I feel anything but hostility toward you."

"I see I'm getting nowhere here—" She turned to leave. But his hand shot out, capturing her arm. She tugged against his constricting hand, and when it remained firmly attached to her arm, she said, "What do you think you're doing?"

"Showing you that I am far from hostile." He pulled her to him and kissed her.

For a moment, she was too shocked to do anything but stare in wide-eyed astonishment. But when the impact of what he'd done hit her, she cocked her hand, ready to slap his face. He caught her wrist up short. "Tsk tsk tsk. Now who's being hostile?"

Incensed, she whirled around and marched out of the room, slamming the door behind her. He didn't follow, but she heard his deep, rumbling laughter echoing behind the closed door.

At the end of the hall, she lowered herself to a bench, hot tears of frustration stinging her eyes. Blinking to clear her vision, she saw a newspaper resting on the bench beside her. The heading ECON-OMY FAILING UNDER CROMWELL caught her attention.

Lifting the paper, she scanned the editorial, reading the words:

> . . . in fact, we honestly believe that the man who will not ask Her Majesty's Government to remove Governor Cromwell and his council is a traitor to his country and unworthy of her protection . . .

Sarah quickly surmised that the author of the editorial was the editor that Esther had mentioned—the political adversary of Jon's administration. Searching for the man's name, she found the peculiar appellation Amor De Cosmos. She contemplated the name, deliberating whether it was genuine. Then, deciding it made no difference, she continued to read, smiling at the conclusion, which described Governor Cromwell's House of Assembly as

> a wizened contrivance which has kept its doors so closed to the refreshing and invigorating popular breeze that it has become asthmatic . . .

A flash of insight sent a burst of hope rushing through her. Mr. Amor De Cosmos would certainly not give a scrap whether one addle-minded female got a business license or not, but she was willing to bet he'd listen to her plight and turn it against the bureaucrats. With a renewed sense of confidence, she left the building and instructed the coachman to take her to the office of the newspaper.

She settled back, and after a short ride around the bay, the coach pulled to a halt in front of a brick building with brass letters on its tall facade that read *The Daily British Colonist*. At first, she made no attempt to leave the secure confines of the coach, reconsidering her brash move. After all, she *was* a guest in Jon's home. But he and his cabinet were also behind the scheme to prevent her from acquiring a license.

"Well, if I am to be a lone sheep among wolves," she mumbled, collecting her parasol and reticule, "then I must learn to defend myself." She stepped down from the coach, raised her chin, and marched into the building.

A tall, lean man with black hair and a short-cropped black beard appeared from a back room. When he saw her, a flash of amusement crossed his face. As he approached, Sarah had the feeling that his dark eyes had taken in every detail of her attire, even though they'd scanned her so quickly, she'd barely caught their movement.

"May I help you?" he asked.

"Yes," she replied. "I'm looking for Mr. De Cosmos."

The man's eyes, luminous in the subdued light, narrowed into a fixed stare. "I am Amor De Cosmos," he said.

A cool sweat broke on Sarah's brow, and she felt a deep, nagging uneasiness. Mr. De Cosmos, she realized, could turn an editorial against her as well, if he so chose. For a moment, she stood in stiff-necked silence, the thud of her heart suggesting she walk out . . .

A deep, guttural sound emanated from Mr. De Cosmos, reminding her that he was waiting. She focused on her reason for being there. Clearing her throat, she passed her tongue over her dry lips, introduced herself, and began recounting the incidents leading to her predicament.

Amor De Cosmos sat, his hip propped on his desk, listening intently while Sarah related the facts surrounding her impasse with the city council. When she'd finished explaining, he stepped to the window and gazed out. After a few moments, he turned and fixed intense eyes on her, "Are you familiar with the many brothels on Humboldt Street?" he asked.

"No, not really," she replied. She looked at him, puzzled. The man seemed to be completely ignoring her problem.

"Sinks of iniquity and pollution," De Cosmos announced, stabbing a finger skyward for emphasis. "Disease in every form, and kindred vices in all their hideous manifestations, lurk there."

Sarah was beginning to see his point. Suddenly, her predicament seemed insignificant. Chagrined, she apologized. "I'm sorry to have taken up your time, Mr. De Cosmos. I'll just be on my—"

"Indian men sell their wives and daughters into prostitution for money to buy whiskey," De Cosmos cut in. "But this is not discouraged in our city. No! Businesses here depend upon the fur traders and prospectors who seek the prostitutes. To sum it up, Miss Ashley, Victoria has laws against brothels. But instead of abolishing the houses of debasement, the city council voted to license them as dance halls."

"But I don't see how that makes the houses any more reputable," she said. "They are still exactly what they are . . . dens of iniquity."

"Exactly!" A sardonic smile curved the man's lips. "And this is the mentality of the present administration. As long as these venal agents of the Hudson's Bay Company continue to rule this colony, the desires of the fur traders and Indians will prevail over the dignity and sensibilities of decent citizens."

"I'm sorry, Mr. De Cosmos, but I really don't know what this has to do with me, nor do I know exactly what you are trying to point out," Sarah finally admitted.

De Cosmos stroked his black beard. "What I'm trying to point out, Miss Ashley, is this administration's scandalous disregard for the moral and legal rights of the citizens. Decent, honorable people have moved into Victoria, people who are offended and outraged by the habitual drunkenness and disgusting language being continually used in public because of the brothels. Yet the city council condones this depravity by issuing business licenses to brothels hidden under the guise of being dance halls, while denying a license to"—with a graceful flourish of his arm, De Cosmos extended an upturned palm toward Sarah—"one enterprising citizen trying to establish a mercantile business."

Sarah relaxed her frown. Was the man on her side? His words certainly suggested that he was. Peering up at him, she asked in a tentative voice, "Then . . . you do feel I have been treated unjustly?"

"Absolutely!" De Cosmos passed his hand in a slow arc through the air, his eyes following its path as he said, "Headline: CITY FATHERS FAVOR BROTHELS. *Several unjust legal enactments have come down from our semi-barbarous city council, the most recent being the licensing of houses of prostitution as dance halls and, now, the denial of business licenses to honest citizens. If prostitutes are allowed to practice their trade in our fair city, certainly one decent, enterprising young woman should be allowed to practice her trade as well . . .*"

Sarah watched and listened as De Cosmos paced, his fiery passion reflected in his eager eyes. She had no idea what the outcome of an editorial such as the man proposed would be, but she knew she did not want to be a guest in Governor Jonathan Cromwell's home when the editorial reached the streets of Victoria. Somehow, she and Mandi must find other lodging before that time . . .

"*. . . by a city council comprised of men who have been all their lives among Indians, swapping baubles and blankets for furs at a profit of two thousand percent,*" De Cosmos concluded. He paused and waited for Sarah's comment.

She smiled. "As Mrs. Amelia Bloomer once said: 'For a new movement, when advertising funds are modest, any publicity is better than none.' I venture to say, my mission will be well-known after the editorial appears."

De Cosmos replied with a contemplative, drawn-out "Well . . . yes . . . And so that the ladies in Victoria are well-informed, what exactly will you be selling in your store?"

Sarah gestured toward her baggy trousers. "Bloomers." She reached into her reticule and withdrew an advertising handbill with drawings and literature about the garments she intended to manufacture. She offered it to Amor De Cosmos. "I'll also be selling an array of overtunics and shirtwaisters, similar to these."

De Cosmos studied the handbill, fingers stroking his beard. A hint of amusement lifted one corner of his mouth. After a few moments, he eyed her costume again, this time more blatantly. "Bloomers," he mused, quietly and introspectively. "May I have this handbill?"

Sarah shrugged. "Yes. I have more."

"Have you a name for your business?"

"Sarah Ashley's Fashions," she replied.

"Splendid." His mouth curved in a rueful smile. "I have an idea which will help your cause . . . and mine. Now, if you will excuse me, I must get back to work." He opened the door for her to leave.

Although Sarah wanted to learn more about what he had in mind, she realized she was being dismissed. She left the office, praising her own good fortune in coming to see Mr. De Cosmos. But once she was in the coach, a vague uneasiness began to creep over her. She'd come to Victoria to start a new life where she could escape the gossip of scandalmongers. She'd also come to elude her stepbrothers. Now she prayed that the issues raised by the *Colonist* would remain in Victoria, that none would turn up in San Francisco and find their way into Hollis's awareness.

There was also the matter of when the editorial would come out—she'd neglected to ask—and where she'd be living at that time. The thought that she might still be a guest in the Cromwell house when the editorial attack on Jon was released brought gooseflesh rising on her arms, and a lump of dread lodging in her throat . . .

Absorbed in thought, she was surprised to find the coach stopping at the legislature building. Rapping on the window, she said, "Why are we stopping here?"

"Governor's orders," the coachman replied.

Sarah fumed as she saw Jon lunge down the steps and stride toward the coach. He'd planned this . . . sent word to his coachman to return for him so she'd be trapped in the coach with him. And she didn't want to face him so soon after their recent confrontation, especially now, knowing what Mr. De Cosmos had in store for him.

Jon swung up into the coach and settled beside her, sitting so close that their shoulders rubbed as the vehicle moved along the uneven road. Sarah attempted to ease away, but he managed to wedge her snugly between himself and the side of the coach. His lips curved in an ironic smile. "You left your papers," he said, proffering the bundle.

She looked down at the wad of papers, snatched them from his hand, and placed them in her lap. "I fail to see what good they'll do, since what they require is unobtainable."

Jon studied her rigid profile and pinched lips. He'd subdue those lovely, pouting lips into soft submission before leaving this coach, he decided. The image of her beautiful face and enticing body had taken root in his mind, and he wanted her, beyond caution and common sense.

Unfortunately, it wasn't a clear-cut case of lust. The fact was, he admired her astuteness, her forbearance, her perception . . . traits that could turn things around and make a man vulnerable. That, however, wasn't an issue at the moment. Bedding her was. Of course, it might take a bit of finesse to get her to submit to him. But he *would* get her to submit, eagerly and passionately.

Then maybe she'd give up her ludicrous plan and, when the infatuation of their impassioned liaison died, return to San Francisco and leave him in peace.

He shifted so his shoulder pressed firmly against hers. "May I offer a suggestion?"

Her delicate fingers toyed with the smooth handles of her reticule, and she stubbornly refused to look at him. "Regardless of what I say, I'm certain you will, anyway."

He leaned so close his lips almost touched her ear, and said in his silkiest voice, "Why don't you find someone who will admire, cherish, and care for you so you won't have to worry yourself with the affairs of a man's world?"

Her eyes darkened and her cheeks flushed with anger as she turned to him. "No one, not even a council of provincial popinjays, will deny me the right to follow my own pursuit. And I choose to manufacture ladies' wear. That being my goal, I shall not be deterred from—"

He raised a finger and touched it lightly to her lips. "I'm certain that no one, not even a council of"—he arched a brow—"provincial popinjays could possible deter you. But maybe this will, at least momentarily." He covered her mouth with his in a long, lingering kiss. When her hand came up to protest, he grabbed it and held it gently but firmly against his chest, until she ceased struggling.

At first, Sarah felt an urge to break away, but the warmth of Jon's hand against hers, and the heavy beating of his heart against her palm, distracted her. For a moment, everything around her faded, until the only thing she was aware of was the impact of his heart against her hand and the feel of his mouth moving sensually on hers. As their lips held, the lingering kiss made her head swim, and a fever of unfamiliar longing filled her.

To her surprise, he was the one to break the kiss. He smiled down at her. "I believe your all-consuming goal is now far from your mind. Am I correct?"

She drew in a ragged breath. A cool sweat broke out on her face, and the air inside the coach seemed suddenly steamy. She touched her handkerchief to her brow and dabbed it to her upper lip. "That is so very typical," she said. "Every man believes that every woman can be overwhelmed by means of physical restraint."

"If you felt physically restrained," he said, with a trace of irony, "you certainly didn't give that impression."

She refused to look at him. She didn't like the way he affected her, the way his dark gaze made her cheeks burn and her throat grow dry. He seemed intent on distracting her. Which made her all the more determined that he would not. "As I was saying, Governor, I shall not be deterred from my goal, in spite of you and your illustrious legislative council." Although she had not intended to do so, she found herself looking at him, and again her cheeks grew fiery hot.

He brushed his finger along her jaw, and his mouth curved with a slow, seductive smile. "We'll see, Miss Ashley. We'll see."

Chapter 4

The following morning, Sarah described to Esther what had happened at the legislature building and showed her the papers containing the restrictions and requirements that the council had imposed. However, she neglected to mention that she'd been to the office of the *Colonist* and enlisted the aid of Amor De Cosmos. Jon was, after all, Esther's brother, and Esther might be offended by an editorial attack on Jon in her behalf. Sarah would tell Esther eventually, but not yet. There was still time.

Empathizing with Sarah, Esther suggested that Sarah accompany her shopping, and while they were about, she could meet some of the merchants in town. Esther felt certain that if Sarah met the men and described her plans to them, they would sign the license application without a fuss. Sarah heartily agreed. She would also transfer her money from Wells Fargo and establish a bank account in Victoria. At least, she should have no trouble obtaining one banker's signature. She had a rather large sum of money to deposit.

Deciding the occasion called for conservative attire, she donned a walking dress of a lightweight russet merino wool with black lace cuffs and collar. On her head, she wore a black Tuscan bonnet with a broad brim that turned up on one side and down on the other, with black ostrich feathers and a cluster of heath blossoms set against the fan-shaped brim.

At the Wells Fargo office, Sarah, to her profound relief, found her money waiting. Now she could dismiss the idea that Hollis might somehow manage to intercept it.

With bank draft in hand, they swept into the Bank of British North America. There Esther, with great aplomb, introduced her to the manager, indicating to him that she was indeed a woman to whom he should show deference. The banker graciously welcomed her to his bank and hastily opened her account. After securing her money, he reminded her that if there was anything he could do for her in the future, she should feel free to call upon him—at which time she thrust the bundle of papers in front of him. To her surprise, he signed.

Stepping out of the bank, Sarah and Esther broke into girlish giggles at their achievement. Feeling triumphant over having obtained her first signature, and sensing a close camaraderie with Esther, Sarah decided that the time had come to confess what she'd done, break the news about the upcoming editorial.

While they walked up the planked board walkway, threading their way between seedy, unshaven prospectors in tattered clothes, Sarah gave Esther a contrite smile and said in an almost apologetic voice, "I'm afraid I've done something that will make Jon quite angry."

Esther looked at Sarah in subdued amusement. "I'm sure Jon has far more to worry about in overseeing the colony than any mischief you might have caused. But since it seems to be worrying you, what is it you've done?"

A faint flush warmed Sarah's cheeks. "I was so angry and frustrated when I left the legislature building yesterday—knowing what Jon and his council had done to make things difficult for me—that I took my grievance to the newspaper. Mr. De Cosmos plans to make an issue of the incident in an edition in the *Colonist*."

Esther laughed lightly. "I assure you, it won't be the first time Jon will have suffered an assault from Mr. De Cosmos. Nor will it be the last. But you're right, of course. Jon will be furious."

Sarah stepped out of the way of a man beating a rug. "Then you agree that Mandi and I should find other lodging?"

"Only if you feel uncomfortable about staying with us," said Esther. "Jon will undoubtedly be upset, but the storm will eventually pass. It always does. However, Mother may be another matter. She'll be highly offended by whatever Mr. De Cosmos chooses to write, especially since a guest in our home is to be its subject." She gave Sarah's arm a reassuring pat. "Personally, I think Jon and his cabinet deserve what's coming. Jon can be most imperious at times."

"I suppose that's a quality to be commended in a governor," Sarah said, a bit illogically, then wondered why she seemed to be defending Jon.

"In a governor, yes," replied Esther, "but in a father, no. He's far too overbearing with the girls. He was not so much that way before Caroline died."

"His wife?"

"Yes . . . the woman in the portrait in your room."

"It's a lovely painting. I suppose it's still very painful for Jon," she said, though his kiss in the coach did not reflect a man still mourning the loss of his wife.

"Oh, heavens no," replied Esther. "It's been years."

"How long were they married?"

Esther pursed her lips before giving a little grunt of derision. "Twelve years." Her disapproval of Jon's marriage was evident. Almost too evident, Sarah surmised, as if Esther were trying to tell her something . . .

Perhaps give her a subtle warning?

Had Jon indulged in a liaison on occasion? He seemed an inveterate rake. But, of course, she couldn't ask Esther. Nor did it make the least bit of difference to her what Jon had done in his former marriage. But she was curious as to how he came to be so far from England.

Glancing at Esther, she asked, "How did Jon happen to end up here in Victoria?"

"He entered the service of the Hudson's Bay Company," she replied. "His first appointment was under Governor Douglas, who was chief factor for Hudson's Bay at the time. Jon was with Governor Douglas when they first selected the site for Victoria . . . he even helped build the fort. He spent several years north of here, on a Hudson's Bay outpost while trading for furs with the Indians. And he loved it."

"Living among Indians . . ." Sarah pondered, aloud. So that explained Jon's untamed, rough-cut demeanor. "Then how did he meet his wife?" She hoped she didn't sound overly curious. She certainly didn't want Esther to think she had romantic designs on her brother.

Esther shrugged. "He was called back to London, where he worked for the company. During that time, he met Caroline. He was quite smitten by her. That's the only reason he didn't return immediately to Vancouver Island. But he always wanted to. Of course, Caroline wouldn't have any part of that. She thrived on London society, and the last thing she wanted was to rub shoulders with men who took Indians for wives . . . or with the wives themselves."

"Then how did Jon get back here?"

"He was appointed colonial secretary to Governor Douglas during the gold rush of '58. When Governor

Douglas retired two years ago, Jon was the logical choice to take his place. Jon had always been sort of a bridge between the new government appointees coming directly from Britain and the Hudson's Bay men, who were essentially fur traders, and who were by then members of Douglas's House of Assembly."

"Then his wife did end up living here?"

"Oh, no." Again, that little grunt of derision. "Caroline was beside herself at the prospect of living in the wilderness among savages. When Jon sailed for Victoria, it was with the understanding that Caroline and the girls would follow on a later ship. But Caroline died. Jon had to turn around and go right back to England. After things simmered down a bit, my mother, the girls, and I joined him. We've been here ever since."

Sarah pondered Esther's comment, *after things simmered down a bit*. It seemed an odd way to describe a funeral. "How did Jon's wife die?"

"In a fire."

"Their house burned down?"

"Not *their* house. The house of some earl. It caused quite a stir. They were alone when it happened."

So it seemed Jon's wife had been involved in a tryst. "It must have been very difficult for the girls."

"Oh, they know nothing about their mother's misadventures. But it *has* been difficult for them, especially Louella. As you might have noticed, your room is a bit of a shrine to her mother's memory. Louella keeps it that way. But Jon rarely goes in there. And he's adamant that the portrait, and Caroline's belongings, remain behind the closed door."

Sarah caught the glimmer of satisfaction in Esther's eyes and, for the first time, understood her overtures: her insistence that she be a guest in their home, her chatter on the ship about her handsome widowed brother, and now her implication that his marriage had not been good. Everything had been quietly and cleverly calculated.

Esther was a matchmaker!

What a poor, droll, drab mouse Esther was, trying to find love vicariously through her brother. But she was wasting her time if she thought she'd found a match for Jon here, if she believed love even existed.

Love. What paltry, futile humbug. Everyone Sarah had loved had betrayed her, or rejected her, or discarded her. The thought of love made her feel disarmed and exposed and bereft. And she refused to dwell on it.

Thirty minutes later, and after receiving less than enthusiastic responses from several merchants to whom she'd proffered the document, Sarah realized the task of acquiring signatures was rapidly becoming a formidable one. But there were still several merchants to approach. Esther directed her toward a book bindery, informing her that the binder was an amiable Englishman with a retiring manner, whom she should have no trouble winning over. If any merchant in Victoria would sign her document, it would be James Moore.

But after receiving a cold shoulder from Mr. Moore, Sarah realized that the man knew exactly who she was, and her purpose. Obviously, Jon or his men had been as quick in spreading the word of her mission to the merchants as he had been in concocting the bogus documents for obtaining her license. The awareness relieved her of the remorse she'd felt over the upcoming editorial attack by Amor De Cosmos. However, it did not discount the fact that remaining in the Cromwell home would be awkward.

As they left the book bindery, she said to Esther, "Mandi and I really must find other lodging at once."

Esther sighed. "Yes, I suppose it's best. Josephine will be very disappointed, though."

"But not Louella," Sarah stated. She'd noticed that shortly after they'd arrived at the house, Louella had become aloof, which was in marked contrast to her demeanor on the ship during their journey from San Francisco. There, she'd been conversant and friendly.

Esther sighed again. "She's upset with me for settling you among her mother's things. I'm sorry to have placed you in such an uncomfortable position, but it's time the room was put to other use." Taking Sarah's arm, she urged her toward a store with the name K. Gambitz displayed across the top of its high brick facade. "If you're certain you want to seek other lodging, we can begin asking here about rooms to let. Kady Gambitz keeps track of everything going on in Victoria. He should know who's moving away. Then we can stop by Bartholomew Derham's bakery. What Mr. Gambitz doesn't know, Mr. Derham does."

When Esther introduced Sarah to Kady Gambitz, Sarah sensed that he, too, knew who she was, which Mr. Gambitz verified by refusing to sign the document. Deciding that she would get nowhere by advocating her cause, Sarah asked immediately about property to lease.

Mr. Gambitz looked directly at her. "It would be best, young lady, if you returned to your family in America where you belong. Victoria is no place for a woman alone."

"I see that Governor Cromwell or one of his agents has paid you a visit," Sarah said brusquely, not even trying to hide her irritation.

Mr. Gambitz raised his brows in mock surprise. "I beg your pardon?"

Esther tugged her toward the door. "Thank you, Mr. Gambitz. We won't be taking up any more of your time."

Outside, Sarah quietly fumed, her anger rising when she spotted Jon's town coach coming toward them, and Jon inside. When she and Esther had been let off at the foot of Yates Street, and Esther had given the coachman instructions to come for them in two hours, Sarah had not expected Jon to join them for the ride home. Nor did she want him to. She had absolutely nothing to say to him.

The coach pulled to a halt and the door swung open. Jon stepped down. "Good afternoon, ladies," he said, although his eyes were on Sarah. Looking at her, dressed so modestly in her high-necked frock, he found it difficult to associate the demure lady she was now with the doxy in the décolleté gown, or the libertine in the bloomer costume. He wasn't sure which Sarah Ashley concerned him the most. Each was beautiful. Each was dangerous.

The doxy could see to his carnal needs while leading him to the gates of hell; the bloomer-clad libertine could turn his colony topsy-turvy; and the demure lady facing him now could have him entertaining thoughts of marriage . . . a fatal mistake. Considering the alternatives, he believed the doxy posed the least threat. And she was the one he most needed at the moment.

"So, have you ladies completed your shopping?" he asked lightly, aware of the stunning green eyes coldly appraising him. Obviously, Miss Ashley knew what some of his men had been up to, and she was miffed.

She moistened her lips. "We were not shopping," she said. "Actually, I was introducing myself to the merchants, hoping that perhaps, unlike you and your venerable council, they were not pigheaded, narrow-minded parochials. But I see your influence precedes me."

Jon's gaze meandered over her jaunty bonnet with

its quaking ostrich plumes, her delicate face blooming with a rosy hue, the dainty lace hugging her slender neck. She was one delectable little chit. A slow smile tugged at his lips. "If it will be of any help," he said, "I'll see what I can do."

"What *you* can do?" Sarah said, nervously fluttering her lashes while attempting to deal with the distraction of the governor's unexpected smile. "I was under the impression that you were the problem."

"I'm only trying to show you that what you propose is not in your best interest," said Jon, his smile holding.

Refusing to allow herself to be taken in by his cocky, patronizing charm, Sarah glared at him. "And you presume to know what *is*?"

He shrugged. "I only know that women are far better off letting men tend to the rigors of earning a living."

"That, Governor, is utter and senseless twaddle. Your attitude is high-minded and arrogant. You expect a woman to be a serf, dependent on her liege lord for survival."

As she raised her chin to confront him, Jon caught the flare in her eyes, the bright afternoon light turning them a rich, almost golden hue . . . like the greens of fresh spring moss. "No one expects a woman to be a serf," he replied, amused. "But if she assumes the responsibilities of filling the larder and running the government, what are we men to do? Stay home and tend the hearth . . . or better yet, bear the children? Isn't that a bit ludicrous?"

"Perhaps, from your narrow viewpoint," said Sarah. "But if you'd take the time to look at the issue objectively, you'd find that without the dignity of employment in whatever field she finds suitable to maintain health and happiness and satisfy her mind and body, a woman soon falls into a state of listlessness and insipidity, her aspirations for nobler destinies crushed."

They stared at each other silently for a long moment, then Jon closed a hand on her forearm. "What a splendid pack of rubbish that is," he said. "Don't you think you're overdramatizing?"

She tried to twist her arm from his grasp, but his fingers remained firmly fixed about it. "I'm only trying to get my point across and demonstrate the injustice of your man-made laws. And will you please release my arm!"

He pulled her toward him, just as a rush of water flew from a window above, barely missing her. She braced her hand on his chest, then looked up into a pair of dark, bemused eyes. "What were you saying, Miss Ashley?" he asked, his lips very close to hers.

Good God! Sarah thought. Certainly he didn't intend to kiss her right here on the street, and with his sister looking on? Yes . . . he did. She pressed against his chest. "I was saying that . . ." She paused. She couldn't remember what she *had* been saying. It had completely escaped her.

He cocked one dark brow. "Have you forgotten your all-consuming goal again?"

She looked at him, miffed with herself that that was exactly what had happened. He seemed to affect her that way, and it was beginning to annoy her . . . immensely.

He gave her a slow, lingering smile. "I believe you were saying something about the injustice of our man-made laws. But I think you missed the point entirely. You fail to see that those laws are made for the benefit of women."

"Fiddlesticks!" She was back on track. And this time she would not be side-stepped. "You know as well as I that you men make the laws with your own aims in mind. And because of them the women of

Victoria are doomed to a life of fashionable dissipation. Unless, of course, someone steps forward and offers a challenge."

"Fashionable dissipation?" Jon's mouth curved in a rueful smile as he was reminded of her alluring but comical bloomer outfit. "As I look around, I fail to see any women in a state of fashionable dissipation."

"Of course you don't!" Sarah said, stamping her foot for emphasis. "You wouldn't know it if you saw it." Annoyed with Jon's ability to irritate her, Sarah determined to say nothing more. Gathering her skirt, she climbed into the coach. To her alarm, she saw that Esther and her boxes of purchases had taken up one entire seat, forcing Sarah to sit opposite her and beside Jon, unless he decided to ride up with the driver, which, of course, he would not.

Jon crowded in beside Sarah, aware of the firm set of her jaw. She had more spunk and determination than any woman he'd ever come up against, he gave her that. And for some inexplicable reason, that intrigued him.

Intrigued him. Hell! It obsessed him.

Just sitting beside her with her warm little body pressed snugly against his and the flowery fragrance of her perfume filling his nostrils made his loins hot and hard. And the thought that she was undoubtedly adroit in the art of lovemaking was becoming decidedly mind-consuming.

"Jon?" asked Esther, drawing his attention from Sarah. "Miss Ashley has expressed a desire to find permanent lodging. Do you know of a vacant cottage, or perhaps some rooms for let, where she and her maid might stay?"

"Yes, I do. Joseph Pemberton has a vacant cottage this side of Cadboro Bay. He's wanting either to sell it or find a tenant as soon as some roof work is completed."

Sarah looked at Jon with a start. "How far is it?"

Jon shrugged. "Perhaps a fifteen-minute ride from the house. But right now a carriage can't get through because a windstorm left some limbs and trees across the road."

Sarah sighed her disappointment.

Esther said to Jon, "After church on Sunday, why don't you provide Sarah with a mare and ride with her to the cottage."

A full smile broke across Jon's face. A splendid idea. There was no question, he wanted to know more intimately the woman who lurked beneath Sarah Ashley's independent facade. Hell! He wanted to know more intimately the woman who lurked beneath her clothes. That was the bare, raw truth. And this would be his golden opportunity. "An excellent idea," he said.

Alarmed, Sarah quickly replied, "I would appreciate the use of a horse, but I'm perfectly capable of finding my way to the cottage ... alone. I assure you, it's not necessary for you to escort me."

"I insist," said Jon. "You're a guest in our home, and I feel responsible for your welfare. Furthermore, an unescorted woman in this country is not safe."

"Thank you for your concern, but as man's equal, I am prepared to go forth with confidence and meet dangers with courage," Sarah said, knowing she didn't really believe that, but annoyed with Jon's condescending attitude.

Steadying his gaze on her, he arched a brow and said in a husky voice, "Nevertheless, it's best I accompany you, so if you wish to see the cottage, you'll have to contend with my presence."

Sarah sighed. "Very well, if you insist." Catching Jon's lazy, devastating smile, and the pair of devil eyes that seemed vibrantly, alarmingly alive, she felt a sudden portentous fear that perhaps she would face a greater danger in the unaccompanied presence of Governor Jonathan Cromwell—a thought that both troubled and tantalized her.

Chapter 5

Mandi set the hairbrush down and stepped back. "Are you sho' you know what you's doin'?" she asked.

"Don't fret so," said Sarah. She stood and slipped into the light wool jacket of her riding habit and buttoned the coat. "Besides, Governor Cromwell is a"—she started to say "gentleman," then reconsidered—"a man who would never take advantage of a lady." At least, she didn't think he'd take advantage. But she couldn't dismiss the devil-look in his eyes when he'd insisted on accompanying her to the cottage. Nor could she banish thoughts of his stolen kisses. But he'd kissed her only to prove a point. Which was to show her how weak and dependent the female sex was.

Hah! She'd show him weak and dependent!

"Ah'm not worried about the guv'nor takin' advantage," said Mandi, "but the folks in Victoria might start gossipin' if you's ridin' alone with him."

"We're only riding a short distance," said Sarah, smoothing the folds of her skirt. "We'll be gone less than an hour. Certainly, there's no harm in that?" She angled her beaver hat on her head, then turned to view herself in the mirror, wondering what Jon would think of her new riding habit with its crisp, tailored lines. She had to admit that in spite of his arrogant and ofttimes condescending demeanor, she found him extremely attractive ... dangerously attractive.

Mandi stepped back to admire her. "You sho' do look pretty," she said, flashing a bright smile.

Sarah gazed at her own reflection. "Do you like my hat better like this?" She squared it on her head. "Or this?" She tilted it slightly to the side.

"Ah reckon to the side," said Mandi. "Mind you don't knock your hair loose, though."

A capricious smile tipped Sarah's lips. She'd actually like to do just that. Hats, like layers of garments, were confining. And one day, she determined, she'd doff her hat, allowing her hair to flow free, slip into a pair of breeches, and ride astride, like some of the more venturesome women of San Francisco were doing. Wondering what Jon's reaction would be to *that*, she had to repress a chuckle.

A series of quick, sharp knocks resounded. "Miss Ashley," Ida called through the closed door. "Governor Cromwell is ready to take you for your ride."

"Thank you." Sarah hesitated in front of the mirror for one last glimpse. On impulse, she snatched off her hat and tossed it on the bed. Jon would be shocked to find her going out hatless, but she didn't give a scrap. It would be her second public gesture in the name of dress reform. Reaching for her gloves and riding crop, she left the room before Mandi could admonish her for her impetuous behavior.

At the head of the stairs, she paused. When she looked down, her heart rate quickened with a suddenness that made her painfully aware of each heavy beat. Jon stood just inside the front door. Tall and strapping, he wore an open-necked shirt that hugged his broad shoulders and thick chest and tapered into tight breeches that clearly defined his maleness.

Standing with feet apart, hands on hips, the man exuded an aura of power and strength, a kind of raw, untamed bearing that she found dangerously compelling.

Trapped in his dark gaze, she started down the stairs. "Good afternoon, Governor," she said, pulling on a black kid glove to occupy her restless hands.

Jon nodded, mulling over the fact that Sarah Ashley wore no hat. Which didn't surprise him. According to his mother, via Harriet Galbraith, Sarah had fled San Francisco because of a scandal. Although he usually placed no credence on the prattling from Harriet Galbraith's wagging tongue, this time there could be a measure of truth in it. If so, perhaps Sarah's lack of proper attire was meant to hint at a daring that went beyond mere dress to a carnal adventurousness . . .

His blood heated at the mere thought . . .

Ever since she'd agreed to let him escort her to the cottage, he'd been consumed with prurient thoughts of stretching out beside her on a bed of cool moss and losing himself in her soft, feminine curves. He imagined her breathless and eager in his arms, her lithe body writhing against him and sizzling with passion, the taut nipples of her bare breasts hot against his chest . . .

He released a long, hot breath. Ah, yes. He definitely hoped it would be like that. It would be a ruddy shame if he'd misread this provocative little minx. He was apt to get his eyes scratched out.

As she descended the stairs, he was all too aware of the tantalizing woman beneath the form-fitting riding habit. The jacket might be cut and tailored like a man's, but on her, it was unquestionably feminine. Not only did it pinch in the middle to reveal a tiny waist, but it pulled snugly and alluringly across her high, full breasts, making him vividly aware of her rounded curves.

On the porch, he offered his arm, and she placed her slender gloved hand into the crook of his elbow. As they walked toward the stables, he said, "I sincerely hope you're not seeking other lodging because of my mother's comment the other night."

She glanced uncertainly at him. She couldn't even remember his mother's comment—so many things had happened since that night. "Oh, no," she replied, aware of their proximity, finding it necessary to walk uncomfortably close to Jon while negotiating the narrow pathway. "I assure you, it has nothing to do with your mother."

He looked at her askance. "Then . . . me?"

She gave him a devious smile. "Why should I seek other lodging because of you? After all, you claim that in making things difficult for me, you're actually looking out for my best interests—me being a poor frail woman and all. The truth is, I'm seeking other lodging because I feel things could get a bit . . . cramped in a few days."

He arched a brow. "Are you expecting more trunks?"

She touched her fingers to her lips to stifle a smile. "No," she said. "I don't mean things will get cramped for me, but rather for you."

His brows gathered into a frown. "Maybe you'd better expand on that. You've left me in the fog."

She realized she'd been baiting him, but he deserved whatever Mr. De Cosmos might write in his forthcoming editorial. However, she had no intention of giving Jon even the slightest hint of what was in store.

Shrugging indifferently, she said, "Actually, what I meant is that once Mandi and I start unpacking the trunks with the bloomers and shirtwaisters, there will be garments spread all over the house." Switching subjects, she asked, "Have you any idea when the cottage will be available?"

"Two or three days . . . maybe sooner," replied Jon. He guided her toward the stables where Peterson, the head groom and coachman, appeared from the darkened interior, leading a sorrel mare. The animal's head bobbed as it pranced along on white-stockinged feet.

"She's a right lively one, mum . . . loves a good run, she does," said Peterson, leading the mare toward Sarah. "But if she knows ye're boss, she's as gentle as a lamb. Are ye sure ye can handle 'er?"

"I'll look out for Miss Ashley and see that she has no problem with the mare," said Jon.

Sarah digested that statement.

Well, she mused, Jonathan Cromwell would soon learn that all women were not helpless, hapless creatures, that there was at least one who was *not* in need of, or desirous of, his male patronage. However, since he believed her to be helpless and hapless, that's what she'd give him . . . for the moment. "I'd appreciate that," she said, giving him a meek smile. "Horses can be so . . . unpredictable."

"Well, don't let Peterson's comment about the mare frighten you. She's not that unpredictable or I wouldn't have allowed you to ride her. But if she gets out of hand, I'll be right there."

Sarah repressed a giggle. Jon's cavalier attitude was almost too much. She stroked the mare's smooth neck while admiring the animal's fine head and alert brown eyes, then she exhaled gently against the mare's flared nostrils, and the animal bobbed its head in response.

Sarah propped her foot in the stirrup, and Jon placed his hands on her waist, then with a swish, he raised her effortlessly into the sidesaddle. "Thank you," she said, gathering the reins and positioning her leg around the leg horn.

A gust of wind tugged at the hair creeping from her chignon and ruffled her skirt, sending it fluttering against the mare's withers. The mare began snorting and pawing the ground. "Oh, my," Sarah said, then gave a helpless little cry as the mare arched her tail while dancing restlessly.

"Peterson, hold her steady until I'm up," Jon snapped.

"Yes ... please do," said Sarah, turning away so Jon wouldn't see her grin of devious pleasure.

Jon swung into the saddle and moved his blood bay gelding forward, then leaned over and grasped the bridle of Sarah's mare to steady her. "We'll head straight out this road toward Cadboro Bay," he said, pointing. "The road's wide and well-graded, so you should have no trouble. And where the trees are down, we'll leave the road and follow the beach to the cottage. Then, if you're up to it, we can take a short ride through the woods to see Mystic Spring."

"That sounds lovely," said Sarah, familiar with the woodland spring Josephine had described, its curative powers and its legend. According to the legend, if a man looked into the pool, he'd see the face of the woman who'd say yes to his proposal of marriage. And a woman looking into it would see the face of the man she loved. A silly notion spawned for idealistic, castle-building dreamers, Sarah thought.

She studied the long, wide road ahead while inhaling deliciously cool air fragrant with wild roses. Her eager anticipation, and the heady aroma of the blossoms, was almost intoxicating. Tightening her leg around the horn, she urged the animal into an easy lope.

Jon was immediately at her side, his gelding straining at the bit. "Don't let the mare have her head," he said, his words more a command than a warning.

Sarah slanted him a wry smile. "Why not, Governor; she's as eager as I." With that, she clicked her tongue and laid the crop on the mare's rump. The animal bolted forward. Leaning over the mare's withers, Sarah pressed the horse into a full gallop. The animal extended its stride, hooves beating a thrumming rhythm, mane flowing back and slapping Sarah's hands as the horse raced along the road.

Guiding the animal off the hard-packed route, Sarah cut through a sunlit glade that rippled with grass. The wind whipped tendrils of hair from the coil at her nape and loosened her chignon until the tresses broke free and flowed as unrestrained as the movements of the galloping horse.

Jon urged his mount on, smoldering inside as he watched the easy motion of Sarah's lithe body as it moved in concert with the surges of the galloping mare. The little minx! She was a damned skilled horsewoman . . . one who enjoyed making a fool of a man. Well, beautiful, willful Sarah Ashley was about to have her comeuppance, just as soon as he could catch her . . .

But when he'd almost reached her, she turned the mare sharply and the animal lunged up a slope. At the crest of the hill, she tugged on the reins, but the mare protested, rearing, pawing the air, eager to keep going. Sarah let the animal have its head, and they galloped along the ridge overlooking the bay, then descended the slope and met the road again. Abruptly, the mare turned onto a wide trail that cut between giant oaks, and they headed into the woods.

Sarah caught Jon's cry of warning. Glancing over her shoulder, she saw him racing toward her and waving. When she turned back, she understood: directly ahead, a tree lay across the path. Leaning over the mare's withers, she gave full rein. The mare soared over the log and landed gracefully on the other side. Sarah reined in beside an enormous maple tree with spreading branches rich with bright green foliage. At the foot of the tree, a spring bubbled up to form a clear, moss-lined pool. The mare lowered its head to drink, and Sarah shook out her hair, sending a wealth of curls rippling down her back.

Jon brought his horse up short. *"What the bloody hell do you think you're doing!"*

Sarah gazed into eyes sparking with anger. "You needn't get your hackles up," she said. "I was just enjoying the ride."

"Enjoying the ride! You were running that mare like she was in a damned steeplechase!"

"Goodness, but you exaggerate. And the mare loved it. Besides, if I had been running in a steeplechase, I would not have reined in at the crest of the hill, nor would I have held the mare back on the downgrade."

Jon's blood raced hot in his veins. "So you ride like a lancer and no doubt smoke like a blackguard and handle a pistol like a dragoon."

She gave him a waggish smile. "As a matter of fact, I can handle a pistol quite skillfully. And on one occasion, I did puff on a cigar ... to prove a point." She shifted in the saddle, prepared to dismount. "Would you please help me down?"

"Me ... help *you* down?" He gave a short, ironic laugh. "You seem an independent little hellcat. I'm surprised you'd ask for a man's help."

"I wouldn't," she said, "if I were permitted to ride astride instead of being forced to perch on the side of the horse like a wood tick."

Jon jumped from his horse and tethered it. Standing below Sarah, he raised his arms. She braced her hands on his shoulders, and he lifted her to the ground.

His eyes darkened. "Now *I* intend to prove a point." He tangled his fingers in her hair, drawing her head back and her lips up to meet his. His mouth came down hard on hers, and he pulled her to him, crushing her breasts against him. She wedged her fingers between them and pushed against the rock-hard wall of his chest. But he drew her tighter, and his lips became more demanding. Her nostrils filled with the musky male scent of leather and warm wool and spicy soap, drugging her senses, making her limbs feel weak and her heart thrum heavily in her bosom.

Then, abruptly, he broke the kiss.

She looked up in startled surprise. Her cheeks burned. "What exactly did you prove by that?"

He released her. "You decide."

She touched her fingers to her tingling lips. "I'd say you proved you could overpower me. Which really proves nothing at all. I have never claimed to have the strength of a man, only the intelligence and ingenuity."

He sucked in a long breath. "Then why don't you use that intelligence and ingenuity for something important instead of wasting it on your damned bloomer crusade!"

She planted her hands on her hips. "I'll have you know that it is because of Amelia Bloomer's ingenious costume, and my crusade, that the women of Victoria might one day be free from the bonds of archaic dress." She went to sit on a log where she could doff her gloves, boots, and jacket. All of a sudden, she felt almost overcome by a muggy warmth, her body feverish and damp with perspiration.

Jon folded his arms. "I'd hardly say the fashions

here are archaic," he said, watching her slip out of her coat.

"That's because you've never been forced to trip over lengths of skirts and petticoats while climbing stairs, nor have you had to drag yards of hem through mud and dirt. If you had, you'd change your view of how a woman should dress." She loosened the ties at the neck of her blouse and fanned her throat. "Further, a woman cannot move or breathe comfortably, nor can she engage in healthy exercise, with every vital organ displaced by whalebone."

Jon watched with mounting expectation as her dainty fingers untied the laces of her boot. The chit seemed intent on disrobing. And he sure as hell wasn't about to stop her. But with this particular hellcat, a bit of finesse might be advised. He didn't relish the idea of returning home with claw marks down his face. And no doubt she would fight him—just to prove a point—if he took her while she was completely off guard.

"It didn't look like you were having too much trouble engaging in healthy exercise on the way here," he said.

"I assure you, only the exhilaration of the fast ride enabled me to forget the restrictions of my dress." She slipped off her boot.

Jon watched intently, eager to see a creamy white foot emerge as she removed her silk stocking. "Another of Mrs. Bloomer's preachings?" he said, disappointed when she went to the other boot instead. "Females shedding their clothing to expose their limbs?"

Sarah slipped off the other boot. "There's nothing immoral about exposing one's limbs," she said, feeling a rush of feverish excitement at her own brazenness in referring to parts of her anatomy she'd never spoken of with any man before. "Men expose their limbs all the time, so why shouldn't women?"

Jon smiled. "Good point."

Sarah waited for him to turn. "Well?"

"Well what?"

"I have no intention of removing my stockings with you ogling me, so would you please turn around?"

He gave her a knowing grin, then reluctantly and slowly turned his back to her.

Sarah quickly rolled down her stockings and tucked them into her boots. Lifting her skirt to clear the water, she stepped into the pool, sending ripples radiating. "You may turn now," she said, glancing over her shoulder to see if Jon had. To her alarm, she saw him coming toward her while shrugging out of his shirt. Hiking up her skirt, she turned and backed into the pool until she could feel cold water up to her calves. "What are you doing?" she asked, nervously eyeing a pair of thick, muscular shoulders and a broad, strapping chest.

"It's fairly obvious," he replied, moving closer. "I'm removing my shirt."

Her heart pounded with awareness. "Why?"

A slow, diabolic smile curved his lips, and his dark eyes shone with intent. "Why not?" he said, tossing his shirt to the ground. "Don't we men have the same privileges as you women?"

"Well . . . yes . . ." She continued backing away until she knew that if she stepped further, she'd sink up to her thighs. "What do you intend to . . . do?" she asked, blood pumping through her veins as the gap between them narrowed.

"I intend to ravish your beautiful body."

A thrill of desire raced through her, which quickly turned to fear when he marched into the pool and scooped her up in his arms. "No," she cried, kicking her feet. In vain, she tried to pull her skirt down to cover her legs. "Governor! You are no gentleman!"

"I don't intend to be a gentleman," he said. "And I certainly don't want you to be a lady—at least not a proper one. Out here in this untamed land, we relax the rules of propriety. And from your unconventional views about women's dress, it's clear you, too, are beyond that nonsense. And right now you're driving me wild."

"I demand you put me down at once!"

He laughed heartily. "I'll put you down on a bed of cool ferns." Lowering her to the ground, he dropped beside her, bracing his arms on each side of her. He pressed his lips to the tender flesh behind her ear.

"No!" she cried. She pushed against his bare chest, her palms meeting hard, brawny muscles as she struggled to get out from under him. His lips moved toward hers, and she abruptly turned her face to ward off his kiss. "Stop!"

Jon found her efforts uncomfortably arousing: the twisting of her hips against his hardened loins, her breasts moving sensuously against his chest. He brushed her hair aside and darted the tip of his tongue into her ear. The heavy scent of blossoms filled his nostrils. Curving his hand beneath her, he pulled her to him and whispered in her ear, "Sarah, my sweet, don't fight me."

Something in the way Jon had spoken—perhaps the sound of her name and the endearment in his low, silky voice—made Sarah feel protected, almost loved. And for the moment she allowed him to cover her mouth with his, even tease her lips apart with the tip of his tongue. And when he slid his tongue inside her mouth and caressed her tongue with his, she felt a rush of wild sensation.

Then his hands seemed to be everywhere: on her leg, across her ribs, covering her breast.

And her mind slipped back to a coach in San Francisco. Her dress ripped, her breasts exposed. Her cries smothered by demanding lips. Horrible hands fondling her breasts. The coach door opening . . .

She jerked her mouth from Jon's and abruptly turned her head. "No," she whispered, trying to find a voice that seemed caught in her throat. "Please . . . don't do this . . ."

Jon realized she was trembling like a lovely, skittish filly. He looked into confused eyes that clearly contradicted her bold, risque behavior.

So the lady was an innocent tease.

Well, he had no intention of playing entirely by her rules. He brushed her bottom lip with the pad of his thumb and trailed his finger down her neck. "So you don't want me to do this . . ." His hand moved down her arm and across her rib cage, stopping dangerously close to her breast "Or this . . ." He tipped her face up with the crook of his finger, and his mouth slowly and gently covered hers, lingering for a moment. "Or this . . ." He kissed her again; this time the tip of his tongue traced her lips, teasing, coaxing, until her lips parted without protest. Their lips still holding, he moved on his side so she was no longer trapped beneath him, and Sarah curved her hands around his neck.

Concealed in the shadowy stillness of the forest, and tangled close in Jon's arms, Sarah felt as if a pristine world of sensation was awakening inside her, and for the moment, she had no desire to break from his embrace. Drugged by his kiss, she yielded her lips to his, and as she did, her exploring hand moved across his heavily muscled chest . . .

Then a kaleidoscope of dire warnings whirled in her head, and in spite of the hot passion growing inside her, a cold sweat dampened her brow. She broke the kiss and looked up at him. He lifted a lock of hair from her shoulder, and trailed the curl across her lips. He smiled. "I apologize for changing the rules of your game."

She pushed against his chest, and to her surprise, he moved off her. She sat up abruptly. "I have no idea what you're talking about," she said, although she had a fair idea what he meant.

"To spell it out to you, Miss Sarah Ashley from San Francisco, you're playing a very dangerous game."

"If you mean because I removed my stockings, I have a perfect right to do so without you taking it as an invitation to plunder my body."

Jon stretched onto his side and propped his head on his hand. "That wasn't the only invitation you sent out. Only minutes after you left the ship, you managed to make some kind of plans with a total stranger. Do you deny that?"

"If you're referring to that seedy merchant down on the waterfront, he all but propositioned me when I only asked him if his building was for lease. I'd hardly call that an invitation."

"Then there was the gown you wore at dinner—a very enticing and revealing gown. I'd say that was a definite invitation. A doxy displaying her wares."

"A doxy! My dress is the latest style of the haut monde in San Francisco. If you were to attend the opera there, you'd see for yourself."

"And undressing in front of me here? Is that also the style of the haut monde?"

"I was not undressing! I merely removed my stockings, away from your view, so I could cool my feet after the ride. Many women in the States display their limbs. It's the fashion."

Jon's eyes moved over russet-gold tresses that gleamed in the sunlight sifting through the evergreens. "You're not in the States," he said. "You're in a wild, untamed country populated by restless lonely men. Merely smiling is an invitation. So I suggest you conceal your naked limbs and save your sultry smiles for the one you wish to find sprawled atop you."

Sarah tugged at her skirt still trapped beneath him. "Nevertheless, you've clearly taken advantage of me."

Jon rolled away slightly, allowing her to retrieve her skirt. "And you have to admit, you burned like a torch in my arms. As for me taking advantage of you, you made it damned near impossible for me to get off you, as you had me pinned quite firmly against you."

Sarah ignored his comment, busying herself with trying to straighten her blouse and smooth her rumpled skirt. She had not intended for things to get so out of hand. She only hoped she could rectify the damage before anyone saw her. "However will I explain my appearance when we return?" she said, combing her fingers through her hair, searching for lost pins.

Jon watched the sunlight catch her hair, igniting it like fire as she attempted to tame it with her fingers. "It's simple," he said. "You fell from your runaway horse."

Her nostrils flared. "I have never fallen from a horse in my life! It would be degrading to admit that I had, when in fact I had not."

"Ah, yes. You mustn't muck up your reputation as an excellent horsewoman."

Sarah looked into his dark, mirthful eyes. "You're making very light of this," she said, sliding her gaze to a firm, masculine mouth. For a moment, she said nothing, pondering the still too vivid feel of those lips on hers. She'd never experienced such a strong reaction as when he'd kissed her. An urgency that seemed to start where their lips met rushed downward to twine like a giant coil low in her belly. Her cheeks blazed.

"And perhaps you're making *too* much of it," said Jon, "and instead should consider it a learning experience. As an unmarried woman—a very beautiful one at that—aspiring to run a business in a man's world, you must be prepared to deal with men's unwanted advances. Unless, of course, you plan to marry to avoid them."

"Absolutely not," she replied, nervously picking specks of forest matter from her skirt and blouse. "A woman gives up all her rights when she marries. She becomes a mere appendage of her husband. She's even expected to give up her name."

"She should want to do that," said Jon. "A wife is, after all, a man's most prized possession, and the world should know who's responsible for her comfort and her well-being." He knew he was needling her, but he enjoyed the way her eyes sparkled with indignation when she was irritated.

"Poppycock!" she said, smoothing her hand along her skirt, trying to press away the wrinkles. "Marriage is a man-made institution inherently unjust to wives, especially wives in business. When I'm successful, I shall never turn over my earnings to someone less capable than I, either to invest as he sees fit, or to squander as he chooses."

Braced on one elbow, Jon looked up from his reclining position. "I'm certain, Miss Sarah Ashley, that married or not, you will allow no man to squander the vast fortune you intend to accrue in your business."

Sarah shrugged into her jacket. "You insist on making jest of my plans," she said. "Well, that's about what one should expect from a provincialist." She reached for her boots. Tucking a finger inside to retrieve one stocking, she added, "Would you mind turning away?"

Jon arched a brow. "I thought there was nothing immoral about a woman's limbs. Besides, after what we've shared, it seems contradictory that you should want to hide yourself from me now."

"We shared nothing but a brief moment of indiscretion," she replied. "I assure you, it won't happen again." She waited, and after a moment, Jon rolled onto his stomach, presenting his back to her. But in his peripheral vision, he watched her stand, slip the stockings up her long, smooth legs, and pull on her boots.

"You may turn now," she said, vigorously slapping at her skirt, to which every particle of moss and dried debris in the forest seemed to catch and cling.

Jon looked up, entranced by the full mane of hair cascading over her shoulders as she bent to brush off her riding habit. Merciful saints! This hadn't turned out at all the way he'd planned. He'd intended to get lost in that hair, feel it trailing across his chest, see it curling around creamy white breasts with dainty rosebud nipples . . .

And the bloody truth was, he found the idea of relieving himself with any of the doxies in town entirely unappealing. He wanted Sarah. That was the whole, hard truth. He wanted her more than he'd ever wanted any other woman.

However, he'd definitely use more finesse. It had been crass of him to scoop her up out of the water and try to bed her right then and there . . . no teasing her into eager submission, no whispering sweet nothings until she writhed in his arms. Well, he *had* whispered one sweet nothing, and she had responded—a tactic he'd keep in mind. But by the time he'd uttered the word, it was too late. He'd already botched things . . .

Sarah gathered her hair at her nape, her brow pinching into a worried frown. "I have no idea what to do with my hair. I can't ride to your house with you at my side while looking like this. And I certainly can't ride there alone," she said, her voice rising and falling in singsong gravity.

Jon pulled himself up and stood beside her. "Here, let me . . ." He reached into the tangle of coppery hair and pulled out a hairpin, then another, and another . . .

He looked into her beautiful green eyes and started to plunge his mouth on hers again, then caught himself up short. Finesse, he reminded himself, then kissed her lightly and handed her the pins.

She looked at them and gave a despondent sigh. "There are just not enough of these to hold my hair in place," she said, "so I guess I'll just have to leave it loose and hope no one sees me." Turning from him, she walked over to the mare, which stood patiently waiting where it had been left, and started to mount. "If you will, Governor."

As Jon moved toward her, he noticed the fir needles and tiny particles of moss tangled in her hair and pondered the vision they brought: moist lips on his, her full breast in his hand. He sighed, dismissing the images, but unable to ignore the aching pressure in his breeches. It was going to be a damned uncomfortable ride home. "I hope we can at least dispense with the formalities," he said. "After all, you must agree we're no longer strangers. So I insist you call me Jon."

Recalling the intimacies they'd shared, Sarah felt her face grow hot. "Very well then . . . Jon," she replied. She placed her foot in the stirrup and Jon clasped her waist, lifted her easily, and set her in the saddle. She gathered the reins and waited while he mounted.

Once up, he eyed her dubiously. "Am I to assume we'll be racing hell-bent for the cottage?"

Sarah laughed lightly. "No, I've had quite enough racing for one day." Her eyes focused on the curve of Jon's lips, and she realized, with some misgivings, that he had a very sensuous mouth. The thought that she wanted to taste it again bothered her immensely. Turning the mare, she urged it up the path, and Jon fell in beside her.

They followed the beach to the cottage—a modest white wooden house with a covered front porch supported by turned-wood posts. Nestled in cool, moist shade, the cottage stood on a rise overlooking the bay.

Sarah contemplated the small dwelling. Tools littered a roof that was in the process of being patched, honeysuckle and morning glory choked rosebushes with withered yellow blooms, and window boxes with dead flowers hung beneath windows obscured by blue-gray shutters.

The place looked terribly neglected, yet Sarah could envision shutters thrown open to reveal lacy curtains ... and window boxes lush with pink petunias ... and white clematis climbing up the posts ... and the evening breeze off the bay bringing with it the fragrance of roses. She didn't need to go inside to know that this was where she wanted to live.

But when she turned to tell Jon of her decision, she caught sight of a carriage moving toward them, rocking as it traveled over the uneven dirt road. She looked at Jon in alarm. "I thought you said no carriages could get through."

"Apparently, I was wrong," he replied. "It seems the road has been cleared."

While Sarah deliberated whether to turn her horse

and dash behind the cottage, the coachman guided the carriage toward them and eased it to a stop. The door swung open, and Lady Cromwell stared at them, her face blanched, her tongue immobile. Harriet Galbraith peered around Lady Cromwell, giving her a discreet nudge. Sarah knew that her own appearance was, at best, disheveled. She could only imagine what both women must be thinking.

Harriet displayed a decorous smile. "You seem to have gathered a good portion of the forest in your hair during your ride, Miss Ashley."

Sarah raised a hand to her hair, her quivering fingers dislodging fragments of forest matter. "The trail gets quite narrow where Governor Cromwell was kind enough to take me," she replied. "The area where I asked him to point out available plots for purchase."

"And did the governor show you something that could"—Harriet's lips twisted with a serpentine smile—"satisfy your needs?"

"Mrs. Galbraith," said Jon, "I resent your base insinuations, and I think you owe Miss Ashley an apology."

Harriet shifted her gaze to Jon, and her eyes rested on his rumpled shirt. As she stared, Sarah mulled over what ill luck it had been to be traveling along this particular road at this particular time. And what an enticing piece of gossip Harriet Galbraith now had to pass on to the ladies of Victoria.

"Very well, Miss Ashley," said Harriet, with great aplomb, "I apologize if I offended you in any way." After a moment, she added, "And by the way, you might try sponge-rubbing some spirits diluted with two parts water on those grass stains. You'll find it very effective. Good day." She nodded. "Governor."

"Jon," Lady Cromwell croaked, having at last found her voice. "I would like to see you in my chambers upon your return." Ignoring Sarah, she closed the door, and the carriage rolled on.

Sarah stared after the buggy while holding in her mind the image of Harriet Galbraith's accusing eyes with their drooping red-rimmed lids, and Lady Cromwell's reproachful gaze as it had surveyed her with disgust.

Her stomach knotted. Had Hollis been behind this . . . set her up so her name would bring scandal again? It seemed beyond coincidence that another incident of a sexual nature would trap her again. But Hollis could not have known where she was yet. Nor could he have acted so quickly.

A terrible awareness swept over her.

Jon could have planned this meeting, knowing his mother and Harriet Galbraith would be along. The gossip they'd initiate would undoubtedly thwart her efforts to appeal to the women of Victoria. Jon had been quick to point out that the road was closed and they'd have to go on horseback.

But the road was indeed open.

And their tussle in the woods seemed suspiciously timely . . . as if premeditated. Was she such a naive little fool that she'd fallen into the same sort of trap again?

Gathering the reins, she held her head high, clinging to what was left of her dignity. "If this is part of your plan to darken my reputation beyond redemption—which would lower my esteem in the community and therefore ruin my chances for business success—let me be the first to congratulate you. You may very well have succeeded."

Jon eyed the buggy as it ambled around a bend. "That's pure rubbish. You know damned well I didn't set it up—though I might suspect my mother of having done so. And, I assure you, I *will* take that up with her."

Jon tightened his jaw. Unfortunately, chastising his mother would not undo the damage to Sarah's reputation. But a gag and muzzle on Harriet Galbraith would. That not being feasible, it would be up to him to clear Sarah's name. Which was not going to be easy. Harriet Galbraith rarely missed an opportunity to vent her suspicions, quickly and exhaustively, regardless of how tenuous their truth. An account of the untimely incident would soon touch the ears of every proper woman in Victoria.

Chapter 6

Jon marched into his mother's room and confronted her. "You deliberately set up that little meeting at the cottage to embarrass and humiliate Miss Ashley!"

Dorothy Cromwell lowered herself into a skirted lady's chair. "I did no such thing. Harriet and I were merely out for a ride."

"Like hell!"

"Please, Jon. Hold your voice down. The servants will hear." She snapped open her fan and began fanning herself furiously.

"I don't give a bloody damn about the servants. And I'll thank you to stay out of my personal affairs."

She gave Jon her most hoity-toity look. "What kind of example are you setting for your daughters?"

"Keep them out of this. Whatever goes on between me and Miss Ashley is our business, and ours alone. And it sure as hell is not to be aired on Harriet Galbraith's dirty laundry line."

"Well, if you were concerned about the moral well-being of your daughters, you'd remove Miss Ashley from the premises at once. I have no idea what Esther was thinking, inviting the woman into our home—and certainly Louella and Josephine should not be exposed to her. But it is unspeakable what you are doing, a man in your position. Let me remind you that we are the first family of Victoria. You may be certain that every move you make is noted, and every individual with whom you associate is scrutinized—"

"Enough!" Jon snapped. "I refuse to listen to another tedious lecture on my position. I've long since outgrown such ministerial diatribes." He'd known at once from the pinched white look about his mother's mouth that she'd been primed for such a discourse.

Her eyes flickered with impatience. She snapped her fan shut, slapped it down, and reached for her sewing caddy. "Very well, I will not lecture you. But you might at least explain your questionable demeanor and Miss Ashley's shameful appearance this afternoon."

Jon leveled his gaze on her. "I don't intend to explain anything." He went to his mother's bed table, poured a shot of brandy, and swallowed it.

"Well then, I shall assume . . . what I shall assume. You give me no reason to believe otherwise." Lifting the pince-nez dangling from a black ribbon around her neck, she propped it on her nose and plucked a darning egg from her sewing caddy. "And I shall also believe what Harriet told me about why Miss Ashley left San Francisco . . . that she left because of a scandal."

"A scandal that Harriet Galbraith no doubt conjured while she was there!"

"Don't be ridiculous. Harriet said everyone on the ship was talking about it. It had something to do with Miss Ashley and a married man. Of course, Harriet didn't have the details."

"Of course not. *She bloody well never does!* But I'll tell you this much . . . Miss Ashley is a woman of high morals. And if you base your opinion of her purely on what a bunch of hypocritical scandalmongers say, then you're no better than they. And to set the record straight, the only reason Miss Ashley looked as she did was because I forced myself on her and kissed her against her will."

Dorothy pursed her mouth into the shape of a prune, drew in a long breath through flared nostrils, and launched into a terse narrative. "Surely, Jonathan, you do not expect me to believe such a preposterous claim. You have been raised to be a gentleman, and I refuse to accept that you would force yourself on a woman without provocation. And I would appreciate it if you would sit down while I'm speaking to you."

"No, I will not. I'm too damned mad to sit down."

"Then, if you expect me to believe that you kissed Miss Ashley against her will, I must assume you did so because she clearly flaunted herself. Wearing those shockingly revealing gowns at dinner and exposing herself to your view . . . I can only imagine what she might have exposed while alone with you in the depths of the forest."

"What happened in the depths of the forest is none of anyone's damned business but ours. And I'll thank you to remember that."

"Humph." Dorothy's mouth twitched with distaste. "Beyond the woman's disgraceful behavior with you, there is also the matter of those dreadful trousers she had the audacity to wear to the legislature building. It would be bad enough for her to parade around in the privacy of her own home dressed in such an offensive costume, but to make a public spectacle of herself before government officials by wearing trousers is unthinkable."

"She did not wear trousers, she wore a bloomer costume. There's a distinct difference," said Jon, surprised to find himself defending Sarah's unorthodox dress. "As for making a public spectacle of herself, that's really immaterial—" But true, he mused. The men had enjoyed a rollicking good laugh after Sarah had left. Giving his mother a droll smile, he added, "Although the style might not be to your liking, it covered her . . . quite thoroughly."

"It's improper . . . not Christian."

"Come now, Mother," he said, his anger waning. "You know you don't truly believe that bit of folde-rol. In Genesis it's stated, 'Unto Adam also and to his wife did the Lord God make coats of skins, and clothed them.' Nothing is said that their coats of skins should differ in any way . . . that Adam's should be bifurcated while Eve's must drape from her like a tent."

Dorothy jerked on the thread. "Don't talk to me in parables. Besides, that's not the point. The fact that Miss Ashley is so boorish as to wear such atrocious dress is reason enough that you should not be seen in her company." She raised her nose as if a disagreeable odor hovered beneath her nostrils. "At best, she is the daughter of a commonplace merchant—a man of no background or position. While you were born into a noble family which proudly traces its ancestry back to royalty—"

"To the Cromwells, Mother. Any connection to the Stuarts is baseless. And might I remind you that Oliver Cromwell was a commoner. It's only through marriage that we gained title. I also suspect there are numerous skeletons in our aristocratic closet, some of questionable parentage, I daresay, who never made the family Bible."

Dorothy's bottom lip quivered with outrage. "That allegation is preposterous! You arrived in Victoria with impeccable credentials and are considered a man of excellent character, as was your father and is your brother."

"My brother?" Jon laughed heartily. "Dear Charles's moral standards fluctuate widely with the occasion, Mother. You're just not in London to witness it."

"That is simply not so," Dorothy insisted. "However, be that as it may, this appalling incident will undoubtedly demean your good standing in this community."

"If it were not Harriet Galbraith's malicious mind and frenzied tongue, this incident would go no further than her carriage."

"The only thing malicious is the effect Miss Ashley seems to be having on you ... and on your reputation. Need I remind you that your position as governor is most unstable right now? Even you have pointed out that if it comes to confederation, Frederick Seymour is clearly the choice of Her Majesty's government."

"*If* it comes to confederation, which will probably not happen." But Jon knew that union with British Columbia was imminent, especially with De Cosmos urging the assembly to agree to unification under any terms, proselytizing that Victoria would be doomed should it continue to struggle as an isolated British colony. "But if it should come to that, Victoria has a greater chance of becoming the capital city than New Westminster."

"Of course it does," Dorothy agreed, "but with Frederick Seymour as governor instead of you, unless you present yourself as a gentleman of faultless character."

Jon laughed heartily. "If Her Majesty's government uses character as ground for selection, Frederick Seymour, with his voracious appetite for drink, should not stand a chance."

Though he knew that was not the case. Even with Seymour's penchant for drink, he'd presented on paper to Her Majesty's government what appeared to be a thriving capital city—though one far from prosperous to the eye. Whereas Jon's public accounts might look somewhat bleak, Victoria boasted a wealth of new and improved civil services, the Common School Act had been passed, real estate taxes were being collected, and Victoria remained a free trade port. But it had been damned hard uphill work, especially having to battle De Cosmos's attacks every step of the way.

Dorothy looped the thread and snipped it, then reached for another sock. "Nevertheless," she said, raising her eyes to Jon, "I hope Miss Ashley will find other lodging soon. I cannot impress upon you strongly enough the extent of the vicious gossip in which the town will be indulging if you do not stop this folly."

"Thanks to your bosom friend."

"Harriet Galbraith has nothing to do with this," Dorothy said, ruffled. "She is the wife of a preacher—a woman of the highest ethical and moral principles—who would not spread undue gossip."

"Oh, that's riotously funny," said Jon. "The old shrew has a tongue like a whipsaw. Not only would she spread undue gossip, but she'd salt and pepper it with all manner of indecent implications as well."

Dorothy shot Jon a censorious look. "I am appalled to hear you degrade a woman of Mrs. Galbraith's standing in our community."

"Harriet Galbraith maintains her lofty standing only because she's the one who grubs up the dirt you women seem to need to keep the parlor gossip going. And that's exactly what she's done with Sarah ... drudged up a lot of baseless, unfounded muck."

Dorothy's mouth compressed in a harsh line. "So, Sarah it is now. When did you drop the formalities?"

"Come now, Mother. Why should that surprise

you? After all, Sarah and I have spent some time together. Besides, you have no objection to my referring to Miss Windemere as Mary Letitia."

"That's completely different." Dorothy's eyes glowed with renewed intent. "And speaking of Mary Letitia—"

"I'd rather not."

"You are being a thickheaded ninny. Mary Letitia Windemere comes from a socially prominent family, and her father is in a position to aid your political career; she is a cultured, sophisticated woman who would see to the proper guidance and upbringing of your daughters; and she is in love with you."

"She's in love with the idea of being the governor's wife," said Jon. "Should Seymour become governor instead of me, then you'd see how anxious she'd be to marry me."

Dorothy stabbed her needle in and out of the sock. "You are behaving like an utter gooseberry. Before the Ashley woman arrived, you were a reasonable-thinking man, courting a reasonable-thinking woman. Mary Letitia would make an excellent wife for you and a model mother for your daughters—"

"Stop! I don't want to discuss Mary Letitia, nor do I intend to marry her or anyone else."

Dorothy tightened her mouth and said nothing, but Jon knew she had not dropped the issue of Mary Letitia Windemere.

"As for Sarah finding other lodging," he continued, "she plans to move to the Pemberton cottage in a few days. Until then, you'll have to bear her presence. And as long as she remains a guest in our home, she *will* be treated with deference and respect."

"Very well." The darning needle went in and out, in and out, in short, quick stabs. "I have just one last thing to say on the subject, and then I will say no more." She paused from her darning and looked up.

"The Ashley woman has obviously bewitched you, just as Caroline bewitched you, and you see where *that* got you."

Jon set the brandy snifter down abruptly and pinned his mother with a steely gaze. "Do not *ever* compare Sarah to Caroline. And do not *ever* mention Caroline to me again!" He turned and left the room, slamming the door behind him.

He'd overreacted, of course. But he wanted it to be damned clear to his mother that there was no comparison between the two women. True, Sarah was beautiful as Caroline had been—more beautiful. And both women possessed high-spirited natures. But Sarah, for some reason, had sworn off men. Caroline had thrived on them.

Oddly, until now, he'd never really thought of *why* Sarah had sworn off men. She'd explained why she was opposed to marriage, but not why she harbored a deep distrust for men. But whatever the reason underlying her unconventional views, it worked to his advantage. By pursuing her, he would never find himself in another conjugal trap because she would not lure him into being that fool again. Now all he needed to do was gain her trust by showing her he cared—that she was important to him—then awaken her sexual appetite through diligent and attentive guidance, and ultimately teach her the fine art of lovemaking so they could thoroughly enjoy each other. And he looked forward to every delectable moment of it.

By the ocher light of several wall fixtures, Mandi dipped a small pail into the washtub and poured warm water over Sarah's head. "Ida said she heard at the bakery that someone saw you comin' out the Pemberton cottage with the guv'nor earlier this afternoon ... that you'd been mussed up quite a bit."

Sarah pursed her lips. "I see that the good preacher's wife is doing her part to help spread the word."

"Ah don't know 'bout that, Ah only know what Ida said." Mandi poured another pail of water over Sarah's head, then said in a worried voice, "You sho' do have a lot of stuff caught in your hair. It's a good thing you's takin' supper here in your room tonight, 'cause we'd never have gotten it all out by then. Ummm . . . ummm. . . . Ah knew you shouldn't have gone ridin' without a hat, or with the guv'nor, you playin' up to him the way you was."

"I never played up to him," said Sarah. "I guess I just didn't discourage him." She squeezed her eyes tight and leaned forward as water cascaded over her hair and drained into the tub. She hadn't told Mandi everything about what had happened, only that Jon had kissed her, and that she hadn't exactly fought him off.

Mandi soaped her hair again. "Ah think you's sweet on him," she teased.

Sarah didn't respond. The word "sweet" seemed incongruous. She couldn't banish thoughts of the kiss they'd shared: of the salty-sweet taste of Jon's tongue as it entwined with hers, the gamy aroma of leather and earth on his hands, the raw male power behind his embrace. At first she'd been terrified, knowing too well the strength and power of a man moved by lust. Then . . . somehow Jon had calmed her fears. She wasn't certain how he'd done it, but the next moment, she'd allowed him to hold her and kiss her while she stretched out with him on the ground. And it was so different from before, so completely different . . .

Mandi scrubbed vigorously. "Well?"

"Well what?"

"Are you sweet on him?"

Sarah shrugged. "I admit, I find him . . . attractive."

Mandi poured another pail of rinse water over Sarah's head. After Sarah's hair had drained and was wrapped in a soft flannel towel, Mandi asked, "What do you intend to do?"

Sarah stood. "About what?"

"About startin' your business?"

"Nothing has changed," said Sarah. "Tomorrow, I plan to look for a building to lease so I'll be prepared when I have completed the papers for my license."

Mandi handed her another large flannel towel. "You still plannin' on lookin' down near the waterfront?"

"Possibly. I saw several likely buildings when we were leaving the ship."

"Well . . . Ida said that's where all the women keep disappearin' from . . . that the last one went outside for a few minutes—even left clothes boilin' on the stove—and she never came back. Ida said the guv'nor said the police are lookin', but he don't think there's much chance findin' them if they's shanghaied to the goldfields 'cause with all the miners up there, a woman's real easy to hide."

"Well, I can't live in fear of what might happen," said Sarah. "If I find a nice store, I'll take it." She stepped out of the tub and onto a braided rug. While waiting for Mandi to bring a chemise and drawers, Sarah scanned the Berlin wool work hanging on the wall, and the antimacassars on the backs of the chairs, and the tapestry-covered letter basket—pieces she suspected Caroline Cromwell had done.

Needlework, as she'd been taught in school, was a respectable pastime for the leisure hours of a woman whereby she could show her love for her family. But Sarah had had no patience with the needle. Riding horses or sketching or chasing butterflies were much more appealing pastimes ...

"The guv'nor sho' is handsome," said Mandi, handing Sarah the drawers. "You figurin' on ridin' with him again?"

"Of course not," replied Sarah. "I only went with him to see the cottage." But she couldn't deny that merely thinking about the passionate kiss they'd shared caused a warmth to spread through her. However, these new sensations would pass, and she refused to dwell on them. She had far more important things to consider. After donning the chemise, she moved to the dressing table.

Mandi started brushing her hair to dry it. "Ah 'spect then you won't be seein' much of him," she said, forlorn.

Sarah eyed Mandi in the mirror. "You're a hopeless romantic. And I fully intend to discourage the governor. He *is* the enemy, you know."

Mandi sighed.

Sarah caught the doleful look in her dark eyes. "All right, if it makes you happy, I just might see him in town tomorrow. And, before I go in the morning, I'd like you to arrange my hair in plaits ... you know, with the plaits encircling a chignon." She knew the style was particularly becoming, especially with the bonnet she planned to wear.

Mandi smiled. "It don't sound to me like you's tryin' to discourage the guv'nor," she teased.

Sarah reached for her bottle of oil of lavender and dabbed a drop behind each ear. "I am," she replied.

For a few minutes, Mandi said nothing, apparently absorbed in working at a tangle in Sarah's hair. When the brush plowed freely again, she caught Sarah's eyes in the mirror. "Ah didn't mention it, but Ah met a real handsome colored man at the baker's today. He said Ah was real pretty and that Ah'd do any man proud by bein' his wife ... that he 'spects it won't be long 'fore someone snatches me up."

"Well, don't go falling for any of that nonsense," said Sarah. "Besides, you mustn't depend on a man for your happiness, or let a man deter you from accomplishing your goals. When we get the business started and you learn how to sew, you'll be quite independent of them."

"Ah don't know," Mandi mused. "They's pretty nice to have around on cold nights. And Ah 'spect they'd be pretty nice for other things, too ..."

While brushing Sarah's hair, Mandi continued chattering about the man she'd met. Oddly, as she talked, Sarah began to feel lonely ... not the kind of loneliness that comes when a person is simply alone and wanting company, but the kind that can come while surrounded by friends ... the kind that settles in the heart and makes it feel heavy, yet empty. And with that loneliness came a longing for something she couldn't quite grasp.

That night, when she made her diary entry dated September 9, 1863, she wrote:

Dear Diary,
    I refuse to believe that Jon is the cause of my loneliness (though I suspect he plays a part in it) because he simply does not fit into my plans. I cannot chance allowing a man to come into my life, exploit me and ultimately betray me as my stepfather and stepbrothers have done. Nor will I allow Jon to manipulate me to his will. The risk to my emotional well-being is too great, the consequence too devastating.

The following day, dressed in a light wool walking dress, Sarah left the bedroom as soon as Ida announced the arrival of a buggy from the livery. With

haste, Sarah scurried down the stairs, not wanting to
meet Lady Cromwell in the hallway. After the episode at the cottage, she'd avoided the older woman,
even claiming to be overly tired at dinnertime and retiring to her room early. But she knew she could not
hide indefinitely, that eventually she'd have to face
Jon's mother again.

Deciding it would not be now, she dashed out the
front door, hastily walked down the wide steps leading from the porch, and stopped abruptly. Instead of
finding the phaeton she'd ordered from the livery,
she saw a landaulet waiting in the circular drive. A
footman opened the door, and to Sarah's surprise,
Jon was sitting inside. Her first impulse was to turn
and rush for the house. But glancing back, she saw
the small, shadowy figure of Lady Cromwell standing at the parlor window.

Collecting her skirts, Sarah climbed into the carriage and squeezed in beside Jon, who sat sprawled
in the middle of the seat. "Why are you here?" she
demanded.

"It's my rig."

"I ordered a phaeton."

"That's not what I was told."

Sarah fixed her eyes on the hat strap across from
her. "You're supposed to be in your office right now."

"I was," said Jon, "but Esther told me you wanted
a lift."

"Esther obviously misunderstood. I asked her to
have the livery send a phaeton for me while she was
in town," she said, trying to dismiss the vague feeling that Esther was throwing them together again.
"I'd rather not be seen with you. You've caused me
enough grief already, considering what happened on
our . . . ride to the cottage."

Jon leaned heavily against her, his gaze caressing
her face, his breath brushing her temple. "I abso-

lutely agree," he said in a silky-soft voice. "And I want to extend to you the olive branch of peace. I'm a blackguard and a lout, I behaved like a tomcat on the prowl, and even though we had a hellishly good time, the blame for the unfortunate outcome is entirely mine."

Sarah caught the flicker of wry amusement in his eyes. "I don't think you really care one whit about the unfortunate outcome. After all, it's not your reputation that's on the line."

"My reputation is always on the line," he said, "but I choose to ignore that. And I think you should do the same. Besides, since the damage is already done, we might as well make the best of it." He reached over and curled his fingers around her hand.

Sarah tried to slip her hand away, but he held it tight. "How?" she demanded. "By venturing out together? I hardly think that will clear my name."

"Perhaps you're right," said Jon. "I'll have the coachman drop me off at the legislature building, then take you on to the land agent so you can inquire about buildings to lease. That *is* what you want to do today, isn't it?"

"Well, yes." She eyed him dubiously. "Why are you being so accommodating now?"

"Anything to further Mrs. Bloomer's cause," he said. "I admit, I'm devilishly attracted to at least some aspects of her preachings."

"You are? I find that surprising."

"Oh, I'm not exactly for Mrs. Bloomer's cause," he said, "only for her notion that women should expose their feet. Have you ever had a man nibble on your ankle or suckle your toes?"

"*What!?*"

"Your toes," Jon repeated, "each one carefully suckled while your foot and leg are being gently massaged. It's a very sensual experience."

Sarah stared, dumbfounded.

"You have admirable feet: dainty toes and lovely ankles, and long, slender calves that demand a man's attention."

"Governor—"

"Jon."

Sarah pulled her hand from his and drew in a ragged breath to slow the erratic pounding of her heart. "This conversation about my anatomy is totally inappropriate."

"You're absolutely right," he said. "Let's talk about our ride to the cottage instead." He reached for her hand again and curled his fingers around it, idly stroking her wrist with the pad of his thumb. "I cannot ever remember having a more enjoyable time than when we tumbled in the woods."

Sarah stiffened. "We were not tumbling."

"We weren't?" Jon's lips curved in amusement.

"Might I remind you that you forcefully pinned me to the ground. I don't consider that tumbling, unless you're referring to what I was doing while trying to get out from under you." Heat prickled her face as she considered exactly what she *had* been doing. It certainly had not been trying to get free. But realizing it would not do well for Jon to believe otherwise, she said, "The trouble is, through the ages, men have so intimidated women that women often submit to unwarranted physical advances when, in fact, they really don't want to."

"Like my holding your hand against your will?"

"Well, that too."

"Would you like me to release it?"

"Well, no, that's really not the point I'm trying to make. As I was saying, times are changing, and soon we women shall no longer be slaves to men."

Jon eyed her with amusement. "But think about

the ways women enslave men," he said, raising her hand to his lips and planting a kiss against her palm.

Sarah blushed deeply. "I can't imagine any man being enslaved by a woman," she said, looking askance at him, "unless he's a little timid mouse of a man whom no woman would have."

Jon nibbled her finger. "You're wrong," he said. "The more virile a man, the more he can be enslaved by his desires. Take me, for example, and the issue of your feet."

"Governor!"

"Wait, hear me out."

Sarah's heart began to flutter in anticipation of what Jon might say. She sat silently, allowing him to kiss the inside of her wrist while she stared straight ahead, afraid to look into his eyes and see the magnetism she knew would be there.

"You removed your silk stockings in my presence—"

"I did no such thing! Your back was turned."

"In the vicinity of my perusal," he corrected. "I need only to have glanced back to see you lift your skirts and petticoats and roll your silk stockings down your lovely, smooth, white legs. But being a gentleman, of course, I refrained."

Sarah's face grew hot as she considered the gist of their conversation, a subject of which no proper lady spoke. "I don't see what any of this has to do with a man being a slave to a woman."

"You will." Jon arched a dark brow and continued. "Then, after you teased me further by revealing a lovely foot and a very shapely ankle, you offered your sweet lips while pressing your body to mine. Have you any idea what that sort of unleashed behavior does to a man?"

"Unleashed behavior! You forced yourself on me. And I most definitely did not offer you . . . anything." Sarah attempted to compose herself while twittering inside at the image Jon so vividly painted in her mind.

"You offered me a promise," he said, sliding her cuff up. He planted a kiss farther up her arm. "And although I did take advantage of the situation at the time—temporarily overwhelmed with passion as I was—being a gentleman, I cannot use force again. So you see, I am now your slave."

"I repeat. You are no gentleman."

Jon inched closer, pressing his shoulder against Sarah's while taking in the gentle sway of her breasts beneath the bodice of her dress as the carriage rocked along the uneven road. "Perhaps you're right," he said. "No gentleman would have the thoughts I'm having right now." His gaze roamed up to meet a pair of wide, green eyes accented by long, coppery lashes, then passed over smooth, high cheeks heightened by a delicate pink bloom, and settled on two perfectly formed lips. "And you, my sweet little mooncalf, are driving me insane . . ." He curved his hand behind her head and drew her mouth to his, pressing his lips to hers. For a few moments, her eyes remained open.

"Little love," he whispered, raising his lips from hers just far enough to speak. "Close your eyes."

Sarah's eyelids glided dreamily shut, plunging her into a lovely sensual darkness, heightening the sultry feel of Jon's lips moving against hers—warm, sensual lips that now seemed familiar. Angling his mouth, Jon slid his tongue between her lips, flicking it across the sensitive tip of her tongue before entwining and searching deeper.

"Ummm," she moaned, savoring the sweetness of his tongue as she was infused with the taste of him. Her hand crept up his back and around his shoulders, and her fingers curled in his hair. Filled with a

yearning she couldn't quell, she began caressing his
tongue with hers until she had to draw in a breath.

He gazed down at her with hooded eyes. "It gets
better . . . and better, doesn't it?"

She ran her tongue over her lips, finding the taste
of him lingering. "I suppose."

"And did you feel as if you'd been subjected to unwarranted physical advances?"

She shrugged. "I suppose not."

"Then shall we try it again . . . my sweet?"

Her only response was to raise her lips to meet
his . . .

It was some time before she realized the carriage
had rolled to a stop. Breaking from Jon's hold, she
quickly straightened her hat and smoothed the way-
ward curls escaping the braids coiled at her nape.
She glanced toward the legislature building, certain
she saw someone move from the window and into
the shadows. "You have an almost uncanny way of
drawing attention to us when we least need it," she
said in an anxious voice. "Your timing is abomina-
ble."

"I apologize for my poor timing," he said, "but not
for my kisses. I've been wanting to do that all morning."

"You take liberties," she said, "but you forget, I
have no intention of getting involved with anyone."

"My sweet, lovely Sarah," he replied in a low
voice, his warm breath stirring the hair at her temple,
"that thought never leaves my mind. But I suspect it
does leave yours. Am I right?"

As Sarah peered into his eyes, she knew he was
right. She *was* allowing herself to become involved
. . . a thought that had a decidedly sobering effect on
her. "Whether you are right or not is irrelevant," she
said, "because it will not alter the facts: I have no intention of becoming any man's wife; I *will* see my

mercantile business become a success; and I *will* maintain my earnings, my independence, and my integrity."

Jon traced the contour of her bottom lip with the pad of his thumb, and as he did, she licked her tingling lips, the tip of her tongue touching Jon's thumb. He raised his moist thumb to his own tongue and tasted it. "It's true," he said, holding her gaze. "You are sweet . . . very, very sweet. And I have a craving for sweets . . . a craving for you—one I have every intention of satisfying." He kissed her lightly and climbed down from the carriage.

As Sarah watched him march up the stairs to the legislature building, she touched her fingers to her lips. They felt cold. Just as her body, where Jon had pressed against her, felt cold. Maybe not cold as much as . . . bereft.

Why was he doing this to her? And why was she letting him? She was making herself such an easy victim. Enabling him to toy with her affections, strain her sensibilities. Allowing him to quell the restless, unnamed loneliness that haunted her. He was manipulating her. And she refused to give in to him, to surrender her heart and her soul on the blind chance that love might be waiting for her, that it might even exist. No matter how much she wanted to believe.

For now, there was only one path for her to take. And it most definitely did not lead into the arms of Governor Jonathan Cromwell. It led to the mercantile district, where she intended to find a building to let.

Tapping rapidly on the driver's window, she motioned for the coachman to proceed.

Chapter 7

Sarah peered out of the bedroom window and through a veil of drizzle, watched the hazy outline of the *Mariah* ease away from the wharf under tow by a longboat. For a few fleeting moments when she'd seen it arriving from San Francisco two days before, she'd toyed with the idea of leaving Victoria and returning to San Francisco. But the notion had quickly passed. She remembered only too well what awaited her there. Lies . . . lies . . . and more lies.

Horrible, hateful lies.

How could Hollis and Tyler have set her up as they had? How could they have betrayed her so? Worse, how could her friends—people she'd known all her life—have believed the appalling gossip?

She should have seen through it all, should have been suspicious when Hollis said the real estate broker wanted to meet her in his coach to discuss the sale of the business. She'd never met the man, and before she had even introduced herself, the trap had sprung, and she'd been caught like a dumb, trusting animal. The man believed she was a high-class whore that Hollis had sent to him, and in her struggles to convince him otherwise, he'd torn her bodice from her and ripped off her chemise. The man's wife, who had been alerted by an anonymous note, had arrived to find her husband sprawled atop Sarah and Sarah stripped to the waist.

The horrible gossip that had followed had been intended to destroy Sarah's good character and show her as unscrupulous in the eyes of the judge—Hollis's attempt to sway the case in his favor in his lawsuit to gain her money . . .

So there was no question of returning to San Francisco.

Now she just wanted to put the nightmare out of her mind. Yet everything in Victoria was still so uncertain.

She'd arrived about a week ago, and by now she had expected to have leased a shop and be living temporarily in the rooms above, to be in the process of setting up sewing machines and garment tables, and to have arranged a display window with her garments. By the second week, she had expected to have hired two women to operate the sewing machines for the manufacture of her garments while she and Mandi took orders and sold the bloomers and shirtwaisters that filled the two large trunks she'd brought from San Francisco.

How far away those objectives seemed now.

Not only was she still roosting on Jon's doorstep, but it seemed that no one would lease a building to her until she had obtained her business license. At least, that had been the excuse. But she sensed there was more to it. Had word of the incident with Jon at the cottage circulated so quickly? Was that why the merchants had refused?

Or, worse, had word of her questionable past sifted up from San Francisco? If so, the city council would certainly twist the requirements in an effort to prevent her from starting her business. However, for the moment, that wasn't her gravest concern. Which was to be out of Jon's house before the editorial appeared.

She looked across the rain-soaked lawn at the muddy road. Another miscalculation. She had not anticipated the weather turning on her, too. But it had. However would they move to the cottage now? The road looked almost impassable.

With a despondent sigh, she turned from the window and walked over to the armoire. She lifted one of her evening gowns from a hook on the door and draped it across the bed.

Mandi glanced up from her packing. "If we don't get out soon, Ah 'spect there'll be a heap o' carryin' on around here, what with Lady Cromwell so gravitated about what happened with you and the guv'nor out at the cottage."

"Gravitated?"

"That's what Ida said. She heard Lady Cromwell fussin' at the guv'nor about what happened . . . said she sounded real gravitated."

"Well, if Lady Cromwell is aggravated now," said Sarah, gathering an array of fichus, scarves, and cravats, "then I can only imagine what she'll be like after she reads the editorial. All I know is, we'd best pack a little faster and make sure we're out of here first thing in the morning."

"Ah suppose you's right." Mandi opened the top drawer of the bureau and began lifting out undergarments and placing them on the bed. She opened the drawer below, gathering nightcaps, corsets, and chemises. Gradually, her movements grew unhurried, and her dark eyes brightened.

She bundled a stack of corsets and chemises to her bosom, looked off with dreamy eyes, and said, "Yesterday, when Ah was in town helpin' Ida with the shoppin', Ah saw that same man again. Ida said his name is Wellington Brown. He sho' is a handsome fella, and he was smilin' at me like Ah was real special. He's not married, either—Ida told me that—so

Ah 'spect he's lookin' for a wife . . . just like the guv'nor's lookin' for a wife." She gave Sarah a rueful smile.

"You can forget that last absurd fancy," said Sarah, wanting quickly, logically, and decidedly to dismiss such a ludicrous notion. "Even if the governor were considering marriage, he certainly would not marry a woman who was starting a business. His idea of the exemplary wife is one who either stays at home tatting and crocheting, or trails along on his arm as a decoration. Since there are any number of eligible women in the colony from whom he might choose, it's obvious he's not after a wife."

"Oh, he's lookin' all right," said Mandi. "Ida says he's been seein' lots of women, but none seem to fit what he wants. So he jes' keeps on flittin' from one to the next."

Sarah began layering basque waists between tissue paper and placing them in the trunk. "Just because he's seeing a few women doesn't mean he's looking for a wife." A feeling of melancholia settled over her. Until now, she had not pictured Jon with any woman but herself. The thought of him holding another woman in his arms—kissing her the way she knew he kissed, calling her his "little love" or his "little mooncalf"—made her chest feel tight.

"Ah 'spect you's right," said Mandi, wrapping a lace parasol in tissue paper. "Ida says the guv'nor will never find someone as right for him as Lady Caroline—that's how his wife was called since she was the daughter of an earl—"

"I *know* who Caroline Cromwell was," Sarah snapped. "And you and Ida should not be discussing the governor's wife. It isn't proper to talk about the dead like that."

"But Ida wasn't sayin' anything bad. She never says anything bad about Lady Caroline . . . only that she was pretty, and clever, and a special good mama. And that she could do just about anything with a needle. Least that's what Ida heard from the guv'nor's daughters—Ida didn't work for the guv'nor's family until they came here."

Sarah grabbed a stack of camisoles and shoved the bundle into the trunk. "There is nothing particularly extraordinary about being able to stitch!" She shoved another stack into the trunk, and another. "And I doubt if Caroline Cromwell could ride a horse, or shoot a pistol, or even play croquet, for that matter—"

"Miz Sarah?" Mandi looked at her, puzzled. "You sho' you want to pack like that? Those camisoles will get real mussed up."

Sarah stared at the untidy heap of undergarments, then looked at Mandi's curious expression. Giving her a bland smile, she said, "I'm just overwrought about . . . how poorly things are going right now . . . the problem with the business license and all."

Mandi lifted the camisoles out of the trunk and began folding them into a neat pile. "What happens if you don't get the license?" she asked, repacking the garments.

Sarah's shoulders drooped in a weary slump. "I'm not sure . . . yet. But since I can't lease a building without it, I'll have to figure out a way to get around it. Meanwhile, if I could maybe rent some space from one of the merchants, just to display my handbills and some of my garments, I could at least introduce the shirtwaisters and bloomer costumes to the ladies here. But, thanks to Governor Cromwell and his esteemed cabinet, no one will rent to me."

"You know that fella Ah been tellin' you about? He might let you put some things in his store—"

Ida appeared in the doorway. "Miss Ashley? There

are two gentlemen here to see you. They are waiting in the parlor."

"Who are they?" asked Sarah.

"They said they are old friends," replied Ida.

Sarah looked at Mandi, bewildered. "I can't imagine who they could be since no one knows I'm here. Meanwhile, keep packing and I'll go see."

Sarah listened on the landing, but, hearing no voices, she descended the stairs. When she stepped into the parlor, her stomach lurched, her heart began to pound erratically, and beads of cold perspiration dampened her brow.

"Well, well now, Ty. If it isn't our little sister," the older man said.

Sarah stood, back stiff, chin raised, eyes riveted on her brother. "Hello, Hollis," she said, struggling to keep her voice flat, devoid of emotion. She saw that even here among ragged prospectors, Hollis had painstakingly anointed his brows with salve and combed them into place. His bristly side whiskers were freshly trimmed, and his dark hair was dressed with Macassar oil.

She looked past Hollis to Tyler—a younger version of Hollis—who maintained a bored and studious calm. One side of Tyler's mouth quirked upward in aloof recognition, then he turned away, appearing to peruse the books in the bookcase behind him. Sarah wouldn't expect Tyler to say much, if anything. He was merely a craven hanger-on to his brother; Hollis was the instigator of whatever they were up to. She turned her gaze on him.

Hollis strolled across the carpet, trailing a finger along the carved rosewood back of an armchair and over the smooth marble surface of a library table. Then he paused to contemplate the elegant, hand-painted globe of a table lamp. After a moment, he turned. His mouth curved in a scornful smile. "Well,

little sister," he said, allowing his gaze to roam the
surroundings, "it looks as though you're doing reasonably well for yourself. But then, you were never
one to lack for material comforts, were you? Your
mother always saw to that."

Sarah noted the hard line of Hollis's mouth and
the venom in his steel-gray eyes. "How did you find
me?"

The lines slanting from the sides of his nostrils and
around the corners of his mouth lifted in an ironic
smile. "Even the most trustworthy servants talk
when confronted with . . . certain consequences. And
once we were here, it wasn't too difficult to find
you. I showed this"—he flashed a daguerreotype—
"around town. Almost every merchant seems to
know you. But it did take several stops to learn that
you were living with the governor. Of course, I'm not
surprised that you've taken up with a man, considering your . . . past behavior."

The brusque remark succeeded in raising Sarah's
ire, as it was meant to. But she refused to humiliate
herself by acknowledging it. She intended to confront
Hollis with as much pride and dignity as possible.
Fixing her chilliest gaze on him, she said. "Why
don't you get to the point. What exactly do you
want?"

"Want? Why . . . only to wish you well. I must
hand it to you. You've managed to hold out for a
very"—he swept his hand in a grand circle—
"opulent lifestyle. None of your suitors in San
Francisco held such high estate, nor did any own a
town coach with four whites."

"You know as well as I that you didn't come all the
way to Victoria to wish me well. So get to the point."

Hollis shrugged. "The point is, since you're the
governor's mistress—"

"I'm not the governor's mistress," Sarah cut in.

"I'm staying here until I can find other lodging." She couldn't discern whether Hollis had made up the aspersion that she was Jon's mistress or if he'd heard it in town—Harriet Galbraith in her tattling about the cottage incident could certainly have intimated such a notion.

Hollis cocked a glossy brow. "You expect us to believe that you're living in the governor's home as his guest, without consideration . . . of any kind?"

"I don't expect you to believe anything. You and Tyler have no scruples. Therefore, it makes no difference what you believe, since what you say to others bears no relation whatsoever to what you know to be the truth."

Hollis's lips curved in a cunning smile. "Don't you think it's a bit surprising for you to talk about scruples? After all, anyone who would bed a married man, get pregnant by him, and destroy the unborn child is certainly lacking scruples by any standards. It's just fortunate that your dear, devoted stepbrothers were willing to forfeit their business to cover the costs of your expensive abortion, then allow you to slip away from the city."

Sarah's eyes blazed on hearing Hollis reiterate the base lies he and Tyler had broadcast in San Francisco. "Get out," she said in a tight voice. "Both of you, get out."

Hollis gave her a cold, hard look. His voice remained smooth, detached. "Oh, but we couldn't do that. I'm not finished with you yet. I warned you what would happen if you refused to turn over the money. You could have married any one of several suitors, and by now be living quite comfortably. But Tyler and I weren't so fortunate. We needed the money to save the business. And now, because of you, we have nothing."

"You know that's an outright lie," said Sarah.

"Any money that ever fell into your hands, you gambled away."

"I admit, we do enjoy faro," said Hollis. "But then, most gentlemen indulge in gaming. It's to be expected."

"Then losing is also to be expected." Sarah looked from Hollis to Tyler and back. "Why don't you for once in your lives take responsibility for your own actions?"

"Oh, how noble we are," said Hollis. "But the fact is, we *are* taking responsibility. We're here to claim what's ours. So if you don't want to face ugly litigation and have a lot of filthy laundry aired, I suggest you make out a bank draft for, say, half the money—since I'm in a generous mood—and we'll be on our way."

"And if I don't?"

"It would be a shame for your sordid past to follow you here, particularly since you seem to be so comfortably cared for by the governor."

"If I am his mistress, as you claim," she said, hoping he wouldn't detect the shakiness in her voice, "then my reputation could hardly be sullied now. So you might as well leave. I have no intention of giving you anything."

Hollis folded his arms. "I suggest you give this matter further thought. I doubt if the good people of Victoria would look favorably upon an unmarried woman who"—he arched a glossy black brow—"got herself pregnant, then stooped to abortion."

Sarah's jaw clenched tight. Knotting her fists at her sides in an effort to keep from thrashing Hollis with them, she said in a restrained voice. "I would say that you are demented, but I know otherwise. You were always cunning and devious. But somewhere along the way, you took a different path and became less than human."

Afraid that the stinging in her eyes would emerge as tears, Sarah turned, and when she did, every muscle in her body went slack. Jon stood in the doorway, his eyes smoldering. She had no idea how long he'd been there, but from the look on his face, she knew he had not just arrived. He stalked across the room in four long strides and stood beside her. "Would you introduce me to your guests?"

When he rested his hand on the base of her neck, Sarah's heart felt as if it were about to leap from her chest. The nearness of him seemed solid, reassuring. Yet she had to swallow before words could come. "These are my stepbrothers, Hollis and Tyler."

Hollis extended his hand, but retracted it when Jon made no move to take it. "My brother and I have some business with our sister," Hollis said. "So we will just step outside and continue."

"There's no need," said Jon, his eyes unwavering. "Unless, of course, Miss Ashley chooses to." His mouth curved in a wry smile. "My home is . . . her home."

Sarah caught the flicker of triumph in Hollis's steely gaze and watched the sullen resentment drain from his face. "Well then," he said, "since she's established here with you, you'll understand when we demand that she relinquish the money she holds . . . money that is rightfully ours."

Sarah's eyes blazed. "That money is from a fund left to me and me alone, and you know it. You have absolutely no claim to it."

Hollis gave a kind of grudging laugh and looked at Jon. "What she says isn't exactly correct, Governor. She neglected to mention that she managed to liquidate a fund that was in litigation, after which time she left San Francisco . . . quite hastily. But then, that's a common course when absconding with another's money, isn't it?"

"That's a strong accusation," said Jon in a lethal tone. "Are you prepared to back it up?"

"We have no legal papers with us, if that's what you mean," replied Hollis.

"Then I suggest you and your brother move on," said Jon.

"We can't," said Hollis. "We don't have enough money to return to San Francisco."

"You're gamblers," said Jon. "Go north to the goldfields. Gamble your last dollar on the chance that there might be a fortune waiting for you there. If not, you'd better find a way to go back to where you came from, because if you stay here you might find it eminently . . . unsafe. You see, Victoria has a policy concerning the presence of rats in sinkholes. We shoot them."

A muscle twitched in Hollis's jaw. "Is that a threat, Governor?"

Jon dropped his hand from Sarah's neck and faced Hollis squarely. "You'd bloody well better believe it is. And there's not a soul around here who'd give a damn if a couple of paltry bastards like you disappeared."

"You seem to be confused, Governor," said Hollis. "Sarah's the only bastard in the family. Didn't she tell you about her elite heritage?" He eyed Sarah with disdain. "No, I don't imagine she'd mention anything about her mother's broomstick marriage to our father . . . Would you, Sarah?"

Before she could respond, Jon's fist cracked against Hollis's jaw with swift and deadly aim, sending Hollis sprawling backward. As Hollis started to pull himself up, Jon grabbed him by the lapels, jerking him to his feet. "You goddamned bloody bastard. There are two ships sailing out of here tomorrow— the *Revelation* to the goldfields and the *Eliza Anderson* to New Westminster. You be on one of them." He released his hold, sending Hollis stumbling backward toward the front door. "Now, you and your brother get the hell out of here!"

Hollis rubbed his jaw and dabbed his handkerchief at the blood seeping from the corner of his mouth. He shifted disdainful eyes from Jon to Sarah. "Just keep in mind that you won't always be able to hide behind the coattails of your paramours. When you're tossed into the streets again, we'll find you ... and we'll get what's ours." He shoved his handkerchief into his pocket, snapped open his umbrella, and swept through the door, Tyler on his heels.

After the door had closed behind them, Sarah went to the window and parted the curtains. "They won't leave," she said in a weary voice. "You may have stopped Hollis for now, but he won't go until he gets what he came for."

Jon peered over her shoulder and watched the men climb into a plain black buggy that he recognized as one of the cheaper vehicles for hire from Parker's Livery. At least some of what he'd heard was true. The men were gamblers. He'd noted the crisp sheen of their frock coats, the ornate gold stickpins securing their silk cravats, the embroidery of their waistcoats. The men had obviously known wealth and lost it, and were holding on to a facade of affluence.

He also knew that the rest were lies. Sarah's behavior at the spring—her response to him when he'd taken her by surprise—was not the demeanor of an experienced woman, but rather of one who still had much to learn.

"How much did you hear?" she asked, continuing to look out the window.

Jon caught the shakiness in her voice, but suspected it was more from outrage than anxiety. "Enough to hope your brother will have a damned sore jaw for a hell of a long time to come."

Sarah kept her back to him. "I suppose you believe everything they said."

Jon couldn't dismiss the incongruous feeling of pleasure that settled over him on realizing that it mattered to Sarah what he thought. The odd thing was, he almost wished she *had* done the appalling things she'd been accused of doing, because then he might be able to banish her from his mind. "Do *you* care what I believe?" he asked.

She shrugged. "I care what the people of Victoria believe, since I hope to solicit their business."

"You didn't answer my question." He turned her around to face him. "I asked if you care what I believe."

She arched a delicately winged brow slightly. "I suppose I care . . . a little. So . . . do you believe what Hollis said?"

"Had it been the day of your arrival, I might have believed at least part of it," replied Jon. "You certainly wouldn't have been the first raspberry tart to arrive in Victoria. But now I know different. So, to answer your question, no, I don't believe what your brother said. What I don't understand, though, is why they'd fabricate such vicious lies about you."

"Because I wouldn't turn my money over to them, and they were angry."

"Why do they feel they have claim to the money?"

"Because it's money my mother put aside for me from earnings from the business. They feel it rightfully belonged to their father—my stepfather—and therefore to them, since they were the heirs. My mother saved up the money because she knew my stepfather had not included me in his will. When I turned twenty-one, she put the money in a secret account in my name, then passed it on to me just before she died. Hollis and Tyler learned about the money when my stepfather died, and threatened litigation. But before they could start proceedings, I liquidated the account and came here."

"And your relatives in the East?" asked Jon, his gaze taking in the sensuous curve of her lips. "Do they endorse this venture of yours?"

"They don't know about it," she replied.

Catching a hint of ruthlessness in her tone, Jon looked into her darkened eyes. "Is there a particular reason why?"

A trace of desperation crept into Sarah's voice as she replied, "Yes. Because I have no contact with them."

"Why not?" Jon asked, curving his fingers more firmly around her shoulders.

"It's a long story, and I'm certain you'd be quite bored with it," she said, ducking from under his hands.

He caught her arm, turning her to face him. "Nothing about you has bored me so far. Now . . . tell me."

She stared at him for a few moments, then shrugged indifferently. "They want nothing to do with me."

"Let me guess," said Jon, his mouth curving with a faintly indolent smile. "They're a bunch of strait-laced prudes, and you insist on parading around in those bloody bloomer costumes."

Chin raised, eyes unblinking, Sarah replied in a flat voice, "No. Because I'm a . . . love child. You see, some of what Hollis said *was* true. My real father was a captain in the British navy, and he never married my mother. When the family learned about it, they made it clear that I was not to come East and pollute their good name. I'm really quite the blue blood, don't you agree?"

Jon ignored her cynical remark. "What happened to your real father?"

"It's not important."

"I think it is. He caused you a lot of pain, and I want to know why." Jon saw her chin quiver slightly and her eyes brighten with unshed tears.

"He called my mother a whore, denied being the father of her unborn child, and sailed off. My mother's family shunned her, so they certainly would not welcome me stepping forward after all these years and reminding them that I still exist. So what do you think of my aristocratic birth now?"

The bitterness of her words and the undisguised pain in her eyes sent blood pulsing through Jon's temples with a low, steady throb. At last he understood why she'd turned from men and marriage. The disarmed, vulnerable woman beneath the dauntless facade had been betrayed by all the men who mattered to her. That she'd turned from marriage was of no concern to him. But he *would* change her opinion of men. She needed love and passion to make her life whole, and he intended to give them to her.

But to penetrate the wall she'd built around her heart, he'd have to approach her with far more understanding. "I think your father was a damned spineless fool."

She gave a short laugh. "I suppose I have to agree with you. But then, he wouldn't want to claim as his the child of a soiled woman who had been tossed aside by her own family."

"That's a blamed piece of humbug," said Jon. "Besides, look what came of it: a ravishingly beautiful, thunderingly courageous, exasperatingly charming woman," he said, the pad of his thumb tracing the hard line of her mouth, attempting to coax a smile.

Her lips softened and she looked up at him with wide, probing eyes. "What I told you doesn't seem to bother you."

He curved his arms around her and clasped his hands behind her waist. "It doesn't. If your mother had not fallen in love with your father—spineless fool that he was—you would not be here in my arms." His eyes meandered across her face, paused at length on her lips, and moved up to hold her gaze.

"Well, no . . . I don't suppose I would be . . ." Sarah said, distracted by the sparks of desire dancing in Jon's eyes.

He cupped her chin and tipped her face upward. "And if you were not in my arms, I would not be able to taste your sweet lips . . ." He flicked his tongue over her lips. "Or feel your warm, enticing body against mine . . ." He pulled her to him so her breasts pressed against his chest. "And do this . . ." His mouth covered hers.

Sarah closed her arms around him and held him tightly, the hard, muscled contours of his back familiar to her now. Slowly, sensuously, his tongue stroked her lips, teasing a response, then urging . . . insisting. She parted her lips and yielded to him, and when he opened his mouth to her, she timidly slid her tongue inside.

Gradually, she became bolder, until her tongue stroked and glided over his in slow, sensual caresses. The scent of him filled her. The warm bouquet of his mouth invaded her—smoke and brandy, salt and sweet licorice. She tangled her fingers in his hair, wanting more . . . demanding more. His hand moved up to cup her breast, his fingers teasing her nipple into a ripe bud. An odd kind of pleasurable pain spread through her, the effect heightening in her loins until it seemed a hot, moist ache burned there.

He drew her closer, thrusting his tongue into her mouth with urgent need, his desperate drugging kiss and the tight, breathless feeling in her chest making her light-headed and disoriented. He rotated his hips, pressing her to him until she felt a rocklike hardness moving against her, low where she ached.

At first she was confused. Then a sudden awareness began to creep into her fogged mind. Abruptly, she broke the kiss, and her eyes popped open.

Jon's breath rushed against her face as he said in a ragged voice, "Don't be shocked, little love, it's just my body's way of telling yours that I want you ... desperately."

His blatant statement and the sudden thud of her heart reminded Sarah that she was swooning in the arms of her adversary. Pressing against his chest, she said in an agitated voice, "I've got to finish packing since we'll be moving in the morning."

Jon looked down at her with hooded eyes. "You'll never get through. The road's a mire. You'd better plan on staying another day or two ... at least until the road dries a bit."

"No, I can't. That's out of the question," she said, contemplating the editorial Amor De Cosmos had proposed, which should be out any day. "Mud or no mud, I *will* leave tomorrow."

"But there's just no reason," said Jon. "Besides, I want you to stay."

Sarah slipped out of his embrace. Licking her lips, she managed an ambivalent smile, then, giving him a long, lingering look, she said, "You won't for much longer." Turning abruptly, she left the room.

Chapter 8

Sarah awakened to a low, protracted rumble in the sky and, to her dismay, rain pelted the window. It had drizzled throughout the night, and now she feared that the road would really be the mire Jon had predicted. But somehow she'd get the wagon through and be settled in the cottage by late afternoon.

Although Jon had instructed his stablemen to load her trunks and drive the wagon, she had insisted on driving the wagon herself. Certainly, driving on a muddy road would present no more of a challenge than negotiating the hilly cobblestone streets of San Francisco.

Knowing she had little time to spare if they were to be out of the house and into the cottage before the newspaper editorial appeared on the streets, she quickly dressed in a plain shirtwaister and working boots, then set about closing the trunks. Before she packed her diary, she made one last entry, dated September 14, 1863:

Dear Diary,
  I have no idea what to expect from Hollis and Tyler. For the moment I am safe from their harassment. But once Mandi and I are in the cot-

tage, I feel certain they will find me and press me for the money. I have little hope that they will leave as Jon has insisted. They have come all the way to Victoria to find me, which they have managed to do, and they are not likely to give up and leave so easily.

As for Jon's indifference on learning the circumstances surrounding my birth . . . it doesn't appear to matter to him in the least. But then it wouldn't, because he knows, just as I do, that there can never be anything serious between us. Still, having told him everything somehow seems to lighten the burden of my sordid past . . .

"May I come in, Miss Ashley?" Josephine appeared in the doorway. "I want to talk to you before you go."

Sarah quickly closed the diary and tucked it in the trunk. "Yes, of course."

Josephine looked down the hall both ways before slipping into the room and quietly closing the door. "What I wanted to talk about was this." She offered a scrapbook.

Sarah took the book and slowly fanned the pages, scanning the numerous articles clipped from the *New York Tribune*. "How did you get these?" she asked, noting the care with which the orderly collection had been cut and pasted.

"From Mrs. Dewig-Gertz. Her husband owns Gertz's Drug Store," Josephine said, excitement bringing a rosy flush to her face. "Mrs. Dewig-Gertz is quite in favor of suffrage for women, and has even insisted on maintaining her former name—her last husband, Mr. Dewig, died. Anyway, Mrs. Dewig-Gertz has a cousin who sends her the clippings, and when she finishes reading them she lets me have them. Of course, Papa and Grandmother don't know

I'm keeping this scrapbook. They'd be frightfully upset."

"Yes, I suppose they would be," said Sarah, lowering herself to the bed. Perusing the articles, she recognized the writings of Elizabeth Cady Stanton. "So this is where you get your rebellious bent," she said, raising amused eyes to Josephine and catching her furtive smile.

"Yes," replied Josephine. "I mean, I don't believe I am being rebellious—although Papa and Grandmother seem to think so. But now you see why I was so happy when I learned you were coming to Victoria to make things right for women."

"Well, I don't know about that," said Sarah, giving Josephine a sideways glance. "It doesn't appear I have been doing very well so far."

"Oh, but you will. And I'll help you." Josephine dropped to sit on the bed, tucked her feet under her, and gathered her skirt about her knees. "I've been reading about temperance and suffrage and education for women," she said in an excited voice, "and also about Mrs. Amelia Bloomer's costumes. Of course, I had never seen one before, so you can see how terribly thrilled I was when you mentioned you had brought some. And twice I have worn the bloomers you gave me ... when I was alone in my bedroom at night."

A sense of uneasiness settled over Sarah on hearing Josephine's announcement. "Maybe you should refrain from doing that, at least until your father and grandmother become a little more accustomed to the idea of women in bifurcated outer garments."

"They are so behind the times," Josephine said in an exasperated voice. Moving close to Sarah, she reached over and flipped the pages of the scrapbook. "Look, right here it says that there is a woman doctor with the Federal Army who wears trousers and a tunic when she tends the soldiers on the battlefield, and that several nurses are considering the idea." She pursed her lips and added, "I just imagine that if Grandmother were there, she would expect the nurses to wear layers and layers of petticoats so they'd be properly dressed. I truly must not let her see this book."

Sarah mused over what Lady Cromwell's reaction might be on learning about her granddaughter's collection of newspaper clippings. "Does your Aunt Esther know you've been reading such controversial things as this?" she asked.

"Well, no," replied Josephine. "I've thought of telling her, but I was afraid she might say something to Papa or Grandmother, even though she holds with most of my opinions. And I would simply die if I were told I could not study these writings anymore."

"Then I believe you're quite right to keep it to yourself," said Sarah, "at least for now." She handed the scrapbook to Josephine and stood to continue her packing.

Josephine's eyes sparkled with curiosity. "Do you know anything about the Women's Rights Convention in New York?"

"Well, yes, as a matter of fact, I was there," Sarah replied, while slipping a kid boot into a muslin bag. "We were still living in New York—that was before my father moved to San Francisco—and although I was only twelve at the time, my mother thought it was important for me to hear Elizabeth Cady Stanton."

"Oh, please. Do tell me about it."

Sarah smiled at Josephine's enthusiasm. Remembering how excited she'd been that day, she replied, "All the roads leading to the church were jammed with carriages and carts, and there was a huge crowd gathered on the lawn when Mother and I arrived—

someone had locked the church so no one could get in. But someone crawled through the window, and soon people filled the pews. The men, although uninvited and unwanted, refused to leave, but that didn't stop the women from debating issues, sometimes quite heatedly. Of course the entire convention was denounced by the newspaper as a motley gathering of fanatical mongrels, old grannies, fugitive slaves, and lunatics. But, as my mother pointed out, it started people thinking and questioning, and that's the first step toward progress."

"How terribly exciting that must have been," Josephine said, clapping her hands with glee. "I should like to stand before a crowd of woman someday and do just as Mrs. Stanton did—I have read that she is an eloquent speaker."

Sarah looked into eyes kindled with the first, almost imperceptible, sparks of fanatical fervor, vaguely reminding her of Elizabeth Cady Stanton herself. "I believe your father and grandmother would be mortified if you ever did such a thing," she said, resuming her packing, tucking her boots into the trunk.

"Yes, I suppose you're right," said Josephine. She sighed heavily. "Grandmother absolutely insists that we be proper ladies. Being proper doesn't bother Louella though. She fashions herself as being exactly like Mama. But it bothers me greatly." She gave another despondent sigh. "I am so weary of hearing how a well-bred lady must conduct herself."

"It does get a bit tiresome at times," Sarah agreed.

Josephine smiled brightly. "You and Mrs. Dewig-Gertz are the only people in all of Victoria who truly understand. Grandmother is so . . . well, so behind the times. She says—" Josephine hopped to her feet, strolled theatrically across the room, and pressed her lips into a smirk, while reciting with great eloquence,

"A proper lady must wear a smile, have a graceful bearing, a light step and"—she tipped her body forward—"an elegant bend. And she must sink gently into a chair." She carefully lowered herself into the lady's chair. "And, of course, retain an upright position."

Sarah chuckled at Josephine's melodramatic parody and added, "And the well-bred lady must also"—she dabbed at her hair—"avoid smoothing the tresses or arranging the curls"—she tugged at her bodice, wiggling as if she had a terrible itch—"or pulling at the dress. And the proper gentleman must assume a stiff and unnatural bearing, simper and frown, quirk his little finger, and dance with ridiculous precision." She danced about the room, stiff-legged, her little finger cocked in the air.

They both broke into girlish giggles.

After a few moments, Josephine stood, and her face sobered. "I must go before Grandmother learns that I'm with . . . uh . . . I mean, learns that I have not . . . tidied my room. But I'll stop by the cottage to see you the first chance I can get away."

Sarah gave Josephine a sedate smile. "I think it would be best if you didn't come to the cottage . . . at least for a while. I don't want your father or grandmother to think that I put these unconventional ideas in your head, and how else could you explain them without disclosing your scrapbook?"

"But we have so much work to do. I mean, spreading the word about women's rights and dress reform. I truly want to help you. And I'll work in your shop without pay. Please, Miss Ashley, I do so want to do it."

Sarah eyed her in amusement. "I'd certainly have no objection," she said, "but I'm afraid your father and grandmother would feel otherwise, wouldn't they?"

"I'm almost seventeen," said Josephine. "I should

be allowed to make my own decisions." Raising her chin, she added, "I may even tell Father and Grandmother so."

Sarah eyed her dubiously. "Perhaps you should wait a bit, at least until you *are* seventeen ... and I am safely away from your father's house."

Josephine's eyes warmed with laughter. "Yes, I suppose you're right. I'll wait until you're away from here. But perhaps not until I'm seventeen."

Sarah studied Josephine's eager face. How easy the job of selling bloomers would be if every woman in Victoria felt as Josephine did. Opening the door for her to leave, she said, "I tell you what. When I have set up my store, then you might drop by and say hello. And maybe when things are going well, and your father and grandmother have become more accustomed to the idea of women in business, then perhaps you might approach them about working for me. Meanwhile, continue to act like a proper lady, because a woman with poise, dignity, and grace has far more power to persuade than one who is unschooled in such matters." She wasn't certain she truly believed that, but it seemed appropriate to say it to Josephine.

"I suppose you're right," said Josephine. "And I *will* talk to Papa and Grandmother about working for you in your store ... later, of course. Now I must go." She gave Sarah a quick hug and scurried off.

Sarah looked across the hall at the door to Louella's room. Ever since her arrival, Louella had been avoiding her, and she wanted to talk to her about occupying the room where her mother's possessions were kept. Deciding that now might be her only opportunity, she knocked lightly. "Louella, may I come in?" she called through the closed door. "I'd like to say goodbye."

When she heard no reply, she knocked again, this

time a little louder. "Louella? I will just take a minute of your time. Please, may I come in?"

The door opened slowly. Louella peeked through the crack, then stepped back, allowing Sarah to enter. She stared at Sarah, her china-blue eyes cool and clear, as she waited in aloof silence for Sarah to speak. Sarah reached out to touch her shoulder, but Louella backed away and tightened her lips.

Sarah sighed. "I had hoped we would continue to be friends, as we were on the ship."

"You should not have come here," Louella said bitterly, her eyes darkening with anger. "Nor should you have stayed in my mother's room." She turned and walked over to the rain-streaked window.

"Yes, perhaps you're right," said Sarah. "I certainly didn't mean to stay where I was unwelcome. And I truly hope I didn't disturb your mother's things. I tried not to."

Louella refused to look at Sarah, and instead stared out the window, her embittered face reflected in the glass against the darkened sky. "My mother was a well-bred, fashionable lady," she said in a quiet but caustic tone. "She knew all the rules of conduct, and the importance of proper dress. There was not a place my father could take her where she would be anything less than a proper lady."

"I'm certain you're right," said Sarah. "And you must be very proud to have had her for a mother."

"Then why are you trying to take her place?"

"Where did you get that idea?"

"It's true, isn't it?"

"No, it's not true," said Sarah. "As a matter of fact, your father and I disagree on many issues."

"I don't believe you. I think you plan to marry him because he's governor and has lots of money. Well, you're not anything like my mother, and he won't marry you no matter what you do."

Sarah peered into resentful eyes glistening with tears. "Believe me," she said, "I have no romantic designs on your father. But you must face the fact that someday someone will, and your father will care for her, too. Then you'll have to let him go."

"You're wrong," Louella said, adamant. "He'll never love anyone like he loved my mother. And no one will be as pretty, either." She turned toward the window again.

Sarah stared at Louella's flaxen hair and her narrow shoulders. "You and your father have a very special relationship. But if you really love him, you'll allow him to have a life beyond you and Josephine."

"My father doesn't need that," Louella replied, refusing to look at Sarah. "He likes things just the way they are. And as soon as you're gone, everything will be fine again."

"I'm sorry you feel that way," said Sarah, "and I truly hope we can eventually be friends." When Louella didn't respond, Sarah turned and left the room, closing the door quietly behind her.

Thirty minutes later, having donned cloak, hat, and gloves, Sarah waited, looking out the window. Soon, up the road came a man who drove a large open wagon pulled by a pair of unmatched, dingy brown horses, with a saddle horse plodding behind. Sarah had contracted for use of the wagon for moving, but once she and Mandi were settled in the cottage, she intended to exchange the wagon for a buggy.

After the man from the livery had gone, two of Jon's stablemen started moving trunks from the bedroom to the wagon, stopping between loads to stand on the porch, out of the rain. Sarah tried to urge the men to move faster—she desperately wanted to be gone before Jon returned from the legislature building—but the men seemed to be in no hurry. When they had loaded the last trunk, they covered everything with a canvas. But before they had secured it with ropes, it began to rain harder and they moved under the porch again. Anxious to be on her way, Sarah dismissed them, deciding that she and Mandi could finish the job themselves.

"Come on," she said to Mandi, who was standing with her on the porch.

Mandi hesitated. "It's raining mighty hard right now."

"Well, we can't wait," said Sarah. "Those ropes aren't going to get tied by themselves, and Governor Cromwell isn't going to stay the night at his office. So we're running out of time."

Mandi sighed. Holding on to the hood of her cloak, attempting to protect her head from the unceasing rain, she followed Sarah to the wagon.

Sarah started crisscrossing ropes over the canvas and fastening them in a web of knots. "We'll be at the cottage in fifteen minutes," she assured Mandi, flicking her tongue up to catch a droplet dripping from the end of her nose. "Then we can build a fire and have something warm to drink. And since the stablemen won't be coming to unload the trunks until later, we can spend a nice, quiet afternoon." She tugged her hood over her head.

"Ah sho' hope you's right . . . Ah mean about bein' in the cottage and bein' warm in fifteen minutes," said Mandi. "Ah'm 'bout frozen clear to my bones."

"Then work faster and you'll get warm," said Sarah, tugging on the last rope and fastening it with cold, wet fingers.

"Ah 'spect things are goin' to get warm sooner than that," said Mandi, gazing in the distance. "Here come the guv'nor on his horse, and he look plenty angry."

Sarah glanced up, and to her alarm saw Jon galloping toward her, mud flying, his rain cape billowing.

From his reckless pace, she suspected that the editorial had appeared and he had read it.

Reining to a halt beside the wagon, he flung his leg over his horse's rump and dropped to the ground. "What the bloody hell do you think you're doing?"

Sarah tugged on the rope. "Leaving, as I told you we would," she replied, surprised that his first words had not been about the editorial. She'd expected an immediate outburst.

He gathered his cape around himself and tipped his hat forward in an attempt to deflect the rain from his face. "Why are you so damned determined to leave today?" he demanded. "Is it because of my mother?"

Sarah looked at him, puzzled. Obviously, the editorial had nothing to do with his behavior. If not for that, why had he been racing home like the devil was on his tail? "Your mother?"

"About finding us at the cottage," he said. "In spite of it, she doesn't expect you to leave in this downpour. No one does."

"Well, I *do* expect to leave," she said. With cold, stiff fingers, she tugged on the wet rope, looped it around itself, secured it, and snapped it to test the knot. Pulling her hood lower on her forehead, she trudged around to the opposite side of the wagon, the soggy hem of her skirt dragging along the wet, muddy ground.

Jon tossed a hand up in exasperation and slogged around the wagon to stand ankle-deep in mire. He peered down at her with fierce determination. "You have a head as thick as gutter mud! Overlooking the fact that the roads are impassable, you'll no doubt catch pneumonia and we'll have that on our hands, not to mention our consciences. Now, for Christ's sake, go inside and forget this lunacy."

Sarah parted her sopping wet hair so she could

look up at Jon. "I simply must get moved so I can get on with my life and my business."

"There's damned little you can do in this rain!"

"That's not the point!"

"Then what the hell is?"

"You'll find out soon enough."

The muscles in Jon's jaw tightened. "Exactly what is *that* supposed to mean?"

Sarah shoved her hair out of her face, propped her hands on her hips, and glared up at him, squinting against the rain. "Look, I didn't ask to be in this position; you put me here. If it hadn't been for you and your council, by now I would have my business license, I would have a store leased, and I would be somewhere warm and dry instead of standing out here in this deluge. What I don't understand is why you're showing such concern for me now."

Jon flailed a hand in the air. *"Because you'll catch your damned death of cold! That's why!"*

"You needn't raise your voice to me, Jon. My hearing is quite sound." Gathering her skirts, she trudged back around the wagon.

"At least you have that to be thankful for," Jon called over the top of the load. "I fear your mind might not be so sound!"

"You may not approve of what I'm doing," said Sarah, flashing angry eyes at him, "but the least you can do is refrain from insulting me."

"Bloody hell!" He pounded his fist against the wagon, swept his rain cloak closed, and marched around to confront her. Drawing in a steadying breath, he took her by the arms. "Look at you. Your teeth are chattering, your lips are blue, and your hair is soaked to your scalp. Come in the house where we can reason this out."

"There's nothing to reason out," Sarah said, shrugging from under his hands. "The wagon's ready, so

Mandi and I will be on our way. Come along, Mandi."

Sarah removed the whip from the whip bucket, threw the ends of the reins over her arm, and gathered her skirts. Then, grasping the handle of the footboard, she propped her foot on the hub, mounted the box, and waited until Mandi had settled beside her.

Jon backed away a few steps. Cupping his hand over his eyes to shield them from the rain, he yelled, "I don't know why the hell you're running off like this, but since there's no talking any sense into your thick head, go on. Get the wagon stuck in the mud. Catch your damned death of cold and die. Maybe then I'll have some peace around here." Wheeling around, he stalked toward the house while muttering a string of expletives under his breath.

Sarah shook the reins, flourished the whip in a loud crack, and gave the command, "Harr harr ... giddyap!" The horses sprang into action, rearing and jibbing, but refusing to move forward. Swinging the whip in an arc, Sarah gave the command again. The horses seesawed and then settled into their collars, pulling in unison, and the wagon moved forward. Laboring and creaking under the heavy load, the wagon wobbled down the road.

They hadn't gone far when Mandi peered over the side board and said in a worried voice, "The mud is sho' creepin' high on the wheels."

Sarah felt the horses straining and the wagon gradually sinking deeper into the muddy ruts, which surprised her. In San Francisco, she'd driven larger wagons than this on roads that appeared similar, but the roads there seemed to retain a solid base, even in the foulest weather. She certainly hadn't anticipated the road being such a slurry. "It looks better up ahead," she said, hoping she sounded more optimistic than she felt. "If we can just get through this slurry, we should be all right."

"I don't know," said Mandi. "It looks mighty bad to me. Maybe we should turn back . . . do like the guv'nor say and stay until the rain stops."

"Even if it means sleeping in the mud under this wagon," said Sarah, "I refuse to stay in that house another night."

Mandi sighed. "Well, at least we got away before the newspaper came out. Ah 'spect that's worth somethin'."

The horses began straining, then seesawing again, but the more they pulled against each other, the deeper the wagon seemed to sink, until at last, mud up to the hubs, the wagon tilted at an uncertain angle.

Feeling herself slipping sideways on the box, Sarah drew in a sharp, startled breath. "Quick! Jump off before we topple over," she yelled, struggling to hold her balance as the wagon settled further. Gathering her cloak about her, she started to climb down, but, losing her footing, she slid off and fell into the mud. Moments later, Mandi collapsed beside her.

Grabbing Mandi's arm, Sarah dragged her from under the dangerously listing wagon. Mortified as the realization of what had happened gradually took hold, Sarah began to weigh her options. She couldn't leave the rig settled at such an angle with the horses still hitched, but she wasn't sure she could unhitch them, either.

"What are we goin' to do?" Mandi asked, her voice weak, almost pitiful

"Well, I suppose we'd better try to back the horses so we can get the wagon out of these deep ruts, then we'll try to turn it around without tipping it over."

Mud oozing into her boots, Sarah trudged over to take the horses by their bridles, then she began urging them backward. The horses tossed their heads, jerking on the leathers, and began backing up. But instead of pushing the wagon out of the ruts, the horses balked and reared. Sarah jumped out of the way.

Hopelessly viewing her situation and knowing she mustn't chance spooking the horses and toppling the wagon, Sarah realized she had no choice but to send for help, which also meant facing Jon. "Damn!" Looking into Mandi's wide eyes, she said, "Go fetch Peterson and have him bring along a couple of stablemen and some horses to pull us out."

Mandi enfolded herself in her muddy cloak. "Then are we goin' back to the guv'nor's house?"

Sarah peered through the unceasing rain at the vague outline of Jon's house in the distance, furious with herself at the thought of having to face Jon while looking as she did, and allowing him to remind her of how right he'd been. But she had little choice. "I suppose we'll have to," she said, wondering why every plan she had formulated had gone awry. Was this some kind of punishment for daring to stray from convention?

"You sho' you be all right?" asked Mandi.

"I will be if these horses stay calm . . . and the wagon remains upright," she said. "So hurry."

While Mandi trudged down the road, Sarah talked softly to the skittish horses. Gooseflesh rose on her arms, and her muscles felt cold and stiff. Beyond rectifying her current predicament and facing Jon again, all she could think of was a warm bath, a dry bed, and a hot drink.

Twenty minutes later, Peterson returned with two stablemen, each leading a stocky dray horse. Peterson took one look at the wagon and said to Sarah, "Ye've done a right good job o' boggin' her down, mum. Now it's best ye get back to the house and get yerself warm. Jess and Tooley and I will see to unhookin' the pair and pullin' the wagon out. And we'll bed down the horses in the stables and park the wagon there, too."

"Thank you, Peterson," said Sarah. "And if it won't be too much trouble, would you please see that the high-topped trunk just behind the seat is returned to my bedroom."

Peterson gave a weary sigh. "Yes, mum."

Pulling her drenched hood over her head and clasping her cloak around herself, Sarah slogged through ankle-deep mud, her boots squelching with each step as she made her way toward the house. Although she was soaked through, when she climbed the porch steps ten minutes later and was met by Jon at the door, her mouth felt so dry she could barely swallow.

For a few moments, Jon said nothing, but simply stood there inspecting her. Then his mouth quirked in an ironic smile. "Ah, a little mudlark at my doorstep," he said. "What are you selling, miss? Nails? Wood? Perhaps a few spots of coal?"

Sarah bristled at his jest. Knowing there was nothing to do now but go through the motions of redeeming a situation that was already beyond redemption, and hoping the tears of chagrin gathering in her eyes wouldn't brim over and slide down her cheeks, she replied, "I suppose you're pleased. Not only am I trapped here for the night, but you have the satisfaction of knowing that you were right, and I was wrong."

Jon pulled a limp tress of wet hair from her face and brushed a smudge of mud from her cheek. "On the contrary, I'm not pleased at all," he said. "I fear you'll catch your death from exposure. However, a hot bath is prepared in your room, a warm comforter is waiting on your bed, and Ida is at this moment fetching a tray with soup and toast and hot buttered rum for you."

"You were pretty damned sure we wouldn't make it, weren't you?"

He merely smiled.

After removing her boots on the porch, Sarah lifted her skirts and traipsed up the stairs, anxious to shed her soggy clothes, take the hot bath, and remain in her room until morning.

On the slender chance that perhaps the newspaper with the caustic editorial would not be released for at least another day, she allowed herself the luxury of optimism.

Chapter 9

Glancing out the window late that afternoon, Sarah saw two men ride furiously up to the house and rein their horses in an abrupt halt. A knot twisted in her stomach. "I don't know who these men are," she said to Mandi, "but they are surely in a hurry. I just imagine they're here to bring Jon the news."

Mandi stepped to the window. "Ah 'spect you's right. That big fat bald one's Mayor Harris, and the other one's Attorney General Cary from the governor's office."

Sarah looked at Mandi with a start. "How do you know that?"

Mandi shrugged. "Ida pointed them out when we was in town. They's always together."

Sarah looked at the mayor, an immense man sporting a beard with silver streaks, and the attorney general, a small man with pale brows and a wispy beard, and wished she could somehow slip away from the house without being seen. That being impossible, she stepped to the door, opened it slightly, and listened to the men who were gathered at the foot of the stairs.

For a few moments, all was quiet, then Jon's voice

echoed through the house. "CITY FATHERS FAVOR BROTH-ELS! What the hell is De Cosmos about this time?"

"You'd better keep reading," said Mayor Harris. "Not only has the editorial challenged your integrity and worthiness as governor—as well as the qualifications of the rest of us—but it will undoubtedly cause strong dissent among the citizens. Word is, the Ashley woman plans to hire only women to work in her business. The men fear she'll be a bad influence on their wives and that she'll lure their daughters away from marriage."

Jon focused on the editorial, his face growing hot as he silently read:

Several unjust legal enactments have come down from our semi-barbarous city council, the most recent being the licensing of houses of prostitution as dance halls and, now, the denial of business licenses to honest citizens . . .

" 'If prostitutes are allowed to practice their trade in our fair city,' " Jon continued aloud, " 'certainly one decent, enterprising young woman should be allowed to practice her trade as well!' " He slapped the newspaper against his palm, and a separate sheet fluttered to the floor. "What the devil is this?" He retrieved the paper.

"It's a handbill," replied Harris.

"I can see that," Jon snapped, "but what's it doing in the *Colonist*?"

Harris shrugged. "It seems that De Cosmos has included one in every copy of the newspaper. It contains quite a bit of propaganda."

Jon turned his attention to the one-page handbill that had been tucked inside the newspaper. He briefly scanned the fashion plates of bloomer-clad women, then read words he recognized as purely and unequivocally Sarah's:

> A woman should not burden herself with clothes to the detriment of her health, comfort, and life. Her dress should be compatible with her needs and suited to her wants and necessities, which are individual, not something dictated by man or church . . .

One corner of Jon's mouth lifted slightly. He could almost see the fiery glint in Sarah's eyes and hear the fervor and enthusiasm in her voice as she spoke the words.

Harris smoothed his mustache and stroked his beard. "It has caused quite a stir among the ladies," he said. "Some are even in favor of the preposterous garments."

"I'm surprised," said Jon. "I would have thought our women much more provident."

"Yes, my thoughts too," said Harris. "But, as Mrs. Harris pointed out, the garments are more suited to tending household duties than house dresses. I'm afraid she, too, has expressed interest. Of course, I've discouraged her."

"Ummm. Well, you continue doing that," said Jon, undecided whether to throw Sarah out the house bodily or commend her for her marketing ingenuity.

"Perhaps you'd better read the other side," said Harris. "That's where the real problem rests."

Jon flipped the handbill and read the block of print, which gave him clear, definitive insight into the woman he intended to seduce into eager submission:

> With present-day laws, women are forced to be dependent on men. Universities and colleges

deny entry to women, so there is little for a woman to do but sew and stitch or teach for wages far below those of a man; nor can she practice law or hold public office. She can own property, yet she must pay taxes without representation. As it stands, all manner of men—drunkards, rowdies, and immoral and ignorant men—have the right to vote, yet the same is denied sober, moral, righteous, and intelligent women of the community. We must band together and demand our rights—our right to reform our dress, to pursue our education, to seek our choice of employment, to acquire equality under law, and to obtain the elective franchise . . .

Attorney General Cary gave Jon a hard-edged look. "It's this sort of thing that creates discord and starts revolts . . . women with their proclamations and indoctrination, preaching ceaselessly until the established is put up for debate, the traditional becomes anomalous, and the system collapses under dissension."

"He's right, Jon," said Mayor Harris. "The last thing we need at the moment is the Ashley woman stirring up the women here. Soon we'll be facing a mob of willful women dressed in breeches, demanding the same rights as men. Then we'll find wives leaving husbands and family, and marching to rallies and holding conventions. It's happening in the States right now. The woman's an agitator, and she's got to be stopped!"

Jon felt the first twinge of trouble brewing. Sarah's self-appointed crusade *could* create problems, especially if the men of Victoria took the same position as Cary and Harris, which is what they'd undoubtedly do.

Cary pulled a paper from his leather folder. "This

just arrived, and, frankly, Jon, things aren't looking too good right now, especially if this thing with the Ashley woman gets out of hand. We could end up facing a minor female rebellion—the type of thing that must not get back to the Crown."

Jon took the paper Cary offered, noting at once the gold-embossed insignia of the royal government. A scowl knitted his brow as he read the dispatch informing him that the assistant to the colonial secretary would be arriving in two months. His mission: to ascertain the state of the economy of both Victoria and New Westminster, evaluate the situation, and make a recommendation to the royal government regarding confederation. If union was indicated, he would also advise the Crown which city was better suited to become capital of the province, and which governor should head the expanded colony.

Cary arched a brow. "De Cosmos jumped at the chance to use the incident with the Ashley woman to push for union, and for the removal of you and the rest of us from office."

Jon returned the dispatch to Cary. "Calling us a council of cock-headed imperialists doesn't help a hell of a lot, either," he said, wondering why fate had sent Sarah bursting into his life at this critical time. But for the arrival of the Crown delegates and the impending threat of unification, she would certainly not have been of any real consequence in the colony . . . just more of an inconvenience.

Mayor Harris dabbed the moist crown of his balding head with his handkerchief, then shoved the wadded cloth back into his pocket. "Maybe we should reconsider our objectives for the moment . . . let the woman have her license just to keep things quiet. I doubt if anyone will lease a store to her anyway, so she'll still be up a tree, so to speak. Maybe then she'll decide to give the whole thing up and return to the States."

Jon gave a short grunt of derision. "That would sure make things a hell of a lot quieter around here." He glanced up the stairs in the direction of Sarah's room, and Sarah quickly closed the door.

"Return to the States!" she said to Mandi. "They'd like that, all of them, including Jon. Well, we might be stranded in his house for a day or two longer than expected, but I refuse to let those days slip idly by. Maybe I have no license, and no one will lease a building to me, but if there is truly an interest in my garments as the mayor said, then I want at least to try and find a place to display them and begin to take orders. And I think I shall start by talking to Mrs. Dewig-Gertz."

"Who's she?"

"Someone Josephine told me about . . . a lady who might be able to help us. And we'll start our search by calling on her tomorrow morning. For now, locate the governor's courier and have him deliver one of my calling cards to Mrs. Dewig-Gertz. Then notify Peterson to unload the footlocker with the bloomers and the small trunk with my walking dresses—"

A sharp knock interrupted her. "Miss Ashley," Ida called through the door. "The governor wants you to come to his library at once."

"Oh . . . he does, does he," said Sarah, nettled at what appeared to be more of a command than a request. "Then, by all means, please inform him that I shall be right there." Of course, she wouldn't be. Some women might jump to the snap of Jon's fingers, but she refused to be one of them.

Deliberately procrastinating, she sat at the dressing table and fiddled with her hair, dabbled with her cap, and trifled with the lace at her throat. His imperial highness could just sit on his lofty throne and wait, and brood, until *she* was ready to see *him*.

Jon paced impatiently, irritated at being kept waiting. Sarah was a clever bit of baggage, he gave her that. To reverse her setback and use it to her advantage by appealing to Amor De Cosmos—the man who had the greatest power to skew and distort an issue—was a master stroke. One couldn't help but admire her pluck.

Maybe Cary and Harris were right. Maybe she *could* stir his female population to the brink of insurrection, if not poise it on the razor's edge of civil disorder. Which would also place his cabinet in a dangerously vulnerable position politically. And now, with De Cosmos on her side and primed for editorial attack, any further grievances from her, however incidental, and the integrity of his administration wouldn't be worth a tinker's damn.

And the little minx knew it.

But despite the discord she was causing, he couldn't put her from his mind. The thought of her warm and naked in his arms wouldn't be pushed aside. He also realized, with some misgiving, that his feelings went deeper than simply lust for a beautiful woman. But he'd hold those feelings in check—not be the mooncalf he'd been with Caroline—because he had plans for Miss Sarah Ashley . . . erotic plans designed to relieve an ongoing problem of late.

As for her moving to the cottage, the sooner the better. Staying here, she'd just continue to bring chaos. As it was, Louella refused to come out of her room as long as Sarah remained in the house; Josephine was becoming increasingly headstrong and unmanageable; and his mother viewed Sarah's opinionated, unfeminine assertiveness as ill-bred, vulgar, and profoundly unattractive. He could only imagine her outrage on reading De Cosmos's editorial and Sarah's damned handbill.

Hearing light, quick steps and the swish of skirts, he stepped behind his desk—a strategic move to keep a buffer between them, keep her out of reach, until he'd said what he intended to say. And he would not offer so much as the courtesy of rising when she entered the room. Even that small gesture could distract him.

She appeared in the doorway, her hair tumbling about her shoulders in a mass of coppery waves. Dressed in a wrapper of rich indigo velvet with white lace at her throat and a white muslin breakfast cap trimmed with dainty tucks and delicate embroidery, she looked soft and enticing, and exceedingly feminine. The sight of her made his blood thrum and his body harden.

Noting the firm line of her mouth and the sparks of indignation in her eyes, he realized with a gratifying sense of relief that she was ready for combat.

She gave him a cool, crisp smile. "You summoned me, your excellency?"

Vexed by her sarcasm, Jon replied, "You're damned right I summoned you. You could have let me know in advance that you planned to slip a knife between my shoulder blades. Do you have any idea what your recent visit to the newspaper has done?"

She batted her lashes in what Jon recognized as a carefully planned attack. "Why no, but I'm most anxious to find out. Unlike you and your political puppets, Mr. De Cosmos was most willing to come to my assistance." In a voice laced with spurious sweetness, she added. "Did his editorial help my cause?"

Jon's fist came down hard on the desk. "You know damned well it did!" He waved the newspaper, then slapped it on his desk. "It could also help tip the fragile balance of the colony's economy!"

"Tsk tsk tsk," she clucked, shaking her head with feigned empathy. "How terribly worrisome that must be for you." She stepped around the desk and peered over his shoulder. "May I read what Mr. De Cosmos has written?"

As she leaned close, Jon caught the warm woman-scent of her: the fresh, clean aroma of soap and the sweet fragrance of lavender water. He shoved his chair back and stood. "By all means. Please be seated." He turned from her, fighting the urge to grab her and assault her with brutal kisses.

Sarah lowered herself into the armchair and noted, with growing excitement, that a copy of her handbill had been included with the editorial. "What a novel idea," she said, perusing it with delight. "Now, why didn't I think of that? It should advance my advertising efforts significantly. Mr. De Cosmos is an absolute genius, don't you agree?"

Jon let out a short grunt of derision.

Sarah set the handbill aside and picked up the editorial. She tried to suppress her smile as she read, sensing that Jon's threshold of tolerance had just about peaked, but the image the words evoked triumphed, and she could no longer withhold the snigger. "I'm sorry," she said, "but you have to admit, the image of a city council sporting rooster heads and gathered around a long table in the ridiculous-looking birdcage structure you call the legislature building is quite comical." She glanced up. The hard look on Jon's face left no question as to how unamused he was. "Really, Jon, you're making far too much of this," she said, parodying his words in the forest. "Why not consider it a learning experience? After all, as a man in a man's world, certainly you don't believe that one frail little female could tip the fragile balance of the colony's economy?"

Jon's jaw went tight. He shot her a baleful glare.

"You'd better enjoy a rollicking good laugh while you can," he said. "You might not find things quite so humorous if the colonies unite and free trade goes by the wayside. Free trade, as you may not be aware, is the means of keeping the trade in Victoria. The end of it would adversely affect *all* merchants."

Sarah shrugged indifferently. "My being denied the right to trade, by the advocates of free trade, does not leave me worrying too terribly much about the state of affairs in Victoria," she replied. "Nor do I feel remorse over the editorial."

"Yes, I can see that," said Jon. "But then, I should not expect you, being a woman, to concern yourself with affairs of state."

She smiled. "On the contrary. If one defenseless woman can stand between independence and unification, think of the power an entire cabinet composed of women could bring to bear. Perhaps you should consider appointing such a body."

"You feel pretty cocksure, don't you?"

She gave a noncommittal shrug. "I must admit, things have certainly taken a different turn. Why, just a few days ago, I was considering returning to San Francisco while I still had funds to reestablish myself there. Now . . . Well, I'm encouraged to continue my crusade here."

Jon eyed her dubiously. He seriously doubted that she had contemplated returning to San Francisco. Still, the thought of her leaving Victoria troubled him. It appeared that he had, through his own creative doing, acquired an adroit but beautiful and enticing political enemy—he was damned if she stayed, and damned if she left. And the realization that one woman could have that hold on him didn't sit well. He also wondered what her next move would be. "Then should I assume you're making progress toward the completion of your papers?"

She stood. "That, Governor, you will learn in due course." She gave him a wicked grin. "Now that Mr. De Cosmos has been so very kind as to distribute news of my endeavor—and include copies of my handbill—you shall have to wait and ponder how my presence may affect your constituency."

Jon folded his arms to keep from reaching for her, although he was uncertain whether his intent would have been to pull her to him or to shake her senseless. She was intent on badgering him. Well, he could play this game, too. "I doubt if I'll give it much thought," he said, catching the light that flared in her radiant green eyes. "It's just not that important. Meanwhile, Peterson's not at all happy with the added burden to his work load, so for the remainder of your visit here, will you try to stay out of trouble? Of course, given your predisposition for mischance, that might be difficult."

"I assure you, I will remain unobtrusive," she said. "As a matter of fact, I'll be leaving early tomorrow to call on someone about a matter of great importance for my cause."

"De Cosmos?" asked Jon, before he could check himself.

Sarah's eyes shown bright beneath their thick fringe of coppery lashes. "Are you worried?"

He held her gaze. "Should I be?" He tried to sound detached, indifferent. But he saw a muscle twitch in her cheek as she suppressed a smile, and caught the flicker of wry amusement in her eyes, and knew that his concern had not escaped her.

"Worrying would be in order, perhaps, if I were going to see Mr. De Cosmos," she said. "But you can rest easy, at least about that. My plans tomorrow do not include a visit to the *Colonist*."

"May I ask where you *are* going?" Jon immediately castigated himself for sounding overly curious, giv-

ing fodder for her already too confident state of
mind.

She smiled provocatively. "That's really none of
your business. After all, a soldier doesn't let the enemy know his strategy . . . unless, of course, the enemy is ready to join his side."

Giving her an ironic smile, he asked, "Is the enemy
ready to join the other side? Give up the crusade?"

She looked up at him, her eyes twinkling with
mirth. "You're the enemy, Jon, not I. So perhaps I
should ask you that question." She placed her hand
over his and smiled. "Have I found a chink in your
armor? Are you ready to concede?"

He whipped an arm around her waist, pulling her
close. "This game has rules," he said, "and I intend
to play by them. Complete your papers, and you'll
get your license." Tangling his fingers in her hair, he
pulled her head back, lifting her chin and raising her
lips to meet his.

At first, he felt steadfast resistance, then her lips
softened, surrendered, grew supple and willing. He
sliced his tongue between her lips, seeking the moist,
sweet warmth of her mouth, and she yielded, stroking his tongue with hers while curving her hands
around his shoulders. Her fingers toyed with the
hairs at his nape, their feathery-light touch making
his pulse throb. She was all woman—soft, fragrant,
inviting, her quickened breath warm and heavy
against his lips. The feel of her in his arms aroused
him, and the ache in his loins grew stronger, intensified until the need for her was foremost in his mind.

She drew back and looked up at him, her eyes
dewy and bright with passion. "You may be an autocratic, overbearing provincialist," she said, lacing her
fingers behind his neck, "but I do like the way you
kiss. What a pity we're on opposite sides."

"We don't have to be," he said, kissing her brow

and the curve of her cheek. "You could give up this foolish notion and be the elegant, desirable lady you are." Pushing her hair aside, he tasted the delicate rim of her ear and darted the tip of his tongue inside.

She moaned and drew in a ragged breath. "It's not a foolish notion," she replied, tilting her head slightly, yielding to his exploring tongue. "And I have no wish to be an elegant, desirable lady."

"You already are," he said. "Even in those bloody bloomers, you send my blood pumping." He pressed his lips to the tender skin behind her ear while his thumbs traced the swell of her breasts straining against her velvet bodice.

She tipped her head, allowing him to send a trail of kisses down the side of her neck. "Ummm . . . But the fact remains," she said in a breathy voice, "we *are* on opposite sides." Moving her head from his lips, she pressed against his chest and looked at him. "And you are distracting me."

He peered into the glistening green depths of her eyes and saw in them the unmistakable flicker of passion. "That was my intention."

"Well, it doesn't coincide with mine, which at the moment is launching my business. Meanwhile, I must get prepared for tomorrow. After all, a still bee gathers no honey." Turning out of his arms, she sashayed out the room, leaving Jon thoroughly frustrated, and more determined than ever to bed her before the week was up.

Chapter 10

During the night, the rain stopped, and morning brought sun streaming through the windows. If the weather held for one more day, Sarah felt certain she and Mandi could get the heavily laden wagon through to the cottage. Anxious to leave for Mrs. Dewig-Gertz's as soon as possible, she sent Jon's courier to the livery to request a covered two-seater be sent out. A short time later, a small phaeton arrived.

At Mrs. Dewig-Gertz's house, Mandi remained in the buggy while Sarah went to the door and presented her calling card. The maid ushered Sarah up a flight of stairs, down a long hallway, and up another much narrower stairway. As Sarah ascended, the air grew warm and musty. The maid swept open the door to what appeared to be an attic, announced Sarah's arrival, and left Sarah standing in the doorway.

"Miss Ashley, I'm delighted you've come to call." The voice rose from behind a large artist's canvas resting on an easel. A patch of blue-gray light sifted through the hazy panes of the window and shone on the top of the woman's breakfast cap. "The governor's lovely daughter has said so many fine things about you. Please, do come over here where we can chat a bit."

Sarah made her way among canvases propped against boxes, crates, trunks, and footlockers, noting that most of the paintings depicted rather amateurish portraits of men. She could not discern whether it was the same man—each face seemed somehow different. But every man had a black mustache and a full set of black whiskers. Having surmised that they were in fact the same man, Sarah said, "I didn't realize you were an artist."

"Yes," said Mrs. Dewig-Gertz brightly. "Mr. Dewig passed away several years ago, and I'm trying to capture his likeness before it fades from memory. Sometimes I feel I have come very close. Very close indeed. Such as now, which is why I mustn't stop. I hope you'll forgive me for not receiving you in the parlor." She peeked around the canvas.

"That's perfectly all right," said Sarah, picking her way over to the woman.

Sarah looked around, and finding a velvet-topped stool, she lowered herself upon it. She studied the woman's rapt profile. Were it not for her unplucked brows now pinched tightly in concentration, and her slightly receding chin, she would be almost pretty. Appearing to be in her late fifties, she wore a morning wrapper of faded blue cretonne and a plain cotton apron with deep pockets from which several brushes splayed. She stepped back, raising her spectacles to study her work. Her eyes shone with glee. "Yes," she said, half-breathless with excitement. "I've almost got him." After a moment, she turned and gave Sarah a long look, as if seeing her for the first time. "I must say, I'm disappointed you didn't wear your bloomer costume."

"Well, under the circumstances," Sarah replied, "I felt it was best to wait until things settled down a bit."

"With your handbill circulating about, I truly

doubt if things ever will again," said Mrs. Dewig-Gertz. "That was a terribly clever idea." She leaned forward and touched the tip of the brush to the canvas, dragging it slowly.

"Well, actually it wasn't my idea," said Sarah. "Mr. De Cosmos took it upon himself to introduce my garments in such a clever way."

Mrs. Dewig-Gertz slanted Sarah a sideways glance. "Some feel the man lives on the narrow edge between genius and madness. Until now, I chose to believe him quite mad. But I must say, his idea was most ingenious. What are your plans now?"

"That's why I've come," said Sarah. "According to Mayor Harris, some of the women who have seen the handbill are interested in my garments, but since the merchants won't lease a building to me unless I have a license—which I am yet unable to obtain—I have no place to display them. All I need is a corner of a shop where I can install a table and exhibit some bloomer costumes and perhaps a shirtwaister or two. I thought you might be able to direct me to a merchant who could be swayed to my cause."

"*Our* cause," Mrs. Dewig-Gertz corrected, peeking around the canvas to give Sarah a supportive smile. "And I think perhaps the most likely person for you to call upon would be Mr. Wellington Brown."

Sarah looked at her with a start. "Wellington Brown?" The man who had so thoroughly captured Mandi's heart?

"A very respectable colored man," Mrs. Dewig-Gertz said. "He moved here to escape oppression in America. If anyone would understand your plight, it would be Mr. Brown."

Sarah smiled, elated. "Perhaps he'll even sign the document issued to me by the city council. I must secure the signature of six merchants and two bankers in order to get my license. It's been an almost impossible task. So far I have no merchants and only one banker."

Mrs. Dewig-Gertz dabbed at the palette with her brush, then, leaning close to the canvas and peering through the thick lenses of her glasses, she touched the paint-laden bristles to the picture, applying what appeared to be a series of short lines. Satisfied, she stepped back and smiled. Her eyes flickered with admiration. "Yes . . . it's him. This time I have truly captured Mr. Dewig. If only he were here to share this moment . . ."

She set her palette on a small table beside the easel, tipped her brush into a glass with spirits of turpentine, and stepped back to admire her work again. "Would you care to step over here and meet Mr. Dewig?"

Her curiosity piqued, Sarah rose and walked over to stand before the painting. Her lips parted, and she stared at the portrait, speechless. Two wide round eyes that were not quite on the same level were fixed straight ahead in a blank blue stare; every hair of Mr. Dewig's eyebrows, mustache, and whiskers had been tediously scrawled; and his face was a network of purplish-red character lines—tracks crossing his forehead, crow's feet splaying from the corners of his eyes, crevices tapering from his nostrils and around his mouth. Sarah bit her lip to keep from smiling. "You certainly have captured all the details of his face," she said.

"Yes," Mrs. Dewig-Gertz agreed. "I do hope my present husband, Mr. Gertz, will not object to my hanging Mr. Dewig in my chambers." She brushed her hands together, took Sarah's arm, and led her toward the door. "Now, you were saying something about needing signatures. Have you brought the papers with you?"

"Well, yes."

"Then I will see that Mr. Gertz signs them. He's just in his chambers, resting."

"But why would he sign when every other merchant in Victoria has refused?" asked Sarah.

Mrs. Dewig-Gertz reached behind herself, untied her apron, and draped it over a chair. "I have special ways of dealing with my husband."

Sarah was curious. "Well, if you don't mind"—she dragged the papers out of her carpetbag and paged through them—"have him sign . . . right here."

"Just give me a few minutes . . ."

Mrs. Dewig-Gertz directed Sarah into the parlor, ordered the maid bring tea and biscuits, and left Sarah sitting alone. After what seemed like a half-hour or longer, Mrs. Dewig-Gertz returned, a rosy flush to her cheeks, a grouping of red blotches on her neck, and the row of buttons on her wrapper misaligned. "He signed," she said, breathless. She handed the papers to Sarah.

Rising to leave, and noting the tiny beads of sweat above Mrs. Dewig-Gertz's upper lip, Sarah said, "I do appreciate it. I hope we didn't disturb your husband too terribly much."

"Oh, no. He was pleased to do it," Mrs. Dewig-Gertz said, blushing deeply. Flipping her fan open, she began waving it briskly as she walked with Sarah to the door. "Have you decided where you want to be located yet . . . after you get your license, of course?"

"Well, I've inspected several locations."

"I suppose you've heard about the women disappearing?"

"Oh, yes . . . several times."

"Well, be careful wandering around. A woman's just not safe anymore—most go out in threes or fours. It's terrible how things have changed here since the prospectors began swarming in. It never used to be like this. A woman could leave her home without any worry. But now . . . Well, just be careful."

"I will. And thank you."

In the buggy, Sarah explained to Mandi what had happened, and ten minutes later, they pulled to a halt in front of Brown's Domestic Dry Goods. "Why are we stoppin' here?" asked Mandi, eyes wide.

Sarah smiled, ruefully. "To see Mr. Brown, of course."

"Oh . . . lawdy sakes alive!" Mandi snapped open her parasol. "Mr. Brown, here Ah come."

A bell on the door announced their arrival. A tall, handsome man holding a bolt of fabric saw Mandi and smiled broadly. Mandi nudged Sarah and giggled.

"Shush, now," Sarah whispered, "or you'll make a fool of yourself." She glanced around, surprised to find such a wide array of fabrics and laces. Bolts of linens, flannels, muslins, and wools in several shades lined the long shelves behind the counter. And rolls of cottons in stripes, checks, and plaids stood propped on two long tables.

Wellington Brown walked over and smiled, his eyes on Mandi. "Ladies," he said, nodding. "May I help you?"

Sarah placed her carpetbag on the counter. "My name is Miss Sarah Ashley," she said, opening the bag, "and this is my . . . associate, Miss Amanda Jackson."

Mandi giggled, and Sarah stepped on her foot.

Sarah explained their needs, even pulled a pair of bloomers out of her carpetbag and displayed them on the counter, concluding, ". . . and women who want them will also need fabric to make waists to wear under their tunics. And, of course, the garments alone will draw women into your store . . . out of curiosity . . ."

Mandi sashayed around, fingering bolts of material while stealing glances at Wellington Brown, and Sarah noted that Mr. Brown's eyes kept shifting to Mandi as he listened.

Finally, Sarah handed him a handbill. "I need just a small spot where I can set up a table for handbills like this, and also display a bloomer costume and a shirtwaister. Of course, Miss Jackson will be helping me," she added.

"Miss Jackson?" Wellington Brown's face brightened, and his lips spread in a wide grin.

Sarah's eyes shifted between Mr. Brown and Mandi, who stood smiling back and batting her eyelashes. "Yes," Sarah said, "as my assistant, Miss Jackson will be passing out handbills while I tend the table . . ."

By the time they left the store, Sarah was about to burst with excitement. Not only had Wellington Brown agreed to give them space for a table, but he'd also signed the document and set up garment racks for displaying a bloomer costume and a shirtwaister.

The following afternoon, while Jon was at work, Lady Cromwell was calling on friends, and Esther was shopping with her nieces, Peterson reloaded Sarah's wagon, and he and Tooley followed Sarah and Mandi to the cottage and helped them move in. That afternoon and half the next day, Mandi scrubbed the kitchen and outhouse, beat the rag rugs, and shook out the gingham curtains. Sarah swept and mopped the floors and made up both bedrooms with linens and quilts that she'd brought with her from San Francisco.

Once the cottage was clean and tidy, Sarah and Mandi agreed that it was charming. The floral wallpaper, though somewhat faded, was not in the least worn, the floors shone a deep golden brown, and the kitchen housed a large tin-lined sink, a hardwood refrigerator with a porcelain-lined water cooler, and a nickel-trimmed cookstove with two towel rods and a high closet with a reservoir.

Mandi's bedroom faced the tall, stately evergreens behind the cottage, but Sarah's looked across the road toward the bay, where silvery waves rolled upon the sandy shore and the breeze brought the fragrance of late summer roses mingled with the damp saltiness of the sea.

Gazing out the window at jewellike islands rising against a backdrop of snow-capped mountains, Sarah at last felt a sense of belonging.

"Miz Sarah!" Mandi called from the parlor, "it's the guv'nor. Looks like he's comin' a-courtin'. Ummm . . . ummm. He sho' looks like he's comin' a-courtin', all right. He's even bringin' flowers."

Sarah rushed to the parlor and pulled Mandi back from the window. "Don't stand there gawking." But she peeked out the window herself to see Jon walking in long strides toward the cottage. He looked so utterly masculine with his shirt open to mid-chest and his tight trousers emphasizing his maleness. He also looked somewhat silly carrying a bouquet of yellow roses in one large hand.

She swept open the door and looked at the bouquet. "Have you come bearing a peace offering?"

His smile was rueful and lopsided. "You might call it that. I might call it a bribe."

"For what?"

"To entice you into strolling on the beach with me."

Sarah regarded him dubiously. "Why?"

"Because I want to take a walk with you."

"I mean, why now, at this particular moment?"

Jon combed his fingers through his hair. "Good God, woman. Why not?" He looked past Sarah at

Mandi and waved the flowers. "Here, pretty lady. Put these in water while your mistress here decides whether or not I plan to seduce her on the beach."

Mandi giggled and took the flowers, then disappeared behind the kitchen door.

Jon raised his palms in feigned submission. "Do I look like a man who intends to ravish your beautiful body? All I want to do is stroll leisurely on the beach, chat a little, and enjoy the nice weather."

Sarah almost laughed at his attempt at wide-eyed innocence. Of course, she should refuse. It was obvious Jon planned to take at least a few liberties. But she did want to spend some time with him, and she'd be safer on an open beach than in the cottage—which Mandi would no doubt vacate at the first opportunity, in order to leave them alone.

"Well, I suppose we could go for a few minutes. But then I must get back to finish tidying things here."

"Of course."

Sarah looked into his dark, devilish eyes, which clearly told her she would *not* be returning in a few minutes. But she was uncertain if it was his decision, or hers.

Outside, Jon took her hand and they crossed the road and followed a path that led to the water. They strolled along a narrow sandy beach edged in wave-washed rocks, but once hidden from view of the cottage, Jon pulled Sarah into his arms and kissed her. It wasn't a long, lingering kiss as she had expected, but rather a quick, playful one. Then Jon hiked up his leg and tugged off one boot, then the other.

Sarah looked at him with a start. "What do you think you're doing?"

"Removing my boots so I can cool my feet in the water."

She stared in uncertain silence as he stripped off

his socks. She could not remember ever seeing a man's naked feet so close up before—not that she was shocked. She'd just never seen male feet ... exposed like that. She'd also never thought of a man's feet as being sensual. But there was something sensual about Jon's. They were so broad and sinewy, the skin on them surprisingly pale, almost translucent, the top of each toe bearing a little dusting of black hair.

Jon wiggled his toes, and when she looked up, she knew he'd seen her staring. He gave her a wicked smile. "Aren't you going to join me?" When she made no motion to remove her own shoes, he said, "You're not getting timid now, are you? You're the one who so boldly announced that women should be able to display their limbs just as men do. Well, I'm displaying mine. Are you beginning to question your own doctrine?"

"Of course not." Sarah sat on a drift log and removed her shoes, then looked up at Jon and waited for him to turn his back.

He raised his hands in acquiescence. "Right. I know the rules now." He turned away from her and said, "It's not as if I haven't seen your feet before though, or thought about them. Or your beautiful legs ... about how slender and white they are, and how splendidly narrow your lovely ankles are. And your shapely feet ... Ah, and those dainty little toes—very suckable toes, I might add. So it's not as if you're hiding anything from me."

"If you don't stop talking like that I shall go back to the house."

"Very well. I will say nothing more. But I can't control the nature of my thoughts. And right now they seem focused on your ... suckable toes." He sighed, then added in a pitiful voice that rang of mocking amusement, "It's difficult being a slave. But I suppose it can have its rewards . . . at times."

When Sarah spoke again, her voice, muffled by the sound of the surf, came from the direction of the water. "You may turn now," she called out.

Jon glanced around to find her wading ankle deep in the surf, her mass of golden-red hair snapping in the breeze, her skirt raised just enough to clear the water. He crossed the beach in several long strides and marched into the water after her. Seeing him coming, she hiked up her skirt and scampered away, water splashing around her legs as she ran. Cupping his hand, he shot a spray of water at her. She let out a little yell, lifted her skirt to her knees, and rushed through the surf where it lapped against the shore.

Jon raced after her, scooping her up in his arms. "So you think you can get away from me," he said, bundling her against his broad chest and carrying her out of the water.

She clasped her arms around his neck. "You are mad, you know. Really quite mad."

"You're right," he said, eyeing her smooth calves and lace-edged drawers as the wind billowed her skirt. "Mad about you." He carried her to an embankment which rose high, shielding the beach from the road above, then set her down on a driftwood log. "And being mad," he said, stripping off his shirt, "I have worked up a lather."

Momentarily blinded by the sun, Sarah raised a hand to shade her eyes and was immediately aware of how powerful he was, how strapping the build outlined in shimmering gold as sunlight splashed over his thick shoulders, muscular arms, and lean torso. She seemed unable to take her eyes off him.

And he didn't move.

He just stood there looking down at her. Except for the breeze ruffling his hair, he was like a golden-edged statue. And as she stared, the heat that filled her cheeks moved downward to settle like hot embers in her loins.

He pulled her up, and she braced her hands against his bare, damp chest. Her palms grew feverish as she felt the heavy beat of his heart beneath them. He smiled, but his eyes held a glint of something far from mirth. They told her he wanted her, and he intended to have her.

He closed his hands around her waist and peered down at her. "You have beautiful green eyes," he said, his voice smooth and sultry. "I don't believe I've ever told you that. But it's true. And right now they're sparkling like fresh-cut emeralds." He kissed one eyelid, then the other. "And your skin is as soft as the underside of a dove's wing."

His deep, husky voice, and the image his flowery words evoked, made Sarah suddenly start giggling.

He pursed his lips. "I can see that my efforts at romancing you with poetic nothings are falling on deaf ears."

"No," she said, a smile playing about her lips. "It's just that it occurred to me that the underside of a dove's wings would be its . . . wingpit."

"Ummm . . . well, perhaps that's not very romantic. I'll use a more direct approach." He trailed kisses down her face and nibbled at her neck, and while he did, he began unbuttoning her blouse.

"What do you think you're doing?"

"Unbuttoning your blouse so I can kiss your lovely neck . . . just your neck, Miss Ashley. I have no intentions of going beyond this button." His finger touched the button at her cleavage, his hand resting firmly on her breast as he unfastened first one button, then the next. Then he did go beyond her cleavage, and she made no move to stop him. She couldn't. It was all she could do to remain standing.

He pushed her blouse open and lowered her chemise, exposing the fullness of her breasts to his eager gaze. Cupping one in his hand, he bent down and took the sensitive nipple between his lips, flicking his tongue over it until moans reverberated in her throat and pains of hot delight shot through her, intensifying in her feverish loins, making her want something urgently and desperately, yet not quite knowing what it was.

He released her breast and kissed her lips. Not a light, playful kiss as before, but one hard and demanding that made her feel dizzy and confused and aching with need. With one hand, he teased her nipple until it was a throbbing core. His other hand clasped her buttocks, pressing her to him until she felt him hard and insistent against her heated loins. His tongue filled her mouth, searching it, thrusting in and out of it hungrily, passionately. One hand tugged up her skirt. The other slipped beneath the lacy trim of her drawers and glided up the inside of her bare thigh.

The cool air on her sweat-dampened legs seemed to have a sobering effect, the harsh onrush of reality reminding her of exactly what she was allowing Jon to do, and where she was allowing him to do it. At once, she broke the kiss and tugged his hand from her thigh. "No," she said, almost breathless. "Please don't. Someone might be watching."

Having said the words, she had the horrible feeling that someone *was* watching—someone with hateful evil eyes that held a hideous delight in what they saw. She jerked up her chemise to cover her breasts. "You should not have done this," she said, fumbling with her blouse, trying to ease it over her shoulders.

"Perhaps you're right," said Jon. "However, I'm the one who took you apart, so I'll be the one to put you back together." He moved her hands aside, kissed her breast, then began buttoning her blouse. "I propose we send Mandi into town on an errand."

Sarah looked up at him, puzzled. "Whatever for?" Then her face flushed with the sudden realization that she had not chastised him for *what* he'd been doing, but rather for *where* he'd been doing it. The sharp glint in his eyes told her he had picked up on that error and would continue where they left off the first chance they were alone . . . like now, in the cottage . . . with Mandi in town on an errand . . .

He would do it, that is, unless she made up her mind *not* to allow him to do so.

She brushed his hands away. "I am perfectly capable of dressing myself," she said, fumbling with the buttons. "And I don't want you doing what you did again. Kissing me is one thing, but what you were doing is quite another." She started toward the log where she'd left her shoes.

Jon followed, commenting pragmatically, "What I was doing was fondling your beautiful breasts while awakening the sensual woman inside so she could learn the true pleasures to be found in her own body."

Sarah's face flushed. "I don't want you talking like that, either." She quickened her pace, her feet kicking up sand as she marched in determination toward the log.

"You're the one who said that a woman soon falls into a state of listlessness and insipidity if she is without employment suitable to maintain health and happiness, and to satisfy her mind and body. Had you ever considered that perhaps it's not the lack of suitable employment that makes a woman feel unsatisfied, but the lack of something else, something much more basic?"

Sarah's cheeks burned. "That's ridiculous."

"What are you afraid of?" said Jon, lengthening his

strides. "Discovering that there is a part of you that might become dependent on a man—a secret part that might awaken and, God forbid, become dependent on a man to pleasure it? That you might even start to lust after a man for that pleasure?"

"That is disgusting. I will never lust after a man. Nor will I be dependent on one for ... what you said."

"I didn't say it. But it's called—"

"Stop!" She covered her ears. When she knew he wouldn't say the forbidden word, she sat on the driftwood log and snatched her silk stocking from her shoe, then waited for him to turn his back.

He planted his hands on his hips. "No, Miss Ashley, I will not turn around. Either you put on your stockings while I watch, or you return to the cottage on naked feet. Your choice."

Hot tears of anger and humiliation stung her eyes. But even as he angered and humiliated her, she ached for him. Turning slightly, she lifted her skirt and rolled one silk stocking up her bare leg, her entire body feeling on fire as his gaze burned into her. She reached for her other stocking. "Why are you doing this?"

He kept his eyes riveted on her. "Because you're lying to yourself. Because you refuse to acknowledge your own wants and needs. Because you're a witless little ninnyhammer. Take your pick."

"I see. You didn't get your way with me, so you're angry. How typically male."

"You're right. It is typically male. I get that way when I'm frustrated as hell! I also get that way when dealing with illogical, muddleheaded females!"

"Oh ... so now I'm muddleheaded and illogical. And exactly what do you base that assessment on? Your own muddleheaded, illogical, frustrated mind?"

"Believe me. It's not my *mind* that's frustrated!"

"Then I suggest you go to one of those dance halls that Mr. De Cosmos talked about and find a woman there to take care of your problem, because this muddleheaded, illogical female has no intention of doing so!"

"Fine. Maybe that's exactly what I'll do!" He yanked on his socks, pulled on his boots, shrugged into his shirt, and left Sarah standing on the beach staring after him.

"Damned, single-minded man!" With several sharp yanks, she shook the sand from her skirt, then headed back to the cottage, furious at Jon for twisting everything she said into something sexual, and enraged with herself for allowing him to arouse in her an ache she couldn't seem to quell.

His male tantrum had accomplished one thing, however. From now on, she'd find it infinitely easier to maintain her distance. It was obvious he wanted her for only one reason, and that certainly wasn't to be his wife! Not that she would ever consider such a preposterous idea anyway!

Being any man's wife was inconceivable.

Unthinkable.

At least it seemed unthinkable . . . at the moment . . .

Crossing the road, Sarah was surprised to find Mandi standing on the porch. On seeing the distraught look on her face, Sarah assumed it was because she'd seen Jon marching off in a huff. Then she realized it was something much more serious. "What's wrong?"

Mandi handed her what appeared to be a hastily scrawled note. "Ah found it fastened to the front door with a knife," she said. "Ah couldn't help but read it."

Sarah took the note in uncertain hands and read:

We read with interest Mr. De Cosmos's recent editorial. It seems you have found at least one advocate here. Hope you enjoyed your little romp on the beach with the infamous governor. Perhaps Mr. De Cosmos would find your dubious behavior of interest—along with other things. Will be keeping in touch.

H and T

"They're still here," Sarah said, almost in a whisper. Her stomach knotted, her face burned as if on fire, and she felt suddenly light-headed. *Dear God. What had they witnessed on the beach?* Hot tears of shame welled. "I hate them," she said. "I wish they were both . . ." She paused, but the thought still hung.

Mandi took her arm and guided her into the house. "It'll be all right," she said. "There's nothing you and the guv'nor could've done out there on the beach that would make no mind no how. So don't fret. Besides, from the way the guv'nor went racin' off on his horse, Ah 'spect he didn't even get a kiss. And even if he did, there ain't no one who cares about a little kiss."

Sarah forced a smile. "No . . . no one would care about a little kiss."

If only it had been just a little kiss . . .

Chapter 11

The next day, Sarah and Mandi set up a table and arranged displays, launching Sarah Ashley's Fashions from the front corner of Brown's Domestic Dry Goods. Sarah's excitement on at last being able to display her garments was tempered with apprehension over what Hollis and Tyler would do next, and anger at Jon for stripping her of her dignity and walking away, leaving her feeling alone and bereft and empty . . . and filled with the terrible loneliness that seemed to haunt her more frequently of late.

What was happening to her? She didn't want Jon to want her—yet she did. He didn't want her as a wife—yet the realization made her feel disappointed. And she couldn't dismiss the indecent thoughts that kept invading her mind, thoughts of him looking at her breasts, suckling her nipple until she felt hot with need and damp with desire. And the thought of his hand on her leg, high on her leg where no man should ever touch a woman who was not his wife . . .

She felt incensed and shamed and dissatisfied at once.

Worse, she wanted him to do all the things he'd done again . . . and again . . . and again . . .

And she was too ashamed even to tell her diary.

* * *

175

Word of Sarah's enterprise spread quickly, and two mornings later, a small group of women organized by Mary Letitia Windemere waited anxiously for the store to open. When nine o'clock struck, Wellington Brown unlocked the door and quickly stepped out of the path of the eager women.

Mary Letitia was the first to enter. With a select group of women trailing behind her, she walked up to the table and eyed the bloomer costume on display, taking care to focus on the costume, not the copper-haired woman sitting behind the table. She ran her hand over the ceil-blue, poult-de-soie tunic and traced a finger over the fine silk embroidery. It wasn't anything like she'd expected. It was really quite lovely . . . at least the fabric was. The costume itself was most unconventional. Indeed, quite garish. But then, the woman behind the table was obviously not a member of Anglo-Saxon aristocracy. She'd arrived in Victoria in a great gale of typically middle-class American boorishness.

Not to seem too eager, Mary Letitia let her gaze pass quickly over the woman, taking care not to goggle, but pausing just long enough to meet a pair of large green eyes.

So this was Miss Sarah Ashley.

Also not what she'd expected—the woman was far more attractive. Perhaps even . . . beautiful, which bothered her greatly. But then, Jon had once told her she was beautiful . . .

And he would again, she vowed.

Had this woman truly smitten Jon? Rumors were that she had. But seeing her in person, Mary Letitia seriously doubted that anything would ever come of it. The woman was far below Jon's station, destined to be only a paramour, or perhaps she already was, if there was any truth in the gossip circulating. Jon would, after all, take only a gently bred woman for a wife, which Miss Sarah Ashley was most certainly not. A gently bred woman wouldn't make a spectacle of herself by sitting behind a cheap little table and peddling clothes.

Giving the woman a cordial nod, Mary Letitia asked, "When would a person wear such attire?"

Sarah Ashley's enthusiastic smile was really quite dazzling. "The costume can be worn for playing croquet and all manner of lawn games," she said. "It's also appropriate for strolling the beach. And I predict that bloomers will soon be worn with a fitted jacket as part of the riding habit, so women can ride astride like men."

Soft murmurings rustled through the group.

Although mortified at the thought of such a suggestion as riding spread-legged on a horse, Mary Letitia resolved to maintain a friendly, pleasant facade. It really wasn't too difficult now. Miss Ashley was clearly a temporary diversion for Jon. Before long, he'd come to his senses, and when he did, she resolved to be there for him. After all, the silly little spat that had served to drive the two of them apart would by then be forgotten.

"Please," said Sarah Ashley, glancing around, "help yourselves to the handbills. As you will note, bloomers are convenient and comfortable, especially as a working dress; they can be worn inside boots which rise above the ankle, they can be trimmed in fur or fancifully embroidered at the cuffs, or they can hang loose about the ankles."

Mary Letitia noted that the advertising circulars resembled the tawdry thing that had appeared in the *Colonist.* Actually, it wasn't so much tawdry as it was tasteless, she decided. Imagine, presenting to the women of Victoria such nonsense as wanting to vote or hold political office. How utterly ludicrous!

She watched with mocking curiosity as Sarah

Ashley dragged a rather disreputable-looking trunk from under the table. "I also have some sample bloomers that I would be willing to give out free of charge to anyone interested in wearing them," she said, lifting the scuffed lid.

"Really . . . free?" How gauche, Mary Letitia thought.

"Yes," said Sarah Ashley, whipping out a pair of black bloomers. "Here you are."

Mary Letitia took the bloomers and held them against herself. "How . . . comfortable they look," she said, turning briefly to check the others' reaction.

Sarah Ashley grinned in agreement. "Why don't you take that pair home with you and try them?" she suggested.

Mary Letitia glanced around at the group, who seemed to be waiting for her response. "Well . . . yes. That's a splendid idea," she said, "and dreadfully nice of you. They do seem most practical." She stepped back, allowing the others access to the table. As she had expected, Flora Pickering accepted a pair . . . then Charlotte Potts . . . and, of course, Elizabeth Thurman . . .

Noting the women's enthusiasm, Mary Letitia flashed them her brightest smile, and in her most exuberant voice, suggested, "Why don't we wear bloomer costumes to the town picnic and horse races at Beacon Hill Park this weekend? Absolutely everyone will be there . . . including the governor himself. I daresay, if we all show up wearing bloomers, what can the men say?"

Gasps and giggles rose from the group, and after a few minutes' deliberation, along with Sarah Ashley's most accommodating urges, all three women agreed to do as Mary Letitia had suggested. Of course, Mary Letitia knew from the start they would—she'd hand-picked the group. She, of course, being much too

genteel to descend to such crassness, would arrive at
the picnic dressed as a proper gentlewoman should
dress for such an occasion—wearing an outfit of
which Governor Jonathan Cromwell would definitely
take note.

Nor had she overlooked the fact that Jon's mother,
who would undoubtedly be there, would be shocked
and appalled by both Sarah Ashley and the whole
disgraceful episode. That thought gave Mary Letitia
great pleasure—she knew that Lady Cromwell fa-
vored her as a match for her son.

And afterward, the unquestionably caustic editorial Mr. De Cosmos would write, and the subsequent
problems his words would create for Jon and his cabinet, would displease Jon immensely. But then she'd
be there to offer words of sympathy, whisperings of
endearment, and a warm feminine shoulder to cry
on—the things Jon needed to bolster his fragile male
ego. Yes . . . Just a little while, and she felt reasonably
certain she'd have Jon eating right out of the palm of
her hand . . . again.

Sarah raised the window of her bedroom. The air
was sweet with fall blossoms, and the trees seemed
alive with the chitter and warbles of countless birds.
From the road came the clatter of horses' hooves and
the creaking of wagons, buggies, and carriages, all
heading for the horse races and picnic at Beacon Hill
Park.

Gazing toward the bay, Sarah wondered if Hollis
and Tyler would be there. They'd had ample opportunity to approach her by now. But other than the
note pinned to her door four days before, she had
seen neither hide nor hair of them. But she would.
Hollis was predictable. For the moment, she was safe
from any gossip he might spread, because if he

started a rumor too soon, he would lose the leverage he needed to extract the money from her.

She also had not seen Jon. But that was for the best. The indecent thoughts had begun to subside, and she didn't want to be distracted by them again. Besides, she had far too many other things on her mind.

Turning from the window, she hummed as she stepped into a pair of pale pink bloomers and donned the matching foulard tunic with its dainty rose embroidery. She could barely believe her good fortune, and she owed it to one attractive, genteel, and affluent lady: Mary Letitia Windemere. Mary Letitia, she'd learned, was the daughter of Lord Charles Alexander Windemere III, an admiral retired from the Royal Navy. Lord Windemere was also one of the colony's largest landholders. Mary Letitia's endorsement of bloomers would carry quite a bit of weight within the community.

But Mary Letitia wasn't her only newfound advocate. After the other women had decided to wear bloomer costumes, Flora Pickering proposed that the women ride together to the picnic, and Charlotte Potts quickly asked Sarah to join them. Then Elizabeth Thurman generously offered to pack extra food. The women were all truly nice people.

But the excitement had not ended there. Wellington Brown had asked Mandi to join him for the day, and since that time, Mandi had been drifting about as if on a cloud. Unfortunately, Mandi was so busy primping and preening for the occasion that Sarah had been forced to put herself together unaided.

At her dressing table, Sarah positioned atop her head a white batiste bonnet trimmed with rose satin ribbon. As she peered in the mirror and arranged the spray of pink roses with moss-green leaves, she pondered the day ahead and wondered what Jon's reaction would be on seeing five women arrive at the picnic wearing bloomer costumes.

Initially, she had intended to wear more conventional clothes, having decided that she'd been a bit premature in her efforts to promote her bloomer costume. But after Mary Letitia's suggestion, it had seemed appropriate. Sarah had loaned each of the women tunics of fine embroidered India silk, so even though the unfamiliar fashion might cause a stir among the picnickers, no one would be able to deny the beauty and quality of the fabric.

Hearing a carriage draw to a halt outside the cottage, Sarah peeked through the curtains and saw a canopied spring wagon with Flora Pickering driving and Charlotte Potts and Elizabeth Thurman sitting behind. Sarah tapped on the window and waved, then gathered her reticule and white lace parasol and scurried out the front door. She climbed into the wagon beside Flora, and after a warm greeting from the women, she looked around and asked, "Where is Mary Letitia? I thought she was coming with us."

Flora jiggled the reins and guided the horse into the stream of traffic. "She sent word that there has been a change of plans . . . that she'll meet us at the park. Mary Letitia is sometimes not too reliable."

Charlotte leaned forward and, above the clatter of hooves and the jingle of harness, said, "I just imagine it has something to do with the governor. She must think that by wearing bloomers today she'll attract his notice . . . which she probably will. Mary Letitia doesn't give up too easily when she wants something. And I know for a fact, she's still got her eyes on Jon Cromwell."

Sarah looked at Charlotte with a start, feeling as if the wind had been knocked out of her. "Jon Cromwell and Mary Letitia?" Just linking Jon's name with that of another woman made her heart lurch.

Although she could not, at this point in her life, see herself romantically tied to Jon or any other man, the thought of him with another woman troubled her. But then, she could not expect him to remain unattached. He was a very handsome and eligible man, and many women would naturally be attracted to him.

Charlotte shrugged. "For a while Mary Letitia fancied them as being affianced, but then something happened between them—a lovers' quarrel, I suppose—and, well . . . after that, the governor just seemed to lose interest. Since then, Mary Letitia has been quite melancholy about it . . . until she discovered your bloomer costume," she said, giving Sarah a light tap on the shoulder. "Since then, she has been optimistic about things. I guess by dressing so boldly, she fashions herself as appearing venturesome in the eyes of the governor."

Sarah considered what she'd just learned. Had her arrival in Victoria coincided with Jon's apparent loss of interest in Mary Letitia? From what Charlotte had said, it seemed that way. "How long ago?"

"How long ago what?" asked Charlotte, frowning.

"How long has it been since the governor withdrew his affections for Mary Letitia?"

Charlotte shrugged. "I don't know . . . two, maybe three weeks. Mary Letitia doesn't always present us with the unvarnished truth, especially if it doesn't make her look good. And she certainly wouldn't want it to appear that the governor was the one to withdraw affections."

Sarah stared ahead. If Mary Letitia was truly after Jon, perhaps even in love with him, and she suspected that Sarah was involved with him romantically, then her outward friendliness could be just a facade. She glanced back at Charlotte and, forcing a smile, asked, "Is the governor seeing any other ladies now? I mean, do you think Mary Letitia will win back his affections?"

Charlotte looked directly at Sarah. "Perhaps you'd be better qualified to answer that than I."

Sarah's face felt as if it were on fire. "I don't know what you mean," she said, wondering exactly how much Charlotte, Flora, and Elizabeth knew. They obviously knew something.

Charlotte shrugged. "You were a guest in his home, weren't you?"

"Well, yes," said Sarah, "but he certainly didn't talk about his romantic trysts." Beads of perspiration dampened her brow. Had these women set up this little gathering to question her? Or perhaps embarrass and humiliate her?

Elizabeth nudged Charlotte. "Oh, for heaven's sake, Char. You don't really think the governor would discuss his liaisons with his sister's houseguest, do you? After all, he *is* a gentleman."

Charlotte gave Elizabeth a wry smile. "He may be a gentleman, but he did, in fact, mention something about one of his liaisons to my brother."

"He did?" Elizabeth moved closer. "What did he say, and about whom?"

Sarah's stomach churned. Would Jon possibly have said something to Charlotte's brother about what had happened on the beach?

Charlotte raised her hand to hold her bonnet in place. "I'm afraid I'm not at liberty to say," she said. "I gave Henry my word."

"Char, you know you're going to tell us—you're dying to," said Elizabeth. "So why not just go ahead and say it."

Charlotte hesitated for a moment, her eyes glowing with suppressed excitement. "It was about Mary Letitia ... that she suggested to Jon that they marry."

When Charlotte offered nothing more, Elizabeth said, "That's all?"

Charlotte blinked several times. "Yes, that's all. But don't you know what that means?"

Elizabeth pursed her lips. "Well, I imagine it means that Mary Letitia wants to marry Jon and she had to ask him since he didn't ask her."

Charlotte sighed. "Sometimes you can be very thickheaded, Elizabeth. What it means is that Mary Letitia has most probably compromised herself. Perhaps she's even ... with child."

Flora glanced at Sarah, a contrite smile on her lips. "Please don't think Elizabeth and Charlotte are busybodies," she said. "But sometimes Mary Letitia really gets our dander up. And I agree with Char. It wouldn't surprise me if Mary Letitia went so far as to compromise herself just to get the governor to wed her, if she truly believed there was no other way."

"From what Henry's said," Charlotte added, "there *is* no other way. Henry says the governor's not about to find himself married again."

Sarah gave Flora a weak smile and said nothing. She tried to dismiss the disturbing thought of Mary Letitia wed to Jon ... his kissing her in the way Sarah knew he could kiss ... holding her ... making wild, passionate love to her ...

"No!" she burst out suddenly.

Flora looked at her with a start.

Sarah blushed. "I mean ... no, I can't imagine she'd do that." She swallowed hard, trying to dislodge the lump in her throat.

"Oh, she would all right," Elizabeth assured her. She leaned forward, resting her hand on the back of Sarah's seat. "When Mary Letitia goes after something she wants, she doesn't stop until she gets it. You just watch her today. I'll venture to say she'll lure the governor onto her blanket—which will be spread some distance from the activities and, of course, out of sight. Then the governor will find himself eating from her picnic basket, which will undoubtedly contain an array of delicacies that no man could resist. And who knows what will happen behind the cover of the bushes, especially if Mary Letitia has already compromised herself with him." She smiled brightly. "I do believe it will be an interesting day."

Sarah fixed her eyes on the road ahead, trying to maintain an indifferent facade, when in fact her stomach was tied in knots. But she refused to allow speculation about whether Jon was involved in a romantic liaison with Mary Letitia Windemere to dampen her day.

They turned into Beacon Hill Park, and Flora pulled the wagon to a halt. Immediately, Sarah spotted Jon's elegant midnight-blue coach. Parked behind the coach was a black-and-green phaeton that she recognized as Jon's. Apparently, the entire family was there, including, she suspected with some apprehension, Lady Cromwell.

For the moment, no one made a move to climb down. Scanning the crowd for Jon, Sarah noted the ladies in their ginghams and calicoes, and she contemplated the wisdom of joining the picnickers dressed as she was. But perhaps Mary Letitia had already arrived and paved the way for what was to come—four more women in bloomer costumes—and the crowd's shock at such a display would have passed.

A short distance from the wagon, Sarah noticed several young men nudging one another, whispering and pointing in their direction, though they actually seemed to be amused by something just behind them.

"Psst! Miss Ashley?" Josephine's voice came from

out of nowhere. She stepped from behind a tree, and to Sarah's shock, she was wearing the pair of black bloomers Sarah had given to her. "May I join you?" she asked.

Sarah bristled. "No, you may not," she said, knowing what the repercussions would be when Jon and his mother discovered that Josephine had defied them in such a brazen way. "Go home and change into a dress at once."

Josephine scurried up to the wagon and peered over the sideboards. "But you're wearing a bloomer costume," she protested. "Please, may I join you?"

"Absolutely not! Your father and grandmother would be shocked with you and furious with me for having allowed you to join us. Now, have Peterson take you home at once and be quick about it before anyone sees you."

Josephine's face fell with a sober frown. She drooped her shoulders and started across the road, where Peterson stood waiting by the coach.

Satisfied that Josephine would do as she'd been told, Sarah turned to find Flora staring in the distance, eyes narrowed, lips pressed in an angry slash. "Well, ladies," she said, disgusted, "it appears that we've been duped mightily by one Mary Letitia Windemere. And guess who she's with?"

Sarah glanced in the direction of Flora's gaze and froze. Leaning with one hand propped against a tree, the other holding a cigarette, was Jon. Beside him stood Mary Letitia. She reached up and brushed something from Jon's lips and laughed, and Jon didn't appear to mind the flirtation. It was obvious where he had been for the past four days.

It was some moments before Sarah's attention was drawn to what Mary Letitia was wearing. Not the silk tunic and bloomers as planned but, instead, a stylish promenade dress trimmed with ruches, rosettes, and tassels.

Twirling her black lace parasol against her shoulder, Mary Letitia chatted with Jon while making little feminine gestures with her hand. Whatever she was saying seemed to interest him—his eyes appeared fixed on her.

Lady Cromwell, who stood opposite Jon and Mary Letitia, also seemed charmed by Mary Letitia. Sarah had never seen the older woman wearing such a gracious smile.

"I don't understand," said Flora. "Why would Mary Letitia talk us into wearing bloomers, and seem so anxious to wear them herself, then not do so?"

"It's fairly obvious," said Charlotte. "She intended for us to look like fools so she'd stand out as the perfect lady. That's typical of Mary Letitia."

Elizabeth pursed her lips. "I told you so. I told you she'd do *anything* to turn the governor's head."

Sarah felt anger coiling inside as she considered how eagerly Jon had bestowed kisses on her when he obviously had another woman waiting in the wings ... one whom he'd thought enough of to escort to the picnic. "Well, Mary Letitia Windemere might take us all for fools"—Sarah's eyes narrowed when she saw Mary Letitia take a small tidbit from her picnic basket and stuff it into Jon's mouth—"but I refuse to let her put a damper on my day. And I hope the rest of you feel the same as I."

"I certainly do," said Elizabeth. "I came here to enjoy myself, and that's exactly what I intend to do." She glanced around at the others. "Shall we go have the time of our lives, ladies—show that peagoose Mary Letitia that her little ploy didn't work, that we will partake in the croquet tournament and the sack race, while she can do nothing more but stand around in her fancy dress and ogle the gòvernor."

Outwardly, Sarah forced her lips into a smile and nodded in vague agreement, but inside, she felt as if all the luster had gone out of her life. If Jon had withdrawn his affections from Mary Letitia, why had he changed his mind and asked her to accompany him to the picnic? Was it because of what had happened on the beach? Had he been so upset and angry because he hadn't had his way with Sarah that he'd rushed back into Mary Letitia's arms?

Deciding she would ignore Jon for the duration of the picnic, Sarah turned to help the women gather the parasols, blankets, and picnic baskets from the wagon. Walking in a tight group, they headed toward the concessions, and before long, a gathering of mocking male followers accompanied them. "Hey, ladies," one bellowed, "how about joining me in a smoke . . . maybe share a nice fat see-gar?"

"They'd probably rather share a chaw," another shouted.

Husky laughs erupted, followed by heckles and wolf calls. Another man yelled, "Looks like Jeremy's no longer wearin' the pants in the family . . . eh, Flora?"

When it became evident that the men, with their snide remarks, were intent on making them as uncomfortable as possible, Sarah said to the women, "Hold your heads high, keep your eyes focused straight ahead, and ignore them. They'll soon get bored and leave us alone."

Flora nervously scanned the faces of the men parading along with them and said in an anxious voice, "I surely hope Jeremy doesn't change his mind and decide to come. I left him home working in the garden."

Charlotte looked at her in surprise. "I thought he knew about the bloomers . . . that you told him. You always boast that he's such a reasonable man. Or do you just say that to impress us?"

"He *is* a reasonable man," said Flora. "I just ... didn't get the chance to say anything. Did you tell Ned?"

Charlotte shrugged. "I started to. But you know how Ned is, always worrying about his patients and their ailments and all. I didn't want to cause him any more worry then he already had."

Elizabeth pursed her lips. "Ned would absolutely die if he knew you were here in bloomers, and you know it."

Charlotte's eyes darkened. "I suppose you told Charles."

"Of course I didn't tell Charles," said Elizabeth. "I'm not a fool. Charles would skin me alive. But he's in Esquimalt," she said, "so he'll never know."

"That's what you think," said Charlotte, eyes fixed straight ahead.

Elizabeth froze. "Oh ... my goodness! He's here!"

Sarah gazed in the distance and saw a man approaching, his long strides quickly closing the gap between them. From the look on his anger-reddened face, she knew he was anything but amused by his wife's display. "Now don't let him bully you," she told Elizabeth as Charles Thurman drew closer. "Just stand your ground."

"Stand my ground! He's furious!"

"That may be," said Sarah, "but you have a right to dress as you wish, without your husband's approval. And you must let him know that he simply cannot dictate your fashion." Seeing the scowl on Charles Thurman's face, Sarah wasn't sure she was giving Elizabeth the best advice, but then, Elizabeth must learn to stand up to her husband.

Elizabeth drew in an anxious breath. "All right. I'll

try." Planting a smile on her face, she stepped from the group. "Charles, I can explain—"

"You can get the hell out of here, that's what you can do!" said Charles, muscles standing out in his neck like taut cords. He reached for her arm, but Elizabeth shook his hand away.

She moved to stand between Flora and Sarah. "I'm sorry you feel this way," she said, her voice faltering, "but the fact is, I intend to stay at the picnic with my friends."

"Not in those, you won't!" said Charles, his enraged eyes sweeping down Elizabeth's bloomers.

Elizabeth raised her chin. "You cannot dictate my fashion. I'm a grown woman, and if I choose to wear a bloomer costume, then that's exactly what I shall do."

"Like hell you will!"

"Please lower your voice. You're creating a scene."

"Good! Now, either come with me quietly, or I'll bodily carry you off."

"Attaway, Thurman!" a man called from the crowd that was quickly gathering around the women.

Laughter broke out.

Charles Thurman looked around at the hecklers, and his face grew livid. Grabbing Elizabeth's arm, he tugged her away. "When we get home, I'll personally rip those clothes right off you."

"What are you gonna to do then, Thurman?" another voice shouted. "She's the one wearing the pants now."

"He'd better show her while he still can who's the man in the family," someone else called. "Looks like she needs a little taming."

Charles Thurman said nothing, but Sarah had an uneasy feeling that once home, he'd indeed show Elizabeth who was the man in the house. She didn't think that Charles Thurman had ever beaten his wife, so Sarah assumed he would assert his masculinity in the only other way she could imagine.

For an instant, she had a quick mental image of Jon ripping off her bloomer costume and asserting himself in that way. In her fantasy, she visualized her naked back and Jon's naked front, but she had trouble filling in the details. She'd never seen an actual naked man before.

"Flora!"

"Charlotte!"

Sarah turned abruptly to find two angry-looking men pressing through the crowd, and from the panicked looks on the faces of Flora and Charlotte, she felt reasonably certain that Jeremy Pickering and Ned Potts had just arrived ...

Jon chewed the cracker with goose pâté that Mary Letitia had just stuffed into his mouth, all the while scanning the crowd for Sarah. He'd already seen Mandi, and she'd assured him that Sarah planned to come to the picnic. But as yet, Sarah had not made her appearance.

He wanted to apologize for his behavior on the beach. He'd set out to court her properly, and to do it with compassion and understanding—mindful of the faithless bastards in her life—and instead, he'd behaved like a first-rate ass. If she never spoke to him again, it was no less than he deserved.

"... like the salmon pâté better, Jon?" Mary Letitia's voice seemed far away as Jon focused on a small group of women dressed in bloomer costumes, a group that appeared to be causing a disturbance—at least one of them seemed to be having a problem with her escort. He had her by the arm and was dragging her from the group.

"Jon!" His mother's voice was quite close.

He blinked and looked at her. "Yes?"

"Mary Letitia just asked you a question." Dorothy Cromwell's face held a tolerant smile.

Jon looked at Mary Letitia, who batted her long lashes as she repeated, "The goose pâté . . . It is your favorite, isn't it? Or did you like the salmon better?"

Jon shifted his gaze to the group of women again. "Well . . . yes, I suppose."

"You suppose what?" Mary Letitia sounded annoyed.

Jon caught a flash of pink and red—pink bloomer costume and red hair. There was no question of who it was. He'd recognize that rich, coppery hair anywhere. "I suppose you're right," he said distractedly. Ever since their steamy encounter at the beach, Sarah's face had mocked him daily. He yearned to feel her arms curved about his neck again, her lips pressed to his, her body firm against his body . . .

"Jon!" said Mary Letitia, annoyed. "You are not making any sense at all. I asked you a question."

He met Mary Letitia's smoldering gaze. "You did?"

"Honestly, you are simply not here with us." She pursed her lips, and when Jon said nothing, she sighed. "I'm sorry I snapped at you, but I had hoped we could spend some time together"—she gave his mother a knowing smile, then focused on Jon again—"just enjoying the day, visiting and talking."

Jon eyed her dubiously. "Talking about what?"

Dorothy stamped her small booted foot to capture Jon's attention. "You are being ungracious and rude to Mary Letitia," she said. "She has packed a lovely picnic especially for you, she has set aside this day from her busy social schedule to spend it with you, and you are being absolutely insufferable."

"I'm sorry," said Jon indifferently, his gaze shifting back to Sarah and the two remaining women, whom he now recognized as Flora Pickering and Charlotte Potts. He also noted that Jeremy Pickering and Ned

Potts had appeared on the scene and were dragging Flora and Charlotte away.

"Sorry isn't enough," said Dorothy. "You owe Mary Letitia the courtesy of a response to her question."

"It really doesn't matter," said Mary Letitia, giving Jon's mother a tight smile. "Why don't we just find a nice quiet place off to ourselves and have lunch . . . Jon?"

Jon noticed that Sarah seemed to be having trouble with a group of men who appeared to be teasing her mercilessly. One had her bonnet perched on his head, another was prancing about with her parasol over his shoulder, and several others were jousting among themselves, perhaps not completely in humor. From the looks of it, things could get nasty.

"Excuse me, Mary Letitia . . . Mother," he said, breaking from the group. Ignoring his mother's gasp of outrage and Mary Letitia's lamentable appeal, he left their side and strode toward the crowd.

Chapter 12

As Jon closed the distance between him and the group surrounding Sarah, he saw Mayor Harris, Sheriff George Heaton, and Israel Needham—one of the members of the city council—approaching from the opposite direction. Sheriff Heaton arrived first on the scene. He rapped the brawling men across their backs with his billy club, halting what promised to be the start of a sizable skirmish. "Break it up, gentlemen. The fun's over. Give the lady back her things."

The men handed Sarah her bonnet and parasol, then stepped back, leaving her to face the sheriff, Mayor Harris, and Israel Needham. Sarah settled her bonnet on her head and snapped shut her parasol. Then she tightened her lips and waited. George Heaton tucked his billy under his arm and assumed a surly stance while confronting her. "I could arrest you," he said, eyeing her bloomer costume with obvious disapproval.

"Arrest me for what?" she asked, incensed.

"For inciting a disturbance."

Jon paused, then stepped out of view. Knowing that Sarah was in no danger now, he decided to watch, to see how she would talk her way out of her predicament. She seemed to be adept at that sort of thing. And he didn't imagine she wanted him waltzing in and rescuing her—being the independent woman she fancied herself to be . . .

"Me inciting a disturbance!" she exclaimed. "I was merely walking across the green with my friends, tending to my own business, when those ruffians accosted us. We did nothing to precipitate their callow behavior or immature actions."

"But you did have the choice of turning around and leaving the area," said Heaton. "You had been given clear warning by their actions that things could get out of hand."

Sarah glared at the sheriff. "In other words," she said, "I am expected either to submit to degradation and leave the scene, or carry the burden for the actions of a group of infantile men. That is most typical of the times."

"Miss Ashley," said Israel Needham, "Sheriff Heaton could also arrest you for selling your garments from Wellington Brown's store without a business license."

"If you're referring to the bloomer costumes that Mrs. Potts, Mrs. Thurman, and Mrs. Pickering were wearing," she said, her voice rising with ire, "I did not sell them. I gave them away."

"How do we know that?"

"You don't. But that's the way it is."

"I don't believe you, nor, I imagine, do any of the other men here."

Sarah's eyes darkened and her lips pinched tight with resentment. Scanning the faces of the men, she leveled her gaze on Heaton. "By not possessing the vote, I, as a woman, have little influence over you male politicians, and so I must submit to laws from which I have no redress." She held out her hands for the handcuffs. "So arrest me."

While the sheriff stared at Sarah's outstretched

hands, seeming at a loss, a man bellowed. "Go ahead and arrest her, Heaton. Then maybe our women will settle down again."

"That's right," yelled another man. "If she's not stopped, our women will be paradin' around in our trousers, makin' us do the cookin' and cleanin'."

"Yeah, Heaton. Arrest her!"

The crowd began to push and shove, pressing ever closer. Sheriff Heaton raised his billy and whirled it about his head. "Here here, gentlemen," he yelled. "Let's just calm down." But the crowd ignored him. Then one man took a jab at another, and before long, Sarah stood in the middle of a circle edged by brawling, pugnacious men.

Seeing Sarah's plight, Jon shoved his way past the onlookers to where two men seemed determined to beat the living daylights out of each other right at Sarah's feet. He grabbed one man by the back of his collar and the seat of his pants and hurled him out the way. Then he pulled the other from the ground by his lapels and shoved him aside. Taking Sarah by the arm, he said, "Come on."

She jerked her arm loose. "I will not!"

"What do you mean, you will not?"

She lifted her chin a notch. "Exactly what I said. I refuse to go with you." Not only did she feel outraged by the attitude of the men who had put her in this position, but she also resented Jon's interference. He'd only done it to prove a point—that a woman was helpless without a man. "I'm quite capable of taking care of myself."

Jon took her arm again, this time more firmly. "You're more capable of making a damned fool of yourself. You just about got yourself thrown in jail."

She tugged against his firm grip. "That's my business, not yours. You have no right to continually interfere in my life."

"Someone had better interfere," said Jon, dragging her through an amused crowd that parted for them to pass. "You're not doing a hell of a good job on your own. If you had any sense at all, you'd pack away that ridiculous outfit you're wearing and let the moths have it!"

She took a deep breath. "Ridiculous outfit!"

"Yes! Ridiculous outfit! It makes you look like a damned clown." He tugged her, fighting and stumbling against his grip, toward his coach.

She tried to shake off his hand, but couldn't. Glaring up at him with burning eyes, she said, "I suppose I should strive to dress more like Mary Letitia!"

"That might be a start!"

Sarah bit her lip to stop its trembling. "If she is so . . . perfect, then why aren't you with her?"

"Because I would rather be with you," said Jon. "But for the life of me, I have no idea why."

"Nor do I. And would you please release my arm."

"Not until I have escorted you safely to my carriage and taken you away from here."

As he ushered her toward the coach, Amor De Cosmos intercepted them. He tipped his hat to Sarah. "Good afternoon, Miss Ashley. It's nice to see you again. I hope my editorial was helpful."

In spite of Jon's firm grip on her arm, she managed a gracious smile. "Yes, thank you, Mr. De Cosmos. It was most helpful."

Jon tugged her away from him. "Beat it, De Cosmos."

De Cosmos ignored Jon and fell into step beside them. Peering around Sarah, he said, "Tell me, Governor Cromwell, have you changed your views on confederation? Have you even given it any thought in the past few weeks?"

"Get the hell out of here, De Cosmos."

"May I quote you on that?"

"Only if you want that pretty mustache shoved up your nose. Now get out of here before I lose my temper and forget I'm a gentleman."

"You're not a gentleman. Actually, you're little more than a somewhat civilized savage. However, I believe I have enough for my next editorial." He looked at Sarah. "Oh ... by the way, Miss Ashley. Your brothers stopped by my office. Nice chaps."

Sarah gave him a rueful smile. "No, Mr. De Cosmos, my *stepbrothers* are not nice chaps. They are a couple of boorish charlatans, as you will undoubtedly learn very soon. But perhaps they'll be of some use to you. Good day."

"Good day, Miss Ashley ... Governor." He stopped, and Jon and Sarah continued on.

Jon kept his eyes straight ahead. "You didn't tell me your brothers were still here."

"I only just found out."

"Well, I'll do something about that."

"No! And I'll thank you to just leave me alone. It's because of you and ... what happened on the beach, that they have more mud to sling."

"Nothing happened on the beach."

"Maybe from your single-minded viewpoint it didn't."

"We'll talk about that later."

"No ... we won't!" she said, her heart pounding in hammerlike thumps.

Jon said nothing but continued to tug Sarah toward his coach. Passing the place where Flora had parked the spring wagon, Sarah saw that the ground looked if they'd made a hasty retreat, and she suspected that Jeremy Pickering had hustled Flora away in a fit of temper. Across the road, a group of young women was gathered near Jon's coach. With great enthusiasm, they were cheering something or someone hidden from view.

Jon eyed the young women with concern. "What the devil is going on?"

As they approached, a female voice delivered a stirring oration from behind the coach: "We are not senseless, weak-minded creatures without opinions of our own. We are man's equal, not his slave. So we must go forth with confidence and meet obstacles with courage . . ."

Blood rushed from Sarah's face, and her voice caught in her throat when she realized who the speaker was. As they rounded the coach, she spotted Josephine—still wearing her bloomer costume and gesticulating from atop the stump of an ancient red cedar—about the same instant Jon did.

Jon sucked in a sharp breath and bellowed, "*Josephine!* Get in the coach at once!"

Josephine looked at him in wide-eyed surprise. "Papa!" Standing rigid, she faced her father and said in a contrite voice, "I was only telling Nettie and Glory and Annie and the others about my bloomer costume. No one else saw me."

"And no one will, is that clear?"

"Yes, Papa."

Jon turned to Peterson. "Take her home at once, then return here to collect the others. I suspect that very shortly Lady Cromwell will want to return to her quarters." He turned to Josephine. "And you, young lady, are to go to your room and stay there until I get home, is that clear?"

"Yes, Papa." Obediently, Josephine jumped down from her stump pulpit and climbed into the coach. As the vehicle pulled away, she peered out the window and waved to her friends. The consternation Sarah had seen on her face moments before was quickly replaced with a sanguine smile, and Sarah had the uncomfortable feeling that Jon had not had the last word with his headstrong, independent daughter.

Jon shoved Sarah into the phaeton, and she sat stiffly while he took the reins. He gave the command, and the big bay gelding bolted forward. "I'll thank you to stop filling Josephine's head with such nonsense as wearing bloomers and touting women's rights."

Sarah saw the sullen resentment in his face. "I never encouraged Josephine to wear bloomers to the picnic; that was solely her idea."

His eyes darkened, like thunderheads before a storm. "But you sure as hell gave her the idea . . . and the damned bloomers."

"I gave her the bloomers, not the idea to wear them to the picnic. She managed that on her own. And I gave her the bloomers with the understanding that she would not wear them unless she had your approval—which she has obviously not received. She's a very independent young woman, in case you haven't noticed."

"Too damned independent."

Sarah rested smoldering eyes on Jon's firm profile. "I should think that you, being the father of two daughters, would be more concerned for their plight. With present-day laws, they're compelled to be solely dependent on men."

Jon snapped the whip, driving the horse to a faster clip. "They'll be dependent on men of my choosing. I assure you, my daughters will be treated with the utmost respect and kindness by their husbands, or the men will have me to deal with. But if Josephine persists in following your path, no man will have her."

"Then, according to you," Sarah said in a tight voice, "if a woman aspires to anything greater than tending a house, dressing as her husband dictates, and devoting herself totally to his wants and needs, she's not even deserving of a husband."

"That would be a start!"

Sarah clamped her mouth shut and glowered at Jon. The man was intolerable. Insufferable. His words were an outright insult. Feeling her anger rising, she said, "Just because a woman chooses to have a mind of her own, you consider her unworthy of having a husband. Well, maybe you deserve a simpering little fool like Mary Letitia Windemere, with her highborn airs and her shallow demeanor."

Jon turned the phaeton into the lane leading to Sarah's cottage. "Who the hell's talking about Mary Letitia?"

"She seems to have been occupying your spare time adequately," Sarah said with detached indifference.

Jon pulled to a halt alongside the cottage. "I've spent more time trying to avoid her."

"Your mother seems to approve of her," she said somewhat incongruously, distracted by the fact that Jon had pulled into her driveway instead of parking out front.

He looked at her steadily. "My mother won't be selecting my next wife ... should I be that foolish again."

Sarah digested that comment. "You object to your mother selecting your wife, yet you insist on choosing your daughters' husbands. Isn't that a bit inconsistent?"

"I know what's best for my daughters. They don't."

"Then that should be true for you as well. So your mother should be the one to choose a woman for you," she parried in wry amusement. "After all, who knows you better than your own mother? I'm certain she'd select someone who would be an asset to your career and your home."

Jon's lips curved in a sardonic smile. "But not one who would enjoy warming my bed."

Sarah pursed her lips, annoyed that Jon placed such high priority on the marital act. "Another of your requirements for a proper wife," she said. "She must eagerly warm her husband's bed. I doubt you could find any woman who truly enjoys warming a man's bed. That sort of thing is one of the crosses we women must bear."

Jon gave her a disarming smile. "You believe that because you have no idea what the hell you're talking about. For a libertine, you're rather inexperienced in some areas."

Sarah shrugged. "I know enough."

"Do you? Do you know that when I do this"—he brushed his thumb across her cheek and over her lips—"your eyes dilate and your breath quickens, and that sends me signals?"

"Nonsense. You read signals into everything I do simply because you want to." But she couldn't deny that she savored the musky aroma filling each quickened breath.

"And when I do this"—he trailed a finger along her throat, then slowly, deliberately moved his hand to cover her breast—"you can't breathe at all?"

Her body came alive under his caress. She released the breath she was holding and pushed his hand away. "You're distorting things."

"No ... you're distorting things." He kissed the sensitive skin beneath her ear and sent a trail of kisses along her neck. "Silly mooncalf," he whispered, "haven't you learned to play your own game?" His mouth moved over hers in a lingering kiss.

Instinctively, Sarah parted her lips, allowing him

access. He deeply explored the inside of her mouth, his tongue stroking hers in a slow, rhythmic parody. His palm glided up her rib cage to cup her breast, his thumb brushing her nipple, sending tingles radiating as he teased it to a pinched bud through her silk tunic.

With his knee, Jon gently urged her thighs apart and slid his hand down her belly to stroke her most sensitive area through the soft silk of her bloomers. She glided her hands around his neck and trembled in his arms, unprepared for the arousal his intimate touch brought. As the kiss deepened and his tongue became more demanding, he began a firm, rhythmic movement, stirring her to heights she had never before experienced.

He took her hand and guided it to the hard bulge in his breeches, moving her palm in a slow, sensual rhythm. While she shyly caressed the hardness of him, something strange was happening deep inside her, seeming to build with Jon's stroking until she felt as if a spring inside her was about to uncoil and burst. The sensation was unlike anything she'd ever known.

Then, suddenly, without warning, a rush of ebullient relief surged through her, followed by a series of incredibly delightful spasms that coursed over and over, seeming to center in her privates. "Ooh . . . ooh . . . ooh!" Short, ecstatic gasps burst from her mouth with each glorious surge. Clinging to Jon, she yielded to his intimate caresses. But all too soon, the wondrous sensations diminished and passed, leaving her weak, her arms aching, and her heart beating so rapidly she was unable to catch her breath.

After a few moments, Jon raised her chin so she would have to look at him. When her fogged vision sharpened, she saw a slow, dangerous smile. "That, my precious little peagoose, is the cross you women must bear. Can you honestly tell me you'd never want to endure it again?"

Sarah blushed deeply as unexpected tears of jubilation pricked her eyes. She'd had no idea such a thing could happen. It was beyond all her wildest expectations—or blackest fears—of what the marital act embraced. It was beyond anything she'd ever experienced before . . .

She looked at him with wide-eyed wonder. "I had no idea. I mean, it happened so . . . suddenly."

"That was just the prologue," he said. "The act itself is much more intense, the response you felt, far stronger."

She eyed him curiously. "Did that happen to you, too?"

He arched a dark brow. "Unfortunately, no. But I intend to put great emphasis on that . . . next time."

She looked at him in alarm. "No . . . there won't be a next time. That was a very brash, untimely move on your part, and it was unwise of me to let you continue what you were doing."

"Wisdom had nothing to do with your response, sweet, innocent Sarah."

"Regardless," said Sarah, "it can't happen again." *Won't happen again*, she silently amended, lest she lose all control and her virginity as well . . . and to a man who had no intention of marrying her. "Besides, we mustn't forget that we are adversaries," she added in an effort to quell the provocatively erotic thought of losing her virginity to him—recklessly, impetuously, and with complete abandon.

"Ah, yes, our own little Armageddon," said Jon. "And since my first duty is to the colony, I'd better get back to the picnic and perform the important governmental task of handing out trophies after the horse race."

"Back to the picnic?" Sarah found the thought of

Jon rejoining Mary Letitia disturbing, even though Jon had indicated that the woman meant nothing to him. And Sarah realized, with startling clarity, that she was jealous—utterly, intensely, undeniably jealous of the woman. And envious of the fact that Lady Cromwell wholeheartedly encouraged and welcomed Mary Letitia into Jon's life.

Jon reached for Sarah's hand. "As much as I'd like, I can't give out trophies from here." He kissed her palm. "So, my sweet, inexperienced little love, I'll have to temporarily give up the idea of instructing your beautiful body in the fine art of lovemaking."

Sarah's breath grew heavy with the realization that she wanted him to teach her those things . . . and end the burning ache that was building again. She was so vulnerable to his silly endearments—so damned vulnerable. It was all rubbish, of course, manipulative rubbish to get her to surrender to him. She knew it, yet it worked. She desperately wanted to surrender. "But . . . you can't go back," she said bluntly.

Jon gave her a disarming smile. "Why not? You're the one who said we're adversaries. I, of course, view our relationship in an entirely different light . . . as you will, too, in time."

She looked at him and pondered the profound longing that filled her, just wanting to be held in his arms again. It seemed that whenever she was with him, she craved his embrace. And when she was away from him, she thought of him constantly. Could she possibly be falling in love?

A preposterous idea!

Love was foolish and risky, a state one must not allow oneself to fall into, especially when it could lead to deception. And she refused to succumb to such nonsense.

But she knew that when Jon had caressed her so intimately, if he had wanted to go further she would have let him. For a few vagrant moments, he'd had complete control of her body.

He was absolutely right. It was their own little Armageddon. And if she wasn't careful, he'd entice her to destruction . . . or to a fool's paradise. So she must maintain her distance, for she feared that once in his arms again, she would not have the strength to resist him.

He'd given her a sample of what he had to offer, and now she found it wasn't enough.

Chapter 13

Dorothy Cromwell marched into the library and slapped the latest edition of the *Colonist* on Jon's desk. With a grand sweep of her arm, she said, "Perhaps *now* you'll come to your senses and get rid of that woman!"

Jon wasn't in the mood for his mother's theatrics. His mind was on other things, specifically Sarah and her ardent response to him in the carriage. Now, she at least had an inkling of what it was she'd been missing, of the passion that smoldered inside her. A passion, it appeared, that he could ignite with the slightest provocation—a thought that made him even more obsessed with making love to her.

Wild, impassioned love—over and over and over.

Dorothy stabbed the editorial with a stiff finger. "In case you have not read this yet," she said, her thin nostrils flaring, "Mr. De Cosmos says . . ." She snatched up the paper, propped her spectacles on her nose, and read:

"THE FACTIOUS GODDESS OF FASHION HAS AGAIN RAISED HER FIERY HEAD. Miss Sarah Ashley created quite a stir at Beacon Hill Park by parading about in reform dress. The bloomer costume, which proved obnoxious to some, was seemingly not obnoxious to our esteemed governor, who rescued Miss Ashley from certain imprisonment at the hands of scandalized constabulary. Should Governor Cromwell show as much concern for the affairs of state as for the affairs of Miss Ashley, he would no doubt realize that Vancouver Island is facing a major political crisis . . ."

Dorothy folded the newspaper and slapped it again on Jon's desk. She fixed stormy eyes on him and pointed her index finger upward as if preaching from a podium. "I cannot see how such ridiculous dress could possibly help bring about the emancipation of women from the tyranny of prejudice and fashion, as Miss Ashley so aptly stated in her handbill."

Jon studied his mother's parody in subdued amusement. She was not all convention and propriety. There was also a touch of the rebel in her. His mouth curved in a cynical smile. "I'm surprised you even read the handbill. Did you do it out of curiosity, or perhaps . . . interest? I remember, when I was a boy, hearing Father reprimand you because you dared to wear pink stockings."

Dorothy's cheeks flushed. "That is beside the point," she said. "I read the handbill so I could prepare myself for whatever nonsense might fill Josephine's head because of it. I assure you, I am not in the least bit interested in Miss Ashley's ridiculous bloomer costume. It is abhorrent. But her dress is not the issue here. Have you any idea what people must think . . . you, the governor, making a spectacle of yourself at the picnic like that?"

Jon rested back in his chair, steepled his fingers, and looked steadily at his mother. "I don't much give a damn what people think."

Dorothy bristled. "That is quite evident! But you

should. Not only has Amor De Cosmos portrayed you as a complete ninny, but he is creating ill-feeling toward you in many of the merchants and citizens. The matter of women wearing bloomers has now become a political issue. There would be no dissension if it were not for Miss Ashley."

Jon poured a brandy and took a swig. Too true. De Cosmos's editorials *were* creating problems for him and his cabinet, at a time when their attention should be focused on preparing for the arrival of the Crown representatives. The past week alone, on top of his usual work load and duties, he'd had to tend to details in the laying of the water pipes on Yates Street so the job would be done on schedule, he'd had to meet with the Land and Works Committee regarding the installation of more gaslights, and he'd had two conferences with the hospital committee to review the plans for the new lunatic asylum—all tasks that needed to be completed before the arrival of the Crown representatives. And his council was in the throes of formulating a new taxing base.

And now his cabinet wanted Sarah out of the colony by whatever means it took—the first being to deny her the business license through whatever reason they could invent.

He took another swig of brandy, set the snifter down with a clatter, and fixed his gaze on his mother. "You know bloody well, if it were not Sarah, De Cosmos would find another way to attack me."

Dorothy pursed her lips. "Well, besides that, there is the issue of Mary Letitia. She was absolutely mortified when you walked away from her to rescue the Ashley woman. Then you didn't have the common courtesy to rejoin her after you returned from wherever it was you vanished to with the woman. In fact, upon your return, it appeared you made every effort to avoid Mary Letitia."

"That's because I did." Miffed, Jon looked at his mother. "As a matter of fact, I made it damned clear before the picnic that we would *not* be spending the day together. She chose to ignore that, so I felt no obligation to stay with her. Nor do I feel any remorse over my actions with Sarah. Now, if you'll excuse me, Mother, I think I'll go do something impulsive, primitive, and infinitely gratifying." He shoved his chair back and strode out of the room.

His mother called after him, "Where are you going?"

"To see Miss Ashley," he called back. "Where else?"

In the dining room of the cottage, surrounded by a group of enthusiastic admirers comprising Charlotte Potts, Flora Pickering, and Elizabeth Thurman, Sarah demonstrated one of her new Singer sewing machines. Although initially the picnic episode had seemed devastating to her cause, she realized now that because of it, she'd actually gained ground in her pursuit.

Word had spread quickly that she had been rescued from certain imprisonment by Governor Cromwell, who had left Mary Letitia Windemere's side to do so, and now it seemed she had gained three bosom friends—Charlotte, Flora, and Elizabeth. The women were ecstatic that Mary Letitia had received her just reward, and they also seemed to have smoothed things over with their husbands. What's more, Elizabeth's father, a prominent commission merchant, and Flora's husband, Jeremy, a grocer, had each agreed to sign the business license application.

Slowly working the treadle of the sewing machine, Sarah demonstrated to her three new friends how quickly and uniformly a seam could be stitched. She held up the fabric to display its straight seam. "It's as simple as that," she said. "You can even regulate the length of the stitch by turning this little thumb-screw"—she demonstrated briefly to the wide-eyed women—"and you'll find it's really very easy to master stitchery on the machine. As you saw, all I did was operate the treadle and guide the fabric under the little foot."

Flora took the fabric from Sarah and studied the seam closely, while Charlotte and Elizabeth peered over Flora's shoulder in awe. "That is positively incredible," said Flora. "A person could make a garment in mere hours."

Sarah smiled brightly. "The bloomers that I gave each of you were fashioned in less than a half-day each. As I see it, with one woman cutting patterns, and two working the machines, we could turn out over forty pairs of bloomers in a week ... or fifteen complete bloomer costumes with matching tunics in that same amount of time."

Flora clapped her hands in glee. "How terribly exciting to be a part of such a movement—actually making garments that will change the course of history."

Sarah chuckled at Flora's enthusiasm. "I don't know about that," she said, "but they should at least change things for the women of Victoria."

"Absolutely," said Flora. "And if I work in your emporium, perhaps Jeremy will even allow me to keep some of the money I earn and put it in my own bank account ... as you mentioned some wives in the States are doing."

"Are you saying that you would really work for me when the business is going?" asked Sarah.

Flora batted her eyelids nervously. "Well ... yes. That is, if Jeremy will allow it."

Elizabeth looked askance at Flora. "You know perfectly well he won't."

"But that's where you're wrong," said Flora. "After we got home from the picnic and Jeremy had calmed down, he agreed that my bloomer costume was practical. He even said I could wear it in the garden and around the house. He said he liked the way the trousers clung to my ..." She paused, her face a bright scarlet. "That is ... he just didn't want me to wear it in public where other men would ... you know, see my ... shape."

Elizabeth smiled knowingly. "But do you really think he'd actually agree to let you go to work for Sarah?"

"He wants to pay off the farm," said Flora. "We have even talked about taking in boarders, but the place is so small and the walls so thin, we decided against it."

Baffled, Sarah looked at Flora. "What do thin walls have to do with taking in boarders?"

Flora looked at her, wide-eyed. "Don't you know?"

Sarah shrugged. "Don't I know what?"

Flora looked at Charlotte, then at Elizabeth.

When no one responded, Sarah scanned the flushed faces. "Does it have anything to do with ... well ... you know, what married people do?"

"Of course it does," replied Elizabeth. "I mean, some men are very noisy."

Charlotte nudged Elizabeth. "Only the men?"

Elizabeth chuckled. "Well, sometimes women are, too ... so I hear."

Sarah pondered her sudden and unexpected reaction to Jon's intimate caresses in the carriage. It had been all she could do to contain the little moans of pleasure that had threatened to erupt in her throat. Actually, she wasn't at all certain they hadn't slipped out when the unexpected bursts of sensation had coursed through her. And Jon had emphasized that the real act was much stronger, the sensations more intense.

She could imagine that lovemaking might be quite noisy, at least if it were she and Jon ...

"Sarah?"

She looked at Flora, then at her seam, which was now a mass of tangled thread. She blushed deeply. How easily distracted she was. But the indecent thoughts had begun to bedevil her again. Actually, the thoughts didn't seem as indecent as they were risqué.

Deliciously risqué ...

"Sarah?"

Sarah's eyes refocused on the puckered seam. She'd been so preoccupied with thoughts of Jon, she'd neglected to guide the fabric beneath the presser foot. She pulled the fabric loose and clipped the thread, then proceeded to untangle the knot. "This rarely happens," she said. "My mind wandered."

"To Governor Cromwell?" asked Elizabeth pointedly.

Sarah shrugged. "Well, not exactly. That is ..."

"He is a handsome devil, isn't he?" said Charlotte. "And we think you two would be perfect together."

"You do?"

"Yes. And you do, too."

Sarah brushed away the pieces of thread she'd cut loose and pulled on the bobbin thread. "I really have no time to even consider him—"

A series of firm knocks startled her. She looked toward the door. "Who in the world can that be?" Gathering her gingham skirt and slipping from behind the sewing table, she swept open the door. "Jon!"

He chucked her under the chin and walked in without waiting to be invited.

"Do come in," she said ruefully, catching the smell of horses and leather and sweet hay as he passed. Male and earthy, he had no lingering trace of soap or cologne on him.

She looked at his broad back and lean hips as he stood gazing around the room. He was so sure of himself. So damned certain she wanted him there.

Scanning the women, he smiled and said, "Don't rush off on my account, ladies."

Flora's eyes shifted between them, then she quickly gathered her reticule and parasol. "We were just leaving."

Sarah moved to stop her. "But we aren't finished yet—" She scowled at Jon, who responded by giving her a furtive smile. "Really, you needn't go . . . any of you. Jon is *not* staying." She glared at him.

Before she could stop the women, all three marched out of the house and headed toward Flora's spring wagon. For a moment, Sarah stood staring after them, then she turned to Jon, her hands on her hips, her eyes burning. "You have your nerve . . . marching into my house like you own the place, and all but sending my guests away. That was incredibly audacious of you."

"Audacious, yes. But effective."

"Well, you're not staying."

He stepped around her and closed the door.

"Why did you do that?" Her heart began to pound.

"Because I don't want to shock your lady friends by what I do next." He stalked toward her.

She stepped behind the dining table, using it as a buffer between them. "Stay away from me." She braced her hands on the table surface.

Jon smiled. "Do I present that much of a threat? I have never taken a woman by force, and I don't intend to start with you. So you have nothing to fear

. . . at least not from me. But maybe I'm not the one you're worried about."

Sarah breathed deeply, trying to calm the erratic beating of her heat. "You are vain and arrogant to even suggest you have such an effect on me. What happened in the carriage was purely a result of . . . surprise. It won't happen again. I am now wiser, more experienced, and capable of controlling my . . . desires."

"Ah, so we're finally talking about desires. We *are* making some headway."

"That changes nothing." She continued to move around the table. "Will you stop this! What do you intend to do?"

"I intend to lift you in my arms, carry you off to the bedroom, and remove your clothes, garment by garment." He slowly circled the table. "Then I will lower you to the bed and feel your warm, naked body against my warm, naked body while I teach you the fine art of making love. I will start by suckling your sweet toes. Then I will make my way up your smooth young body, covering every inch of it with hot kisses. Every inch, Miss Ashley. Every single soft, warm, delectable inch—stopping, of course, to pay particular attention to certain sensitive areas—until you are crazed with passion and crying out with need, at which time I will lustfully, thoroughly, and unremittingly satisfy that need."

Sarah stared across the table in stunned silence. The picture Jon had so vividly painted sent a sultry warmth pulsing through her. And deep inside, a feverish and insistent ache began to throb. She hated what he did to her . . . what he made happen inside her. The aching throb and the thoughts it brought to mind were ones no respectable woman should have. She hated it, yet she wanted it. She wanted him. She wanted him to do precisely what he'd said he'd do. That was the pure, simple truth. And afterward?

Afterward . . .

There was no *afterward* beyond more lovemaking without commitment. And since she did not plan to marry, she could not chance having a child—a decision which precluded lovemaking. And she would not allow Jon to change her mind.

"Please don't do this, Jon. You're scaring me."

Jon looked into eyes that moments before had burned with desire, but that now reflected mistrust. What had triggered the change? He'd been completely honest with her about his intentions . . . no misconception there. And she wanted him. Even as she stared at him with those wide, wary eyes, he knew. But . . . she looked so vulnerable.

The vulnerable woman behind the dauntless facade.

And he was acting like a bloody rutting buck again, when what she needed was some tenderness, and a hell of a lot more understanding. She didn't need another deceitful bastard in her life. He moved cautiously around the table. "You don't need to be afraid of me," he said soberly as he edged his way toward her. This time, she didn't move, and he took her in his arms and held her. "I don't want you to ever be afraid of me, love . . . not me. I won't do anything you don't want me to do."

She tucked her arms between them and let him hold her. "Then please don't do what you were doing."

He stroked her hair. "What . . . telling you how it would be with us? I thought it would help ease your apprehension. I want to be the first man with you . . . I want to be the one to teach you everything about lovemaking."

"Well, I'm not ready for that."

"You're ready," he said. His hand moved around

her neck, the tips of his fingers pressing lightly. "Your pulse is racing, your breath is quick"—he brushed a finger along her face—"and your cheeks are on fire."

"That's not what I meant."

"All right. We'll go slower. Take things a little at a time until you get used to the idea."

"I don't seem to be getting through to you, Jon—"

He touched his finger to her lips. "Enough. You *are* getting through to me. I understand." His thumbs came up to lightly stroke the undersides of her breasts. "Now, tell me how you are doing with your . . . enterprise."

She looked up at him, distracted. "My . . . enterprise?"

"Your mercantile business." His thumbs continued to stroke.

She removed his hands from her and held them at arm's length. "Are you curious or interested?"

"Both."

Her face, which moments before had been tight with apprehension, became animated, and she said with enthusiasm, "Oh . . . it's so exciting. I've had favorable responses from many of the women here—and even some of the men—and the application for my license is almost ready. I have also obtained signatures from several merchants and two bankers. And a few of my new women friends have told me that their husbands will endorse the application as well. So I expect to deliver my papers to the city council shortly . . . perhaps even by the first of next week."

Jon sighed. She was so confident, he didn't have the heart to tell her that her battle had not yet ended, that the council had no intention of simply granting her the license. That, in fact, they had no intention of stopping short of seeing her on a ship bound for the States.

He did make up his mind, however, that when the battle was over, he *would* be there to nurse her wounds in the way he knew would most quickly and completely heal the hurt ...

Chapter 14

S arah sat at her dressing table, preparing for her
meeting with the city council—a confrontation
she and Esther had wryly come to refer to as the in-
quisition. Peering into the mirror, she adjusted her
straw bonnet at a jaunty angle so the small bird
perched among the cluster of silk flowers would not
appear to be sitting squarely on top of her head.

Esther stood looking over her shoulder. Sarah
glanced at her friend's reflection and noted that her
features were really quite good: nicely contoured lips,
straight nose, well-defined cheeks ...

Something was different.

True, Esther was about to make a bold, brash statement against her brother and his cabinet. But there
was something else ... something about her eyes.
Eyes that looked suspiciously as if they wore a touch
of ... brown bister?

Looking more closely, trying to discern if Esther
was, in fact, wearing coloring on her eyes, Sarah said,
"Are you certain you want to march with us?" Joining the small group Sarah had collected to parade to
the courthouse would definitely place Esther in jeop-
ardy with both her mother and Jon.

Esther gave her a confident smile. "Yes," she replied. "I think it's appalling what the city council is

doing to you. And I think Jon is being an utter goose-berry to allow them to do it. So I just want them to see that you're not alone in your crusade."

"I appreciate that," said Sarah, leaning toward the mirror slightly. Was Esther also wearing a trace of rouge on her cheeks ... and perhaps a touch on her lips? Her face definitely had more color.

Esther's brows gathered in a frown. "Jon doesn't suspect what you have planned, does he?"

"No," replied Sarah. "I haven't seen him in the past few days." Five days, to be exact. Although collecting the last of the signatures had kept her mind occupied during the day, at night Sarah had not been able to dismiss thoughts of Jon ... the way he'd described how his lovemaking would be ... or the way she had responded to his caresses. Every time she thought of what had happened in the carriage, her face grew hot, as if on fire. The mere thought of Jon placing her hand against his privates, while he did what he had to hers ...

And the memory of the incredibly glorious throbs, and the wild, frenzied sensations that had coursed through her ... Goodness! Just thinking about it was like a potent aphrodisiac ...

Nor could she dismiss their candid exchange in the cottage. How embarrassed she felt now to have revealed to Jon the extent of her yearning. Well, she hadn't actually revealed it—not in so many words—but he knew.

As she visualized the detailed, hedonistic scene that Jon had described, her eyelids fluttered closed, her heart accelerated, and damp heat scalded her cheeks.

"You'd better pull yourself together." Esther's voice seemed far away. "Or you'll look like a wilted flower by the time you get to the meeting. Just remember, since Jon rescued you at the picnic, I imag-

ine he'll rescue you from the city council as well, if
need be."

Sarah flushed even deeper at Esther's wrong assessment. "I won't need rescuing," she said, touching
her handkerchief to her damp brow. "Everything is
in perfect order. So the council will have no choice
but to grant my license."

"Don't be too sure," said Esther. "Mrs. Harris told
me that the mayor let slip that the city council is going to try and make you look so foolish you won't
even want to stay in Victoria."

Sarah stood and adjusted the blue scarf fichu at her
shoulders, then smoothed the skirt of her matching
poplin walking dress. She really had no idea what to
expect from the city council. But whatever their decision, she would be dressed in a manner that would
not detract from the issue at hand. "Well, at least I
won't be facing them alone," she said, fluffing the
lacy ruffles at her wrists.

Esther smiled widely. "No, you certainly won't be
alone. I suspect we'll have half the city behind us by
the time we get there. I sort of let the word out that
anyone wanting to join us was welcome."

Sarah beamed with delight as she visualized a parade of determined women marching to the fateful
meeting.

Forty minutes later, Sarah and Esther walked in
long purposeful strides toward the stone jail building where the city council held its meetings. Accompanying them was an entourage of Charlotte Potts,
Elizabeth Thurman, Wellington and Mandi, Flora and
Jeremy Pickering, Mrs. Dewig-Gertz and Mr. Gertz,
and four men and eighteen women whom Elizabeth,
Charlotte, and Flora had enlisted for the occasion.

As they paraded through the streets, curious onlookers fell into step behind them, and by the time
they reached the jail building, the flock had grown

considerably. En masse, they marched into the anteroom, where a nervous little man sat at a desk. The man looked up in shocked surprise, then rose, scurried into a back room, and shut the door. A few minutes later, he returned, accompanied by Mayor Harris and Israel Needham.

Sarah stepped forward. "My appointment is at eleven o'clock." She glanced at the clock on the wall and saw that she was exactly on time. "I trust you're expecting me."

"Well, yes." Mayor Harris stroked his jowls as his eyes scanned the crowd. "If you'll step this way."

Sarah and her flock followed Mayor Harris into a large room where six dour-looking men sat lining one side of a long table. While Mayor Harris and Israel Needham took their places, people crowded into the room, filling the six pewlike benches, standing against the walls, and packing into the hallway.

Mayor Harris called for quiet in the room.

Sarah faced the formidable assemblage. Reaching into her carpetbag, she pulled out the papers of the application and offered them to Mayor Harris. "As you will note, I have answered all the questions and obtained all the required signatures."

Mayor Harris took the papers and perused them while the two council members flanking him looked on. Although the men exchanged murmured comments, Sarah was not able to discern what they were saying. At once, the men's voices died, and all eyes focused on the door. Sarah turned to find Amor De Cosmos stepping into the room. He leaned against the wall, a sardonic smile curving his lips.

Mayor Harris whispered to each of the men beside him, and they passed his words along in both directions. That done, he turned his attention to Sarah's papers and silently reviewed them, brows drawn, mouth set in a pugnacious line. When he'd finished perusing the document, he passed it to Israel Needham, who gave it a fastidious examination.

Sarah noted the meticulousness with which the men inspected each page. "I'm certain you'll find everything in order," she said.

Mayor Harris looked up. "That, Miss Ashley, is for us to decide." His tone warned her to be silent. He reached across Israel Needham and pointed to a particular item on one of the numerous pages, then mumbled something.

Israel Needham nodded, and Sarah caught a glint of wry humor in his eyes. "It seems, Miss Ashley, that you have not completely answered the question about the removal of offal matter. Could you be more specific as to what offal matter you will be removing, and by what means you will be removing it? That is, will you use a shovel? Perhaps a tin pail? You have not included these details."

Sarah glared at the man. "I clearly stated that the offal matter would be from slop jars on the premises, and periodically from the privy. I assume you gentlemen are aware of what is contained in both."

"But you have not stated on this application *exactly* what that is," Needham pressed. "If you will simply explain in detail to the council at this time, I'll note it on the document and complete the question for you."

Sarah's eyes narrowed as she gazed around the table at the mocking faces. It was just as Mrs. Harris had warned. These men intended to make a public spectacle of her. Well, she could play their insidious little game, too. Glaring at the man, she replied, "Human excrement, Mr. Needham. If you wish a more detailed description, then I'll have to depend on you for that. Holding such a lofty and eminent position on the town council as commissioner of sanitation, you must know the precise composition of the matter in question."

A whoop from Jeremy Pickering was followed by robust laughter from the rest of the spectators.

Israel Needham's face deepened to a rich shade of red. When the laughter died down, he muttered, "Then we will just fill in the answer as human excrement."

"Why so formal, Needham?" Jeremy Pickering shouted. "Why not just call it sh—"

"Jeremy!" Flora jabbed her husband in the ribs, sending him into a fit of coughing—and the crowd into roars of laughter.

"Order! Let's have order in here," said Mayor Harris, rapping the table with his gavel. When the crowd had settled down, the mayor scanned the faces. "If there is another outburst, all spectators will be asked to leave." He turned to Israel Needham, who appeared to be the spokesman for the group, and nodded for him to continue.

Needham cleared his throat. "About the nature of your business, Miss Ashley. You state that you intend to manufacture women's garments. Could you be more specific?"

"More specific?" Sarah felt a nagging uneasiness. She could not guess what the catch was this time, but she was certain it had something to do with bloomers. Aware of the men's antagonistic eyes on her, she said, while attempting to maintain a steady voice, "It is stated quite clearly on the application. I plan to manufacture bloomer costumes, overtunics, and shirtwaister dresses."

Whispering and shifting glances brought Sarah's head around, and to her surprise, she saw Jon standing in the doorway. The shock of seeing him took her breath away. The faces around her faded. The whispers and stares receded. All she was aware of was how incredibly handsome he looked standing tall and commanding in a top hat, tan frock coat, and brown leather breeches. The coat emphasized the breadth of his shoulders, and the tight breeches made her aware of how lean his hips were . . . how powerful his thighs . . .

Gradually, it dawned on her that perhaps he, too, had come to take part in her ordeal . . .

Jon held Sarah's gaze, aware of whispers rustling through the crowd. Then he peeled off his gloves, removed his top hat, and walked through the crowd, which parted for him to pass. Scanning the faces of the councilmen, he said, "Don't let me interrupt this cozy gathering." He lowered himself into a chair at one end of the table and rested his gaze on Sarah.

Wisely, she'd worn conventional dress. He'd thought of suggesting she do so, but deciding she'd no doubt take it as meddling, he'd tossed that idea. He focused on her bonnet and the dainty bird perched atop it. Catching the worry in her eyes, he smiled his support. She flushed deeply, fanned her lashes several times, and licked her lips, leaving them shimmering and wet.

Jon fixed Israel Needham with a wry smile. "As you were saying, Commissioner . . . something about the nature of Miss Ashley's business . . ."

Needham glanced around at the other men, cleared his throat, and proceeded. "Miss Ashley, you led the council to believe you would be fashioning women's garments, yet it clearly states here that you plan to manufacture trousers."

"Bloomers," Sarah corrected.

"Is there a difference? As I see it, both accommodate a man's needs, that being to have the freedom to move about unrestricted while"—he leveled his gaze on her—"earning a living to support a family."

"You're absolutely right about that," said Sarah.

"The loose garment does allow one to move about freely, much more freely than trousers." She gave him a contrite smile. "And I do see your point completely."

The councilmen nodded to one another their minor success. For a moment, Sarah didn't respond, and Jon grew uncomfortable, suspecting she was stymied. Then he noted that she didn't waver beneath Needham's gaze: there was no frown on her brow, and in her eyes he saw triumph.

She gave Israel Needham a cynical, lopsided smile, and said with a trace of irony, "I apologize for restricting my garments solely to women. If you, or any other man on this esteemed council, would care to purchase a bloomer costume, I'd be happy to take measurements and see that you receive exactly what you want. I'll have a complete line of silks and fine wools. But, of course, if you prefer ginghams or plaids, or perhaps checks—that's quite a rage among men now—that can certainly be arranged."

Again the room filled with laughter, and Mayor Harris banged his gavel on the table until the voices died.

Jon saw the mayor's eyes flicker with amusement ... and, he thought, perhaps even admiration? But maybe Mayor Harris had no choice but to concede. His wife, Jon noted, was among Sarah's supporters.

Israel Needham's eyes narrowed as he said slowly and deliberately, "That, Miss Ashley, is not what I meant."

"I know exactly what you meant," said Sarah, her thin nostrils flaring, her eyes glittering like shards of glass. She leaned forward, fingers splaying on the table as she scanned the faces of the men. "How ready the distinguished members of this council are to raise a bugbear by turning their attention to insignificant details on my application in an attempt to embarrass me and publicly ridicule my utilitarian garments. But perhaps I should give you the benefit of the doubt and assume that your impression of what I propose to do is distorted: that you view my plans through glasses fogged by prejudice and hear my proposal through ear trumpets blocked by prejudgment! Gentlemen, I respectfully suggest that you cease these dilatory tactics and proceed with good-faith consideration of my application and the issuance of my license!"

Applause and cheers erupted, and again Mayor Harris rapped his gavel. Jon grinned widely, amazed at Sarah's capacity to survive in the face of adversity. Silence stole over the room as everyone waited for whatever would happen next. Sarah seemed relaxed now. Perhaps too relaxed.

Maybe even ... overconfident.

Jon saw the slight curve to her lips and caught the baleful look in her eyes as she waited. But he knew she hadn't won the battle yet.

Israel Needham passed the papers to Samuel Eckstein, another council member, who looked at the item to which Needham pointed with a stiff finger, nodded, and said, "The location of your building, Miss Ashley. You stated that it will be on Wharf Street, but you didn't indicate where on Wharf Street it will be."

"That's because I have no idea where on Wharf Street it will be, since I am unable to lease a building from anyone until I have my license ... a recent directive, I suspect. My plan, however, is to find a building near the waterfront. But now I suspect you'll object to that, too, for whatever reason, so perhaps you might be so kind as to give me an idea where I *will* be allowed to operate. A location some distance from Victoria and up a muddy little lane accessible only by mule should meet with your approval." She tightened her mouth and said nothing more.

Samuel Eckstein gave a short, cynical grunt, but didn't pursue the issue. When Needham whispered and pointed to another item, Eckstein nodded and said, "And your schedule for shaking rugs? You have stated only that it will be done after business hours. You must be more specific. We have to know exactly what time you intend to shake your rugs."

Sarah bristled, wondering how long the interrogation would last. She suspected it would continue until they managed to back her into a corner, at which time they would deny her license.

Well, she'd had enough.

She squared her shoulders, raised her chin, and said in a voice filled with purpose. "You gentlemen are so vain and high-minded, you have appointed yourselves as keepers of beings you hold lower than yourselves. You believe women should stifle their intellect and ignore the faculties given them by their Creator. You expect us to have no greater wish than to gossip or read, or dance and flirt in order to obtain a husband, when we would much prefer to be educated and occupy our minds with useful occupations." Gathering her carpetbag, she careened and started out of the room, aware of angry protests aimed at the councilmen from the crowd.

"*Wait!*" A man's voice brought Sarah up short.

Her anger faded, replaced by puzzlement when she looked up to see who had spoken. A shrewd-looking man, with dark, luxuriant sideburns that met under his chin, stood. Sarah recognized him at once as Mr. Babington, the lawyer in the building next to Wellington Brown's store.

Facing the councilmen, Mr. Babington said, "Miss Ashley has raised some valid points. However, the fact remains that nowhere in the city Bill of Incorporation is it stated that the mayor and council have the power to collect money from the person or property of the inhabitants for municipal purposes. Therefore, the city has no legal authority to impose a license tax at all. If Miss Ashley is not granted a license, I suggest she bring action against the city to rescind this tax. Since the city has already collected in excess of $12,000 in license taxes, possibly illegally, that raises the question of refunds, should the case be decided in her favor. In light of this, I respectfully suggest that the esteemed city council contemplate their final decision in this matter most carefully."

Mayor Harris pounded his gavel. "Mr. Babington, would you please sit down. This is not an open hearing." He turned to Sarah. "Miss Ashley, perhaps you misunderstood our motives." His gaze shifted from her to Mr. Babington and back again. "We are not your adversaries; we are only attempting to determine the suitability of your proposed business enterprise for the city of Victoria. If you'll give us a few minutes in chamber to review the papers, we will return with our decision." He nodded to the other councilmen. "Gentlemen . . . shall we adjourn to my office?"

The councilmen filed out of the room behind Mayor Harris, and ten minutes later they returned and took their seats.

Mayor Harris remained standing. "We have carefully considered your application, Miss Ashley, and we have reached an agreement. However, we are curious why you believe that women are oppressed by men. A gentleman always relinquishes his chair to a lady, she is given the best seat in the carriage, and she enjoys the warmest place in winter. Her dress costs thrice that of a man's, and with the prevailing fashion, she occupies three times as much space. It would seem, if there be any oppression, men are the ones who suffer. Yet we ask no redress for having assented to the destiny given us by our Creator: that women are to be obliged and cared for. But since you have chosen to give up these amenities and privileges, and suffer the discomforts and adversities borne by men over the ages, then we are prepared to issue a business license to you."

Sarah stood in stunned silence when she saw Jon signing the document. As she waited for her license, Mr. Babington passed a card to her. "If you need me further, Miss Ashley, please contact me at my office."

Sarah studied the card imprinted with the name David Babington, Attorney. "Perhaps I will," she said, but found herself talking to his back as he dashed out of the room.

The excitement over, the crowd quickly dispersed, and Sarah was left standing in the middle of a closed circle of Charlotte Potts, Flora and Jeremy Pickering, Elizabeth Thurman, and Esther Cromwell. Sarah looked down at the card and said to Esther, "Do you think there's anything to what he said about the license tax being illegal?"

Esther shrugged. "You'll have to ask Jon, who's coming this way right now." Bidding a quick farewell, she left, and Sarah suspected she hadn't wanted to be intercepted by her brother.

Jon nodded his regards to the group surrounding Sarah and took her arm. "If you folks will excuse Miss Ashley, she and I have some business to attend to."

As he ushered her away from the group, Sarah gave him a sharp look. "Did it ever occur to you that perhaps I don't want to be dragged away from my friends by you?"

A lazy smile crossed his suntanned face. "Of course not, because you do."

She pursed her lips. "I would say that you are

cocky and conceited, but you already know that, and it doesn't seem to matter to you."

"Right."

She stared at him. He was so impossibly arrogant. So incredibly sure of himself. She wanted to feel incensed by his haughty behavior, but the feeling wouldn't come. Instead, she found herself eyeing his attire with amusement and thinking he looked rather like a big, not so tame wolf in sheep's clothing. "Why are you all dressed up? I've never seen you wearing anything but shirts and breeches."

He smiled wryly. "I always dress for hangings."

"Then you knew what was going to happen to me today?"

"Vaguely."

"Why didn't you say something?"

A smile touched the corners of his mouth. "Would you have listened to me if I'd told you to throw in the towel because the council had no intention of issuing your license and there was no point in your even trying to get it?"

"No."

"That's why I dressed for a hanging instead."

"Sorry to disappoint you."

"Believe me, my sweet, you didn't disappoint me. The last thing I wanted was to see your lovely neck in a noose. I have other, much more interesting plans for that neck."

"Forget them."

"Never." He led her into a shadowy office that appeared to be in disuse. After shutting the door, he lifted her carpetbag out of her hands, placed it on the desk, and curved his arms around her. She braced her palms against his chest. "You're not being very discreet," she said. "I can't imagine what everyone must be thinking right now."

He laced his hands behind her waist. "Why should

they think anything more than that you're absorbed in important business with the governor? After all, you're going to be one of Victoria's merchants now, so naturally there are important governmental issues we need to discuss ... behind closed doors." He gathered her closer, forcing her to bend her arms and rest her hands against his chest.

Sarah felt the tingle of his warm breath on her forehead. "I thought you agreed not to do this sort of thing," she said, aware of the tight, breathless feeling that seemed to come whenever Jon held her.

His eyes filled with amusement. "This isn't what I agreed not to do," he said, giving her a wicked grin. "I agreed not to do this ..." His finger meandered across one breast, lingered on the ripe bud straining against the bodice of her dress, then trailed away. "But I will try to control my animal lusts long enough to enjoy one chaste kiss ... to celebrate your overwhelming victory here today."

A faint flush rose in Sarah's cheeks. Trying to force from her mind the thought of what his touch could do, she said, "Why would you want to celebrate my victory? Not too long ago, you were clearly against me."

"I have never been against *you*," he said, "only against your cause. But since you've managed to gather in your behalf an impressive group of dedicated followers—including my sister, I noticed—and you are determined to carry on with your plans in spite of my efforts to convince you otherwise, I have little choice but to step aside and give you my official sanction." He kissed her.

Sarah pulled away before the kiss could deepen. "Then you agree that a woman is equal to a man in labors, duties, honors, and offices ... and that she should be allowed to deposit her vote in the same ballot box?"

He looked at her, confused. "I never said that."

"But if you gave me your sanction, that's what you would have to mean. And you must also accept that a woman should marry out of choice, not economic necessity, and that the only fair marriage is one in which husband and wife are equal partners and lead equal lives with equal privileges and restraints."

"I don't have to agree with you to wish you well," said Jon, wondering how the conversation had taken such a dramatic turn. It seemed he still had a bit of work to do if he expected to make her understand that what she wanted was unattainable. He admired her independence to a point, but he refused to let her wear the pants—be they bloomers or otherwise. He might acknowledge that marriage was a partnership, but the burden of support fell to the husband. And that was that. And why the hell was he thinking about marriage? It had nothing to do with them. "I'm merely wishing you well," he said, "nothing more."

"But if you wish me well," Sarah pressed, "then you must be on my side."

"I don't have to be on your side to wave my white flag," he said. "Consider it a sign that I am no longer in combat with you, that I have conceded to the enemy and I'm willing to accept my punishment."

She eyed him dubiously. "You don't seem to me a man who would throw himself on the mercy of the enemy. What do you expect to gain by doing so?"

"My punishment." He gave her a dark, devious smile. "What will it be, Miss Ashley? Feverish kisses branded into my naked chest? Scalding hands blistering my bare back? Fiery lips blazing a scorching path down to my . . . path's end? Whatever you plan for me, my wicked little love, I will bear like a man." He bent close to her ear where he could nibble the soft lobe, then kissed the side of her neck, inhaling the warm fragrance of lilac.

He curved his arms around her and drew her to him. Slanting his mouth on hers and parting her lips, he touched the tip of his tongue to hers, tasting, teasing, deepening the kiss until she moaned her pleasure.

"Do you have any idea what you're doing to me right now?" he said in a ragged voice.

Sarah tipped her head back to give him access to her throat. "Yes ... ummm," she moaned. "I'm allowing you to express your animal lusts."

"No, you're not ..." Jon trailed kisses up her neck and cupped her breasts. "You're making me hard and hot and frustrated as hell." He stepped back to sit on the desk, pulling her to stand between his legs. "I have a mind to barricade the door, disrobe you, and express my animal lusts right here. And that's not exactly what I have planned for you the first time we make love."

"You talk as though it will take place," Sarah said in a wavering voice. "You already agreed that—"

"I only agreed to wait a little longer. Nothing more." He pressed her palm firmly against his arousal. "I want you, quite desperately, as you can plainly tell."

Heat rushed to Sarah's face, turning her cheeks a rosy pink. She pulled her hand from beneath his. "You must stop doing that," she said.

"My sweet, innocent little mooncalf, I can no more stop that from happening than stop the sun from rising. As long you're near me, that *will* happen."

"That's not what I meant," she said. "I meant ... what you keep doing with my hand."

"Why should I stop that? You've already admitted in more ways than one that you share my desires. I'm simply guiding you toward the next step in our relationship."

"Relationship?" Sarah stiffened. "For us, that

would be unthinkable, given your closed views about what a woman should and should not do."

"Closed views! Who gives a bloody damn about views?"

"You needn't raise your voice to me, Jon. After all, we are simply discussing the relationship between a man and a woman, which, as I said, would be unthinkable with us, given your unreasonable and inflexible views about a woman's place."

Jon tightened his jaw. "You have some harebrained idea that a man should step aside while a woman engages in all manner of enterprises, none of which seem to include keeping a home, raising a family, and tending to her husband's needs."

Sarah's eyes glowed. "And you have not listened to a word I have been saying. I never said that a woman should not be willing to keep a home, raise a family, and tend a husband. I only said that she should expect her husband to share in all of those activities so that she might pursue a business as well. And she should also expect to voice her opinion in matters of importance and not be obliged to endorse her husband's sentiments solely because he is a man and she is a woman. With close-minded views such as you possess, entering into a relationship with you would be tantamount to self-imposed slavery!"

"*Self-imposed slavery!* Is that what you feel when you're with me? Good God! Maybe you're right. Maybe we should give up the whole damned idea."

Sarah looked into his unyielding eyes and saw the hard line of his mouth. He'd be satisfied with nothing less than a conventional wife, a dutiful wife who would run the house and tend her husband's wants—someone content to be an extension of her husband.

But her philosophy simply would not allow her to be that person. But then, the subject of marriage was not an issue between them. There had been no mention of marriage—Jon had been careful to avoid that. Nor had her feelings on the subject changed.

And Jon's attitude was the very reason she never intended to give up her freedom.

"I believe this little meeting has come to an end," she said. Grabbing her carpetbag, she turned and left the room. The door slammed behind her, followed by Jon's string of expletives and something else that crashed against the door and fell to the floor.

Narrow-minded, single-minded, infuriating man!

Chapter 15

The following Monday, Sarah marched out of the office of J. D. Caravello, commission agent, Mandi close behind her. On the board walkway outside, Sarah rested her hands on her hips and glared at the closed door. "No buildings for lease, my foot! I know for a fact that there are two vacant buildings on Wharf Street and one on Yates. And I'm certain the small warehouse on Waddington Alley is also available."

"On Waddington Alley?" Mandi's eyes grew wide with apprehension.

Sarah stared at her. "What's wrong with Waddington Alley?"

"Plenty." Mandi's brows gathered in a worried frown. "You remember what Ida said 'bout the women disappearin'? Well, Wellington told me when Ah was tendin' the table this mornin' that two nights ago another woman disappeared. It happened near Waddington Alley. He said the police came 'round questionin' all the folks up and down the street, and that no one saw nothin'. He's real worried 'bout us roamin' around down here."

Sarah pursed her lips. "Well, we wouldn't have to roam around if someone would lease me a store. Obviously I'm still being manipulated by the men of this town. Maybe we *should* pack up our bags and leave."

"We can't do that!" exclaimed Mandi. "What about Miss Charlotte and Miss Elizabeth and Miss Flora, and all the other folks who are wantin' to see your business get goin'?"

"And Mr. Wellington Brown?" Sarah looked askance.

" 'Specially him." Mandi looked at Sarah in alarm. "You really aren't thinkin' of leavin' here, are you?"

"No," Sarah assured her. "We've come too far to give up now—although I suspect it would give Jon great pleasure if we did leave." She still felt angry over the quarrel they'd had in his office three days ago.

How could a man who was so perfect in every other way be so steadfast and narrow-minded when it came to the issue of rights for women? Actually, it wasn't so much that he was against rights for women. It was more that he simply didn't think the issue important. He wasn't against dress reform, either. Beyond calling her bloomer costume ridiculous, he didn't seem to mind if she wore it. And he'd certainly stepped in at the picnic in her behalf.

The fact was, Jon was unlike any man she'd ever met. And he seemed to have captured a permanent place in her heart, and in her dreams . . .

Mandi looked at her, baffled. "Why do you say the guv'nor would be pleased if you left? Seems to me like he's pretty sweet on you . . . him walkin' away from that highfalutin Windemere woman so's he could rescue you at the picnic. And comin' a-courtin' with flowers and all."

Sarah gathered her skirt and started walking down the street. "Well, perhaps he doesn't want me to leave," she said, "but he does want me to quit what I'm doing and be an ordinary woman engaged in ordinary activities ... like Mary Letitia Windemere, I suppose."

Mandi scurried along. "She is that, all right. From what Ida said, when the guv'nor was a-courtin' her, she was always flittin' over to the house doin' this and that, makin' pretty things that pleased the guv'nor."

"I really don't want to talk about her," Sarah snapped, determined to delegate thoughts of Mary Letitia Windemere and Jonathan Cromwell to a lesser position of importance in her mind. "If *you* want to stay in Victoria, we'd better turn our attentions to finding a building to lease ..."

After two hours of walking, searching, and questioning every banker, merchant, and land agent in Victoria, Sarah gave up. Every available building was either too expensive, in too bad a state of disrepair, or too far from the mercantile district. It became evident that they'd have to come up with an alternative plan.

When they stopped at a cross street for a large, ungainly produce wagon to pass, an idea came to Sarah quite suddenly. "I could lease a delivery wagon and peddle my garments along the waterfront to the prospectors' wives," she said excitedly. "Living in tents and shanties as they do, they should be most anxious to get rid of their cumbersome clothes. That way I'd be generating operating capital while waiting for a building to become available."

Mandi looked concerned. "Would we still keep the table at Wellington's store?"

Sarah gave Mandi a reassuring smile. "Yes, we'll keep the table at Wellington's store. Now, let's go see about a wagon."

At the livery, Sarah leased an elderly dray horse named Judd and a carmine-red delivery wagon with the words "Royal Pie Company" scrawled in faded gold and green letters across its tall, broad side. It was the only wagon available that came close to satisfying Sarah's needs. She'd selected it from among three others—a timeworn milk wagon with missing floorboards, a huge two-horse furniture delivery wagon, and an undertaker's wagon that had been stripped of its accessories.

Sarah packed three footlockers of bloomers, shirtwaisters, and overtunics, and she and Mandi lifted them into the pie wagon. After dropping Mandi off at Wellington Brown's store to tend the table, Sarah set out along the waterfront. As she urged old Judd onward, she pressed repeatedly on the foot-operated bell mounted under the toe board, and in a very short time a sizable crowd followed along beside her. After pulling Judd to a halt, Sarah stood and faced the women—most of them drab, tired-looking women whom she surmised were prospectors' wives.

"You're the lady in the newspaper," one woman shouted. "I heard about them things you're wearin'."

"They're called bloomers," said Sarah, turning slowly. "And yes, I'm the lady from the newspaper. I've come to relieve you of the burden of restrictive dress so you can tend to your duties in comfort. Any woman who spends more than four hours a day washing clothes, cleaning the house, and cooking should own a bloomer costume such as the one I'm wearing." She turned around slowly so that everyone could get a good look at her sturdy gray poplin bloomer outfit with its crocheted lace cuffs and collar. "You'll find bloomers especially comfortable for house duties. They can be purchased in plain fabric and unadorned, or in ginghams and calicoes fancifully trimmed with crocheting at the collar and cuffs. And the price of these attractive, utilitarian garments is within reach of every woman here."

"How much for that outfit you're wearing right now?" one woman asked.

"The complete costume, which is made of fine poplin, is two dollars if purchased without the crocheted cuffs and collar, and three dollars with the crocheted trim. But I have others of plain weave cotton for as little as one dollar and seventy-five cents."

While Sarah distributed handbills, a woman called out, "Can I get one of those outfits right now?"

Sarah smiled brightly. "Yes, you certainly can. Step over here where I can estimate your size, and I'll get you just what you want." The woman pressed her way through the gathering. Sarah scanned her briefly, then ducked into the wagon. While crouched over a trunk, sorting through the stacks of bloomers for the appropriate size, Sarah was aware of a woman's voice in the background.

". . . not only do men dictate our fashion," the woman was saying, "but they make laws that we must submit to and for which we have no redress . . ."

Sarah ceased her rummaging and listened.

No. It couldn't be. Not again . . .

". . . so if there must be rules by which the vote is cast, let the ignorant, drunken, and immoral be denied, and the intelligent, educated, sober, and moral of both men and women be given the right—"

"Josephine Cromwell!" Harriet Galbraith's voice cracked like a whip. "Your father and grandmother will certainly hear of this!"

Sarah stood abruptly. "Oh, my God!" Stepping out of the wagon, she looked over the crowd, now turned toward Harriet Galbraith and Josephine, who faced each other a short distance away. Climbing down quickly, Sarah pushed her way through the crowd, listening with helpless horror to Harriet's attack.

"It is an abomination for a woman to speak in public on any subject!" said Harriet, aghast. "If you had studied your Bible lessons, young lady, you would know that because woman was so great a sinner in the Garden of Eden, she must forever be excluded from oration and be subservient to man."

"If that is so," Josephine challenged, "then how is it that Queen Victoria sits on the throne of England ruling over men?"

For a moment, Harriet stood in disbelieving silence, too shocked to respond. Then, looking at Josephine out of the narrowed slits of her eyes, she replied, "You are an impertinent, disrespectful young woman."

"And you are nothing but an old biddy—"

"*Josephine!*" Sarah pressed her way between two women to get to Josephine. "Leave here at once!"

Josephine looked at Sarah, her face displaying a blend of hurt and chagrin. "But . . . I was only trying to help you," she said. "Why are you angry with me?"

"Because you should not be here. Why aren't you in school?"

"I *am* in school. My class is just over there"—she pointed toward the water—"on the beach. Madame Pettibeau brought us to gather driftwood."

"Then return to your class at once," Sarah demanded.

Josephine looked at Sarah, contrite. "I'll rejoin my class for you"—she glared at Harriet Galbraith—"and not because *she's* going to rat on me to my father. I still say she's an old biddy."

Harriet bristled. "You should repent for your sin of insolence," she said. "If your father was a God-fearing man, he'd thrash you for it as the Bible says he should. But then"—she fixed her icy gaze on Sarah—"he, too, has strayed from the path." She looked past Sarah, and her lips curved with an ironic smile. "Seemingly, the Lord has answered my call and sent Madame Pettibeau to administer the punishment this girl's father has neglected."

From the direction of the waterfront, a woman marched toward them, a scowl on her face, a willow stick in her hand. Josephine broke from the group and made her way toward the woman. "Madame Pettibeau—"

"Qu'est-ce que c'est?"

"I just stepped over here to—"

"Mon Dieu!" Raising her willow stick, she whacked it sharply across her own hand, then fluttered it at Josephine, who turned abruptly and left the scene.

As Josephine and Madame Pettibeau walked briskly away from the gathering, Harriet felt a surge of satisfaction. After a few moments, she turned, removing from her view the lurid sight of Dorothy's disgraceful granddaughter. Dorothy was to be pitied—the girl had been corrupted, perhaps beyond redemption.

Harriet realized she, too, was in danger of being drawn from the path and into the snare of the devil by adverse influences like Sarah Ashley. But with her dedicated and lustral mission she could feel herself growing in heavenly wisdom. Merely thinking about her calling made her eyes fill with tears of gratitude.

She studied Sarah Ashley, who was again soliciting customers for her wicked garments. She'd come seeking these wretched woman under the pretense of selling pies, luring them from propriety with her evil raiment. Next she'd have them touting carnal favors . . .

Stepping over to the wagon where a flock of poor, naive souls fondled the garments while chattering in excited voices, Harriet pointed an accusing finger. "That woman should be cast from respectable society."

The voices around her died.

Ignoring the shocked faces, Harriet continued in a voice filled with purpose, "If we could but look into the woman's mind, I'm certain we'd see vile and sinful thoughts. She has been lured by debase pleasures, and now she's luring you down the same path."

Sarah glared at Harriet Galbraith, whose malevolent gaze moved down her bloomer costume like evil, touching fingers. Deciding that she could not allow the woman to degrade her in front of these promising customers, she countered, "A woman does not break divine laws and commit grievous sin simply by reducing the unwieldy burden of present-day fashion." She was aware of sniggering talk, but she realized quickly that it was aimed at Harriet Galbraith.

Harriet's lips tightened. "You will be punished for your transgression." She glanced around at the unfriendly faces. "You will all be punished if you yield to vile temptation and wear these immoral garments."

"The dress distinctions between the genders have been made by man, not God," said Sarah. "There's no command saying that women must submit to the constrictions of corsets, tight bodices, and heavy skirts while men don comfortable garments."

The angry breath that Harriet had been holding burst forth. "That is blasphemy!"

"What is blasphemous is your demeanor," said Sarah. "You stand there draped in a cloak of respectability while all manner of caustic falsehoods spring from your tongue."

Cheers and applause swept through the crowd.

Harriet's face turned as while as a bleached bone, her lips quivered, and condemnation burned in the shadowed pits of her eyes. "Despicable woman!" She pivoted and strode off, her skirts whisking up a billow of dust.

Shifting her gaze beyond Harriet, Sarah noted a small sternwheeler docked in the direction Harriet was marching. She eyed the steamer—a fancifully decorated vessel with cherubic gargoyles, ornate wooden scrollwork, and the name *Revelation* inscribed cursively in gold letters on its stern—and wondered if it was some sort of church.

Her view was soon obstructed as enthusiastic women gathered around the wagon once again.

Forty-five minutes later, as she repacked her trunks to leave the waterfront for the day, Sarah felt elated. She'd sold more garments and collected more orders than she had ever imagined she could. But since she hadn't yet found a building from which to operate, she'd have to set up her sewing machine at the cottage and make her garments there. She only hoped Flora had been serious about sewing for her, because several of the women who'd ordered bloomer costumes would soon be moving on to the goldfields with their husbands, and she had little time to fill the orders.

Smiling with satisfaction, she'd just closed the last trunk and moved to the box to take the reins when she spotted Jon's coach heading toward her, the fast clip of the horses suggesting that he had recently heard from either Harriet Galbraith or Madame Pettibeau.

He jumped out of the coach and fixed stormy eyes on Sarah. "Where is she?"

Sarah climbed down from the wagon. "Where is who?"

He pinned her with a steely gaze. "You know damned well who. Harriet Galbraith just paid a surprise visit to my office. Where is Josephine?"

Sarah raised her hand in protest. "Before you say

anything more, Jon, I must emphasize that you have undoubtedly received from Harriet Galbraith a very distorted picture of what happened."

"The hell I have! Given the fact that you *are* indeed peddling those bloody bloomers from a pie wagon, I believe I've received a very accurate picture. Now, where is Josephine?"

"I suppose she's with her classmates."

"You suppose! You mean you don't know?"

"Stop yelling!"

"Do you know how many women have disappeared from here? Do you have any idea? Ten! That's how many! Ten women have been shanghaied to who-knows-bloody-hell-where, and you don't even know where Josephine is? You were with her not more than an hour ago."

"Calm down, Jon. Josephine rejoined her classmates. And it's not nearly as bad as you've been led to believe. Josephine simply stepped over here for a few moments to see what I was doing. You're really making far too much of it."

"Did Josephine not stand here with you while delivering a lecture on giving women the right to vote?"

"Well, yes, actually she did . . . sort of. That is, she mentioned something about it."

"*Mentioned it!* According to Harriet Galbraith, she delivered a damned sermon on it!"

"Calm down. Josephine did not give a sermon. She merely made a few passing comments on the subject."

"I'll just bet she did. And if you didn't stop her from speaking in public, then I assume you encouraged her."

"I did neither. I had no idea she was here until I heard her from inside my wagon. And I didn't have any idea it was she until I heard Harriet Galbraith berating her."

"And did Josephine not speak with total disrespect to Mrs. Galbraith?"

"For heaven's sake," Sarah said irritably. "You know how Harriet Galbraith is. She exaggerates."

"Did Josephine call her an old biddy?"

"Harriet Galbraith *is* an old biddy."

"That's beside the point."

"Frankly," said Sarah, "I think Josephine handled herself rather well. The crowd was certainly amused. But really, you've overblown the incident—which didn't last more than a couple of minutes when Madame Pettibeau came for Josephine—"

"Madame Pettibeau!"

"Will you stop yelling as if I were deaf!"

Jon sucked in a breath, then said in a tight voice, "Madame Pettibeau has strict rules regarding the young women at the seminary. If Josephine violated those rules, she could be asked to leave."

"Well, what Josephine did hardly warrants expulsion from school. Believe me, there's nothing to worry about. It was a very trifling, insignificant incident that has undoubtedly been forgotten by now. And I did not encourage Josephine in any way. As I said before, she's an independent and determined young woman. You should feel proud of her, and of the strength of her convictions. Were she a man, she'd make an excellent governor."

Jon cast her a sidelong glance, and Sarah was certain she saw laughter flicker across his features. "As for what you call an incident," he said, "I hope that's what it was, because if it wasn't, Josephine would not be the first student to be expelled from Madame Pettibeau's for ill conduct."

Sarah rested her fingers lightly on Jon's arm. "I'm

certain it has been forgotten," she reassured him.
"Now stop worrying."

Jon gazed off toward the bay and released an extended sigh. "Sometimes I feel at such a loss as to how to handle the girls. They're each so different: Josephine so strong-willed and assertive, and Louella quite the opposite."

"Like her mother?" said Sarah.

Jon's eyes narrowed with disdain. "No, she is not like her mother." He reached in his pocket for a cigarette and shoved it between his lips. Striking a match against the side of the wagon, he cupped his hand around the flame, drew heavily, and exhaled a plume of blue smoke.

A long silence hung.

Sarah noted the sullen slant of his lips as they closed around the cigarette, the tension in his features as he looked off in the distance.

So . . . what Esther had implied was true. Jon's wife had committed adultery. And he was still bitter.

Undoubtedly why he avoided marriage.

Of course, he was quick to entice Sarah into having a relationship with him, with never a mention of marriage. But then, in no uncertain terms, she had expressed her adverse feelings on the subject as well, and that would, of course, preclude discussing it . . .

While she stared indifferently at a group of ragtag men leaning against several water barrels on the wharf, the memory of a portrait of a golden-haired women with embroidery clasped in her hands swam into Sarah's mind in a blur of dark, macabre light. Such cold eyes. One would think the artist might have softened them a bit. But perhaps he had . . .

"What was she like?" Sarah asked, curious about the woman with whom Jon had fathered two children.

Jon flicked the ashes from the cigarette with his

thumb. "She was a beautiful, charming, well-bred bitch." He exhaled another plume of smoke.

Sarah was shocked by his choice of words.

"Why did you marry her?"

"Because I was a fool."

"Then why did you stay with her?"

"Because she was the mother of my daughters."

"Yes, I suppose that would be a reason to stay," she said inanely, since it was evident he didn't want to discuss his dead wife.

After another long pause, Jon flipped the cigarette into the street and said, "I don't want you coming to the waterfront anymore."

"What do you mean, *you* don't want me coming?" She planted her hands on her hips. "You cannot tell me what I can and cannot do. That is precisely what I was trying to point out to you after the city council meeting."

"Well, *someone* had better tell you what to do, or you're apt to get yourself kidnapped."

"That's ridiculous," she said. "I don't plan to come here at night. And I hardly think I'd be kidnapped in broad daylight with so many people around."

"That's where you're wrong." His face darkened. "Just yesterday another woman disappeared . . . during the day. She left her house to meet someone on the waterfront and never returned. That's ten women in less than two months."

"Was she a . . . ?"

"Prostitute? No, she worked in the dance hall, but not as a prostitute. So it's not just the prostitutes anymore. That's why I was so concerned about Josephine."

"Well, I had nothing to do with that."

"Besides the fact that she's in awe of you and will do anything for you."

"That's just not so. And I refuse to stand here defending myself for something over which I had no control. And now, for the very reasons I walked out of the room the other day, I would like you to leave."

Jon lapsed into a thoughtful silence. "Well, I've been thinking about that." Thinking, hell! He'd been obsessed with it. The fact was, Sarah had swept him off his feet just like Caroline had. And like Caroline, she, too, renounced a woman's place in the home. Although their motives were disparate, the result was the same: Sarah diminished a woman's importance in the home; Caroline had made a mockery of it by committing adultery.

But . . . there *were* other differences.

Sarah was perceptive and intelligent and passionately altruistic compared to Caroline's taxing self-indulgence; and Sarah was candid and undesigning and deeply intense compared to Caroline's frivolous superficiality.

Caroline would have considered Sarah boorish and uncultured. But he found her charming . . .

He saw the guarded yet confused look in her eyes. The look of someone about to flee, yet not quite able. "I think we need to talk about what happened," he said. He took her hand, and she didn't protest as he drew her around behind her wagon, out of view of his coachman.

He gathered her against him. "I've missed holding you in my arms. I've missed doing this . . ." He curved his finger under her chin, tipped her face up, and covered her mouth with his in a long, lingering kiss.

Sarah savored the feel of being in Jon's arms again, and for the moment she couldn't bring herself to move away. Her eyelids drifted shut and her heart began to thud as she felt the solid force of his mouth on hers, the hot smokiness of his tongue caressing hers. He slid his hand down to the small of her back and splayed his fingers, pressing her against him. His warm breath filled her mouth, sending her senses reeling, until she felt light-headed and dazed and immersed in him, and she had to cling to him while her world spun ... and spun ... and spun ...

Gradually, her senses sharpened again. She opened her eyes, braced her legs to keep from faltering, and looked up at Jon. "Please, not here," she said, pulling his arms from around her. "Harriet Galbraith might see us. She was just over there." She pointed toward the *Revelation*, and to her shock saw Hollis and Tyler standing on the prow talking to Reverend Galbraith. She hadn't heard from them since the day Mandi had found the note impaled on the door, and seeing them now made her stomach knot.

Jon followed her gaze. His jaw tightened. "What the hell are those bloody bastards up to now?"

"I'm sure I have no idea."

His eyes smoldered. "Well, the *Revelation* should be heading up the Fraser any day now. Maybe they took what I said to heart and will go with it to the goldfields."

Sarah stared at the ornately trimmed steamer. "The *Revelation* goes to the goldfields?"

"It's a mission ship," said Jon. "Reverend Galbraith preaches to the prospectors."

Sarah seethed as she looked at Hollis and Harriet Galbraith, who had now joined the group. "Good riddance to the lot of them," she said. She eyed the spiteful old woman, visualizing her pitiless face as it had been during their confrontation earlier. It was hard to imagine that someone as intelligent as Lady Cromwell could actually like the woman. She glanced at Jon. "What I don't understand is how your mother can be friends with Harriet Galbraith."

Jon shrugged. "Harriet is solicitous of her ... tells her what she wants to hear. And my mother is impressed by the fact that Harriet's a woman of strong religious conviction."

"Strong religious conviction! She's a fanatic! Maybe the boat will run aground and they'll be forced to remain in the goldfields permanently."

Jon smiled. "Now there's an entertaining thought. It would certainly cut down on the amount of gossip around here. Meanwhile, I'll hope nothing comes of Josephine's shabby conduct today."

Sarah gave him a blithe, confident smile. "I'm certain nothing *will* come of it," she said. "So you can relax. Meanwhile, I must get started on my orders."

He tipped her chin up and kissed her lightly. "I have to go to Westminster for a few days," he said, "but as soon as I get back, I'll be over to see you. We need to talk . . . and other things."

"No!" she said quickly. If he came to her with roses and kisses and silly little words of endearment, there was no question how she'd respond. The mere thought of what could happen sent chills of trepidation racing up her spine and hot waves of desire settling in her loins. She felt her face turning crimson.

A full smile broke across his face. "Yes," he said. "I *will* be over." He squeezed her hand and left.

"No . . ." she called after him, wondering desperately how she could prevent him from coming. But he only waved and smiled and shook his head, and she knew there was no way she could stop him. He was a man who went after what he wanted. And he'd made it clear. He wanted her.

Chapter 16

Josephine hastily tucked *Madame Bovary* under her mattress as the sound of footsteps in the hallway drew closer. Quickly, she reached for the piece of embroidery she'd been working on during the past week. Ever since she'd started reading about the shockingly exciting affair of Madame Bovary, painstakingly in the French she'd learned at Madame Pettibeau's, her progress on the embroidery had almost ceased. At least the book made the hours of her after-school confinement pass more quickly.

Madame Pettibeau had wasted no chance telling her father about what had happened on the waterfront—which was most unfortunate. One more day and her father would have been away on business. And that old shrew, Harriet Galbraith, had scurried to inform both her father and her grandmother.

In only nine days she'd be able to resume her after-school activities—a small price to pay for the excitement she'd felt on addressing the women at the waterfront about having the right to vote.

Glancing up from her embroidery, she saw Louella standing in the doorway, hands behind her back, an excited look on her face—the portent of another of Louella's secrets. Louella looked up and down the hallway before stepping into the room. "I'll tell you something if you promise you won't tell Papa or Grandmother."

Josephine shrugged. "I won't tell. What is it?"

Louella tiptoed over to the bed, her hands behind her back. "Millie O'Shaunessey asked me to go over to her house, and I told her I would."

Josephine looked at Louella with alarm. "You can't go there," she said. "Her father's a drunkard. And besides, Papa has forbidden you to go." She realized there were other things about Mr. O'Shaunessey that Louella obviously wasn't aware of: that he beat his wife, and that he'd taken improper liberties with Millie—although she wasn't sure exactly what that meant. She'd only heard it from Jenny Barker, who had heard it from Emily Norton. But whatever it was, it was dreadfully bad.

Louella's eyes darkened. "Millie's father is not a drunkard," she countered. "Millie says he only drinks because he has a bad leg and it sometimes hurts."

Josephine started to tell Louella about the improper liberties, but deciding that being an imbiber was probably worse, she focused on that issue instead. "Mr. O'Shaunessey hurt his leg falling down the stairs of a saloon. Everybody knows that. And everybody also knows he's a drunkard."

"Well, they're wrong," Louella insisted. "And I *am* going to visit Millie. I plan to tell Ida that I'm going over to see Clarissa, so if Papa or Grandmother should ask where I am, you tell them the same thing."

Josephine gave Louella a sharp look. "Millie's father *is* a drunkard, even if you don't think so. Besides, if you go near the waterfront where Millie lives, you might get kidnapped like those other women."

"No, I won't. I heard Ida tell Esther that all the

women were bad women and that so far no respectable women have disappeared. So I'm not worried."

"Well, if you go, I'm going to tell Papa, because you shouldn't be over there."

Louella shot Josephine a smoldering look. "You promised you wouldn't tell."

"I did not. I *said* I wouldn't tell. I didn't promise."

Louella pressed her lips into an angry slash. "Well, if you tell, I'll show Papa this." She held Josephine's scrapbook just out of Josephine's reach.

"Give me that, you sneaky little snake." Josephine rushed after Louella.

Louella darted around the bed. "Not unless you promise you won't tell about my going to Millie's."

Ignoring Louella's plea, Josephine jumped onto the bed and marched across the mattress in bouncing strides, hoping to corner Louella. But Louella ducked under Josephine's arm. Panic-stricken at the thought that her precious scrapbook might fall into the wrong hands, Josephine grabbed Louella's arm, ripping her sleeve. "You know what Papa said about going through my things. Give me my scrapbook or I'll—"

Louella darted around the bed. "You'll what? Tell Papa that I found it? If you want it back, you'd better promise you won't tell on me, or I'll give it to Papa and you'll never see it again."

"You will not!" Josephine lunged after Louella, who scurried over the bed, jumped down, and rushed for the hall, meeting her grandmother headlong in the doorway.

Dorothy Cromwell's eyes shifted between the girls. "What on earth is going on?" She noted that Louella was holding something behind her back. "What is that?"

"Nothing," said Louella.

Dorothy held out her hand. "May I please have it?"

"No!" exclaimed Louella. Then her face went ashen and her lips quivered. "I mean ... it's really nothing."

Shocked, Dorothy stared at Louella. It was not like her to be disobedient. Obviously, whatever she held was vital—the girls had been engaged in a most unladylike fracas moments before. And the sleeve of Louella's dress was torn quite raggedly. "Must I call your father?"

"He's home?"

"Yes, he just walked in the door. And this is a most unpleasant way to greet him, after being away all week. Now, the book, please."

Louella handed her the book, shot a brief, penitent glance toward Josephine, then hung her head.

Dorothy opened what was obviously a scrapbook and stared, flabbergasted, at what was pasted on the pages. "I assume this is yours, Josephine?"

The girl squared her shoulders. "Yes, ma'am."

Dorothy paged through the scrapbook, scanning the clippings, then closed the cover and tucked the scrapbook under her arm.

"What are you going to do with it?" asked Josephine, her brow gathering in a worried frown.

"I'll give it to your father and let him decide," Dorothy replied, feeling that it would be best for Jonathan to handle this matter. But she, of course, would counsel him beforehand about the impropriety of such tomfoolery on the part of a young lady, particularly the governor's daughter. "Louella, go change your dress. And Josephine, I suggest you work harder on your stitchery. It's progressing dreadfully slowly."

"Yes, ma'am," replied Josephine. She lowered herself resignedly to the bed and picked up her embroidery.

Dorothy closed the door and walked slowly down

the hall, her eyes moving with curiosity over the clippings. Obviously, the book belonged to Sarah Ashley, and she'd given it to Josephine to read—undoubtedly, it was the reason that Josephine had taken it upon herself to do what she'd done at the waterfront. Well, Jon would hear of this immediately. Esther, too. Somehow, they must all band together to stop Josephine's insufferable behavior.

After sending Ida to summon Jon and Esther, Dorothy waited for them in her chambers. Esther was the first to arrive. "You wanted to see me, Mother?" she asked, appearing in the doorway wearing a pair of black bloomers and a blue gingham overtunic with black lace cuffs.

Dorothy stared in shocked surprise. "Go and remove those trousers at once!"

"No, Mother, I will not," replied Esther. "They are practical and comfortable. I can move about unrestricted like this." She squatted to a crouch, rose onto her toes, and stooped several times. "And I don't have to wear a corset or drag around layers of petticoats. Besides, I'm only wearing my bloomer costume in the privacy of our home."

Dorothy looked at Esther, flabbergasted. Why . . . she had openly defied her own mother! Mortified at the almost unthinkable realization that her own daughter had undertaken the same audacious behavior as her granddaughter, and feeling light-headed over that awareness, she snapped open her fan and fluttered it furiously. "Those trousers—"

"Bloomers."

Dorothy clamped her bottom lip between her teeth to stop its trembling. For the moment, she could not find the words to express her horror at Esther's inexcusable demeanor. "That garment you are wearing is obscene, and I insist you change your clothes at once."

"I am long beyond childhood, Mother, and quite capable of making my own decisions. And I choose to wear bloomers in the privacy of our home."

Dorothy recognized Esther's self-assured tone as an echo of Sarah Ashley. "Has everyone in this house been bedeviled by that Ashley woman?"

"Oh for pity's sake!" said Esther. "Now you sound like Harriet Galbraith. Sarah has only opened our eyes to other options. And although you refuse to recognize it, she has also opened Jon's eyes to other options."

"I hope you're not implying what I think you're implying," said Dorothy, her lips quivering in dismay.

"I mean exactly that," said Esther. "Mary Letitia Windemere may be your choice of a wife for Jon, but the simple fact is that Jon has his eyes on—"

"Did someone mention my name?" Jon strolled into the room, smiling as he regarded Esther's bloomer costume. He'd never expected her actually to wear one. And he sure as hell never thought he'd see the day she'd stand up to their mother and hold her ground. But moments before, he'd heard her most definitely hold her ground. Somehow, by wearing that silly bloomer outfit, she'd also gained courage. He rather liked that in Esther—she'd been under the domination of their mother for far too long.

Esther returned his smile, and in her eyes he saw the sharp glint of chicanery. "I was just telling Mother that Sarah has opened our eyes to other options," she said. "Don't you agree?"

Jon contemplated Esther's remark. Sarah had indeed opened his eyes to other options. He was seriously considering asking her to become his mistress. But he could not reconcile himself to the fact that she was everything a mistress should *not* be—headstrong, independent, in no way subservient. That she didn't like cooking or stitchery or the other little trifles most women enjoyed was not an issue, because he knew that, once initiated into the rites of womanhood, she would attend to another, infinitely more important duty most satisfactorily.

Dorothy offered him the opened scrapbook. "Is this the sort of literature you want your daughter to read?"

Jon took the book and scanned the clippings, surprised at how meticulously they had been pasted. "Would you prefer she read *Madame Bovary*?" he asked and looked up to find his mother's face flushed. "Don't look so surprised, Mother. Esther and I know you have the book hidden around here somewhere. We even knew when you were reading it."

Dorothy flipped her fan back and forth. "I merely perused it to learn what all the hubbub was about. But that has nothing to do with your daughter's recent and very unacceptable behavior. Not only has Josephine been severely reprimanded by Madame Pettibeau for taking part in that disgraceful woman's assemblage—"

"It was not an assemblage," Jon corrected, smiling when he realized he was actually defending Josephine. "It was a small gathering of women interested in buying garments."

Dorothy slapped the fan against the folds of her gown. "That's irrelevant! The fact is, this scrapbook, which has unquestionably influenced Josephine's absurd fancies, was given to her by Miss Ashley, who is therefore responsible for your daughter's audacious conduct. And I trust you'll confront Josephine about the book and take appropriate disciplinary action."

"I scarcely see how Josephine's reading a scrapbook warrants further disciplinary action," said Jon. "She's already been confined to her room for a week now, and she still has another week to go. I can hardly keep her there indefinitely."

"Well, it's imperative that you do something at once to curb her brazen ways. And I should also hope that you'd confront Miss Ashley about sharing with Josephine such rubbish as I find in this scrapbook."

Jon closed the book and tucked it under his arm.

Yes, he would most definitely confront Sarah. Until now, she'd almost convinced him that she hadn't attempted to influence Josephine with her liberal philosophy when, in fact, she had been doing exactly that . . . methodically and furtively.

Following the confrontation about Josephine, and after he and Sarah had a little talk about their opposing views on what a woman should or should not do—approaching it with tenderness, understanding, and finesse—he had something else in store for Miss Sarah Ashley from San Francisco.

Ah, yes . . . what he had in store for her . . .

Chapter 17

⟨⟨⟨∽◯◯∽⟩⟩⟩

The indecent thoughts were back. Just thinking of Jon's return brought heat rushing up Sarah's face and a vision of Jon doing all those things he'd described. She added her own touches, too ... things like stretching out naked on the bed while he looked at her. All of her. And she wouldn't try to cover herself. She'd just lie there staring dreamily up at him and smiling, while he feasted his eyes on her bare breasts, or flicked the tip of his tongue over her ... Oh, my goodness!

She set the scissors down and dabbed her brow and cheeks with a swatch of poplin. Picking up the scissors again, she continued cutting out the pattern.

And then Jon would move his hand down her tummy to where her thighs joined, and with his fingers, he'd do what he'd done in the carriage ...

The insistent ache started again. She blotted her damp forehead with the back of her hand and attempted to finish cutting the pattern. Her hand paused.

And Jon's lips would suckle her toes ... each one slowly while she lay stretched out naked to his view. Then his lips would begin making their way up her calf, over her knee ... along her thigh ...

She shook the scissors from her fingers, loosened

261

several buttons of her overtunic, and fanned her face with the poplin. Today, Jon was supposed to get back from New Westminster, and fighting him off was the farthest thing from her mind.

A carriage rumbled to a halt out front. "Jon!"

She dashed to the window and saw Mandi climbing out of Wellington Brown's phaeton. She appeared concerned. Sarah met her on the porch. "Is something wrong?"

"There sho' is," said Mandi, breathless. "Wellington heard some men talkin' about smuggling rum, and he heard them say your name."

Sarah stepped back to let Mandi pass. "Who were they?"

Mandi shrugged. "Wellington didn't know. He'd never seen 'em before."

"Well, there's no reason why my name should be linked with smugglers. Wellington must have heard wrong."

"No, he didn't," Mandi insisted. "He was in the shed behind the store and he heard the men talkin'. They said your name all right . . . real clear. You'd best tell the guv'nor . . . and the police."

"I'm certain I'm in no danger of being accosted by smugglers," said Sarah, suspecting that Mandi had misinterpreted or misconstrued what Wellington had relayed to her. "But if it'll relieve your mind, I'll mention it to Jon. Meanwhile, you'd best get on back and tend the display table. Have you made any more sales or taken any orders?"

Mandi hesitated. "Ah sold two shirtwaisters earlier."

"Splendid," said Sarah. "Now get back to the store so Wellington won't have to tend the table. He's kind enough to let us use his place, but we mustn't take advantage."

Mandi started for the door, then paused. "About

those shirtwaisters Ah sold," she said, turning to face Sarah.

"Yes, what about them?" Sarah noted that Mandi's hands were toying restlessly with the folds of her skirt.

Mandi shrugged. "Wellington bought them . . . for me."

"Well, you simply cannot accept them," said Sarah. "He's trying to buy your favors. If you allow him to do that, you'll be nothing more to him than his kept woman. And you deserve much more."

"Ah'd never be his kept woman." Mandi's lips curved. "There's something Ah've been meanin' to tell you."

Sarah looked closely at Mandi. She was certain she'd seen her face flush. "Are you blushing?" she asked.

Mandi patted her cheeks and gave Sarah a wide smile. "Ah 'spect Ah am. Ah do that whenever Ah think about Wellington. And he's on my mind most of the time, now that . . . we's gettin' married."

"You're what?!"

"Gettin' married. It all happened so fast, what with you runnin' 'round tryin' to get your business started and me over at Wellington's tendin' the table. Well . . . Ah just didn't get the chance to tell you. But it's gonna happen all right. We's gettin' married in two weeks. That's why Ah didn't come home last night. He's a good man, and Ah know he'll do right by me. And he sez Ah don't even have to work . . . that all Ah have to do is stay home and have his babies and take care of his house."

"That's what you want? Just to stay home and have babies and keep house?"

"Sho' that's what Ah want," replied Mandi. "You's the one who wants to do all the business things. Me,

Ah just want to have Wellington's babies and keep his house."

When Sarah had digested Mandi's news, she gave her a hug. "Well, if that's what you really want, then I hope you and Wellington will be very happy."

"We already is." Mandi blushed again. "And everything Ah thought 'bout what happens when folks do the things that married folks do . . . Well, it's not like Ah thought at all."

"Really?" said Sarah, trying to appear unschooled.

"No, it's like . . . well, things poppin' and cracklin' inside, and funny noises goin' off in your head. Ah sho' hope you find out someday. It's real special."

"I'm sure it is," said Sarah, having a vague idea now what Mandi meant.

Mandi's eyes grew moist with happy tears. "Ah sho' do love that man," she said dreamily.

Sarah squeezed her hands. "Yes, I can see you do."

Mandi gave her a contrite smile. "And Ah'll be back whenever you want to fix your hair or do some sewin'—that is, if Wellington don't mind."

"I'd like that," said Sarah.

"Well, Ah guess Ah'd best get on back. Ah'm helpin' him move things around the house so's Ah can get all my things in. And, Miss Sarah?"

"Yes, Mandi?"

"Will you help me with my weddin' dress? Wellington wants to have a proper weddin' and all, and Ah want to do him proud."

"We'll make a dress that will knock his socks off."

Mandi giggled behind her hand and flushed. "It's not his socks Ah intend to knock off." And she giggled again.

After they discussed Mandi's dress and other wedding plans, Mandi rushed off, eager to get back to the store and Wellington. Sarah tried to adjust to the idea of Mandi as a married woman. Strangely, as she contemplated Mandi's bright face and radiant smile, she felt a twinge of envy. Not that Mandi was to be married, but that she was able to trust a man enough to take that irrevocable step. There had been no apprehension or uncertainty or doubt evident on Mandi's face. Hers had been the face of a woman who knew precisely and absolutely what she wanted.

With thoughts of Mandi's new life foremost in her mind, Sarah continued cutting out the material for her first three orders—bloomer costumes of gray poplin like the one she'd worn to the waterfront, but without the crocheted lace on the cuffs. If she worked diligently, she could complete the costumes and deliver them to her customers by the first of the week, as promised.

And she would *not* allow indecent thoughts to creep into her mind again. She would not even think about Jon, or about toes, or about Jon's lips moving up her leg to her . . .

A tapping at the kitchen window shattered the risqué fantasy that came next. She saw Josephine peering through the glass, and she met her at the back door. "What on earth are you doing here now? It's almost dark, and you shouldn't be out this late."

Josephine rushed through the door. "They've taken my scrapbook," she cried, her eyes glowing with rage. "If they don't give it back, I'll positively leave home."

"Don't talk like that," said Sarah. "Who are *they*?"

"Papa and Grandmother," Josephine replied. "And I *will* leave. They had no right to take it. Can you ask Papa to give it back? He'll listen to you. And Grandmother will do what he says. Please! I simply must have my scrapbook."

"I cannot intervene between you and your father," said Sarah, a rush of hot pleasure igniting her cheeks when she realized Jon was really back in town. "I fear I have caused quite enough problems between the two of you already."

Josephine's brows lowered over pleading eyes. "But can't you just kind of . . . mention it?"

"Well, I suppose I could do that," said Sarah, feeling uneasy as soon as she'd said the words.

Josephine smiled brightly. "You're the only person in the whole world who understands me," she said, "and I do so wish you'd move back to our house."

"You know that's impossible."

"Why? Because of what Grandmother thinks of you?"

"No, that has nothing to do with it," said Sarah, bending over the table to pin a tissue cuff onto the poplin. "I cannot live in your father's house simply because you want me to. I'm not family."

"But you could be, if you married Papa."

Sarah laughed nervously. "Whatever gave you such a silly notion?" she asked, jabbing a pin through the pattern with shaking fingers.

"Papa did."

Sarah let out a sharp cry as the pin pricked her thumb. She sucked her finger a bit longer than necessary while collecting herself, then asked lightly, while her heart beat a staccato rhythm, "Your father said something to you about wanting to . . . marry me?"

"Well, Papa didn't really say anything," Josephine admitted. "But he does want to. Aunt Esther says so . . . just that he doesn't know it yet."

Sarah gave her a tight smile. "Well, regardless of what your aunt says, marrying your father is *completely* out of the question. He has been the source of all my problems since I arrived, and I have caused him grief as well. So the idea that he wants to marry me is preposterous," she emphasized, more for herself than for Josephine. The fact was, Jon showed no signs of deviating from his rigid views of what a woman's role must be, nor did he appear inclined to change his biased view of marriage. Though for her, the idea wasn't quite as unsavory as it had seemed in the past. "I suspect he'd rather see me return to San Francisco."

"No, he surely doesn't want that," said Josephine. "Aunt Esther said Papa has passion in his eyes for you ... at least I heard her talking with Ida about that after you wore your fancy green gown with the front so low. So if Papa has passion in his eyes for you, he must want to marry you."

Sarah let out a short, mortified laugh. "Just because a man feels that way about a woman does not necessarily mean he wants to marry her." Her heart beat erratically, and perspiration dampened her brow.

"I know that," Josephine said, quite worldly. "But the way I see it, if Papa doesn't want to marry you, then you could have an affair with him—just like Madame Bovary—and he could keep you as his mistress here in this cottage and I could come and see you all the time."

Thoughts of toes and thighs and feverish lips brought heat rushing to Sarah's cheeks. She unfastened another button on her overtunic and fanned her lapel. "But Madame Bovary took her own life after she had the affair, so that was not such a good idea," she said, trying to keep her voice steady, surprised that Josephine had managed to get her hands on the risqué book.

Josephine pursed her lips. "But if Papa has passion in his eyes for you—"

"Josephine!" Sarah snapped, deciding she'd heard enough from this sixteen-year-old, who was bringing far too many pointed thoughts to her own feverish mind. "I'm certain your aunt misread your father's ... feelings. He's simply not that kind of man." She blushed again, knowing he was indeed the kind of man who would suckle a woman's toes and . . . other things. "Now, I don't want to hear you talking like this—"

Hearing the thrum of hoofbeats, Sarah looked out the window and saw Jon reining to a halt and dismounting. "Here's your father now," she said, her heart beating wildly as the indecent thoughts seemed to overwhelm her. She felt thankful for Josephine's presence, which would preclude allowing to happen what Sarah knew would happen if she and Jon were alone in the cottage. "Perhaps we can talk to him together about your scrapbook."

"No!" Josephine rushed for the back door. "I mean . . . I'm not supposed to be here. I'm not even supposed to be out of my room. Papa won't know I was here unless you say something. You won't say anything, will you?"

"I cannot lie to your father, Josephine," said Sarah, panicked at the thought of facing Jon alone.

"Please . . . I promise I won't leave my room again. I'll even stay an extra day to make up for this one if you won't say anything." She backed out of the door. "And I'll go directly to my room." She rushed for her horse.

Moments later, Sarah heard Jon's knock. It was more forceful that she'd expected, and she wondered if he'd already discovered Josephine missing and suspected she was there. Drawing in a full breath and letting it out slowly, Sarah planted a smile on her lips and opened the door. Her smile faded as she noted first the scowl on Jon's face, then the broad chest beneath a half-opened shirt . . . and smooth, sinewy forearms exposed by rolled-back sleeves . . . and large sun-bronzed fingers clutching the scrapbook. Managing a half-smile, she said, "You're back!"

He moved past her, turned, and pinned her with a steely gaze. "This, I believe, is yours."

Sarah stared at Josephine's scrapbook, then looked into eyes that, even in anger, set her heart fluttering and sent a fiery warmth coursing through her . . . and brought to mind those menacing, indecent thoughts.

Toes . . . Naked thighs . . . Bare breasts . . . His tongue flicking over her . . .

She licked her lips. "Why do you think that belongs to me?"

"Why would I *not* think that?" His eyes sharpened. "Who else would it belong to?"

She noted the pulse throbbing in his neck and wondered if it was because he was angry or because he was having the same reaction to her that she was having to him: a tightness in the chest that made it hard to breathe, a heart that felt as if it would burst, a sultry, aching heat that demanded release—an inescapable reminder that he was a man, and she was a woman, and together that release would come. There was also an unmistakable bulge in his breeches. "The book belongs to Josephine," she said in a wavering voice, wiping her damp palms on her overtunic. "She's been pasting clippings in it for over a year now."

Jon's jaw tightened, and moisture glistened on his brow. "You really don't expect me to believe that, do you? Half the damned clippings are from New York!"

"That's because they came from New York . . . and from Mrs. Dewig-Gertz," she said, peering into eyes that no longer smoldered with anger, but gleamed with something else . . . something that made her want him to do all the things he'd said he'd do . . . now. Her nostrils flared to ease her heavy breathing, and she again wiped her damp palms on her tunic. He'd caught the gesture, she knew, because one corner of his mouth tipped slightly, and the fire in his eyes burned brighter. In spite of his anger, she knew he wanted her. And he wanted her now.

The ache intensified . . .

Licking her dry lips, she focused on the issue and said, "Mrs. Dewig-Gertz passes her discarded clippings to Josephine. As you can see, Josephine has carefully arranged them in a very complete album. You simply refuse to believe that you have raised a daughter with a mind and will of her own—a very strong will, I might add."

Jon thumped the book against his palm. "She didn't get the scrapbook from you." It was a statement.

"No, not from me." When he said nothing, Sarah asked, "What do you intend to do with it?"

Jon set his jaw. "I don't know yet."

"Well, you should give it back," she said, wondering how long it would be until he took her in his arms. She wanted him to. God, how she wanted him to. "I know it would be admitting you're wrong— which seems to be difficult for you to do—but you *are* wrong. The scrapbook belongs to Josephine. She's worked hard to compile the clippings, she's strong in her beliefs, and she has a right to them, even if you don't agree with her. Don't deny her what's rightfully hers . . . what means so much to her."

Jon thumped the book against his palm once more. "I'll think about it." He tossed the book on the table and looked at her. His eyes rested on her breasts, remained there for a few moments, then moved up to her face.

Sarah toyed with the button at her cleavage, the button beneath the open neck of her overtunic. Why didn't he take her in his arms? Why did he just stand there staring at her with that predatory gleam in his eyes and that hungry look about his mouth, as if he were about to devour her? His burning gaze made her hot and eager and wishing for him to tear off her clothes and take her. She wanted him to take her now. On the floor where she stood. Not slowly as he'd described, but urgently ... lustfully ...

She drew in a labored breath and ran the tip of her tongue along her dry lips. "Well ... while you're thinking about what to do with the scrapbook, I have some good news," she said to break the silence, a silence—she noted from the feral curve of Jon's lips—that he seemed to be taking great delight in prolonging. "Mandi and Wellington are getting married."

"I know."

"You do?" She felt a twinge of jealousy that Jon had learned the news before she had. "How did you find out?"

"Wellington told me when I went looking for you."

"Did he tell you anything else?"

"Like what?"

"Anything about some men talking?"

"No." His eyes feasted on her breasts again, making her heart thud harder. "What did Wellington hear?"

"It may not be anything, really—Mandi has a way of confusing things, or twisting the truth—so I don't take seriously much of what she says, especially if she's relaying something she heard from someone else, in this case, Wellington." She realized she was running on a bit, but Jon's pointed stare was driving her wild.

His smile was sly, cunning. "What did she hear?"

Sarah gave a short, nervous laugh. "It's so far-fetched it's hardly worth mentioning ..."

He cocked a dark brow. "I'm listening."

"Yes ... well ..."

Sarah relayed what Mandi had told her, and when

she'd finished, Jon said, "I want you to stay away from the waterfront."

"That's all well and good for you to say," Sarah replied, realizing that Jon had moved closer, yet not knowing when he'd done so. "But since my place of business happens to be a pie wagon—because no one will lease a store to me—and my customers are women on the waterfront, I have no choice."

"Bloody hell, woman, you win!" He pulled her against him. "I'll use my influence to get you your building." He nuzzled her neck and nipped her earlobe. "But right now, I intend to use my influence to get what *I* want . . ."

He kissed the side of her neck.

She tipped her head back, releasing an impassioned moan as he blazed a burning trail of kisses along the length of her neck and pressed his lips to the hollow of her throat.

"Yes," she whispered. "Yes . . ." He unbuttoned her tunic and slipped it off, then kissed the swell of her breasts above her chemise, his hot, steamy breath rushing against her and sending chills coursing through her. Then he unlaced the chemise and stripped it from her. Cupping her breast, he flicked his tongue over a rosy crest, then suckled until she cried out her need.

She tangled her fingers in his hair, little moans of passion humming in her throat as he dragged her bloomers and drawers down her legs. Covering her mouth with his and filling it with his tongue, he began a slow, rhythmical parody of what was to come . . .

She moaned as their tongues stroked and entwined, the heaviness in the pit of her stomach now a tight, aching knot, a yearning so deep, she knew instinctively that only Jon could ease it. She longed for him, ached to feel his body joined with hers.

"Jon . . . I want you," she whispered in a raspy

voice, vaguely aware that she'd said the words. "I want you ..."

"Sweet Sarah ... sweet, sweet Sarah," he moaned, then covered her mouth with his again.

While their lips clung, he shrugged out of his shirt and tossed it aside. Easing her thighs apart, he found the entrance to her deepest pleasures and teased the moist, pulsating point of her desire, bringing her to the brink of fulfillment, until she writhed in his arms, repeating over and over her need for him.

Lowering her to the rug, he stripped off his breeches, moved on top of her, and lowered himself into her grasping arms. With one slow, penetrating thrust, he joined his body with hers. A short cry burst from her lips, then she exhaled a raspy sigh of intense pleasure.

Slowly, rhythmically, she met his thrusts as she gave herself to him, body and soul. Her heart pounded in hammerlike beats, and the moan of pleasure in her throat exploded into a cry of raw ecstasy as their fiery passions burst into one radiant flame, untamed and pulsating and brilliant beyond all imagining. Tangling her hands in his hair, she clung to him and held him, and knew then that she had at last found total fulfillment ... and that she could never find it with any other man.

Afterward, as she lay in Jon's arms, still languid from their lovemaking, the magnitude of what had happened settled over her. She'd given to him the one thing she could never take back—her virginity. She had crossed the bounds of propriety, without promise of commitment or words of love, and in return, he had introduced her to an ecstasy so potent and euphoric she would cherish it for the rest of her life, regardless of what happened between them.

It was some time before Jon rolled off her, propped his head on his hand, and said, "It seems, my love, that there is at least one woman who enjoys warming a man's bed."

"Yes . . . it seems that way," she said, teasing.

"Good." He gave her a wicked grin. "Now, I will give you your first lesson in lovemaking."

"My first lesson? I feel quite . . . learned already."

"No, my sweet, you are only a silly infant when it comes to lovemaking. You know nothing."

Lifting her in his arms, he carried her to the bedroom and laid her on the bed, then stretched alongside her. He kissed a rosy crest, teasing it with the tip of his tongue until her breath grew rapid. He moved to her other breast. As he suckled, soft moans reverberated in her throat.

He braced his head on his hand and stared down at her again. "You are a most exquisite sight, little love. And you look beautiful clothed in blushing pink . . . and red." He touched a finger to one tight bud.

Sarah shivered involuntarily. As he began making little patterns across her breast, she saw his body changing again: slow, steady throbs that made him grow large and solid and thick. She swallowed hard. The sight of him was like an aphrodisiac. Hot tears of longing burned her eyes, and a fiery ache throbbed in her loins. She didn't realize she was blatantly staring until Jon said, "What you're ogling, my love, is the cross we men must bear. And it gets damned uncomfortable at times." He smiled. "Lesson number one"—he took her hand, curved her palm around him, and began moving it rhythmically—"how to alleviate the discomfort."

He removed his hand from hers, and she continued the slow, sensuous movement. His breath grew heavy. "Enough," he said, removing her hand. "Time for lesson two . . ." With the tip of his tongue, he traced little patterns down her neck and over her breast, making his way down her body to her feet. He closed his lips around her tiny toe and started suckling.

Sarah giggled as he sucked noisily, first one toe, then the next. But when he started up her body in a meandering path, teasing and tasting as he went, her breath quickened and shivers raced through her. Then his tongue began doing wondrous things, and she feared she'd burst with delight.

He flicked his tongue over her nipple until it gathered into a tight bud and she moaned with unabashed pleasure. He traced with the tip of his tongue the swirl inside her ear and whispered, "You, my precious little peagoose, are a very apt pupil."

The rush of his breath in her ear made Sarah feel as if an uncontrolled fire was raging inside her again, and when Jon started a meandering path downward, she writhed against the bed and said, breathless, "You're driving me wild."

"Then you are ready for lesson number three."

"Yes . . . oh, God . . . yes . . ."

Moving on top of her, he brought her to the heights of ecstasy, and at the peak of their union, she cried out her glorious triumph and collapsed in his arms.

They lay together in a room now darkened by evening, hearts pounding, bodies damp and satiated, and for a while, neither spoke. But when their breathing had settled into quiet, easy undulations, Jon kissed her affectionately and lit the lantern on the bedside table. He stood and stretched, the glow from the lantern washing him in gold, and Sarah thought she'd never tire of looking at his magnificent body. Then he strolled into the parlor, took a cigarette from his trousers, and returned to the bedroom. He lit the cigarette and exhaled a plume of smoke. Sitting on the bed, he leaned back, pulled her up to sit beside him, and put his arm around her. "Now, we need to talk. We have a few things to resolve."

Sarah leaned into the curve of his arm and rested her hand on his chest, feeling the heavy thud of his heart. "We do?" She could barely remember what those things were. In one day, her world of bloomers and shirtwaisters and rights for women had changed dramatically, and her goals seemed to have shifted.

She'd never imagined she could feel this way, or that such ecstasy existed. And she'd never imagined a man could be so important to her. Yet Jon had taken a place in her life . . . a very important place. And she wanted him to always be a part of it. "That's funny," she said. "I can't seem to remember what we have to resolve."

He tipped his head back and exhaled a long, slow current of smoke. "It had something to do with keeping you home long enough to warm my bed."

She gave him a devilish smile. "Oh, that."

"Ummm . . . that. I want you in my bed. I want you in my arms when I go to sleep, and I want you there when I wake up. I want to provide for you—and you can still sell your silly bloomers. But I want to know that you're mine and mine alone." He looked at her lovingly and lingeringly, and added in a soft, silky voice, "Sweetheart, I'm asking you to be my mistress."

Sarah froze. "Your mistress?"

"Yes, love. My mistress. I want you desperately. And, of course, if any child comes from our union, I will provide for it, too."

"Of course."

"I'll give you whatever you want. Closets full of bloomers, a fine coach with four horses—or a carriage if you'd prefer. And a house . . . this house if you want. I'll buy it for you tomorrow."

She stared at the wall across the room. "I don't know, Jon. It's a big decision."

"I know, love. Take your time." He ground out his cigarette and turned his full attention on her once again. "It's not as if you have to decide tonight." He kissed her neck and nibbled his way to her throat. "Take your time, my sweet, lovely Sarah. And tomorrow, when you say yes, I'll see to buying this house." He sent a row of burning kisses across her breast and eased her down beside him.

She felt her body awakening again, and as he made his way down the length of her, she already knew what her answer would be. She wanted him. She wanted his love. And she wanted to give him her love in return. But she was afraid.

Love was so vague, so elusive and intangible.

She didn't understand it. She had nothing by which to judge it. The most important men in her life—her father and her stepfather—had never loved her.

But she wanted love desperately, a love that was secure, enduring, unshakable.

Light flooded the sheer curtains in what Harriet Galbraith presumed was Sarah Ashley's bedroom. She shifted on the buggy seat so her husband could view the window more clearly. Shadows moved behind the curtains. "You see, James, it is just as I told you. The governor *is* in her bedroom. That *is* his horse tied out front."

Reverend Galbraith's mouth curved in delight. "Yes . . . I believe you're right. However, I think it best you not tell Dorothy this time."

"Not tell Dorothy?" Harriet looked at him, miffed. "But . . . whyever not? He is, after all, the father of Dorothy's granddaughters, one of whom is already bewitched by the sinful woman and will undoubtedly follow in her evil footsteps if someone doesn't do something."

"Nevertheless, I forbid you to tell Dorothy." He took the reins and snapped the whip, giving the command.

"Very well, James."

As the buggy moved slowly into the darkness, Harriet's cheeks burned and her heart quickened as she visualized two lustful, naked bodies engaged in . . . She could not utter the word even in her mind, but the thought of what they were doing confirmed her suspicions that Sarah Ashley was indeed the governor's mistress. Of course, she would not tell Dorothy—a wife must not disobey her husband.

But wait until the others heard . . .

Chapter 18

S arah completed her orders for bloomer costumes. After inquiring at numerous hovels along the waterfront, she located the women who had placed the orders with her and presented the garments to her enthusiastic customers. She even acquired several more orders from the women's friends.

As she walked back to her wagon, she should have been jubilant. But she wasn't. Her success was tempered by Jon's proposal that she become his mistress. He'd assured her that if a child came of the union, he'd care for it, and she had no doubt that he would. And he'd said she could continue with her business. But faced with the offer, she couldn't bring herself to say yes. Yet she couldn't understand why. She wanted Jon in her life. She couldn't imagine life without him now. But to become his mistress . . .

Just his mistress . . .

True, she'd expressed her feelings about marriage. And she'd given him no reason to believe she'd changed her views on the matter—which she didn't think she had. And it was obvious how he felt about marriage. In truth, she sensed his bitterness toward his dead wife went even deeper than he'd let on. The fact that he refused to talk about her indicated that he'd been hurt too badly to allow that wound to open again. And she would not press him to do so.

But to be just a mistress . . .

It seemed so fleeting. So impermanent.

She needed more time. He'd come tonight for her answer, but she couldn't give it to him yet. Not yet . . .

Relieved that her wagon was in sight, she quickened her pace, anxious to leave the waterfront. She couldn't dismiss the warnings about women disappearing. But when she lifted her foot to the step to climb onto the wagon, she heard crying coming from inside. Swinging up, she dashed inside, then stood in shocked silence at the sight of Louella crouched in the corner, sobbing as if her heart would break.

Sarah noted the scrape on Louella's cheek, the torn bodice of her dress, and the undisguised terror in her eyes. Kneeling in front of her, she combed her fingers through Louella's flaxen hair and pushed it from her face so she could see the scrape more clearly. "What happened?"

Louella raised tear-drenched eyes to Sarah. "It was horrible," she sobbed. "I was at Millie O'Shaunessey's house and Mr. O'Shaunessey came in drunk in his nightshirt and sent Millie off somewhere and . . . and he told me he was going to make a woman of me . . . like Millie."

As terror for the girl engulfed her, Sarah pulled Louella into her arms and held her. When Louella's sobs began to subside, Sarah spoke, trying to keep her voice steady. "Did he . . . hurt you?"

Louella's delicate brows lowered over sorrowful eyes. "He put his hand on me . . . here . . ." She pressed against her small breast while clasping the torn dress to herself. "Then he raised his nightshirt and . . . it was horrible."

"Did he do anything like . . . well, touch you again,

where you didn't want to be touched?" Sarah asked, feeling a need to know.

Louella began to weep harder. "He tore my dress and then he tried to kiss me. That's when Millie's mother came in, and she had a gun. She told me to run, and I did."

Sarah held Louella, rocking her in her arms. "Oh, my poor Louella. Life is so horrid at times, isn't it? But you're safe now . . . safe."

"Am I a soiled woman?"

"Of course not," said Sarah. "You're the same lovely young woman you always were. If you had wanted him to do those things, then that would be different. But you are a lady, and of course you would not want him to touch you like that. No, you're definitely not a soiled woman." She felt Louella's tension ebbing. But after a few minutes, the sobbing started again.

"I disobeyed Papa," she said. "I went to Millie's house when I wasn't supposed to."

Sarah handed Louella a handkerchief and waited while she mopped her eyes and blew her nose. "Did your father tell you why he didn't want you to go to Millie's house?"

"No," said Louella, seeming to have gained some control. "Only that I was not to go. Some people said Mr. O'Shaunessey was a drunkard, but I didn't believe them because Millie said he wasn't. I can't tell Papa what happened. And I can't go home looking like this because he'll ask me what happened. And I don't want to lie to him. I just want to die."

"Oh, my heavens," said Sarah, wiping away a tear that had found its way down Louella's cheek. "If you'd like, I'll explain to your father what happened—"

"*No!*" exclaimed Louella. "He mustn't know what

Mr. O'Shaunessey did. I'll simply die of shame if Papa ever finds out."

"You needn't die of shame," said Sarah. She studied Louella's distraught features, her red nose and quivering chin. Smiling into anxious eyes, she said, "If it bothers you so, I'll omit that part and tell him that you went to Millie's and that Mr. O'Shaunessey was drunk so you ran home . . . and, of course, that you promised me you would never disobey him again."

"I won't ever disobey him again . . . not ever. And I do promise." She knotted her fingers together. "Are you certain I'm not a soiled woman?"

Sarah eyed her dubiously. "Well, perhaps your dress is a bit soiled, and your face and hands could certainly use a good scrubbing, but the rest of you doesn't look too bad. Meanwhile, we'd better take you to my cottage and sew up that dress—I can stitch it quickly with my sewing machine. You can also wash up there, and I'll help you with your hair. Then we'll go to your house and I'll explain to your father what happened . . . that is, almost what happened."

To Sarah's surprise, Louella smiled, and the tension of moments before seemed to have drained from her face.

"For now," said Sarah, "you stay inside the wagon where no one will see you, and after we get you cleaned up, everything will be fine."

At the cottage, while Louella washed in a tub of warm soapy water that Sarah had prepared for her, Sarah stitched her dress and pressed it lightly with a hot iron from the stove. After Sarah brushed and arranged Louella's hair for her, Louella peered into the mirror. Sarah smiled. "I believe we did a rather commendable job, don't you think?"

Catching Sarah's eyes reflected in the mirror,

Louella nodded and smiled back, and at that moment, Sarah realized that although the bond between them was fragile, it was, nevertheless, there.

As they rode toward Jon's house, Sarah found herself commenting spontaneously, "I want you to know that I never had any intention of trying to replace your mother—there is no one in the world who could do that. I just want us to be friends again, like we were on the ship." She gave Louella a sidelong glance. "And you don't have to wear a bloomer costume or be anything you don't want to be. I like you just the way you are. So can we be friends again?"

Louella nodded. "I guess so. Yes . . ."

At the house, Ida informed them that Lady Cromwell and Miss Cromwell were away, that Josephine was in her room, and that the governor was in the stables. Sarah gave Louella a knowing smile, and Louella scurried off to her room.

Sarah headed toward the stables. Now to see Jon. How much should she tell him about what had happened? She could not betray Louella's confidence. But he needed to know enough to protect Louella from her own rash actions, to make sure she never went to the waterfront alone again.

Good God! What if she'd been raped by the man . . . or abducted and taken to the goldfields to be used by the prospectors? Poor, sweet Louella. Poor, innocent child. The thought was too horrible to contemplate. For now, she'd tell Jon just enough to save Louella's pride, but enough to protect her.

Inside the stables, Sarah was surprised to find Jon alone, and in the process of washing a horse. Shirtless and wearing worn breeches and scuffed black boots, he looked more like a stablehand than a governor. His broad chest glistened with moisture, and his tight, wet breeches hugged his lean hips and molded to his . . .

She bit her lip as memories of the night before came rushing back. This was definitely not the time to be reflecting on what lay beneath those wet breeches. She looked up and found him smiling. He cocked a rueful brow. "We can adjourn to the hayloft if you'd like."

"Is that a proposition, Governor?" She reached up and pushed an untidy thatch of wavy, dark hair from his forehead.

"Let me phrase it another way." He curved his arms around her, bent her low, and kissed her soundly. "Step up to the hayloft, my sweet, and I will show you something that will quite take your breath away . . . I trust."

She laughed as he nibbled her neck.

"And after we exchange a"—he smiled wickedly—"tit for a tat, so to speak, we will get down to the serious business of lesson four."

Sarah pulled his arms from around her, but continued to hold his hands. "Right now, we'd better discuss Louella."

"Louella?" Jon sobered at once. "There's nothing wrong, is there?"

"No, not exactly," said Sarah, trying to present a calm facade. "But she is disturbed about . . . disobeying you."

He raised a questioning brow. "What did she do?"

"She went to the O'Shaunessey girl's house."

"*What!* By God, I'll give her a good rattling she won't forget." He started out of the stable.

"Jon, wait!" Sarah grabbed his arm. "Please stay calm. She's very disturbed about it, and I assured her I'd talk to you first."

Jon's doubled fist met his palm. "If that drunken bastard laid a hand on her, I'll kill him!"

"Louella is fine," Sarah said. "She's more upset

about disobeying you than anything, so please don't
ask her a lot of questions and make things worse."

"Make things worse? Do you propose I make
things easy for her when she clearly disobeyed me?"

"No, of course not," said Sarah. "I only hope you'll
approach the situation with some understanding. Try
to look at it from the viewpoint of a blossoming
young woman."

"Forgive me, but I'm a bit foggy as to how you
more mature females think, so you'll understand
why I might be even foggier as to how a blossoming
young woman might think." He flailed a hand in the
air. "Nothing the lot of you does makes any damned
sense!"

"Then if you'll just stop bellowing and let me explain, I'll attempt to help you understand."

"Fine, you do that," Jon retorted. He folded his
arms. "You can start by explaining how Louella happened to confide in you in the first place. The last I
knew, she didn't want anything to do with you!"

Sarah glared at Jon, angered by his cynical, unspoken accusation. "You're treating me as if *I* had
something to do with Louella's recalcitrant behavior," she said. "I assure you, I did not. I merely found
her hiding in my wagon."

"What the devil was she doing on the waterfront
in the first place? I sincerely hope not following the
course of her sister."

"I already told you, she'd been at the O'Shaunessey girl's house, and when Mr. O'Shaunessey came
home drunk, she ran off, spotted my wagon, and
climbed inside. So I brought her home. She's filled
with remorse over the whole thing, and I'm certain
she won't disobey you again. Actually, it was probably a blessing in disguise. Now she understands why
you didn't want her to go to the O'Shaunessey girl's

house in the first place. And she certainly understands the danger of being down at the waterfront."

"She understands nothing, the naive little fool," said Jon. "She's as trustful as a babe. She has no concept of what could have happened to her. None at all."

"Don't underestimate her," said Sarah. "She probably understands more than you think. After all, she's a very intelligent and sensitive young woman. That's why I urge you to be gentle with her."

"I'll keep that in mind," said Jon. "But I will do what I have to do." He disliked chastising the girls, but when they disobeyed, he had no choice. It was his duty as a father. He also knew that for Louella's own safety, he must explain his real reason for forbidding her to visit the O'Shaunessey girl's house, which meant bringing up the matter of men lusting after women—a hellishly touchy subject to explain to a fourteen-year-old girl.

The time he'd ventured on such a course with Josephine, he'd skirted everything but the facts he'd planned to address, and when he'd finished, Josephine had smiled at him in wry amusement and boldly informed him that she knew all about fornication, at which time he was certain his face had turned as red as a turkey cock's waddles.

"A penny for your thoughts?" said Sarah.

He shrugged. "I was just thinking that with Josephine confined to her room, and Louella soon to be confined to hers, I'm beginning to feel like a damned prison warden."

Sarah chuckled. "Looking on the bright side, as long as your girls are confined to their rooms, you'll at least have *some* peace of mind."

"Ummm." He curved his arms around Sarah's waist and peered into her mirthful eyes. "Why is it that in matters regarding my daughters, I always find myself in the position of having to admit you're right?"

"Because you are a man"—she slipped her arms around his neck—"with the leviathan task of raising two charming, impetuous, and occasionally devious daughters alone. And I suspect you often find yourself at your wit's end over having the sole responsibility of doing so."

She was right, Jon realized. If the girls had a mother, he wouldn't be faced with such problems. He could simply tend to matters of state while she tended to the ticklish areas of child rearing.

But mothers came in tidy little packages called wives. No thanks. He'd been that route.

But he *did* want this woman in his life. He didn't care what anyone thought—the lot of them be damned. But he sensed that Sarah *did* care. So he wouldn't press her but, rather, would simply bide his time and wait until she came to terms with his desire. However, while she was deliberating on whether to let him take care of her, he intended to proudly and possessively show her off and let all of Victoria know that she was his. And the upcoming ball was the place to do so.

"Miss Ashley," he said, while making languid circles against her back, "will you grace me with your beautiful presence at the ball in honor of Admiral Windemere at the naval base two weeks from Saturday? I'm asking in plenty of time so you won't accept another invitation. Of course, if you did, I'd simply break the poor fool's neck and insist on taking you anyway."

She toyed with the hair at his nape. "Who will be there?"

He kissed her lightly. "Does it matter, as long as I promise you dancing beneath twinkling stars and among silvery moonbeams?"

"Umm, I'd like that," she said, pondering what it would be like to spend an evening being swept around the dance floor in Jon's arms, she in a gossamer gown, he in a ... She raised curious eyes to his. "What will you be wearing? Your dancing boots and formal stable attire?"

His laugh was deep and rumbling. "Sorry to disappoint you, love, but I'll be dressed to the nines and looking like a bloody peacock."

She contemplated his dark devil eyes and diabolic smile and tried to visualize him in formal dress. "A peacock, my darling? Definitely not. Satan in disguise? Perhaps."

"Perhaps." He kissed her forehead ... her cheek ... the side of her neck. "Which brings up another subject, love. My proposal. Are you ready to say yes? If not, say nothing. I won't accept no." So much for biding his time, he thought.

She gave him a tentative smile, and Jon noticed an interesting little dimple just to the right of her chin—a lovely, delicate chin that was a bit more pointed than he'd realized. And her lips tipped up enticingly at each corner. Ah, but those high, delicate cheekbones and slanted catlike eyes, they were the focus of his attention. Yes, he definitely wanted this woman ...

"I need more time," she said.

"We'll discuss it in bed tonight."

"No, we won't. Mandi still lives with me, you know." Sarah glided her hands down his back, feeling the strain of his hard, sinewy muscles. "It's just fortunate she didn't return until after you left last night."

Jon slid his hands down to cup her buttocks, pressing her hard against him. "Meanwhile, what am I supposed to do about this ongoing problem?"

She looked at him ruefully. "I suppose you'll have to bear it like a man."

"Or like a howling, blathering lunatic. It's not a situation that's easy to ignore."

"I know. I'm having difficulty ignoring it myself." She ran her hands over his chest. "I'm ready for lesson four," she whispered, feeling his muscles flex beneath her palms. Her breath quickened. It was happening again. The tightness in her loins. The aching need. The indecent thoughts. But with Jon, the thoughts no longer seemed indecent, but instead . . . sublime . . .

He eyed the hayloft.

She bit her lip.

He smiled.

She said, "Where are Peterson and Tooley?"

He gave her an evil grin. "So you like that idea, me bedding you on a mound of straw? Well, my wanton little witch, sorry to disappoint you, but Peterson and Tooley are due back in about twenty-five minutes. When will Mandi be moving out?"

Sarah curved her arms around his neck and nibbled his lips. "Not until after the wedding."

He kissed her neck and below her ear and said in a deep, breathy voice, "My sweet, I have no intention of toting around this weighted and burdensome cross for two weeks."

She moaned as his hot breath tickled the inner recesses of her ear. "Ummm . . . no, that would be . . . burdensome," she said, finding it increasingly difficult to follow the gist of the conversation as his hand glided up to close around her breast. He unbuttoned the top several buttons of her blouse and kissed the hollow of her throat. A low, slow, throbbing ache began to build. "Jon . . . you said Peterson and Tooley are due back soon . . . Ummm . . ."

"Not for twenty-five minutes . . . enough time to

do what I intend to do." He released another button and kissed the swell of her breasts, then lowered her chemise and flicked his tongue over the rosy crest.

She moaned as he suckled, her chest growing tight, her breath heavy as his tongue teased a sensitive nipple into a firm bud. She raked his sides with her fingernails and ran her hand down his hips to the ridge of him to cup the hard bulge in his breeches, the heat of him warming her hand. "Jon . . ."

He kissed her hard, then scooped her up in his arms, shifted her over his shoulder, and started up the ladder to the hayloft. "To hell with Peterson and Tooley," he said. "This won't take more than a few minutes."

In the hayloft, Jon tugged off his boots. "So you're ready for lesson four?" he said. He kissed each palm and placed her hands on the waist of his breeches. "Well then, my love, for lesson four, you will learn how to slowly and seductively undress a man."

"That's it?"

He smiled ruefully. "You were expecting more?"

"My darling governor, you must take me for a complete ninny. Even an inexperienced chit can do that without lessons." While unfastening his breeches, she traced little patterns down his chest with the tip of her tongue. "You taste wild . . . like the ocean," she said, savoring the salty taste of his skin. She flicked her tongue playfully across a flat male nipple and felt it gather into a tiny peak.

"Good God, woman, but you're a fast learner."

"An eager one." She dragged his breeches down his legs. Kneeling, she disentangled his feet, and he stepped out of his breeches. Then she eased his drawers down, releasing him. Her gaze meandered over his taut stomach and down the thin line of hair to where it formed a dark nest around the magnificent thrust of his manhood. The musky male scent of him filled her nostrils.

And she had a deliciously erotic thought, one so bizarre and outrageous, she had to catch herself to keep from acting on impulse . . .

Jon curved his palm beneath her chin. "Are you ready for lesson five so soon, my love?"

Blushing deeply, she slowly stood. Gliding her hands up his lean torso, she kissed his chest, the corded muscles of his neck, his broad jaw. Curving her arms around his neck, she said, "I *am* a wanton little witch, aren't I? I never would have dreamed it."

"A delightfully wanton little witch." He inched up the skirt of her shirtwaister, tucked his fingers in the waist of her drawers, and in one sweep, tugged them off. He backed up to sit on a small barrel and pulled her between his legs. Smoothing his hands up her naked thighs, he caressed the essence of her womanhood.

She moaned as he stroked and teased, her fingers curling into his back, her hips tipped to meet his exploring touch, until she could bear it no longer. "Jon . . . hurry . . ."

"I will, sweet." He lifted her until she straddled him and eased her onto him. She wrapped her legs around his hips, and, instantly, wave after wave of hot desire swept through her. And Jon met her ardent thrusts as he soared with her to the pinnacle of fulfillment.

When it was over, all Sarah could think of was being with Jon again . . . of making love with him again.

But when? Where?

She had Mandi's wedding dress to make and her bloomer orders to fill, and for the next two weeks, Jon would be immersed in government affairs, which included several short trips.

But he came to her five days later, immediately upon his return from New Westminster. Sarah slipped out of the cottage, where she and Mandi had been cutting out Mandi's wedding dress, and she and Jon made love at sundown while hidden in the tall grass on a vacant beach, their bodies washed in glorious golden rays.

It was wild, impetuous, reckless . . .

After that, it seemed almost impossible to arrange time together. Sarah and Mandi spent their days and nights busily working on Mandi's dress, and the few times Mandi was gone, Jon couldn't get away. With the representative from the Crown due to arrive soon, he faced increasing pressures with governmental issues.

But three days later, Jon managed to slip away between meetings. He located Sarah coming out of Wellington Brown's store. He only had to open the door of the coach, and she was in his arms. Behind the closed curtains of the coach, and while riding along Cadboro Bay, they made love.

Again, their passion was uncurbed. Again, she wondered when the next time would be . . .

It happened six days later. They met at Mystic Spring. She wore no underwear. She felt delightfully wicked, surprising Jon in such an erotic way. And he was wild with delight . . . crazed with passion. Their lovemaking was even more untamed and uninhibited, and she was bolder than ever before, doing things she'd never dreamed she'd do, delighting in every deliciously lustful moment of it.

She was obsessed with him. Possessed with need.

Chapter 19

The wedding was perfect. Mandi made a beautiful bride, and Wellington was as handsome and happy as a man could be. Guests included Ida and her family, many of the merchants and their families, Mrs. Dewig-Gertz and her husband, and even Mayor and Mrs. Harris. Mandi and Wellington dashed for the coach beneath a shower of rice and cuddled inside, laughing and kissing, as it pulled away.

For a few passing moments, Sarah envisioned the coach as Jon's, and herself as his bride, curled in his arms . . .

A silly, capricious notion, which she dismissed.

Until she swept open the door and greeted Jon for the ball that night. The sight of him took her breath away. From the crown of his black silk top hat to the toes of his glossy black shoes, he was immaculately dressed. His black tailcoat, tailored to perfection, nipped in at his lean waist, accentuating the breadth of his wide shoulders. His close-cut black trousers, with stripes of braid down each side, emphasized his narrow hips and long legs. She eyed his fashionably tied white cravat, crisp white dress shirt with its tiny tucks, and white silk waistcoat.

And all she could think of was how like a bridegroom he appeared. And how dangerous such thoughts were.

Jon slid his arm around her waist, pulled her to him, and kissed her soundly. When their lips parted, he kissed her cheek and her neck where it curved into her shoulder, taking in the sweet scent of lavender water. "Let's skip the ball," he said. "I can think of a much more interesting way to spend the evening."

She smoothed her hands along the satiny lapels of his tailcoat. "But I have an affinity for silvery moonbeams," she said, "and you promised an evening of dancing under the stars."

He smiled into eyes glistening with anticipation. "Then stars and moonbeams you shall have." He took her in his arms and twirled her around. Her gown of apricot duchesse, with its diaphanous overgown of white lisse and trails of poppy garlands and moss-green leaves, swirled around her like a cloud.

She wore her hair pulled high on her head and caught with satin ribbon and clusters of tiny silk poppies, and as they twirled, long curls bounced at her neck, and the tiny crystal sequins interwoven in her curls twinkled like dewdrops among the coppery tresses. He kissed her forehead and each dewy eyelid, and smiled into a pair of exquisite eyes that looked as clear and bright as fresh-cut emeralds. "You, my love, are like a beautiful wood nymph shrouded in a pale apricot mist."

Sarah bit her bottom lip to hold back a smile of pure pleasure. "And you, my darling, look incredibly splendid yourself," she replied.

Settled in the plush confines of the coach and nestled in the curve of Jon's arm, Sarah said, "Who, specifically, is planning to attend?"

Jon arched a dark brow. "Victoria's blue bloods and the high-ranking officers of the Royal Navy."

"Will Esther be there?"

"Yes . . . with Mayor and Mrs. Harris. So you'll have at least two allies."

"I hardly consider the mayor an ally."

"But Mrs. Harris is." Jon patted her hand. "Having second thoughts, sweet? We can still return to the cottage. But then I couldn't be the envy of every poor clod at the ball. Let's see. There will be Judge Cameron; Attorney General Cary; some members of the city council, the House of Assembly, and my legislative council; and their wives. And, of course, our friend Mr. De Cosmos."

"That doesn't bother you?"

"No. It should make the evening interesting. But not as interesting as it will be later, because you, my sweet, are definitely ready for the next lesson. Unfortunately, we have to endure this evening first."

"Don't you like balls?"

"Sure . . . about as much as I like boiling in oil. But then I've never escorted a beautiful wood nymph before, and that makes all the difference."

When they entered the grand ballroom, Sarah felt as if she'd stepped into a fairyland. Candles twinkled through hundreds of crystal teardrops in the wall sconces and glittered through garlands of prisms in the chandeliers.

Sarah gazed around the room at women dressed in wide gowns made of the finest silks and satins, their coiffures lavishly fashioned with flowers and feathers and tiny gemstones. Long tables draped with snowy white tablecloths held glistening ice sculptures, sparkling champagne glasses, and trays with exquisitely arranged food.

"It's truly like a fairyland," she said, tilting her head to gaze up at the chandelier above the dance floor.

Jon smiled at the mirthful, almost childlike look on

her face. "Yes, it is a bit like that," he said, his eyes focused on her. Dressed in her gossamer gown, and with tiny sequins flickering in her shimmering copper hair, she looked like a fairy princess.

She took his arm and they strolled around the room, and almost immediately, Sarah focused on a group of naval officers and their wives surrounding Admiral Windemere. Mary Letitia, who stood beside her father, looked away as if she had not been watching when, in fact, Sarah knew she had been staring pointedly. Standing with a tall naval officer, Mary Letitia fluttered her eyelids and laughed merrily at something the man was saying. But Sarah suspected she was not really listening to the man's words at all.

Sarah took a firmer hold on Jon's arm, and he rested his palm over her hand as he ushered her toward a group of dignitaries who stood sipping champagne near one of the long tables. As they crossed the floor, the talk and laughter seemed to fade, and Sarah became acutely aware of probing glances. Smiling cordially at Jon, as if engaged in casual conversation, she said under her breath, "Is it my gown, or is it simply the fact that the governor has chosen to escort a woman of . . . questionable character to the ball?"

Jon gave her hand a reassuring pat. "Definitely the gown . . . and you in it. You've captured every male eye in the room, and the women are all jealous as hell."

"Thank you for alleviating my apprehensions."

"Ignore them."

"I'll try." She scanned the crowd. "It doesn't appear that Esther and the Harrises have arrived yet, but"—she nodded toward the wall where Amor De Cosmos stood staring at them—"I see that one of my proponents has."

Jon gave De Cosmos a dark look. "He should have sufficient grist for his editorial mill after tonight."

"Doesn't that bother you?" she asked. She waited for Jon's response, and when he didn't reply, she looked up to find him gazing across the room, his eyes wide, his lips parted in surprise.

"Good God!" he said.

She turned and stared, dumbfounded. Standing in the entrance with Mayor and Mrs. Harris was Esther. Dressed in a décolleté gown of shimmering electric-blue satin, her ash-brown hair coiffed in an elegant twist of plaits and curls and bedecked with several iridescent, quaking peacock feathers, Esther was definitely not a drab mouse.

Sarah finally found her voice. "I assume your mother didn't see her before she left to come here tonight."

"That's a safe assumption," said Jon, his eyes fixed on his sister. He had not yet adjusted to her wearing bloomers around the house. Now her appearance was almost too much. But he had to admit, he'd never seen Esther looking lovelier, or younger. His middle-aged spinster sister was turning more than a few heads. He looked askance at Sarah. "You act surprised. I can't imagine you had nothing to do with this."

"I assure you, I did not."

Esther caught them staring and immediately glided over to join them. "Isn't this a lovely ball?" she said, her face glowing with excitement.

Jon's lips curved. "I do believe our butterfly has emerged from her cocoon."

"Then you approve?" Esther asked, eyeing Jon with a touch of uncertainty.

"Of the gown, I'm not sure," said Jon. "But of the emerging butterfly, most definitely. Now, if you ladies will excuse me, I'll get you some champagne."

After Jon left, Sarah said, "Your gown is beautiful. Wherever did you find it? Certainly not in Victoria."

"In San Francisco," replied Esther. "I just haven't had the nerve to wear it—Mother being the way she is." Flares lit her dark eyes. "She will undoubtedly have a fit of the vapors when she hears about it, though. But by then I'll have had a glorious evening, so I refuse to worry about it." Her glance flicked beyond Sarah and fixed on a point across the room. "Isn't the admiral a magnificent man?"

Sarah glanced around. "Admiral Windemere?"

"Yes."

Sarah more closely studied the tall, stately man with the thick crop of silvery hair, and to her surprise found him staring at them, smiling. Esther blushed deeply. Snapping open her black lace fan, she fluttered it at her throat, sending peacock feathers quivering atop her head.

Sarah eyed her curiously. "Does Admiral Windemere, by any chance, have something to do with your decision to wear the gown tonight?"

"The admiral *is* my reason," replied Esther. "But don't tell Jon. I decided that if the man is ever to notice me, it would have to be tonight, because I fear one day soon another woman will ensnare him. It has been over a year since Mrs. Windemere passed away, so he's quite available."

Jon returned with glasses of champagne, accompanied by a stocky, middle-aged officer who eyed Esther with pleasure. The officer muttered a few inane comments as they stood in a circle while sipping champagne, then he asked Esther to dance. After he'd swept her away, Jon's gaze continued to follow Esther around the dance floor. "That's the damnedest transformation I've ever seen. Puzzling, but gratifying, Esther has always been so . . . drab, at least in her appearance."

"Well, she's certainly not drab tonight," said Sarah, smiling at the peacock feathers as they swished around with Esther's twirling movements.

Jon took Sarah's arm. "Now, I suppose we should pay our respects to Admiral Windemere."

"Aren't you afraid he might be a bit out of sorts because you didn't escort Mary Letitia?"

"From the looks of things," said Jon, "I seriously doubt he's given his daughter much thought tonight."

Sarah noted that a bevy of women had surrounded the admiral. When she and Jon approached, the women turned and fixed their eyes on Sarah, and she was aware that she was being studied intently. Two of the women appeared to be slightly younger than Mary Letitia, the third somewhat older. All seemed to know exactly who Sarah Ashley was, as was evident in their cool glances.

Scanning their faces, Sarah nodded and smiled cordially, then quietly ignored them. Within moments, all three women drifted away. While Jon, Sarah, and Admiral Windemere chatted, Mary Letitia walked up. She gave Sarah a baleful smile and turned to Jon. "May I have this dance?"

Jon seemed too stunned to speak. After an awkward silence, Admiral Windemere said, "Please don't leave the young lady standing there, Jon. Do dance with her so that I might steal your lovely lady here and spin her about the floor a few turns . . . if you'd do me the honor, Miss Ashley."

Sarah smiled. "Yes, I would be delighted."

Admiral Windemere escorted her onto the dance floor and swept her into his arms, dancing with practiced precision to the fast waltz. As he spun her around the floor, her gaze shifted from one side to the other while she tried to keep Jon's tall frame in view. Although her glimpses of him were brief, she noted that Mary Letitia's hand rested intimately around the back of his neck rather than on his shoulder, and her eyes appeared to be fixed on his.

"... look lovely, my dear." The admiral's voice seemed to come from out of nowhere. "And I do believe that the governor is quite taken with you."

Sarah looked at the admiral with a start. Why would he make such a statement? Uncertain how to respond, she smiled tentatively. "I believe everyone is ... taken with the splendor of the evening. It's a lovely ball." Her gaze shifted beyond the admiral to where Jon and Mary Letitia had been, and to her alarm, they were nowhere in sight.

She looked past the admiral ... around him ... to the side of him ... and saw Jon and Mary Letitia leaving the room to go out on the veranda. Her heart lurched, and she felt a rush of intense jealousy.

"I hope you'll excuse my daughter for absconding with your escort," said Admiral Windemere.

"You knew?" She had not thought that he'd noticed them leaving the ballroom.

"I beg your pardon?"

"About her taking Jon out on ... that is ..."

The admiral seemed completely baffled, and Sarah realized at once that he had not seen Jon and Mary Letitia leave for the veranda, but was referring instead to Mary Letitia's asking Jon to dance. Chagrined, she pressed her lips into a smile. "Oh, it's perfectly all right."

"Ever since my Mary died," said Admiral Windemere, "Mary Letitia has been ..." He missed a step, caught himself, and fell into time again. "That is ..." He missed another step. Glancing beyond Sarah, his gaze sharpened. "The exquisite young woman standing with Mayor and Mrs. Harris. Who is she?" He spun Sarah around so that the mayor was in her line of vision.

Trying to keep her mind on what the admiral had asked, and off thoughts of what Jon and Mary Letitia might be doing on the veranda, Sarah looked over the admiral's shoulder and, to her surprise, saw Esther. "She's Jon's . . . That is, she's Governor Cromwell's sister, Miss Cromwell."

"Esther Cromwell?" Admiral Windemere's silvery brows gathered into a puzzled frown. "I failed to recognize her."

After a few more turns around the floor, Admiral Windemere asked, "If I may be so bold to ask, who escorted Miss Cromwell to the ball?"

Sarah tore her eyes from the vacant doorway where she'd last seen Jon. "Who?"

"Miss Cromwell. Who is Miss Cromwell's escort?"

"Oh . . . uh, yes," replied Sarah. "She accompanied the Mayor and Mrs. Harris." Determined to concentrate on her dancing partner, Sarah smiled, but the admiral didn't notice her . . . obviously engrossed in thoughts of his own. Catching the gleam of interest in his eyes and realizing where his thoughts lay, she asked, "Would you like to talk to Miss Cromwell?"

Admiral Windemere smiled broadly. "Yes . . . I would indeed."

When the music stopped, Sarah walked with Admiral Windemere to where Esther stood. The admiral lifted Esther's gloved hand and touched his lips to her fingertips. "Lovely lady, you have quite taken my breath away," he said, peering into her sparkling eyes. "May I have the remainder of the dances with you?"

Too stunned to speak, Esther simply stood staring at the admiral, who in turn seemed to have forgotten that he was leaving Sarah quite alone on the dance floor. Tucking Esther's hand into the crook of his elbow, he swept her onto the dance floor and into his arms, where Sarah suspected she would remain for the rest of the evening.

Jon was at Sarah's side at once, with Mary Letitia nowhere to be seen. Sarah looked at Jon, and to her shock, saw the ruddy imprint of a hand on his cheek. Had he tried to kiss Mary Letitia when they were on the veranda? It certainly appeared that way. Feeling queasy fingers curling inside her, she said with more than a trace of sarcasm, "Did you and Miss Windemere enjoy the moonbeams?"

Jon raised his hand to his face and rubbed. "We had a slight ... disagreement. But I'll say this much for her, the chit has one hell of a swing."

"So I surmised."

Jon smiled, which infuriated Sarah. Taking her hand, he placed it in his arm. "Aren't you curious as to what we disagreed about?"

Sarah shrugged. "I imagine it had something to do with you ... forcing yourself on her. Isn't that usually why a woman slaps a man?" She started to pull her hand away, but Jon held it fast.

"It had something to do with my calling her a spoiled, manipulative, sharp-tongued shrew. I'm afraid the lady took offense."

"You called her that? But why?"

"Because that's what she is. And because she said some rather unflattering things about you in very unladylike terms."

"Like what?"

"That, my good woman, I will never tell." He patted her hand. "Now, unfortunately, before we can start dancing, I must make the rounds and offer salutations—one of the demands of my job. But afterward, I intend to have you to myself for the rest of the evening."

For the next hour, Jon ushered Sarah on a circuit of the ballroom, greeting one dignitary after another and exchanging cordial words. Sarah talked with the wives, finding most of them reserved and some a bit staid, perhaps even offended by her presence. Jon appeared impervious to their sideways glances, continuing his exchanges while holding on to her elbow.

They joined the crowd gathered around the long tables and feasted on pâtés, fine cheeses, exotic fruits, and fancy hors d'oeuvres while sipping champagne. At last, when the orchestra began playing a slow waltz, Jon said, "Shall we?"

Anxious to be away from the stodgy dignitaries, Sarah nodded. They stepped onto the dance floor, and Jon slipped his arm around her waist, drawing her close. He smiled into her eyes. "In case you're not aware of it, Miss Ashley, you have been thoroughly ogled by every fire-breathing male in this ballroom."

Sarah's lips curved with pleasure. Resting one gloved hand on his shoulder and curling the other in his palm, she gazed into his dark, smoldering eyes. "I wouldn't know about that, Governor Cromwell, as I am not aware of any man in this room but you."

He pressed his palm firmly against the small of her back and moved her closer to him. "And that, my sweet, is as it should be." He waltzed with her around the floor, guiding her into the current of twirling couples, spinning her round and round beneath the glittering chandeliers.

Entranced by the lilting music swirling in her head, intoxicated with the headiness of being in Jon's embrace, and captivated by the gleam of pleasure in his eyes, Sarah felt bewitched. And as she held his gaze, the people around her receded, the music and laughter diminished, the flicker of candles and the sparkle of crystal faded ...

All she was aware of was the feel of Jon's muscular shoulder beneath her palm, the pressure of his hand firm against her back, and the warmth of his fingers tightly closed around hers.

It was at that moment that she realized she loved him—madly, desperately, totally. Gazing into his mesmerizing brown eyes, she found herself in a world in which nothing existed but her and Jon.

His arm around her tightened, drawing her closer. His movements slowed, and his lips brushed her forehead. "I fear you have charmed me with your magic wand, fairy princess," he said in a husky whisper.

The deep, rich sound of his voice uttering the romantic words drew Sarah deeper into the enchantment of the moment. "No, I'm the one who has fallen utterly and completely under your spell, my darling," she said in a breathless voice, peering into his eyes.

"If you are under my spell," said Jon, his gaze meandering over her face and resting on her lips, "then I have accomplished my goal."

He moved to kiss her.

It was then that Sarah realized the music had stopped and they stood transfixed in the center of the dance floor, swaying slowly to music only they could hear, lips a breath apart, oblivious to everything and everyone around them.

Mortified, Sarah glanced around, aware that all eyes were fixed on them. Flushing hot with embarrassment and humiliation, she dropped her hand from Jon's shoulder and turned out of his arms.

Jon held her hand. "Just ignore them," he said, "and we'll go out onto the veranda. I promised you stars and moonbeams, and we won't find them in here."

Knowing there would be gossip whether they stayed in the ballroom or stepped outside, and wanting to be away from the sharp stares and furtive whisperings, Sarah squared her shoulders, held her head high, and walked with Jon off the dance floor. As they threaded their way between couples who eyed them surreptitiously, she tightened her hold on Jon's arm, uncertain whether her quaking limbs would support her. They walked past a coterie of women whose conversation ceased until they'd passed, at which time a babble of voices broke out. Sarah only half-heard what was said, but she caught the word "mistress" quite clearly.

Then, to her dismay, she saw Mary Letitia standing with two other women near the entrance to the ballroom. Mary Letitia immediately whispered something to the woman beside her, who passed on the comment to another woman, who in turn stared at Sarah with wide, shocked eyes. Sarah knew some perverse information had just been exchanged.

Lifting her chin, she determined to ignore the women, but when she and Jon passed the group to leave the room, her eyes defied her and shifted to meet Mary Letitia's icy gaze and mocking smile. With his hand resting possessively at her waist, Jon nodded politely to the women. "Good evening, ladies. Mary Letitia, I hope your hand has recovered."

Mary Letitia turned crimson.

Jon guided Sarah out the door and onto the candlelit gallery, where couples strolled leisurely in the moonlight. They stood some distance from the others, gazing across the bay. "My coming here with you was a terrible mistake," said Sarah. "Mr. De Cosmos will undoubtedly use his pen to create something quite improper and notorious from our untimely actions on the dance floor. And it will be crafted to have an adverse effect on you."

Jon shrugged. "Regardless of what De Cosmos writes, the people of this colony will be the ones to decide whether or not I'm doing my job. And they can simply look around at the civil services they now enjoy to determine that."

"Then they'll look at me on your arm and forget all of it," she said, pondering the knowing leers and sniggering talk. "And I'm certain that whatever Mr. De Cosmos omits, Mary Letitia will supply. I really think we should leave."

"No," said Jon. "I promised you dancing under the stars, and that's what we'll do." He clasped both hands behind her waist as the distant strains of a waltz floated to them on the breeze. Held in his close embrace, Sarah laced her fingers behind his neck, and, under rays of silvery moonbeams, they glided in easy, unhurried steps, turning slowly to the winsome music and to the sound of Jon's low humming.

When the music ended, Sarah raised her lips to his, and he kissed her lingeringly. Her heart began to hammer, and she felt vibrant with energy, blazing with desire. He kissed her again, harder this time, and she held him tighter. Stroking the side of her jaw with his thumb, he said, "I believe, my sweet, that you share my thoughts."

They slipped into the darkness and made their way to the coach. Behind closed carriage doors, and rocking gently to the motion of the coach, Jon pulled Sarah to him. "At last I have you all to myself."

She drew his arms around her and cuddled against him. "My thoughts exactly. I have endured quite enough pointed stares for one night." She gave him a wicked smile. "And I would very much like to get on with my lessons."

He chucked her under the chin. "That's my girl." He nibbled her neck. "By morning, we should have covered several lessons—you're a very apt student."

She moaned as he kissed his way down her throat. "You can't stay till morning," she said, breathless. "I still haven't made up my mind about us, and I don't want anyone to know you're there. But I do want you for a few hours."

"You'll have me for at least that long." He nuzzled her cleavage. "Peterson can drop me off and return at two."

"But won't he talk?"

"He's gotten me out of more scrapes than I can remember"—he kissed the swell of her breast—"so you have nothing to fear from him."

The way Sarah felt now, even if Peterson *did* talk she was beyond caring. All she wanted was for Jon to hold her, to cover her with hot kisses and end her intense yearning.

Inside the cottage, they doffed their clothes and, in minutes, lay curled in each other's arms. Jon flicked his tongue across her nipple and took the tight bud between his lips. As he suckled, Sarah dug her fingernails into the sleek muscles of his back. He trailed fevered kisses across her breasts and over her tummy, stroking her body, touching her everywhere, lingering to explore, to tease, until she felt she'd go wild with desire. "Jon ... I want you ... now ..." she said in a raspy voice.

"Yes, love. I know ..." He thrust his fingers into her hair, drawing her head back, and crushed his lips to hers. He kissed her harder, deeper, until her mouth throbbed and her body demanded fulfillment. Tears of passion moistened her eyes. Sweat dampened her brow. Her nerves hummed like hundreds of taut wires. "Jon ... now ..."

He cupped her buttocks, the hardness of his arousal moving between her thighs until he found the entrance to her deepest pleasures. She raised her body to meet his, and they joined. Gentleness gave way to urgency as she arched, his raw male power thrusting ... throbbing inside her until her aching need was replaced by pulsating tremors of ecstatic delight, and a warm, languid feeling filled her.

Glorying in the last ripples of her waning desire, she clung to him. It was even more intense, more overpowering than before. And next time? When? How soon? She couldn't seem to get enough of him. She didn't want to let him go, not even for a few days. But for now, she could hold him a little longer. Just a little longer . . .

After a while, as she lay in the curve of his arm, feeling his rhythmic breathing while listening to the quiet beating of his heart, her mind began to wander, she felt herself drifting, and darkness seemed to close in around her.

An hour later, she awakened when the clock on the mantel chimed twice. She hadn't wanted to fall asleep in Jon's arms because she didn't want to lose precious time being with him, but she had fallen asleep.

She slid her arm over his broad chest and shook him gently. "Jon . . ."

He stirred, gathered her to him, and held her. "Yes, love?"

Almost immediately, the sound of carriage wheels rolled to a halt out front. "Peterson's here. You have to go."

He gathered her more tightly to him. "Not until after I make love to you again, sweet. I'll be gone five days, and that's too damned long."

"Yes . . . I agree." She nibbled on his neck. "But we'd better hurry."

"No, love. Peterson can wait. I intend to savor every delectable inch of your beautiful body, and you, my wickedly wanton little seductress, can implement all the enticingly hedonistic things you've managed to learn on your own."

Sarah glided her hand down his belly while visualizing the hedonistic things he was referring to. "Do you think perhaps I'm . . . too wanton?"

He rolled her onto her back and braced his hands on either side of her. "Sweet, there is no way on God's earth that you could be too wanton for me." He covered her body with hungry, ardent kisses, and she responded in the most sensuous way she knew how.

Again, they came together with a fiery passion that, once spent, seemed to sap all of Sarah's strength, yet left her feeling radiantly, exuberantly alive.

After a while, Jon gave her one last, lingering kiss. "I'd ask you to keep the bed warm for me until I get back, sweet, but I seriously doubt it could possible cool off by then." He lit the lantern and threw his legs over the side of the bed.

Sarah slipped into a robe and sat at her dressing table to brush her hair. In the mirror, she watched Jon hastily dress. "Do you really have to go to New Westminster?"

"Yes, love." He tucked in his shirt, fastened his trousers, and came up behind her. Bending over, he kissed the side of her neck. "When I return, we'll make up for lost time. I promise."

She stood and wrapped her arms around his neck. "Jon?"

"Yes, love."

"I'll miss you."

He pulled her to him. "I'll miss you, too, sweet. And as soon as I get back, I *will* see to buying this place and making a proper home for you." He kissed her deeply and left.

Several minutes later, a series of short knocks startled her. Thinking it was Jon, she rushed to the door and swept it open. To her horror, Hollis stood in the doorway. She went to slam the door, but he stopped it with his foot.

Throwing it open, he burst inside and slammed the door. "That was shortsighted of you," he said, whiskey heavy on his breath. "You know I would have splintered the door and walked right through it."

Sarah knew only too well. The last time she'd closed a door in his face and locked it, he'd taken an ax to it, and for a few terrifying moments, she'd thought he intended to take the ax to her as well. "Get out!"

He eyed her with contempt. "Has the governor been screwing you all this time? What a wanton little whore you are. Lying half-naked on the beach, begging the governor to take you. Yes, little whore. I saw the two of you there. And what unsavory things you did. Acting like the slut I always knew you were. Oh, yes, little sister, you are a slut. A wanton little slut, just like your mother was, lusting after the governor's cock like a bitch in heat."

"Get out of here!"

"And what if I don't? Will you kill me, little whore?" He grabbed her arm and pulled her so close that the odor of whiskey burned her throat. "Maybe I should screw you, too. You're just another bastard who doesn't even know who her father is."

Sarah started to scream, but he clamped his hand over her mouth. "Don't worry. I'm not going to screw you. You disgust me. I wouldn't want to sully myself. Does that surprise you? Does it, little whore? That I find you too dirty to screw? *Well!*" Sarah shook her head behind the hand clamped over her mouth. "Now . . . I'll say this just one time." Hollis's tone was controlled, ruthless. "Turn over the money to me—all of it—or you and the governor will be the subject of gossip in every parlor in Victoria. And I promise you, the gossip that circulates will be lewd, explicit, and very detailed. You have just one day, little whore. One day!"

He walked out, slamming the door behind him.

Sarah slid to the floor and closed her arms around herself. She felt so dirty. So horribly, disgustingly dirty. And there was nothing Jon could do to change that.

She was what she was. A wanton little whore who lusted after a man who wanted her only as his mistress.

Chapter 20

Dorothy Cromwell stood, her back ramrod-straight as she stared at the whitewashed door of Sarah Ashley's modest dwelling. When she'd seen the cottage the day she and Harriet had found Jon and the Ashley woman there, it had looked rather disreputable. Now, with the rosebushes trimmed and the flower beds weeded, sparkling clean windows framing lacy white curtains, and a colorful braided foot mat gracing the threshold, the cottage presented an entirely different facade. A snug, homey facade.

But whatever the feminine touches contributed by Miss Ashley, they didn't change the facts. As long as the woman remained in Victoria, she was an encumbrance to Jon's career and a threat to the colony.

Dorothy adjusted her gray crepe bonnet to sit squarely atop her head and straightened her black lace fichu to drape neatly about her shoulders. She could not explain, even to herself, why she must look her best today. She had only a vague feeling that in order to complete her objective, she would have to earn Miss Ashley's respect.

Raising an unsteady hand, she knocked lightly while going over in her mind what she would say, particularly her opening statement. She must not appear resentful or demanding, but rather concerned. She must appeal to the woman's sensibilities.

The door swept open, and Dorothy saw the shock in Sarah Ashley's eyes, large emerald eyes that looked as if they'd recently shed tears. Then she saw shock give way to wariness as Miss Ashley said in a wavering voice, "Good afternoon, Lady Cromwell."

For a moment, Dorothy stared, unable to believe that this scrubbed-clean woman with her modest gingham dress, her starched white apron with its ruffled trim, and her hair pulled up in a tidy knot on top of her head was the same woman who had worn an indecently low-cut gown to the dinner table. "Miss Ashley," she said, "if I might have a few moments of your time?"

"Well . . . yes, of course," she replied. "Please, do come in and sit down." She moved aside, and Dorothy entered.

Stepping into the room, Dorothy glanced around. With the exception of two skirted lady's chairs and a small linen-covered tea table between them, there were no other pieces of furniture. But two sewing machines on two rather crudely built tables dominated the room. Everywhere lay fabric and patterns and snippets of material.

"Please . . . sit down," Sarah said, motioning to one of the chairs. "May I offer you some tea?"

"Yes, thank you. That would be lovely, dear," Dorothy replied, careful to maintain a cordial facade. She sat stiffly on the edge of the chair while Sarah stepped into the kitchen. Several minutes later, Sarah returned carrying a tray holding a small dish with several pieces of shortbread and two dainty china cups with steaming tea. She set the tray on the table, then, offering sugar and cream, said, "I hope you'll excuse my house, but as you can see, it's also my place of business."

Dorothy gave a sympathetic nod. "We must adapt to our circumstances as best we can." She pondered the younger woman sitting adjacent to her. The golden-russet color of her hair seemed richer than she'd remembered, the set of her chin less firm, the lines of her delicate face softer, more vulnerable. She searched for signs that Sarah Ashley was the threat she knew her to be, but found instead a poised, lovely woman whom she knew Jon loved.

But, in time, he'd forget.

Deciding that the reason behind her visit could not be put off any longer, she said tentatively, "I know you must be wondering why I'm here."

"Well . . . yes, I am," replied Sarah. "I'm sorry, but I must assume it's not a social call."

"Unfortunately," replied Dorothy, "I'm afraid you're right. To be frank with you, Miss Ashley, Jon's cabinet feels it's imperative that you leave the colony at once." She paused to allow her statement to be absorbed.

Sarah's courteous smile shriveled. She blinked, took a slow sip of tea, and said nothing.

Continuing in a contrite voice, Dorothy said, "I'm sure you're aware that if the colonies unite, the independence Jon has strived to maintain, and Victoria's position as a free trade port, will cease."

"Jon mentioned something about that," Sarah replied. She took another sip of tea.

"I'm certain he didn't elaborate on it, though," Dorothy said, wishing Sarah Ashley would stop staring at her with those despondent, luminous eyes. "He would not want you to believe that your presence here would have that much influence. Unfortunately, it does." Dorothy waited for the information to be digested, and again, Sarah Ashley said nothing, but continued to stare at her with those wide eyes, which now held a hint of uncertainty.

"You see," Dorothy continued, "with the impending threat of unification, Jon's administration cannot endure the added complication you have brought to the colony. It's an unfortunate situation . . . for both you and Jon."

Sarah finally spoke. "I realize my being here has caused some problems for Jon," she said, "but certainly it has no real bearing on whether or not the colonies unite. I am just not that important."

"But that's where you're wrong. You are a major threat to the colony." Dorothy set the cup down with a clatter. "Only if Jon can maintain a stable economy can unification be prevented. But to do that, he needs the support of his cabinet and the merchants of the community, all of whom are becoming divided over the issue of rights for women!"

Realizing she'd raised her voice, Dorothy drew in a long breath to compose herself. Then she continued in a benevolent tone. "Unfortunately, because of your presence in Victoria and the defamatory editorial attacks of Mr. De Cosmos, Jon has rapidly lost favor with the community, something he cannot afford in light of the current situation, particularly with the representatives from the Crown scheduled to arrive soon to evaluate the economic position of the colony . . . and, of course, to reassess Jon's qualifications as governor of the combined colonies, should they unite." Dorothy saw a flash of intense emotion in Sarah's eyes. Was it love? Did she, in fact, love Jon as he loved her?

After a few moments of quiet contemplation, Sarah said, "I suppose I could cease my business until after the representatives have completed their assessment and left."

Dorothy had anticipated such a response—although she'd rather hoped the Ashley woman would have become defensive instead of complaisant, and that she would stubbornly assert her rights, at which time Dorothy was prepared to dislike her immensely. Now, as she looked at the younger woman with her lovely face and spring-fresh complexion, she found nothing really to dislike. But the fact remained, she was a threat to Jon, and she must go. "Even if you give up your crusade," she argued, "you're still a threat to Jon's political position, as too many of the townspeople look upon you with disfavor for the disturbance you have caused."

"But certainly the townspeople can just look around and see what Jon has done for the colony," Sarah insisted. "And in time, whatever disturbance they feel I've caused will be forgotten."

Dorothy snapped open her fan and fluttered it to cool her flushed face. She'd hoped to establish her point by now, but it was obvious she had not. She'd be forced to bring up other, more personal issues to reinforce her position. "I'm afraid it's not that simple," she said. "There is talk that Jon's horse was seen very late at your house—while your house was quite dark—and there is also talk that Jon remained at your house for an inordinate amount of time after the ball. The fact is, Miss Ashley, there is talk that you are my son's mistress." There, she'd said it.

Sarah's hand shook, spilling tea into her saucer, and she quickly set her cup down. Dorothy chastised herself for being so cruel, but she needed every ploy she had at her disposal. "I'm sorry to have brought that up, Miss Ashley, but you must realize that that sort of vicious talk can ruin a man politically."

"It seems that my private life is an open book in Victoria," Sarah said in an uneven voice. "Is that the case with everyone here?"

"No," said Dorothy, "but anyone engaged in a liaison with the governor is open to censure."

"Yes, I suppose you're right," she replied.

Dorothy wished the woman would become unreasonable, or scream profanities like a fishwife, or simply defend her actions. But her poise never cracked. Continuing, Dorothy said, "In addition, there is the added complication of Josephine's brash actions. You may not be aware, but just yesterday she was suspended from Madame Pettibeau's Seminary for Young Ladies for two weeks. Jon returned Josephine's scrapbook, as you apparently suggested he do, and Josephine took it to school. Unfortunately, Madame Pettibeau found it in her possession. I'm afraid you have much more influence with Josephine than her father does."

"I'm very sorry about that," said Sarah. "Of course, Josephine should not have taken the scrapbook to school, and I would have advised . . . no, insisted, that she not do so. I feel very badly about this, and yes, even responsible."

The sorrowful eyes that met Dorothy's were sincerely penitent, and Dorothy realized that Sarah Ashley cared a great deal for Josephine, a thought that made her feel a moment of profound remorse. Regardless, Dorothy knew that what she was doing was right, and so she proceeded. "Well, that may be, but since Josephine looks upon you as a mentor, striving to emulate you, it has become an acute problem of late."

Again, Sarah Ashley said nothing, simply sat staring at Dorothy with an expression that had changed from remorse to despair. Feeling a vague sense of injustice on her part, Dorothy shifted her gaze to a bouquet of asters on the windowsill. "I'm afraid Louella has also become a problem since your arrival. Before, she never disobeyed her father. But now we learn that not only did she go against Jon's strict orders that she not visit the O'Shaunessey girl, but she faced grave danger because of it ... and you knew."

"But I assure you, I had nothing to do with Louella going to see the girl," said Sarah.

"Perhaps not," replied Dorothy, "but you did hide the fact from her father."

"No, I did not," Sarah insisted. "I told him that very same day what Louella had done."

"But you failed to mention that Mrs. O'Shaunessey had a gun. You may not be aware of it, Miss Ashley, but we have just learned that the O'Shaunessey girl's mother shot and killed the girl's father on that very day and hid the body. It was only just discovered."

"What! Oh ... my God ..." Sarah exclaimed, her face growing pale.

"Yes ... as a matter of fact, the woman claimed that she was protecting Louella from the man," Dorothy said, focusing on Sarah's chin so she wouldn't have to look into those stunned, repentant eyes. "Louella is deeply disturbed by the incident. And she claims that she did tell you about Mrs. O'Shaunessey having a gun."

Sarah's hands twisted in her lap. "Yes," she admitted. "I did know about it. But Louella was so upset, and she begged me not to say anything to her father, so I promised I wouldn't."

"Well, that was not a wise decision on your part," said Dorothy. "Her father should have been told everything, regardless of Louella's wishes. These problems with the girls are added complications that Jon simply does not need right now."

To Dorothy's shock, Sarah's enormous green eyes filled with tears. Sarah blinked several times, then looked away, reaching for a scotchbread to disguise her emotion.

"What is it you want me to do?" Sarah asked,

looking at the pastry she held in her trembling fingers.

Dorothy swallowed hard, fixed her objective in her mind, and replied, "The only thing you can do if you love Jon—and I do believe you love him. Leave Victoria." She said the words slowly, purposefully, and emphatically. "Should you remain in Victoria, not only would you further damage his standing in the community and threaten his position with the royal government, but you would also jeopardize the welfare of his daughters."

"I see." Sarah stood, walked to the window without turning, and looked out. After a few moments, she said, "If you'll excuse me, I must see to some . . . things."

"I understand." Dorothy realized the woman was crying softly. "I'll just let myself out." When Sarah didn't respond, Dorothy gathered her reticule, stepped around the patterns on the floor, and left the cottage.

As the door clicked shut, Sarah moved from the window and blotted her eyes with her apron. How could she have allowed herself to lose control in front of Lady Cromwell? And how humiliating to know that Jon's mother and the entire town seemed to know that Jon had been at her house on at least two occasions.

And no doubt on the beach as well!

Of course! Hollis had already started to carry out his threat. He'd see her driven from Victoria. He'd see her in hell again before it was over . . .

Warm tears flooded her eyes. She felt so empty . . . so hollow. She and Jon had shared acts of love, even though the words had not been spoken. How could she simply walk out of his life? Her previous goal, which had once seemed so important, became secondary to the loss she felt over not sharing a life with him.

But, loving him as she did, what choice did she have?

If she stayed in Victoria, her presence in his life, and the vicious gossip that Hollis would spread, would threaten his career and perhaps even threaten the colony; it would also destroy his daughter's respect for him and alienate him from his family. And she could not take that chance.

Nor could she face another horrible scandal.

She dragged a trunk into the parlor. She'd leave right away . . . on the next steamer leaving the city. Whether it was bound for Port Townsend or Seattle or New Westminster, it made no difference, as long as she was gone before Jon returned. It was the cowardly way out, but her only choice. If she saw him again and he opened his arms to her, she feared she'd lose herself in his embrace. If he returned before she got away, she'd have no alternative but to appear cold and uncaring, because if she floundered he'd see through her actions and simply not allow her to leave. And she could not give him that chance to change her mind.

She blotted her eyes. She'd put thoughts of him from her mind. Yes, she would. After all, he embraced the traditional male attitude about a woman's place. Which undoubtedly applied to his mistress as well. And she just couldn't live with that.

Yes . . . she could. And that was the honest truth. She could live with it. It wasn't his traditional male attitude at all that stopped her.

The truth was, she couldn't bear to raise a child who could one day be accused of being just another bastard who didn't even know its father.

Although Jon had said he'd care for any child of their union, that wasn't enough. Her own mother must have believed that the man she'd given herself to would stay by her. But he hadn't. He'd simply turned his back on her and his daughter and walked out of their lives.

And if a younger, more beautiful woman walked into Jon's life one day, there was no assurance that he might not do the same. Although they'd shared their love, that didn't change the fact: she was just a woman he wanted for his mistress. Nothing more. And never would be.

And she couldn't live with that.

Jon snapped the buggy whip smartly over the mare's rump, urging her on, anxious to get back to Sarah. She'd been on his mind constantly while he was in New Westminster, and he wanted her. The buggy rattled and bumped over the uneven road, a road that would soon be macadamized. Which should give the Crown something to take note of.

This last trip to New Westminster verified his hunch: while the city fathers boasted funds in accounts, the city's ditches overflowed with drainage from cesspools, streams of soapy water ran from the public bath houses into the unpaved streets, and the whole place reeked of rotting fish, pent-up pigs, and carrion from the slaughterhouses.

While Victoria's accounts might fall significantly short of the glorified and somewhat padded accounts of New Westminster, Victoria's streets were being macadamized, gaslights were operating, a free common school had been established, and all butcher shops, tanneries, and slaughterhouses were located outside the city limits. Soon, even an observatory was to be constructed.

If union was advised, and the Crown representatives took all these civil improvements into consideration when reviewing the ledgers, there was no question which city was better suited to become capital of the province, or which governor should head the expanded colony.

What a life! His political position was sound, his daughters were safely confined to their rooms, and a beautiful, fascinating, and intelligent woman was waiting eagerly to warm his bed. Sweet, sensual Sarah. His wanton little witch. Godamercy! How he wanted that woman.

He snapped the whip again. The mare extended its strides, kicking up billows of dust and leaving a brown cloud scudding behind. Ah ... to feel Sarah's hot body writhing in his arms, her smooth skin beneath his palms, her lovely breasts against his chest. The thought was driving him wild. She was his mistress, and he intended to seal their commitment with an afternoon of untamed, unencumbered lovemaking.

He'd undress her slowly, lay her on the bed, and suckle each luscious breast while she gasped those soft little moans that drove him wild, while she begged him to take her. But he'd make her wait until he kissed his way down the length of her and suckled her toes ... then trailed kisses across her ankle ... over her smooth calves ... up her legs where he would slowly and sensuously caress her with his tongue until she wantonly cried out her impassioned need for him.

God! He was as hot as hell!

He snapped the whip again. The damned mare was trotting as if they were on a Sunday outing. If he didn't get to Sarah's soon, he feared he'd split his breeches. Maybe he'd forget the slow undressing ... save the toe suckling for later. Hell, he might just make love to her on the floor of the parlor.

Rounding the bend, he caught sight of the cottage. He ran his tongue across his mouth, the saltiness reminding him of how her damp skin tasted when they'd made love.

Pulling the mare to a halt, he lunged from the buggy, rushed up to the cottage, and knocked. Too anxious to wait for a response, he swept open the door, then froze when he found Sarah bent over a trunk . . . packing!

Her sewing machines were gone, the tables dismantled, and three trunks appeared to be packed. She looked at him, said nothing, and continued packing without so much as a greeting. This was definitely not the welcome he'd expected. Obviously, she had not been waiting breathlessly to be in his arms. "Did you locate a building?" he asked.

"No. I'm moving to New Westminster." Sarah continued to pack the trunk. She dared not look up, knowing that if she gazed into Jon's eyes, she'd crack.

She must stay calm . . . and cold.

"What do you mean you're moving?"

"Just what I said. You and everyone else around here have made it impossible for me to remain in Victoria, so I'm moving to New Westminster where I can make a fresh start."

"Something happened while I was away. What was it?"

"Nothing happened except that I had a week to think about things . . . about us, and about what I want, and I want to leave Victoria. Now, if you'll excuse me, I must keep packing, as I have booked passage on the *Eliza Anderson* for this afternoon, and I *will* be on it." She started around him.

He shot out a hand and took her arm. "The hell you'll be on it! You can't just walk away from me. I won't let you."

She looked into eyes filled with rage and bewilderment, and quickly snatched her gaze away. She must remain cold and uncaring ... not allow herself to falter. "There's nothing you can do to stop me."

"Oh, yes, there is." He pulled her to him and covered her mouth with his.

Before the kiss could deepen, she jerked her head to one side. He attempted to hold her and capture her mouth again, but she forced her arms between them, shoving against his chest. "Stop it, Jon! I don't want this! The fact that we indulged in a few nights of dallying does not mean you own me." Yanking herself free, she dashed into the bedroom and slammed the door.

"*Dallying!* Is that all it was to you?" He burst open the door and glared at her.

"I don't know why you seem so surprised," she said, cradling a stack of fabric to her chest. "I never led you to believe it was anything else. Nor do I want to be your mistress." She brushed past him, knelt down, and continued packing.

"I don't believe you can just dismiss what we have."

"I'm not dismissing it," she said. "I'll always cherish it. But I made no promises and nothing has changed. I *will* see my business become a success, but not in Victoria. And I *will* maintain my earnings, my independence, and my rights as a human being."

"I don't know how the hell you can be so indifferent." He took her arm and dragged her to her feet. "Look at me and tell me you don't want me."

She lifted her chin and said in a firm voice intended to hide her shakiness, "I don't want you, Jon. Now will you please let me get back to my packing? I have a steamer to catch, and you're in the way here."

She tried to pull free, but he tightened his hand, his fingers digging into her arm. "You're leaving me for a goddamned bloody mercantile business!"

"Let me go. You're hurting me."

His fingers tightened, and his words were ruthless. "It seems your brothers were right. You do have means of getting whatever you want. I admit, a man would have to be dead not to respond to your ... charms. It's obvious what you wanted from me from the start. After all, as governor, I should be able to pave some ways for you. But you quit too soon. You should have opted for a letter of introduction to give to Governor Seymour when you get to New Westminster. Now there's a thought. Maybe for another quick roll in the hay, I'd be willing. But then, maybe I wouldn't. I don't relish the idea of having my eyes scratched out by a loose-tailed little hellcat."

Sarah cocked her arm and slapped Jon hard across the jaw. "Get out! Get out of my house!"

His eyes blazed. "I'll get out ... sure as hell, I'll get out. But first ..." He yanked her into his arms and plunged his mouth on hers in a brutal, punishing kiss, one hand tight against her head so she couldn't break loose, the other pressing against her back so her body was crushed hard against his. She struggled in his arms and squealed her protest against his mouth, but the kiss was merciless, unrelenting. Then he released her abruptly. "Goodbye, *sweetheart!*" He slammed his fist against a trunk and stomped out of the house, sending the door crashing shut behind him. Yelling a string of expletives, he cracked his whip and sent the buggy rattling away.

It wasn't until then that every nerve in Sarah's body seemed too snap. Tears rolled down her cheeks, her body began to shake uncontrollably, and she felt as if her heart were being crushed.

Chapter 21

As she'd done several times before, Sarah peered through the window, half-expecting to see Jon's carriage. She envisioned him sweeping open the door again, but this time he'd force her to admit that she'd lied—that she really did want him. And she *would* admit it. Ever since he'd walked out the door, she'd been fighting the urge to go to him. But such a step would be pointless.

Nothing had changed. And nothing would.

She shivered as she envisioned Jon's face when she'd told him she didn't want him. First shock. Then disbelief. She gazed up at a leaden sky churning with dark clouds, a sky that reminded her of the turmoil she'd felt on hearing Jon's cruel words ... horrible, brutal words that made her feel cheap, like the wanton whore Hollis had said she was.

How long would it take to get over the terrible despair? A year? Two years? In time, she would come to terms with it. But for now, she felt lost, her life pointless, the world colorless and flat.

Closing her eyes, she felt as if she were plummeting into an oblivion where she would drift aimlessly through an eternity alone. Teetering on the brink of tears, she opened her eyes, turned from the window, and determined to snap out of her morose mood. She refused to indulge in any more noisy floods of weeping.

She looked around. With the trunks now in the pie wagon—she'd hired two boys to load them—the room seemed so bare. No sewing machines or patterns or lengths of fabric. No lacy curtains on the windows. And in less than two hours, she'd sail out of Jon's life.

Mandi had promised to come visit her. New Westminster was not so terribly far away. She'd told Mandi goodbye the night before, when she'd also told her of her decision to go. A wise move, she had explained, to another city poised on the verge of growth, where Hollis and Tyler couldn't find her and where she could see her business become a success. And she wouldn't be so far away.

She'd been careful not to reveal to Mandi her true motives for leaving; she couldn't face the shame of telling Mandi that Jon wanted her only as his mistress.

The sound of horses' hooves brought her rushing to the door. "Jon!" Instead, she found a boy of about twelve dismounting. He sprinted up the footpath, swept off his hat, and held it between nervous fingers. "Miss Ashley?"

"Yes."

"This is for you." He handed her a note.

Sarah unfolded the paper and read the hastily scrawled words: *Miss Ashley, please meet me on Kaindler's Wharf at three o'clock. I have several orders for you. D.P.*

Sarah couldn't remember which of the women on the waterfront was D.P. But since the steamer wasn't leaving until four o'clock, she would have time to meet briefly with the woman, explain her plans, and obtain the orders, which she would fill when she was settled in New Westminster, and ship back to the woman later. She gave the boy tuppence and a message to tell the woman that she'd be there.

Shortly before three o'clock, she gathered the last of her belongings, closed up the cottage, and headed for the waterfront. She parked the pie wagon a short distance from the wharf and looked for the woman, but found instead only seamen and prospectors. After twenty minutes, the woman still had not arrived, and Sarah realized she couldn't wait any longer. She still had to take her trunks to the steamer dock for loading and return the pie wagon to the livery in time to catch the steamer.

Taking a last look around, she headed for her wagon. Something about the situation brought on a vague uneasiness. She also noticed that another wagon was parked right behind her pie wagon, even though there was ample room for parking all along the street.

Feeling uneasy, she mounted the box and reached for the reins. But before she could move, a large hand darted out from behind and covered her mouth, and a powerful arm clamped around her waist and dragged her backward inside the wagon. She tried to cry out, but the cry was stifled by a brutal slap followed by the twist of a gag clinched fast around her head. Immediately, her ankles were clamped and bound, her hands forced behind her back and wrapped. Struggling against the restraints, she was enveloped by a blanket, which was trussed securely around her until she was virtually unable to move. She felt herself lifted out of the wagon by two pairs of hands. Bucking inside her blanket cocoon, she attempted to scream through the gag, but the numbing impact of something solid and hard struck through the blanket, sending her into darkness . . .

* * *

A mustiness reeking of mold, ferment, and the pungent odor of rat droppings assaulted Sarah's nostrils. Her brain still sluggish from the drug that had been forced down her throat, she opened her eyes and peered into a black void. Her head ached, and she felt a painful lump on the back of it, but she was no longer trussed inside the blanket, and the bindings on her wrists and feet had been removed.

She tried to piece together what had happened, but her memory was clouded. Her last coherent thought was of being seized, gagged, and bound. Then everything had gone dark.

Hearing the staccato hiss of a boiler and the muffled thrash of paddles churning water, she realized she was on a steamer. She sat up, blood pulsing in her ears, a stabbing pain in her head. She touched a tentative hand to the welt on the back of her head and felt a crust of blood. When the pain had passed, she reached out to orient herself, groping around until she located the door, which she found locked.

She had no idea how long she'd been in this fetid cell. It could have been minutes or hours. Perhaps even days. She'd lost all sense of time. In the pitch-black hold of the vessel, there was no day or night.

So ... Wellington really had overheard a plan to abduct her. But she could think of no logical reason why she'd been taken, or why she was being held prisoner. Unless ...

Hollis! He had something to do with this, she was certain. But what would he expect to accomplish by having her taken away?

Amid the din of the paddlewheel, she heard footsteps plodding toward her and the rattle of the latch, and she held her breath. Her chest felt tight, and there was a jittery weakness in her limbs as she waited for whoever would enter. Soon, she realized the sound had not come from the door of her cabin, but instead from a cabin on the opposite side of the bulkhead.

As she peered into the darkness, searching for anything that might give form to her obscure world, dim amber light flickered through a small crack in the bulkhead. Pressing her eye to the opening, she saw a shadowy shape, and when the figure turned toward her, the flame of a single candle brought Harriet Galbraith's face into stark relief.

Sarah stared in shocked bewilderment. She must be aboard Reverend Galbraith's mission ship. So Hollis really was behind this—she'd seen him talking to Reverend Galbraith the first day she'd sold bloomers from her pie wagon. Hollis had obviously paid the Galbraiths to haul her away. But why? What did he expect to gain by having her kidnapped? Certainly not her money. It just didn't make sense.

Harriet Galbraith brought the candleholder closer. Eerie ocher light flooded her face, accenting the bony line of her jaw and heightening the pouches hanging beneath her eyes—excited eyes that glistened with expectation. Moving to one of several upended barrels labeled WATER, Harriet removed a large bung and reached inside, drawing out a small bag ... and another ... and another, continuing to retrieve bags until she sat behind a large mound.

Loosening the ties of one of the bags, she tipped it toward her hand. Shimmering gold dusted her palm. She let out a gasp of pure pleasure, then quickly pressed her hand to her mouth to stifle her cry, leaving her thin lips sparkling with gold dust.

She raised her eyes and cocked her head, then looked at the door in alarm. Muffled footsteps in the passageway beat a slow, steady rhythm as they moved closer. Harriet quickly returned the bags to the cask, but while she fumbled with the fastenings of the opened bag, the door latch rattled and Reverend Galbraith appeared in the portal.

Closing the door, he peered down at Harriet. His bristly brows gathered with outrage. "I thought I'd find you here. You have clearly disobeyed me."

"I was only looking at it, James."

He snatched the bag from her hands. "You indolent old woman. You were to fetch tallow lights, not lust after gold. And when you disobey me, you must be punished."

Harriet's wizened face pinched with distress. "Please, James, I didn't mean to disobey you. I only wanted to—"

His hand shot out and slapped her sharply across the face, sending her falling back. "I shall not listen to the sniveling of a disobedient wife. Now fetch the tallow lights as you were told."

"Yes, James."

The latch rattled, the door slammed, and Reverend Galbraith's footsteps died away.

Sarah felt a twinge of sympathy for Harriet Galbraith. But when she groped into the darkness and located the door latch and found it locked securely, the feelings passed, and fear welled. Knocking on the bulkhead, she called to Harriet Galbraith, "Why am I being held?"

Harriet didn't respond, but Sarah knew the woman had not yet left the cabin. She knocked again. "I know you're in there, and I know my brother is behind this. Where are you taking me?"

After a few moments, Harriet replied, "You have been sold to white-slave traders and are being taken to the goldfields like the other harlots."

"No!" Sarah gasped. "You can't mean that. I am *not* a harlot."

"You are a woman of sin," said Harriet, "and you must pay for your sins. It is our mission to rid the city of evil while acquiring bounty so that Reverend Galbraith may continue God's work." Harriet's voice no longer carried the timbre of pathetic acquiescence that Sarah had heard when she'd spoken to her husband.

Sarah moved so that her mouth was close to the crack. "How can you believe this is God's work?"

"Do not question!" she said in a tone which was a caricature of her husband's. "The Lord speaks through my husband, and the Lord is not to be questioned."

"How can you possibly believe that your husband is a godly man after the way he hit you?"

A portentous silence hung. After a moment, the dim light fluttered and disappeared from the crack, the door to the adjacent cabin slammed abruptly, and Harriet's quick steps sounded in the passageway, gradually fading.

Sarah sat on the pallet in darkness, listening to the slapping of waves on the hull and the sloshing of water in the bilges directly below her. She strained to see around her, but found herself cloaked in a pitch-blackness that was unlike any darkness she'd ever known.

Cold. Foreboding. Tomblike.

To her horror, a series of short gnawing sounds came from just across the cabin. "Oh, my God! Rats!" She scooted back on the pallet, pressing against the bulkhead. "Shoo! Shoo!" The gnawing stopped, followed by the sinister shuffle of diminutive feet. Sarah's breath came fast. She imagined red eyes like polished buttons peering at her through the darkness . . . a quivering nose taking in her scent . . . sharp teeth poised to sink into her flesh . . .

She pulled her legs close, tucked her knees under her chin . . . and waited . . .

The gnawing started again.

"Shoo ... shoo!" she cried, clapping her hands.

The rat skittered across the deck boards, its claws clicking against the wood as it scuttled off.

Hours, it seemed, passed. With the exception of the rat and a silent shadowy figure who reached inside the door and set a slop jar and a tray with bread, cheese, and water on the floor, Sarah was alone. She had no appetite, but hearing the patter of feet coming closer—the rat becoming increasingly bold—she ate the cheese and bread, knowing that if she didn't, the rat soon would.

To stifle her growing anxiety, she shifted her thoughts to the water casks and the gold. Gold acquired through the sale of women ... Wanton whores who lusted after men ...

So Hollis had convinced the Galbraiths ...

She must escape. The sounds of water close below and against the hull meant she was at the bottom of the steamer. And since the thrashing of the paddles was far away, she must be near the bow. She'd break the latch, slip out of the cabin, and hide, then flee as soon as they docked. But if her plan failed, she'd have to convince whoever was to meet the Galbraiths that she was not a harlot.

Would they really care? From the looks of the men wandering the waterfront of Victoria, they most probably would not. To them, a woman served one purpose.

She must find something ... a tool to pry off the latch or wedge open the door. She ventured off the pallet onto the cold, damp floor, groping her way blindly while crying into the darkness, "Shoo! Shoo!" She padded around the cabin, passing a discerning hand over the sharp corners of wooden boxes and the rounded edges of casks, but found nothing with which to pry open the latch. Then she raised her nose to a cask and inhaled deeply. The musty odor of liquor filled her nostrils.

Whiskey!

The Galbraiths were smuggling spirits to the miners as well as women, while operating under the guise of a mission ship. When, and if, she got away, she'd get word to Jon.

Jon . . .

He seemed so far away now. So unreachable . . .

All she wanted was to crawl into his arms and be held and tell him she loved him, that she wasn't those things Hollis had said . . .

Her head throbbing with a steady beat, she curled into a ball on the pallet and closed her eyes.

Some time later, she awoke to the blast of a steamboat whistle and realized the paddles had stopped. From the passageway came men's voices. "Jake, ye take tha whore tae Galbraith and coom back tae 'elp me unload tha casks," one said in a heavy brogue.

"I kinda wanted a piece o' that whore before we let 'er go," replied the man called Jake. "No one 'ould know if we helped ourselves. She's got tits a man could sink his teeth in. Makes me hard just thinkin' about 'em. Whatcha say, Mac? It wouldn't take no time at all. I'm 'bout splittin' outta me breeches already."

"I canna say nay tae that," replied Mac, "but we have ta make it quick. Galbraith dinna like waitin' while we dipped our dicks tha last time."

"I'm ready now . . . jeez, I'm ready. I'll be done by the time you git your dick out."

A wedge of light cut through the gloom. Sarah scooted into the corner, into shadows beyond the light. She crouched and held her breath. The man's large shadow was thrown across the wall. "Where is she?" he asked, his fingers fumbling with his breeches. "Gimme the lantern."

Light flooded the cabin.

"She's over here," said the other. "Here ... hold this." He passed the lantern back, casting the cabin into shadowy darkness. But even with his back to the light, Sarah knew precisely what he was doing. He reached for her, and she shrieked, scrambling off the pallet and onto the damp floor.

"Ya not gittin' away from old Jake," the man said. "Come on, it'll only take a minute. It ain't like ya never did it afore."

"If you touch me," Sarah hissed, her back pressed against the boxes, "I'll claw your eyes out."

"Hey, Mac, we've got a little wildcat here. You hold her down for me an' I'll hold her for you."

Jake started toward her, but when he reached for her, she shrieked, raised her knee, and kicked him soundly in his exposed privates, doubling him over. She rushed out of the cabin and ran along the darkened passageway to an open hatch where a ladder led to a shadowy compartment above. Heavy footsteps accompanied by the vilest of profanities followed in her wake.

Scrambling up the ladder, she crawled onto the deck, only to be caught up short by Reverend Galbraith. Holding her in an iron clasp, he looked down at her, his fleshy nose bulbous and cherry-colored in the light from his lantern. "Where do you think you're going?"

Looking into his malevolent gaze, Sarah felt dread overwhelm her, and for the moment, she couldn't find her voice. Then she said, "Please. You're making a mistake."

Without speaking, Reverend Galbraith dragged her across the deck and thrust her into a cabin, sending her collapsing to her knees. She braced her palms on the floor and gazed across the room at an unkempt man with an unshaved face. Peering into a pair of cold, hard eyes, she said, "No. This is a mistake . . ."

Reverend Galbraith turned to the man. "Here's the whore, brother. You know where to take her."

Sarah backed away from the man, tears rolling down her cheeks. "No, please, I was taken against my will. I'm not a harlot. You can't do this!"

The man's mouth contorted into a hideous grin. Saying nothing, he grasped her arm and dragged her to her feet. A cold, acidlike fear burned through her as she realized, with horror, that she was about to become what Hollis had said she was: nothing more than a whore.

And maybe that's all she was.

Maybe it hadn't been love, after all, but lust she'd felt for Jon. She'd given of herself so freely, and with such abandon. And now she'd never be held in loving arms again . . . never be told she was someone's little love or his precious little peagoose . . .

Never be anything but a mistress . . . or a whore.

With that realization, something died inside her. All she felt was a grim numbness, a spiritless void.

Chapter 22

~~~⟡⟡~~~

J on paced the narrow confines of the stables like a
   caged animal. He had a colony to run, but all he
could think of was Sarah: how her lips curved in that
engaging little smile when she bested him, and the
way sparks ignited the impassioned depths of her
eyes when she was aroused, and how her fingers
drew little patterns on his chest when he held her after they'd made love.

And she'd simply walked out of his life.

Like Caroline, Sarah had swept him off his feet,
then betrayed him. But she hadn't betrayed him for
another man. She'd betrayed him for a goddamned
bloody business.

She'd offered no justification for what she was
doing. She'd callously repeated words he'd exacted
from her . . . and dismissed him. She didn't want him
in her life. And he burned with the desire to possess
her body and soul.

He'd half-expected her to stop to see him before
the steamer left yesterday . . . express some regret
over their angry parting. But she hadn't. Nor had she
changed her mind about leaving. He'd returned to
the cottage later, only to find it empty.

Yet . . . things didn't quite fit. She'd cleared all of
the business hurdles set in her path, and he'd even

agreed to get her a building, so it didn't seem probable that she was leaving because of her business.

Unless something had happened while he was away.

He eyed Peterson, who seemed just as baffled by Sarah's hasty departure as he was. "You must have heard something, Peterson. I'm not accusing you of talking, but I just thought maybe you've heard something—perhaps from Ida that came from Mandi. If you know anything, anything at all, I want to hear it."

"No one's said nothin', leastways nothin' to me. But . . ." He scratched his chin.

"But what? Dammit, man. Talk!"

Peterson shrugged. "It might have had to do with Lady Cromwell's visitin' Miss Ashley."

"Lady Cromwell?"

"While's you was away. It weren't long afterward that Miss Ashley left."

Jon's eyes narrowed. Hellfire and damnation! His mother was poking her nose where it didn't belong again. "Thank you, Peterson. I believe you've just given me some answers." He turned and headed toward the house. Marching into his mother's bedroom, he said, "What did you say to Sarah to make her leave?"

His mother fussed with her fichu. "I have no idea what you're talking about."

"Like hell you don't!"

Dorothy's thin nostrils flared. "Don't look at me as if I'd sprouted horns, a forked tail, and cloven hooves. I did it for your own good. As long as you persisted in dilly-dallying with the woman, your career was at stake. And now the decent folks in this town can talk of nothing but the fact that their esteemed governor has taken a mistress."

"Bloody hell!" Jon's clenched fist crashed down on the dresser. "The lot of them can go to the devil!"

Dorothy flinched. "*Is* she your mistress?"

Jon's eyes bored into hers. "That's no one's goddamned business but mine."

Dorothy's bottom lip quivered with vexation. "What do you suppose your daughters must think . . . hearing that their father has taken up with—"

"The woman he loves!" Jon's chest felt as if it were being crushed, and a dull pain accompanied each beat of his heart. The words sounded uncomfortably permanent . . . too closely linked with marriage. He swallowed a lump that seemed to have lodged in his throat. But marriage had never been the issue. Sarah had made it clear that she intended to maintain her independence . . . that nothing had changed that fact, not his presence in her life or his lovemaking.

But thanks to his mother, Sarah had known that the town was buzzing with gossip about her being his mistress. And she'd been too humiliated to stay in Victoria and face the hypocrites who gossiped righteously during the day and crept into their lovers' beds at night. And he'd acted like all the other bastards in her life, calling her a loose-tailed little hellcat and storming out in a rage, when the truth was, she was a woman who would not feel passion without love. A woman who . . . loved him.

A sensitive, vulnerable woman who was too independent to be a man's wife, and too proud to be his mistress. And he didn't know what in hell to do about it.

He glared at his mother, whose lips had flattened in annoyance. "Stay out of my personal life!" he shouted, and stormed out of the room, colliding with Ida in the hallway.

Ida pulled herself together. "There's a rather disreputable-looking gentleman here to see you. He says his name is Mr. Ely Cooper. Shall I send him away?"

"Cooper? He's from the livery," said Jon, puzzled. "No, I'll see what he wants."

Ely Cooper stood waiting in the entry. " 'Scuse me for disturbin' you, guv'nor, but there's somethin' I think you might want to know."

"Yes?" Jon saw from the nervous way Ely turned his hat in his hands that he was agitated about something.

"When I arrived at the livery this mornin', old Judd had wandered in by hisself and was standin' there with the wagon Miss Ashley had jobbed. The wagon had all Miss Ashley's goods in it, but she weren't nowheres about. I knew from the pile layin' behind old Judd that he'd been there awhile, so I 'spect he come sometime durin' the night." Ely dropped his eyes downward. "Knowin' your fondness for the lady, I thought you might oughta know."

Jon combed his fingers through his hair. There could be any number of explanations. Sarah could have hired someone to deliver the trunks to the wharf and return the wagon to the livery, and the person might have neglected to do so. Or she could have left the wagon parked somewhere and the old horse wandered off with it . . .

"Did the trunks look disturbed, as if something might have happened?"

"Well, yes, sir, they did . . . some," replied Ely. "A small one was toppled, and some goods was tossed about like there'd been a scuffle or somethin'."

"A scuffle?" The chilling possibility that something dire had happened to Sarah hit Jon with the impact of a severe blow. He braced his hand against the wall until the lightness passed.

"You okay, guv'nor?"

"Oh . . . uh . . . yes." Jon sucked in a long breath to

try to calm the aberrant beating of his heart. He fumbled in his pocket and drew out a gold piece. Pressing it into Ely's hand, he said, "Go to the waterfront and start asking questions. See what you can learn about what happened."

"Yes, sir," said Ely. "I know some lads who know just about everything that goes on down there. I'll hustle 'em up and see what they can find out."

Immediately, Jon went to tell Sheriff Heaton what had happened, and Heaton and his deputies began combing the waterfront and searching backstreets and alleys.

Two hours later, Heaton located Jon on the wharf at the foot of Yates Street. "We talked to a woman who said she was one of Miss Ashley's customers," said Heaton. "She claimed she saw two men haul something big from the pie wagon, that it could've been a woman wrapped in a blanket. They dumped it into another wagon and drove off. I'm afraid it looks like she's been shanghaied."

Jon felt his heart squeezed as though in a vise. He had to swallow before words could come. "Those bloody rutting bastards in the goldfields will kill her!"

"It looks bad," agreed Heaton. "Meanwhile, we checked sailing schedules for ships that left port yesterday and today, just in case things turned out this way. Along with the *Revelation*, which we discounted—it being the mission ship and all—there were three other steamers heading for the goldfields: the *Prince George*, the *Vanderhoof*, and the *Lillooet*. Of course, she could have been transported in a smaller vessel."

"Then we'll go after them," said Jon, clenching his jaws with grim determination. "Tell Dudley to make ready the *Hudson*, and tell Burlington to meet me in my office. And I'll need some men."

Blood drummed in Jon's ears. He'd battle his way through hell and throw himself at Sarah's feet if only to beg her forgiveness for the callous—no, brutal— things he'd said to her. Nothing mattered now but finding her and telling her he loved her ... unequivocally. Unequivocally.

As the gangway of the *Hudson* settled against the dock, jagged lightning stabbed through the clouds and thunder cracked with a deafening report, rumbling and rolling and gaining momentum as it feathered out across the sky.

Standing on the deck, Jon tugged his hat lower to fend off gust-blown raindrops that whipped him as if with angry impatience. He gazed at the derelict town, another nameless settlement of tents and shacks and hovels and bawdy hotels dotting the banks of the Fraser River. The hamlet was deserted, save for a few paltry prospectors who slogged ankle-deep in the slurry.

Was Sarah imprisoned in one of the ramshackle hotels overlooking the muddy street? Or perhaps locked in one of the shacks or hovels cluttering the riverbank? Or would this be just another futile stop like all the others?

It had been six hellish days since she'd disappeared.

What kind of barbaric nightmare had she endured? When he found her—*if* he found her—he'd kill the blackhearted bastards who had kidnapped her. He'd kill any who'd ... had her.

"Governor?"

Jon turned to find Daniel Fenster, one of the deputies accompanying him. Fenster handed over the reins of Jon's bay gelding and stood beside Jon while holding his own horse. He pointed north along the river. "Looks like most of the settlement stretches up that trail. I'll head that way and start asking questions, and Derry can head south, if that sounds all right."

Jon heaved a burdensome sigh. "I guess that's about all we can do." Scanning the saloons, dance halls, and hotels, he decided to start questioning at Goldie's Saloon, an ornate, high-fronted building just up the road. It appeared to be the most prosperous of the bunch, and seemed to be packed to capacity.

Jon led his horse down the gangway, mounted, and rode up the road to Goldie's. Inside, he questioned a bartender, who promptly suggested he talk to Goldie.

The scene was almost a repeat of the three previous stops: question the bartender, talk to the madam, and meet Rosie or Kate or any of a half-dozen jades who chucked him under the chin and tried to lure him to her bed.

He knocked on the door labeled OFFICE and was promptly met by a wiry little woman with spectacles propped on her nose and a tangle of peppery-gray hair caught with a tortoiseshell comb on top of her head. "I'm looking for Miss Goldie," he said.

"I'm Goldie." The woman's eyes roamed down the length of him and meandered up again. She smiled, revealing crooked teeth with a lower tooth missing. "Well, come on in, honey. I've been waitin' for you." She tugged his arm to usher him into the room and kicked the door shut.

Puzzled, Jon peered down at the tiny woman. Had word of his mission already reached this godforsaken place? "Do you know something about Miss Ashley?"

Her measuring stare still fixed on him, Goldie appeared to be assessing the breadth of his shoulders. "I don't know no Miss Ashley," she said, "but I've got girls here who'll make you sizzle in more places than you know you got . . . if you know what I mean." Her gaze dropped, and she stared pointedly. "And from the looks of you, big fella, you just might get my girls to sizzlin', too." Her laugh was low and raspy.

"I'm not here to bed your women," said Jon. "I'm looking for a woman—slender, pretty, fiery red hair. She'd be new to the area—would have arrived no more than three or four days ago."

"Was she lookin' for work?"

"No. She was taken against her will. We have reason to believe she may be somewhere around here."

Goldie's painted brows came together with a thoughtful frown. She eyed him speculatively. "Red hair, you said?"

"Fiery red."

"I've heard tell that some of the boys living in a shack on the Dopp claim up Calkins Gulch have a woman with red hair. Word is she's right pleasin' to look at, too. I guess there's men waitin' in line for that one."

"Jesus Christ!" A cold shiver touched Jon's spine. "How long has she been there?"

Goldie shrugged. "Three, maybe four days. Never saw her myself, but I heard talk of a fancy-looker who came in on one of the steamers. Set the town a-buzzin'. My boys—the regulars here—were pretty excited, thought she was comin' here. But I guess that bunch up the gulch have their own place set up."

"How do I get there?"

"Just follow the trail north till it forks—two, maybe three miles up yonder—and instead of takin' the high trail, head east into the gulch and start lookin' for the water tower. It's not more'n a mile or so up the creek."

Jon pulled a gold piece from his pocket and flashed it in front of Goldie. "I need to send word to the government steamer. Who can I trust to do the job?"

Goldie eyed the gold piece. "If you give that to any man around here, you can be sure it'll be used to warm one of my girls' beds. So I'd better go myself."

"Fine." He handed the gold piece to Goldie. "I want you to go aboard the government steamer and tell the deputy exactly what you told me. And tell him to follow me up the creek and meet me at the Dopp claim."

Goldie lifted her skirt and slipped the gold piece into a small pouch tied to her garter. "Consider it done."

Jon thanked her and left the saloon. Heading north on the mucky trail, he pressed his horse into a mud-splattering gallop. Cold rain pelted his face and rolled down his neck inside the collar of his coat. At the fork in the road, he followed the lower trail into the gulch. He couldn't imagine what Sarah's state of mind would be at this point, but he'd soon find out, as the shack at the base of the water tower was quickly coming into view.

Reining in so he wouldn't alert whoever might be inside the shack, he dismounted and approached slowly. A short distance from the cabin, he tethered his horse, scrambled across the clearing, and crept onto the porch. Crouching, he peered through the window.

His breath caught. His heart tumbled.

Sarah stood in the doorway of what appeared to be a bedroom, talking to a man who sat in a chair, his back to Jon. In the haunted depths of her eyes, Jon saw a grim remoteness. And as he stared at her haggard face, the sharp sting of guilt and remorse pierced him. She'd been living in her own private hellhole. He'd free her from it now, but the scars might last a lifetime.

Her hand went up to her chest and her fingers tightened protectively on her bodice as he heard her say, "How long do you plan to hold me here?" Her voice sounded unnaturally passive. Yet it didn't ring of defeat. And when he caught sight of the scornful curve of her lips, he knew the man had not broken her spirit.

The man shrugged. "Who knows? When we're finished here, we might just sell you to the whoremongers and double our profit."

Another man's voice came from inside the bedroom behind Sarah. "Get back in here, you little bitch!" he bellowed. "You're not done yet."

Hate and fear rose up inside Jon, the fear making his hate much greater. All he had to do was walk in there and take Sarah ... and he would. But first, he intended to beat the bloody hell out of two men.

Chapter 23

J on raised his leg and kicked the door at the latch, sending it crashing open. He knocked the man in the chair to the floor and planted his fist hard into the man's face, hitting him repeatedly: square in the nose, under the jaw, in the chin. Then he attacked his belly, the blow sending a whoosh of air erupting. "You bastard!" Jon yelled. "You goddamned bloody rutting bastard." He kneed the man hard where he knew it would do some damage, and was rewarded by a sharp howl of pain as the man attempted to double up under Jon's weight. Then he hit him square in the jaw again, this time feeling him go limp beneath him.

Promptly, Jon felt the sharp crack of a chair smashing and shattering against his back. Jumping to his feet, he turned and landed a punch into the belly of the other man, sending him staggering back and falling to the floor. The man struggled to his feet, but Jon lunged for him, knocking him down. Straddling him, Jon pressed his thumbs to the man's windpipe until he saw veins bulge in his temples.

Sarah backed against the wall, watching in stunned helplessness, when suddenly she glimpsed the face of the man who had burst into the cabin.

"Jon!" she gasped, but knew he was too filled with murderous intent to hear her.

Fearing she'd soon be witnessing a killing if she didn't do something quick, she picked up a bucket and banged it repeatedly against the floor. "Stop!" she yelled. "Stop, Jon, you'll kill him!"

When Jon made no move to stop, she whacked him across the shoulders with the bucket. "Stop!" she yelled, tugging on his arm. "That's Tyler!" For a moment, she thought Jon hadn't heard, and she wasn't certain Tyler was still conscious. But then Jon released his hold and moved away. Tyler sat up abruptly, clasping his throat and coughing, while across the room, Hollis lay unconscious.

His fists still balled, his gaze shifting between the two men, Jon curved his arm around Sarah and drew her to him. "Are you all right?"

Sarah braced her hand against him, fearing her knees might buckle with the relief she felt on being in his arms again, his body pressed securely against hers. "Yes, I'm fine." She looked up and for the first time saw his drawn and weary face: eyes deeply shadowed, mouth heavily downcast, chin shadowed by a beard.

He peered down at her, inspecting her more closely. "Then they didn't ... I mean, no men have ... ?"

"I assure you, Jon, I am untouched."

"But I don't understand," he said, his brows drawn in a frown. "Why were you called back into the bedroom?"

"To finish mopping the floor. Tyler spilled beer all over it." Sarah released a weary sigh. "That was part of their redress. And I had to do it with threadbare rags, which don't work very well."

"I can't believe they went to such extremes just to make a servant out of you."

"They didn't." Sarah looked at Hollis, her gaze

coldly assessing the unconscious man. For the first time in months, she didn't fear him. "They did it to get my money. They said they'd sell me to white-slave traders if I didn't sign . . ." Her voice trailed off as she reflected on Hollis's dire threat. He'd even introduced her to the whoremonger.

"Get your friggin' ass outta here," Hollis had said, dragging her from the back room. "Meet Mr. Ramsey Milligan. He wants whores . . . with healthy appetites. Ones who can screw all night and still beg for more." He'd hurled her against the burly, red-faced man who reeked of whiskey and cheap cigars.

The man had reached out and touched her face, and she'd flinched. His eyes had darkened, and his cigar had bobbed up and down in his mouth as he'd said, "Show me the rest of her. I want to know what I'm buying."

She'd expected Hollis to comply, but to her surprise, he'd said, "If you outbid the others, you'll see her . . . every friggin' inch of her." His mouth had twisted in a serpentine smile that left no doubt in Sarah's mind that she would be stripped naked before money passed hands.

Jon's hand began gently moving up and down her arm. "Did you sign, sweetheart?"

On hearing his endearment, tears misted Sarah's eyes. "No. I knew that as long as I refused, Hollis would hold the men at bay. But the offers were getting higher . . . too high for Hollis to turn down. I tried to escape once, but Hollis had hired a ruffian to guard the cabin—the same man he sent to fetch me from the steamer—and the man caught me and dragged me back. This morning, Hollis gave me an ultimatum. He told me to sign today, or be sold to the man, Milligan. But I knew that signing wouldn't stop Hollis from selling me and getting more money." Just thinking about it sent a rush of bile to her throat, and a cold, clammy sweat breaking out on her brow.

"It's all right now, love," said Jon, when Sarah started shaking. He curved both arms around her and held her. "It's all right, love, you're fine now—"

"Hold it!" Hollis leaped to his feet, a pistol gripped in his hand. Before Sarah could scream, Jon hurled her out of the way and lunged for Hollis, gripping him around the waist and heaving him against the wall. As they struggled for the gun, it discharged, the sound reverberating off the walls. For a moment, both men remained standing. Then, gradually, Hollis slipped out of Jon's grasp and fell to the floor. Sarah stood in shocked silence, too stunned to speak. Then she saw Jon holding his side, blood dampening his shirt. "Oh, God!" She rushed over to him.

Jon raised his hand to stop her. "I'm all right," he said. "It's your brother's blood, not mine." He crouched above Hollis and slowly turned over his lifeless body. Hollis stared at the ceiling with unseeing eyes. As Jon gazed at a face devoid of expression, the anger and hatred he'd felt moments before vanished, replaced by sad regret. Although Hollis had been stricken by his own weapon while attempting to assault Jon, his death was the first in which Jon had been directly instrumental, a thought which caused him certain grief. The man was also Sarah's kin, which added to that distress. But Sarah was safe from Hollis now, and for that reason alone, Jon knew he could come to terms with what had happened.

He looked up at Sarah. "I'm sorry, love," was all he could bring himself to say.

Sarah stared at Hollis, feeling both remorse and relief at the death of the man who had caused her so much heartache. For years, she'd lived in fear of what Hollis could do, and now she was free of him. But her freedom had come at too high a price. Death was so final and terrible. If only things could have worked out differently. If only she could have been Hollis's friend instead of the enemy he'd made her out to be. If only Hollis had not been driven by greed . . .

She closed her eyes, blocking out the horrible scene. Thank God it had not been Jon. How could she have lived with that? Opening her eyes to reconfirm that Jon was indeed safe, she gasped when she saw him inspecting a large, ruddy-black wound at his waist. "Oh, God!" she exclaimed. "You *have* been shot!"

"No," he assured her. "It's just a powder burn." The issue was dismissed when Jon spotted Tyler inching toward the door, primed to flee. Jon quickly stepped in front of him. "Don't plan on leaving," he said. "Kidnapping is a punishable offense."

"Well, I'm not going to jail for something Hollis did," said Tyler. "This was all his idea."

Jon folded his arms and leveled his gaze on Tyler. "You can tell that to the judge. Meanwhile, just keep in mind that if you escape, I'll track you down like the guttersnipe you are, and when I find you, I'll break your goddamned neck."

"But . . . our claim," said Tyler. "Someone will jump it."

"You won't need money where you're going," said Jon. "Victoria sees to all the basic needs of its chain gangs."

"Chain gang?" Tyler looked at Jon incredulously. "Surely you don't mean to commit me to that. As you can see, Sarah is quite well . . . completely unharmed. It was Hollis who planned it all. And I give you my word, I won't see Sarah again . . . ever."

"Oh, you'll see her, all right," said Jon. "You'll see her at the trial. And if you're lucky, you'll see her again in about five years—when you get out of jail. Now, get in that chair and stay put."

While Jon was securing Tyler's hands with a rope, two deputies appeared in the doorway. They questioned Sarah and Jon, and noted for their report that Hollis had been killed by his own gun while Jon struggled with him in self-defense. Then the deputies returned to the hamlet to enlist two men to dig Hollis's grave.

While Jon and Sarah stood guard over Tyler, who was now handcuffed and tied in the chair, Sarah told Jon the whole story about her abduction and imprisonment on the steamer, and about how the Galbraiths had been kidnapping women and transporting them to the goldfields on the *Revelation*, under the guise of its being a mission ship.

When she'd finished her tale, Jon said, "Well, I'll be damned. Who would have suspected that sanctimonious pair? Certainly not my mother," he mused. "But all the signs were there: dear whey-faced Harriet's fixation on purging the city of harlots; the venerable reverend's mission trips up the Fraser; the *Revelation* with its celestial gargoyles and sacred scrollwork. The perfect cover. But how did your stepbrothers become involved with the Galbraiths?" he asked Sarah, his gaze still on Tyler.

Sarah's eyes narrowed. "Hollis and Tyler have always had a knack for joining up with scum. The ironic part was, Harriet Galbraith had already pegged me for a trip to the goldfields. So, in effect, Hollis did me a favor by having me brought to him. Of course, if you hadn't come along, things might have worked out quite differently."

"Thank God for that," said Jon. "I may just recommend this blackguard get off with laying fifty miles of water pipe instead of rotting in a cell."

"The Galbraiths are also smuggling whiskey and gold," said Sarah. "The whiskey is hidden in the forward hold of the ship, and the gold is smuggled in water barrels."

"So that's how they've been getting past our customs inspectors," said Jon. "I'm not certain they've even been checking the *Revelation*, though I'd assumed they had."

Sarah eyed Tyler with cynical satisfaction: sitting there, wan and dismal, miserably hunched in the chair. What a pathetic man he was. And how grateful she was to Jon for coming to rescue her. The import of what he'd done hit her for the first time, and she said with an absurd wobble in her voice, "Why did *you* come?"

He looked at her with affectionate indulgence. "Do you really need to ask?"

In his eyes, she saw a reflection of her own feelings, her own unspoken words. *Because I love you.* Which couldn't be.

Nothing had changed. She still couldn't be a part of Jon's life—mustn't jeopardize his political career, alienate his mother, and threaten his relationship with his daughters.

And she still wouldn't be his mistress.

Her heartbeat drumming wildly in her ears, she said stupidly, "I mean . . . how did you know where to find me?"

"It's a long story, sweet, which I'll tell you about later. Meanwhile, we'd better get back to the steamer and track down the *Revelation*."

Harriet Galbraith cast wary, restive eyes on the two men coming aboard. Dressed in the garb of Victoria's police brigade, they acted as if they had some authority to board the *Revelation*, which they most certainly did not. James would never allow such an outrage. The *Revelation* was, after all, a sacred vessel. She'd summon James at once.

Turning, she saw James emerging from the cabin. "Gentlemen," he said, smiling at the two men. But Harriet knew from the sober look in his eyes that he was displeased. "What can I do for you?"

"We're looking for a woman ... a Miss Sarah Ashley," the taller of the deputies said. "We have reason to believe she may be aboard this vessel, and we'd like to look around."

James squared his shoulders. "I assure you, gentlemen, there is no such woman aboard."

"Was she ever aboard?" the deputy asked.

"No." James's eyes narrowed. "She was not."

"Are you absolutely certain?"

"Absolutely!"

"Then you won't mind if we look around."

James's fists curled at his sides, and Harriet knew at once that he was more than just a little disturbed by the intrusion. "This ship is a sanctuary of the Lord," he said. "I cannot permit you to desecrate it by such a search."

"I'm sorry, Reverend Galbraith, but you can't stop us."

Harriet was aghast. "This is a mission ship," she said, marching over to confront the men. "It is exempt from search. If you defile it in such a way, I shall bring it to the attention of the governor—I am a personal friend of his mother."

"Madam," the tall deputy said. "you may take that up with the governor directly."

To Harriet's alarm, at that moment Governor Cromwell himself emerged from the cabin of the governmental steamer, followed by—Harriet drew in a ragged breath—Sarah Ashley! She pointed a finger at the despicable woman. "She's a harlot! She has sinned! She is unworthy and must make up for it through pain and suffering. That's why we took her to—"

"Shut up, you old fool!" James's voice cracked like a whip. "Have you no sense at all?"

"But, James," said Harriet. "Explain how it is . . . that it is our moral obligation. Tell them why we did it—"

"We did nothing." James enunciated the words clearly, a note of warning in his voice, his eyes as dark as a dungeon.

The tall deputy stepped forward. "Reverend Galbraith, you are under arrest for kidnapping."

"No!" Harriet cried. She clutched her hands to her bosom in despair. "It was all for the church. Explain to them, James . . . explain that all the gold is for the church."

James rounded on her furiously and struck her across the face, sending her reeling to the deck. "You bitch! You stupid bitch!" he bellowed, his face crimson, veins standing out in his temples. "Shut your goddamned mouth."

"Take him away, Sheriff," said Jon. "We'll deal with him later." He looked at Harriet Galbraith, who was slumped against the deck in shocked silence. "Mrs. Galbraith, you can go to your quarters."

Her lips quivered, but she said nothing.

After she'd been escorted below, Jon said to Sarah, "For the first time since I've known Harriet Galbraith, she seemed at a loss for words."

"What will they do with her?" asked Sarah, feeling a strange sympathy for the pathetic old woman.

"Not a thing," said Jon. "But she won't come out of it unscathed. With her husband in jail, she'll face all those wagging tongues she herself loved to set in motion, but this time she won't be the one starting the wagging. Call it a kind of poetic justice." He took her arm. "And now, sweet, you are to go back to your cabin and wait for me. I have some business to attend to here, but when I'm finished, you and I have some serious talking to do."

In a storage cabin on the *Hudson*, Jon shut the door and fixed his gaze on Sarah. "Now, my love, will you be so kind as to explain to me *what the hell is going on!* I have been looking all over the damned ship for you. Why are you hiding in here?"

"Because I am not ready to talk to you," said Sarah, nervously wringing her hands. "But now that you're here, I want to thank you for rescuing me. With Hollis gone, I feel confident that Tyler will stay out of my life for good, and I simply cannot thank you enough."

Jon stared at her composed face. Her words were thoughtful, her tone amiable, but he had the feeling she was telling him goodbye . . . again. "What exactly do you mean by you can't thank me enough? You can thank me by letting me take care of you and provide for you. Why the hell do you think I went up the bloody Fraser River to the goldfields to do a job the deputies could have done, if it wasn't because I cherish you above all else, want you more than life itself, and have no intention of letting you walk out of my life?"

Sarah swallowed back a lump that threatened to lodge in her throat. "I thought perhaps that was the reason," she said, because she couldn't think of anything else to say.

Jon stared at her, speechless. "That's all?" This wasn't going at all as he had expected. Sometimes, she could be as elusive as the wind. Seeing the worry in her eyes and trying his damnedest to understand her, he managed a vague smile. "Why do I get the distinct feeling that you're still telling me goodbye?"

"Because I am," she said. "I still plan to move to

New Westminster. But we can visit back and forth," she added.

Standing no more than a breath away, Jon looked down at her lovely face and lost himself in thoughts of how enticing she looked in the soft light and how venturesome she'd been to come to Victoria with her handbills and her sewing machines and her trunks of bloomers, and how witty and smart she'd been at the council meeting when she'd pleaded for her license, and how he would never tire of being with her . . .

Damn her pigheadedness!

"If it's because of the inexcusable things I said before you were kidnapped, you know I didn't mean them. I was angry. I also know my mother came to see you."

"That may be," said Sarah, avoiding his eyes. "But the fact remains that my presence in your life would hinder your career because your cabinet and the merchants would always disapprove of me."

"Do you think I give a damn about that?" A lazy smile spread across his face. "Besides, you silly mooncalf, you'll be a bloody heroine now. Because of you, the kidnappings have been stopped, the smuggling ring has been broken, and the horde of gold we impounded from the *Revelation* represents a damned good boost to our economy. We estimated over $20,000 in gold alone. There's no question, the Queen's delegates will find Victoria a prosperous colony . . . far more prosperous than New Westminster."

Sarah looked up to find Jon staring at her as if her presence in his life was something halfway between an aggravating enigma and an itch. "But you believe that rights for women and the wearing of bloomers are silly and frivolous," she said somewhat illogically.

"Perhaps," said Jon, "but I rather fancy a potion of frivolity every day of my life for the next fifty years."

"You don't understand. It's just not that simple."

"Isn't it? I ask you to be my mistress. You agree. I buy you a house, and we spend the rest of our days making mad, passionate love together."

Sarah met his gaze. The pull was there, the all-powerful awareness of his physical presence: of his broad-shouldered frame standing solid and real, his strong hands moving up her arms. But the thought of holding a man's love for a lifetime seemed inconceivable. "I'm afraid."

"Of what?"

"Of losing you."

"Losing me?" Jon stared at her. Light through the porthole caressed the curve of her cheeks and softened her lips, making her look childlike. And vulnerable. Of course. What a fool he'd been. It wasn't the political burdens she'd bring to his life, or ambivalence about her own feelings, that was making her hesitate. It was the fact that every important man in her life had deserted her.

He tipped her chin up so she would have to look into his eyes. "How could you possibly lose me? You're the center of my world, the heart of my existence. Being with you brings me such joy. I love your wit and your charm and your cleverness. And I love the way that little dimple appears when you smile . . . and how your eyes light up when you've bested me. How could you possibly lose me? Our hearts and souls are one. Could you lose your heart? Could you lose your soul? Besides, if you won't live with me and be my love, I'll never be able to suckle your toes." He kissed her tenderly on the lips, peered into her eyes, and added in a voice just above a whisper, "Sweetheart, I love you."

The truth came to Sarah quite suddenly. It happened while she looked into his eyes: all of her fancies about fashion and independence and rights for women faded, replaced by a longing that made her chest ache and her throat constrict.

She wanted Jon to gather her in his arms and hold her for an eternity. She wanted him to banish her apprehension for the love she'd never had and help her come to terms with her inability to trust and accept a man's love. She wanted to curl up with him amid down pillows and muslin comforters and feel his arms close around her and his skin warm against hers. She desperately wanted his love—a steadfast, unfaltering, forever kind of love that would endure a lifetime.

The fact was, she wanted to be his wife.

She wanted to be Mrs. Jonathan Cromwell . . .

Taking a long, slow breath, she held his gaze. "You might consider it maddeningly priggish of me, but I don't want to be your mistress. I want to be your wife."

"Wife?" The word lingered in Jon's throat. But he couldn't bring himself to say, *Yes, be my wife.*

True, she'd make an unconventional wife. But that wasn't what was stopping him; it was because of Caroline. And he refused to become the romantic, guileless fool he'd been. Nor would he start building silly castles in the sky . . . castles that could crumble.

Needing time to digest the idea, he said, "I thought you were against marriage."

"I was . . . until I fell in love with you. But no matter how much I love you, I cannot be your mistress. And you can't seem to ask me to be your wife."

"I *was* married once. It wasn't successful."

"And so you intend to be bitter about it for the rest of your life? I find it hard to imagine that your wife did something so terrible that you can never put it behind you."

He folded his arms. "Well, then, let me tell you about Caroline's little *misadventures* so you might understand." His eyes narrowed. "The first time I confronted her with gossip I'd heard about her and another man, she laughed it off, telling me the talk was merely jealous gossip from women who envied her because she had the handsomest, most desirable man in all of England. Her passionate lovemaking that night convinced me unconditionally that I was the only man in her life. Until her next misadventure . . .

"That time she'd been linked with a man who had boasted publicly at a gaming hall about his sexual prowess with my wife. I promptly rose to defend her honor, but the morning of the duel, the man left London.

"The next incident involved a known rake. When I heard the gossip, I got drunk. Totally soused, I demanded my wife prove her love. Which she did. And again I allowed her to convince me the talk had been untrue.

"For the next few years, she played at being the devoted wife and mother. She curbed all her misguided instincts—her coquetry, her vanity—until outwardly she appeared a model of propriety. The memories and doubts surrounding her began to fade, until I was certain it had all been a figment of my jealous, illogical mind.

"And then came the fire. And the truth. Caroline died of smoke inhalation in the arms of another man . . .

"Now you know why I'm bitter."

Sarah placed her hand on Jon's folded arm. "Jon, I am not Caroline. You cannot judge me by what she did, because I simply am not her."

Jon looked at Sarah, long and probing. What he saw was a rare female: strong, yet vulnerable; pragmatic, yet vibrant with love and promise; confounding, yet utterly charming . . .

And he knew she was right.

She wasn't Caroline. She may have swept him off his feet as Caroline had, but he knew now that she would never betray him. She was a more mature and complete woman than Caroline, a woman he wanted to protect, despite her objections; a woman who would enrich his life as Caroline never could.

A woman he wanted to cherish forever . . .

Knowing that to have her he'd have to take that fearful step into the unknown and trust her, because not taking that step and losing her would be far too painful, he curved his arms around her. "Will you come live with me and be my love . . . and my wife?"

"I don't want you to say that just because you have found yourself backed into a corner, Jon."

"Sweetheart, do I look like a man who could be backed into a corner? Besides, if you left me, I would dearly miss suckling your toes."

Sarah stared at him as if she hadn't heard correctly. "Truly? You want to marry me . . . so you can suckle my toes?"

He grinned wickedly. "And other things."

"Then yes . . . I will marry you." She curved her arms around his neck. "You know, I think I will enjoy being the wife of the governor instead of being a bloomer merchant."

"You'd give that up for me?"

"The truth is, I'd give it all up for you. Wearing bloomers, the emporium, the issue of rights for women . . ."

"No," said Jon, "that would be all too exceptional of you, and I couldn't allow it. I fear if I did, you'd take on the dull gloss of an exquisite piece of porcelain sitting on a shelf collecting dust."

"Then . . . you don't mind if I proceed with my plans?"

"Absolutely not," he said with resolve. "Long ago,

a beautiful butterfly convinced me that she'd never be content leading an aimless, frivolous life, and I accepted that."

"So our little battle has finally ended?"

"Whether you realize it or not, you overthrew your opponent and seized power long ago—at Mystic Spring when you kissed me—because it was then I knew I'd move heaven and hell to have you. As for my political future, lesser men than I have survived greater obstacles than complications imposed by a headstrong, independent wife."

Sarah gave him a rueful smile. "And what will you do, Mr. Governor, if I'm forced to go against your wishes because we disagree on certain principles regarding my business?"

A triumphant gleam crept into Jon's eyes. "Probably haul you off to bed."

"Bed?" Sarah echoed vaguely. "Why would you do that?"

"Because, my adorable little bird-wit, whenever you defy me, that's what I feel like doing. And since I still cannot condone women marching from home and family to fight for rights they simply don't need, nor can I openly endorse your wearing bloomers outside the privacy of our home, we should be spending quite a bit of time in bed."

"I like that idea." Sarah kissed his chin, his jaw, his lips. "Now that I'll be proceeding with my plans," she said between pecks, "I'll look into purchasing the little building on Wharf Street that I wanted a while back ... the one next to Sporborg's Grocery. Mandi said Mr. Sporborg told Wellington it was for sale—"

"Just hold it right there. I refuse to let you buy the building—"

"*You refuse!*"

"Flatly. I'm the man in the family, and I'll be the one to buy the damned building. And that's that!"

Sarah took a moment to digest his words. Then she gave him a furtive smile and said dutifully, "Very well, Jon."

He puffed out his chest.

She allowed him his moment of triumph, then said, "Of course, the building will have to be expanded, so when I present my plans, what will your position be?"

"I'm afraid I won't be able to approve them. They'll violate an ordinance prohibiting the expansion of any building on the waterfront." Jon gave her a wry smile. "But I suspect you'll get around that."

Sarah tightened her arms around his neck and raised confident eyes to meet his gaze. "Well, I did plan on having a rather large following with me when I go to face the council: Elizabeth Thurman and her father, Flora and Jeremy, Mandi and Wellington, Mr. Babington—he offered to represent me if I need him. And just in case that isn't enough, I'll also enlist—"

Jon silenced her ramblings with a sound kiss, knowing he'd already lost this round. He chucked her under the chin. "I can see that our bed will never get cold."

She gave a slow, wicked grin. "How lovely."

Epilogue

Victoria, Vancouver Island
Six months later

Josephine glanced up and down the hallway, peeked into Jon and Sarah's bedchamber, and motioned for Louella to follow. "Well, here they are," she said to Sarah. "What do you think?" She offered the black bloomers for Sarah to inspect.

"And look"—Louella pointed proudly at the stitching along the gathered inset—"my seams are ever so much better."

"Your seams are perfect," said Sarah. "Absolutely perfect."

Louella beamed.

Sarah held up the bloomers, her eyes focusing on the U-shaped panel of soft flannel gathered in an inset in the front. "And I think you are positively clever, Josephine. What a novel idea. Lying-in bloomers. Why, every woman who is with child in Victoria will want a pair." She smiled at Louella. "And you, love, have become so proficient with your stitchery that I want you to start right away on the silk outfit for Mandi. She'll be needing it very soon."

Louella grinned widely.

Josephine nudged Louella. "Go on . . . show her."

Louella blushed, then held up something she'd been clutching behind her back. "Well ... these are for you. I hope they fit."

Sarah stared at the bright, flowery silk lying-in bloomers. "For me?" She held the bloomers against her stomach and giggled. "I fear it won't be long before this pouch will be quite expanded."

"How exciting," said Josephine. "A little brother."

Sarah looked askance at her. "It could be a little sister, you know."

Josephine eyed Louella. "Well, I suppose that would be all right, too." After a few moments, she added, "Have you talked to Papa about my working for you yet?"

"I will soon, love," replied. Sarah. "Just be patient. I must address the subject at precisely the right moment. With men, timing is ever so important." She smoothed her hand along her tummy, realizing her timing had been a bit off along those lines. But Jon was delighted. Actually, she'd never dreamed she'd be so excited about such a domestic thing as having a child. But she was. Incredibly and amazingly so ...

"Well, I guess you're right," said Josephine. "Will you show Papa the lying-in bloomers?"

"Of course," replied Sarah. "I'll also point out that they were your idea, and mention how clever you are. And I'll tell him how adept you are with the sewing machine, Louella, and how much help the two of you would be to me in my shop, especially now that I must slow down a bit."

Josephine looked at Sarah, a tiny crease gathering between her brows. "Do you have any notion why Papa wants to see us all in the library?"

"No," said Sarah. "I haven't the foggiest idea."

"I do hope we're not in trouble again," she said. "What if Papa already found out what we've been doing and is angry?"

"Don't worry, love," said Sarah. "Your father's not angry. Actually, he seems particularly pleased about whatever it is. Perhaps it has something to do with the baby."

"Perhaps." Hearing someone approaching, Josephine snatched the silk bloomers from Sarah's hand and tucked them behind her back, then looked up with a start. "Oh . . . Grandmother. We were just leaving." She gave her grandmother a peck on the cheek and took Louella's arm, and they slipped away.

"Lady Cromwell," said Sarah. "Please . . . do come in and sit down."

"Oh, my dear," Dorothy said, moving to sit in a lady's chair. "We must do something about that."

"About what?" Sarah glanced around the room, wondering what she meant.

"My name," she said. "Since you are not only in the family now, but also to be the mother of my grandchild, we must dispense with the formalities."

"Well . . . that would be nice," said Sarah, surprised. Lady Cromwell had not exactly been overjoyed at the wedding. And afterward, she'd seemed a bit indifferent. But ever since Jon had announced the news of the baby, his mother had seemed to take a genuine interest in Sarah. "What do you propose I call you?"

Dorothy tilted her head while pondering the question. "Well . . . perhaps Mother Cromwell. No"—she waved her hand as if erasing that idea—"that wouldn't do at all. It makes me sound like a mother superior. Oh, well, no matter. We'll think of something. Now for the reason I'm here."

"You certainly don't have to have a reason to come to our chambers," said Sarah. "You're welcome any time."

"Thank you, dear. But first, how are you faring?"

"Very well. Actually quite peckish," Sarah said. "I feel as if I could consume several scones with marmalade, a few kippers, and at least two cups of chocolate."

"Then it will most certainly be a boy," said Dorothy. "I felt enormously ravenous with both Charles and Jonathan. But with Esther, I was quite squeamish during most of my lying-in. If it's a boy, Jonathan will be as proud as a horse with bells."

"Yes, I expect he will be," said Sarah. Jon had been talking endlessly about the outings he and their son would take—fishing, hunting, day excursions on horses . . .

"Jon has been most evasive lately," said Dorothy, interrupting Sarah's musings. "And now with his bidding us to congregate in the library at six o'clock . . . Do you have any idea what this is about?"

"No, none at all. But I admit, I'm most curious."

"Yes, we all are. Neither Esther nor the girls know what it is, nor does Ida. But I suspect Peterson and Tooley know, although they deny it—those scalawags have been smiling more than usual, as if they had a secret. But that's not why I'm here." Glancing around, she asked, "Are we quite alone?"

"Yes," replied Sarah. She noticed that Dorothy seemed to be holding several remnants of material, which she dabbed at with restive fingers, arranging and rearranging them, pressing them smooth, nervously trifling with them.

Giving Sarah a contrite smile, she offered the samples. "What do you think of these?"

Sarah took the remnants. Studying them closely, she ran her fingers over the fine silks: an ecru jardinière strewn with orange poppies and foliage, an olive-green foulard with dark myrtle-green shamrock leaves, and a salmon India silk with embroidery of a deeper shade. "They're lovely," she said. "Are you planning a new toilette?"

"Well, not exactly," said Dorothy. "That is, I want to have something made for ... a friend. I'd like to place the order with you."

"How lovely," said Sarah, pleased that Jon's mother held her tailoring in such high regard. "This jardinière with the bright poppies made into a shirtwaister would make a lovely summer frock," she said, smoothing the fabric against her knee.

"Well ... the fact of it is," said Dorothy, "I wasn't exactly contemplating have a shirtwaister made."

"You weren't?"

"No, I was thinking more about"—Dorothy's eyes darted nervously about the room before resting on Sarah—"bloomers."

"Bloomers?" Sarah looked up with a start. She could imagine Lady Cromwell enlisting her to make almost anything for her friend, except bloomers. Was the older woman actually trying to promote the garment?

Dorothy cleared her throat. "The jardinière," she said, drawing Sarah's attention to the remnant. "I thought perhaps it might make a rather nice ... What is it you call the upper garment?"

"Overtunic," said Sarah.

"Yes," Dorothy said. "It would be quite summerish. And the bloomers could be made of perhaps a green foulard. Green is one of my favorite colors. I have always felt it was especially attractive on ... uh ... my friend."

Sarah eyed Lady Cromwell dubiously. "Is this ... *friend* a young person?"

"Well, not exactly," replied Dorothy. "That is, she's about ... my age."

"I see," said Sarah, the outlandish implication almost too outrageous to conceive. "Then I assume her coloring is the same as yours—ivory complexion, silver hair."

Dorothy shrugged and admitted with a wan smile, "Yes."

Sarah stepped over to her desk and retrieved a box of fabric swatches. "May I suggest an overtunic of a rose peau-de-soie such as this?" She offered a remnant with pink and blue brocaded flowers. "The blues would accentuate your silver hair and the lovely rose would bring out the pink of your cheeks. The bloomers could be of a deeper rose faille. Or perhaps we could make the tunic of a ciel-blue poult-de-soie embroidered with silk of a darker shade, and the bloomers could be made of a deeper color of blue such as this sapphire Sicilienne."

Dorothy's brows snapped together over the bridge of her thin nose. "Oh, balderdash!" she said. "You know."

Sarah shrugged. "I only guessed. And I'm delighted."

Dorothy smiled ruefully. "Well, Esther has been parading about the house in bloomers for quite some time now, and although they're most unconventional, they do make good sense. Of course, I will wear the costume only in the privacy of my bedchamber." Her cheeks flushed as she added, "And I would appreciate it if you would not say anything to the girls, or to Jonathan. Naturally, I will tell them in due course, but I prefer to allow a bit more time to pass first. I hope you understand."

"Yes ... of course," Sarah said, sensing that she and Lady Cromwell were on the verge of becoming fast friends.

From the mantelpiece, the clock chimed six.

"Oh, my goodness," Dorothy exclaimed. "It's time."

Sarah and Dorothy met Josephine and Louella in

the hallway, and the procession funneled into the library. Moments later, Esther, dressed in a bright green bloomer costume, with Admiral Windemere at her side, joined them. They gathered in a semicircle around Jon, who stood beside a draped easel.

Jon addressed the group. "I know you must all be wondering why I've called you in like this, but as you can see, we're about to have an unveiling." He winked at Sarah. "As you might guess, it's a painting of my beautiful bride."

Sarah blushed. Now she realized what had happened to the daguerreotype of her they'd found among Hollis's things. Jon had given it to the artist he'd commissioned to do the portrait. She wasn't certain she wanted to see a painting of that particular daguerreotype, but she was deeply touched that Jon had taken it upon himself to have a portrait done.

Jon lifted a corner of the drape. "And now . . ." He swept off the veil.

Everyone stood, speechless.

Sarah stared in open disbelief. She had expected to see a portrait of herself sitting demurely on a sofa, hands clasped in her lap, a slight smile on her face. Instead, what she saw was what appeared to be body parts and multiple faces and large eyes—all less than masterfully painted. The composite was most bizarre. She had no idea how to respond.

"Dear." Dorothy was the first to speak. "May we assume this is a joke?"

Bemused, Jon looked at his mother. "I assure you, Mother, it is no joke. It was done by Mrs. Dewig-Gertz."

"I don't understand," said Esther, her eyes narrowed in thought. "Why is Sarah in pieces like that?"

"Sugar lump," Admiral Windemere said to his intended, "I don't believe Mrs. Dewig-Gertz meant her to be in pieces. She's all there, but in a rather different order. Could you tell us more about it, Jon?" he asked graciously.

"Yes, for heaven's sake, please do," said Esther.

Jon eyed Esther with restrained forbearance. "Mrs. Dewig-Gertz calls the technique totalism. But it was really my idea," he said proudly. "I wanted her to capture as many facets of Sarah's personality as she could ... which she did."

Nibbling absently at her bottom lip, her hands laced behind her back, Sarah silently studied the painting. It was certainly different from anything she'd ever seen. She saw her own profile—somewhat stiff and immobile—but Mrs. Dewig-Gertz had traced the edge of her nose and chin with a kind of sunlight coming from behind. And the wind was blowing wisps of coppery hair across her cheek— every single strand seemed to be there.

And those two huge eyes superimposed on the profile and staring out were really quite ... green. But she also saw her face straight on, smaller than the profile, yet rather cleverly worked in so it seemed to be a part of it. Mrs. Dewig-Gertz had also included bloomers and detached hands and—heat rushed up her face—toes. Tiny little toes.

Looking at Jon, she realized he was watching her. From the amused look on his face, she knew he'd caught the focus of her attention.

While the others gathered around the painting, pointing and chattering, she said covertly to him, "You have some explaining to do."

He chucked her under the chin. "Yes ... I rather thought you'd bring that to my attention."

She pursed her lips. "Just how did Mrs. Dewig-Gertz know about the toes? Certainly you didn't tell her about us ... what you do." She blushed deeply.

Jon patted her hand. "Relax, love. I only mentioned in passing that you enjoyed immersing your

toes in the spring. She took it from there. She's really
a very innovative artist. But enough about Mrs
Dewig-Gertz." He slid his arm around her waist.
"Mother's latest peccadillo: I'm to mollycoddle you
and wait on you and tend to your every need. She
claims I've been very remiss in my husbandly duties
during this delicate time in your life."

"Well, you needn't fuss so," said Sarah. "I'm quite
fit. As for your husbandly duties"—she grinned
wickedly while contemplating making love with Jon
right in the middle of the day—"my toes, and other
more delicate areas, are tingling quite noticeably
right now, and I fear they need immediate attention."

Jon gave her a discreet pat on the fanny. "Wanton
little chit."

"My thoughts exactly." Lacing her fingers in his,
she led him out of the library and up the stairs, leaving his family to ponder the various and enigmatic
aspects of Sarah Ashley Cromwell.

Author's Note

For reasons necessary to the story, the term of office of Governor Douglas has been shortened by two years, and certain events that occurred during the period from 1863 to 1865 are compressed into the year 1863. Several of the townsfolk are actual figures from history, including Mayor Thomas Harris, Attorney General George Cary, and Amor De Cosmos, editor of Victoria's newspaper, *The Daily British Colonist*. Governor Jonathan Cromwell, the hero in this story, is a fictional character.

On September 17, 1863, it was reported in the *Colonist* that David Babington Ring refused to pay his business license fee as a barrister on the grounds that in the wording of the Incorporation Act, the city of Victoria had no legal authority to impose such a tax. The case was brought before Chief Justice Cameron, who, in December 1863, decided in favor of Ring, holding that the city had no legal right to levy any general taxes at all.

Subsequently, the city council, having collected over $12,000 by means of a wrongful tax, faced the prospect of having to meet demands for refunds.

Perhaps David Babington Ring's lawsuit could have been inspired by a certain radical young woman whose innovative garments may have changed the course of fashion in Victoria, and whose chaotic and untimely presence in the colony may ultimately have led to the unification of Vancouver Island with British Columbia in July 1867.

And perhaps this industrious young woman may even have influenced Her Majesty Queen Victoria's decision in May 1868 to declare the seat of the government of the combined colonies to be Victoria.

Who's to say?

Avon Romances—
the best in exceptional authors and unforgettable novels!

LORD OF MY HEART   Jo Beverley
76784-8/$4.50 US/$5.50 Can

BLUE MOON BAYOU   Katherine Compton
76412-1/$4.50 US/$5.50 Can

SILVER FLAME   Hannah Howell
76504-7/$4.50 US/$5.50 Can

TAMING KATE   Eugenia Riley
76475-X/$4.50 US/$5.50 Can

THE LION'S DAUGHTER   Loretta Chase
76647-7/$4.50 US/$5.50 Can

CAPTAIN OF MY HEART   Danelle Harmon
76676-0/$4.50 US/$5.50 Can

BELOVED INTRUDER   Joan Van Nuys
76476-8/$4.50 US/$5.50 Can

SURRENDER TO THE FURY   Cara Miles
76452-0/$4.50 US/$5.50 Can

Coming Soon

SCARLET KISSES   Patricia Camden
76825-9/$4.50 US/$5.50 Can

WILDSTAR   Nicole Jordan
76622-1/$4.50 US/$5.50 Can